NIGHT'S FALL

A WEREWOLF SUPERNATURAL THRILLER ADVENTURE

NIGHT'S CHAMPION
BOOK TWO

RICHARD PARRY

CONTENTS

NIGHT'S END

ISBN-13 paperback: 978-0-473-34986-8
ISBN-13 ebook: 978-0-473-34989-9

First edition

NIGHT'S FALL

Adalia Kendrick sees the dead. It's a gift. Or maybe a curse. Either way, she's had five years to learn that the dead don't always stay quiet.

Her mother, Danny, has spent those years **running from the darkness of the Night's Favor**, trying to carve out a life far from the blood and ruin they left behind. But some things won't be outrun—**especially when the past comes hunting.**

Across the sea, **Talin Moray has heard of the Night's power**, and he wants it for himself. With **Vodou and an army of the dead**, he brings Chicago to its knees, and he won't stop until the world bows with it.

To stop him, Val, Danny, and Adalia must face the truth: **this curse is their only weapon, and the price of using it might be everything.**

If they fail? **Talin won't just take the city. He'll rule its ashes.**

YOU'RE AWESOME

You could have picked any book, but you chose this one. That means a lot.

Your support keeps independent authors like me forging ahead, writing the stories we love (and hopefully, the ones you love too). Whether you're here for the characters, the worldbuilding, or just a little escapism, thank you for being part of this journey.

You. Kick. Ass.

ROLL FOR NARRATIVE
WHERE WORLDBUILDING AND OVERTHINKING COLLIDE

Love stories that linger in your brain long after The End? Ever wonder why some books hit like a natural 20 and others critically fail their way into the 1-star abyss?

Join *Roll for Narrative*, my hub for sci-fi and fantasy lovers. I explore storytelling like a rogue casing a dungeon, review movies, books, and games, and dish out writing tips like a chaotic-good bard with a grudge against bad prose. No spam, just good stuff.

Join the quest:
https://rollfornarrative.parrydox.com

For Julia, because if you want it enough you can have it.
And for my Rae. Thank you for being strong enough for both of us.

CHAPTER
ONE

"What I'm thinking," said Carlisle to the barman, "is that you're a thief."

The barman blinked at her. "Say what?"

"Because I know a thief when I see one," she said, her words slurring just a little. She leaned forward over the bar. "Serious … seriously? Twenty bucks for a shot of Jack is *theft*."

"You could drink somewhere else," said the barman. "Free country."

Carlisle gave a long, lazy smile. "Free country." *Only bar in this town. If you can call it a town.* She'd heard of one-horse towns, and this place was a horse short. No one else was in the bar tonight, the broken-down old jukebox spitting out the same two songs on repeat. She'd had about as much Johnny Cash as she could take. The door to the bar opened behind her, and she felt a gust of cold chase someone inside. She didn't turn to look, still holding her glass of Jack.

"That's right," said the bartender, his eyes lighting up a little as he saw a new potential customer. He started to clean a glass — Carlisle was about to say something else when a man slipped into the seat beside her.

She knew it was a man before she turned, the way he put himself in that chair like he had sovereign land rights. Carlisle spent some time taking him in. Close cut hair, ebony skin, stacked like a Vegas deck of cards inside a suit worth north of a couple grand. *Like.* She kept the lazy smile on. "Well hello, sailor."

"I'm not really a sailor," said the man. "But I'm impressed you guessed that I came here in a ship."

Carlisle let the smile fade away into a frown. His accent was strange. "Where you from?"

"The Caribbean, originally," he said. "More recently, Queens." The man gave the barman a nod. "Rum and Coke. Easy on the Coke."

"Starting hard, or…" Carlisle let herself trail off. *Something isn't right.* That old instinct came back, the cop inside her refusing to die like it should. *Too much damn alcohol, that's your problem. Thought you'd come out, get lucky, and here you are talking to a — a* something. "You some kind of soldier?"

"Not really," said the man, lifting his rum and Coke, breathing in the aroma. He smiled, his eyes closed. "More of a problem-solver."

Carlisle pushed her barstool back a little. "What kinds of problems you looking to solve tonight?"

The man laughed, something easy in it, and turned to look at Carlisle properly for what seemed like the first time. "That depends. You bring any trouble with you?"

"Left all my problems behind," she said, the lie coming easy. "Why else come to a shit hole like this?"

"Hey," said the bartender.

"Maybe your problems are trying to catch up," said Caribbean. "Maybe your problems are only just starting." He gestured with a hand to the air around her. "I can see your problems. They tug at you like needy children."

The bartender took a look around the bar, then moved through a grimy door to the kitchen. It was old and stuck just before it was fully closed. It was funny the things you noticed, just before everything went to hell. "So look," said Carlisle. "I'm here to have some drinks. Maybe get laid. Can you help with any of that?"

Caribbean downed the last of his drink in a long swallow, then turned the glass over in his hand. "Detective Carlisle?"

Fuck. "Not anymore."

"Detective Carlisle, we're trying to track down some friends of yours. Do you know a—"

"No."

"What?"

"No, I don't know anyone. Not who you're looking for. And," she said, as the man's eyes widened slightly, "not her either. And definitely not the next person you're going to ask about."

"That's a shame," said Caribbean. "That's what we call a 'crying shame.' Do you know why it's called that?"

Carlisle tipped her head from side to side, loosening up her shoulders, just getting the kinks out. "Because someone always ends up crying."

He nodded. "Do I look like the crying sort to you?"

Carlisle laughed, and Caribbean looked startled. "No," she said, "but you've made a huge mistake — and I mean, a massive, colossal fuck-up — if you think *I'm* the crying type."

"The name I was going to ask you about," said Caribbean, "was Elliot."

Carlisle blinked at him in the silence left between the tracks changing on the jukebox. Her veins felt like they'd just started running ice instead of blood, her head clearing from the fuzz of the alcohol. She could hear the machine catch, clicking as it tried to drop another disc in. She swallowed. "What did you say?"

"I thought that might get your attention," said Caribbean. "What would it be worth to you if you could see him again?"

"Elliot's dead," said Carlisle.

"Is he, now?" Caribbean reached behind the bar, snagging out the bottle of rum. "I wonder about that."

"I don't."

"Let me ask you something," said Caribbean. "Let's assume he's dead. What if I said I could bring him back to life?"

"I'd say you were crazy in the coconut," she said.

"Well," said Caribbean, "that's not an unusual reaction to get."

"You ask people about their dead friends often?"

"Often enough," he said. "It's a growth industry, in my line of work."

"Right," said Carlisle. *Here's a good one. Guy walks into a bar, asks about your dead friend Elliot...* "What exactly *is* your line of work?"

"I get things done," he said. "The job title changes week to week."

"First you said you were a problem solver. Now you say you can raise the dead."

"They don't have to be different things," said the man. "And I don't raise the dead. I'm more of an intermediary. The woman who stands behind me is the one who can raise the dead."

"Fancy trick," said Carlisle, turning on her stool to lean back against the bar. She took in the room — no one else here, clear exits, she should just get out. This kind of crazy talk wouldn't lead to any good.

"I can tell," said Caribbean, the soft touch of his accent making him easy to listen to, "that you're having trouble believing me."

"You think?"

"Here's a little taste," he said, reaching — slowly, Carlisle noticed — into the breast pocket of his jacket. He pulled out a few items — a small vial of clear liquid, a hand-rolled cigar, an old-style lighter. He placed these on the bar, then splashed a generous portion of rum into his glass. He emptied in the clear liquid, then raised the cigar.

"There's no smoking in here," said Carlisle. "Not that I give a shit, but you know." She pointed at the sign on the bar top, right next to the lighter. *Thank you for not smoking.*

"I see it," said Caribbean. "I don't think they mean this kind of smoke." He picked up the lighter, flicking it open, a long tongue of flame kissing the end of the cigar. He drew big puffs, then blew a stream of smoke towards the ceiling. "That feels right." He puffed a few more times, then blew another stream of smoke over the top of his glass. Instead of the smoke flowing past, it clustered and gathered at the top of the rum. Small eddies pulled the tiny cloud about, which then seemed to be drawn into the dark liquid.

"There's a thing you don't see every day," said Carlisle. "But if you think I'm drinking that, you've got another thing coming."

"Just watch," said Caribbean. He pushed the glass closer to her. Carlisle noticed he seemed ... *drained*, tired around the edges. "It won't be long now."

Despite herself, Carlisle looked into the liquid. She knew it would be some parlor trick, but she had to look anyway. The smoke seemed to bunch just under the surface of the liquid, a small storm in silent motion, then cleared, the liquid reflecting the room. *No. The liquid can't reflect the room, I should be seeing the ceiling in there, if anything.* She could see a room in the liquid, drawn out in shades of brown, and a man stepped into view. It was like she was looking through a peep hole and seeing—

"Jesus fuck," said Carlisle. It was Elliot, standing in there, picked out like she remembered him, even the gut. "Jesus fuck," she said again.

The image of Elliot walked closer, and his voice came out of the glass, blurred, like if it were a picture someone had colored outside the lines. She was hearing him from a long way away. "Carlisle?"

"Elliot," she said. "Is that you?"

"It's me," he said. "It's—"

"What was the last thing you said to me?"

"Hell if I know," said Elliot. "That was a long time ago."

"Take a guess," she said.

"I think we were talking about... It's so hard to remember, Carlisle. I think we were looking at some footage of something—" his face scrunched up as he tried to remember, and the surface of the liquid shimmered. "I can't remember. I'd started smoking again. Can you believe that? Praise no day until it's ended, that's what I always say."

"I can believe that," she said. "I can't believe *this*, though. What is this?"

"It's—" he was cut off as Caribbean knocked the glass over, the rum spilling out.

"What the hell did you do that for?" Carlisle said.

"Just a taste," said Caribbean. "Now we need to make a deal."

Carlisle looked at him, then at the splash of liquid on the bar. *That ... that was Elliot. But Elliot's* dead. "No deal," she said. She pushed off from the bar, jacket already in hand, and turned towards the door.

"Just remember," said Caribbean's voice behind her, "that we offered you a deal. You can still take it."

"Ain't no way," said Carlisle, "that I'm taking a deal like that."

"But you don't know what the trade is," said the voice at her back.

She paused, her hand on the door outside to the street. "I know well enough," she said. She reached up and brushed the tears from the corners of her eyes before she stepped out into the snow.

THE CARIBBEAN WATCHED her step out into the cold and the night and the loneliness of the world, then looked down at the bar. The spilled rum sat there, empty of purpose, but not of power. Not of faith.

He traced a finger through it. He felt the warmth of that power, a spill that had held — just for a moment — the captured soul of a man. He tugged on that faith, scooped his hand through the rum and closed his fist around it.

Liquid leaked and dripped around his fingers, and he looked at the door where Detective Carlisle had gone. What was it that she had said?

I'm here to have some drinks. Maybe get laid. Can you help with any of that?

He breathed deep, opened his hand as he closed his eyes, and blew air through his fingers, spraying rum into the room. Sending it on a path after her.

Maybe get laid.

So lonely, hidden behind that facade. She needed, *longed* with a will. All that she lacked was direction.

Can you help with any of that?

The rum floated in the air, slipped around a table, crossed over the top of a chair, and misted under the door after her.

"Yes, Detective," said the Caribbean. "I can help you with that. And you *will* help me."

Bound. Her need, balanced against the soul of a dead man. He felt the ties as they found their mark. Carlisle would want him. Follow him. Do what he needed, for as long as he needed.

So they could catch a monster, and save the world.

CHAPTER
TWO

"What I don't get," said the man with bad teeth, "is why people don't carry cash no more."

"Sign of the times," said his partner, wearing a low-quality smile under a worse haircut. "They say it's a ... what do they call it?"

"Regression," said Bad Teeth. "That's what they call it."

"Please," said Lacie, backing away. "I don't have ... I don't have anything."

Bad Teeth lifted Lacie's purse up in front of her face, shaking it upside down. A cascade of incidentals fell, some lipstick, her phone, a make-up case, her taser. Lacie watched the taser fall to the grass, just outside of arm's reach. It may as well have been at the end of a football field. She felt so alone, so frightened. Her mouth was dry, her heart hammering. If her taser had been near to hand instead of in her bag... "There's nothing here," said Bad Teeth. "And you know what that means, don't you, pretty thing?"

"It's a recession," said Worse Haircut.

Bad Teeth paused, then shot a glance at Worse Haircut. "What?"

"It's a recession," said the other man. "I think that's what it's called."

"Who gives a fuck what it's called?" said Bad Teeth. "Call it Tinkerbell if you want."

"Tinkerbell's a tiny little woman," said Worse Haircut. "Not a sign of the times at all."

Lacie stared at the two men with wide eyes. *This ... this isn't happening.* Not like *this*. She'd thought she could just cut through Fuller Park on her way to Bridgeport — save some goddamn *time* — and these two had stepped out as she'd been walking. Like they'd been hiding in shadows that weren't even there. She hadn't been talking on her phone. It wasn't even *late*—

"What you think, pretty lady?" Bad Teeth leaned in closer with a leer, the alcohol sharp on his breath. "You think it's a *recession*? Leaves honest men like us out of work."

Her eyes darted between the two men. "I don't—"

"Don't lie!" Bad Teeth's hand slapped her hard across the face. She rocked back, the heel on her Guess Odells twisting. She landed, her head hitting something so hard her teeth ached. Lacie was stunned, her arms moving weakly as she tried to *move*, to just *get away*...

"Now look what you've done," said a voice. It sounded like Worse Haircut, but he was so far away.

"She made me," said Bad Teeth. "You saw."

"I saw," said Worse Haircut. "It's still a recession."

"Jesus, will you give it a rest with the ... you got a problem, buddy?" It sounded like Bad Teeth had turned away. Lacie struggled to make her eyes focus, picked out a man-sized shape, that's all it was, just a shape really, but hope hit her hard. She tried to focus, tried not to throw up.

"No," said the newcomer. Lacie blinked, and when she opened her eyes the man was at her side. "Miss? Are you okay?"

"Hey," said Worse Haircut. "That one's *ours*."

The newcomer didn't look away, his eyes concerned. "My name's Val," he said. "You'll be all right."

"They..." Lacie coughed. "I just want to get *home*." Her words tasted like metal in her mouth, her teeth like hard stones. She felt like being sick, and reached a hand up to the back of her head. It came away sticky and red. "One of them—"

"Don't worry about that," said Val. He leaned in close. "Can you keep a secret?"

Lacie looked up into his face. She didn't know why, but he seemed... *safe*. "Yes."

She was rewarded with a smile, generous and warm, before she fell backwards into black.

"Hey," said one of the men at his back. "*Asshole.* I'm talking to you." Val heard them close in, felt the—

Fear and blood.

—smile that was more snarl come onto his face. He stood, quick and easy, turning to face them. "I hear you," he said.

That stopped them. None of the usual posturing they'd expect. No *what's your problem* or *let's dance the man dance* bullshit. Bad Teeth looked at Worse Haircut, then pulled some tatters of bravado closer to him. "You *hear* us," he said. "You get that? He said he *hears* us."

"Yeah," said Worse Haircut. "Next he'll be—"

"There won't be a next," said Val.

He could see them shuffling, indecisive, but warming to the task. This was more like it, a bit of hidden threat in someone's words. It's what they needed to—

Kill.

—get their blood up. Two minutes ago they'd been about to beat some poor woman senseless, maybe worse, for a handful of dollars and a bad pair of heels. Now they were seeing a man, sure just the one man, not a whole group, but the threat profile was all different.

It took a shift in thinking, and these guys did not look like mental athletes. Val stood with his arms at his side, thinking about relaxing his hands. *Just breathe*, he said to himself. *It doesn't always have to get bad.*

"That sounded like a threat," said Bad Teeth.

Okay. Maybe it does have to get bad. Val shrugged. "Doesn't have to be," he said. "Life's really what you make of it."

"A philanthropist," said Bad Teeth.

"I think it's a philosopher," said Worse Haircut. "That's what you call it when—"

"No one cares," said Bad Teeth. He was clenching his fists at his side. He wasn't trying to relax, and something inside Val—

It wants to die. Let us kill it.

—wanted what was coming next. He held up a hand, a careful distance from touching Bad Teeth. There was a hidden language in this dance; a hand held a certain way said *give me a minute* and held another way said *I'll slap you silly*. He was aiming for the middle ground of *hold up*. "I'm not a philosopher," he said.

"See," said Worse Haircut. "Philosopher, like I said—"

"What I am," said Val, continuing like the other man hadn't even spoken, "is someone who's trying to help."

"No one wants your help," said Worse Haircut. "No one—"

"What kind of help?" said Bad Teeth.

Val's teeth glinted in a smile. "The worst kind," he said. The light was fading from the sky, all the color leaking out as night — *my old friend* — walked closer. The air felt cool and heavy, a blanket held before the coming storm. "Or the best. It depends on your ... your point of view."

"This isn't the first time," said Bad Teeth, "that you've tried to help, is it?" He seemed uncertain, his hands no longer clenched. There was doubt in the way he held his shoulders, the way his mouth turned down at the side. "We're ... we're not the first."

"He's not helping us," said Worse Haircut. "He's helping *her*." The man pointed at the woman on the grass behind them.

"No he's not," said Bad Teeth. "Are you?"

"No," said Val. *There might be a chance.* "I'm here for all of you, one way or another."

"Well fuck you, pal," said Worse Haircut. There was a gun in his hand, a small revolver.

Val looked at it and laughed.

Worse Haircut looked at Val, then at the gun. "What are you laughing for?"

"Sorry," said Val. "It's nothing."

Bad Teeth was backing away. "I'm done," he said. "I'm out."

Worse Haircut ignored him. "I asked you a *question*," he said, stepping forward. "What's so funny?"

"That gun," said Val. "It's more of a ... it's really not your size, is it?"

"Punch a hole in you," said Worse Haircut. "Kill any philosopher."

Val let his face go serious, felt the—

Kill them.

—adrenaline rise. He looked at Bad Teeth. "You better go. Your friend here is going to start something that neither of us can stop. Doesn't matter if he's got a kid's cap gun or not."

Bad Teeth turned and walked away into the falling dusk. Worse Haircut didn't even turn to watch him go, the sound of the other man's passage fading out. "More for me," was all he said. His eyes flicked to the woman behind Val, and he licked his lips. "All for me."

"I'd like—" said Val, as the gun went off. He felt the bullet hit him in the chest, the sharp stab of it coming a second after the sunburst flare of the weapon firing. Something uncoiled inside him—

KILL THEM ALL.

—with the fury of an awakening volcano, and he stepped forward faster than thought. He lifted the other man off the ground as if he weighed less than a wasted thought, heard —*felt*— the light and burn of the pistol firing again and again. His free hand pulled back, slammed forward through the Worse Haircut's chest, grabbing at the—

Flesh. Meat.

—warm wet interior. The other man tried to scream, but no sound came out through a rib cage torn and shredded. The light faded from his eyes like a snuffed candle, and Val dropped the broken body at his feet. He paced left and right, then looked into the darkness to where Bad Teeth had left. He could smell where the other man had gone, the path laid out in scent like a bright arrow. Smell the blood all around him, on his hands. He licked it, the sticky sweetness filling his mind. Val closed his eyes, breathing fast. He could—

Hunt. KILL.

—follow the other man, track him down.

"No," he said into the falling night. "No. We gave him a chance and he took it. We made a *deal.*"

There is only the hunt.

"We made a goddamn deal!" He shouted the words at the empty park around him. His eyes fell on the woman's body on the ground, felt—

There is only the hunt.

"No," said Val. "*No.*" He clenched his teeth, his fists, squeezed his eyes shut until the voice inside quietened. He felt his breath ease, let himself relax a fraction. When he opened his eyes, the evening was the same as it ever was. He bent over in a smooth motion and grabbed the man from the ground, slinging him over his shoulder. Not much he could do about the blood, but she didn't need to see the body when she came around.

When he got back to her, he picked up her purse, a few things from the ground. He found — *thank Christ* — her phone, jabbed in 9-1-1 with a thumb, leaving red marks on the screen. He waited until the call connected.

"9-1-1. What is your emergency?" The woman on the end of the line had that crisp way of talking that he'd grown used to. He'd done this a hundred, a thousand times before.

"Yeah," he said into the phone. "I'd like to report a murder."

"Sir?" The voice sounded more alert. "Are you hurt?"

Val looked at the holes in his shirt, the skin already smooth and clean underneath. "No," he said, then dropped the phone next to the woman. They'd track it, find it, and he shouldn't be here for that. The emergency operator's voice was still talking, made tiny by the speaker, as he walked off into the embrace of night.

LACIE WAS COMING AROUND, her head pounding. She hadn't had a hangover like this since *forever*, and maybe she shouldn't have had that last drink—

Memory slammed back into her and she jerked herself up with a cry. *You didn't have a last drink.* The park sat quiet around her. The two men who'd threatened her were gone. Her purse sat to her side. She held her head with one hand, wanting to throw up almost more than she wanted to run. Lacie took a breath, then another, and looked up. The night stabbed at irregular points by the beams of flashlights. She could hear voices shouting to each other as they moved towards her.

An officer found her, his flashlight feeling like a stab right in the back of her head. She *really* wanted to throw up, but started crying instead. "Found one," the officer said. He crouched down. "Ma'am? Are you okay? Can you tell me what happened?"

Lacie looked past him into the night. She was about to speak when—

Can you keep a secret? She remembered the warm smile when everything else had seemed so *cold*.

"I—" She stammered to a halt. "What happened?"

The officer looked around the park. "You've been attacked," he said. "We've heard that there's been a murder."

"I'm not dead," she said. Her thoughts were lazy and slow, running around like milling sheep. "I'm okay."

"Not you," said the officer. "There's a ... we found a man." He swallowed, his head tipping towards the trees. "That way. What do you remember?"

Can you keep a secret?

Yes.

"I don't remember anything," she said. "I didn't see anything at all."

THREE

When Rex had pulled left onto Wabash, he hadn't been expecting to die.

He'd been thinking about that family — from Arizona, was it? — who'd stopped right in the middle of an intersection. They'd got out of their truck, spent some time dancing on the roof of the Chevy. Been arrested, some such, didn't matter anymore, but Rex had figured it was a shame — the mother, if that's what she was, had a tight body. It was a crime to stop that kind of natural entertainment. He'd glanced up at the Sears, thinking about that tight body, ignored the red, and jammed his foot down on the peddle. His Prius made its sensible, economic way right into the path of a bus. The little car had been picked up, tossed like a toy across the intersection. He'd felt the impact not once, but twice, then a third time, as his car had hit against other cars, the road, God knows what else. There was broken glass flying around inside his car, and his airbag punched him hard in the face.

It seemed hours later that he came around. He could see a slice of the world through the narrow opening in the front of the Prius, the roof tamped down like a piece of tin foil. He could smell smoke, and over the sound of his radio — *This Kiss* playing still through the ruins of the cabin — someone was screaming.

Rex coughed, then tried to claw himself free of the seatbelt. There was something wrong with his arms, they wouldn't — *probably broken*, some part of his mind said, and *get up* another part said — work right. The smoke was getting pretty bad. He could hear movement outside of the car, voices.

"Get back, man. It's going to blow!" Panic, real fear in that voice. Rex was no stranger to that kind of fear, he'd seen more than his share of fires. But a Prius blowing? That'd be something else. Wasn't enough fuel left in this one to start a camp fire. Was there?

"It'll be okay," said another voice. This one calm, relaxed as he spoke over Faith Hill.

Rex thought a little bit about Faith Hill. Now there was a woman who knew how to carry herself, back in the day. He drifted again, then was yanked back to the here and now as the pain shot up his arm, and he screamed.

"Sorry," said the calm voice. Rex pushed his eyes open, but it was hard to see. There was so much smoke in the cab.

He coughed. "It's ok," he said. "Say."

"Yeah?" Calm Voice had a calm face, easy smile.

"I'm gonna die, aren't I?"

Calm Voice frowned. "What makes you say that?"

"I'm all crushed up in here," said Rex, "and I smell smoke. I'm pretty sure I can't get out, and I'm pretty sure my arm's busted good." Faith called to him over the radio again, and he swallowed. "It's okay."

The other man pushed his face a little closer through the broken windscreen. "Why do you say that?"

"My fault," said Rex, coughing again. "Did I hurt anyone?"

Calm Voice nodded, nice and slow. "Yeah."

"Who?"

"Bus driver's pretty banged up. Another car over there smashed through the front window of Sears. They're shook up."

"No one's dead?"

"Not yet," said Calm Voice.

"That's okay then," said Rex. "Hey, pal."

"Yeah?"

"You better get out of here. I'm pretty sure this thing's gonna go up in flames."

"Sure," said the other man. "Can you keep a secret?"

What the hell kind of question— "As good as anyone else."

"No," said the man. "It needs to be better than anyone else."

Rex tried to make out the man's face through the smoke, but it was getting too thick. "Yeah," he said. "I can keep a secret."

"My name's Val," said the other man, "and I'm going to get you out of here."

Rex tried to respond, but he couldn't stop coughing.

VAL LOOKED up from the wreck of the Prius. There was blood all over the ground; the guy inside was hurt pretty bad. The smoke from his car was coming off in thick black clouds, one of the tires on fire. Something in the back of the bus caught with a low *thwump* and flames started to lick out the shattered windows along its side. He caught tall letters written in red, *Damned If You Don't*. Val looked at the writing, then down at his hands.

Yeah. It was then that he looked up and saw a small oval face in the window of the bus, a kid maybe fifteen years old. He was waving at Val, trying to get his attention. Val looked back down at the Prius, then at the kid.

Flame and death.

"Not today," said Val. He took five long steps back from the bus, then pushed himself forward in a sprint, his Nikes gripping the asphalt like claws. Three sprinter's strides saw him moving fast and low, and he jumped into the air, crashing through a window on the side of the bus. The fire at the back coughed with the influx of air, then *whooshed* up loud as it sucked, greedy, eager. *Hungry.* He landed hard against one of the seats, shaking his head as he stood up. The kid was still there, his foot caught between two seats. Pale face, eyes wide with fear. Val looked at the flames that were burning hotter than ever, then back at the window he'd just broken to come in. *Nice move, dumbass.*

"Kid," said Val. "What's your name?"

"James."

"James, huh?" Val walked closer, taking a look at where the metal was caught and twisted around James' leg. "Not Jimmy?"

"No." James had streaks of tears down his face, tracking clear footprints through black smoke dust. "Just James."

"Well, Just James," said Val, "I'm going to get you out of here."

"I've tried," said James. "I can't get out."

"I know a secret," said Val. "But you have to promise not to tell."

"I promise," said James.

"Okay," said Val. "Where're your parents?"

"Dad got off," said the kid. "Step Dad."

"Step Dad, huh?" Val frowned. *What kind of asshole leaves his kid on a burning bus?* "I have to tell you, Just James, that this is going to hurt a little. That okay?"

"Yes," said James. Then, after a moment, "Can you ... if I die, can you tell my Dad to give my Nintendo to Tommy? He's my friend."

"No," said Val. He reached a hand down, felt the metal spar that was twisting around Just James' leg.

"Why not?" The kid's eyes were wide with something, a little shock, a little fear. *Perfect.*

"You can tell him yourself," said Val, muscles bunching in his back as he wrenched the metal aside. Just James screamed, then passed out. Val did a quick check of Just James' leg — *going to be a hell of a bruise, but nothing broken* — before he grabbed the kid from the seat, tossing him over one shoulder and jumping back out the broken window. He landed easy on the ground, glass crunching under his shoes. He ran to the edge of the crowd — *always a crowd, no one wants to get involved, they just stand there* — and handed the kid's unconscious body to a woman.

She looked at him, tugging down the scarf she held against her mouth. "I — he's not my—"

"Lady," said Val, "I don't give a fuck. Take the kid."

She nodded, mute, seeing something in his eyes. She took James from him, staggering under the weight — sometimes it was easy to forget how easy some things were now. Val turned to go, then spun back. "Make sure he gets help for that leg."

"His leg?" The woman looked down at James' leg, seeing the blood for the first time. "My God, how did—"

"You see that bus over there?" Val jerked a thumb behind him.

"Yes."

"He was in there. That's how," said Val, and sprinted back to the Prius. Smoke was all around now, the fire coming off the bus in big sheets. He felt it lick at him, cringed—

Only flame and smoke.

—a little before pushing himself through. He could feel the cotton on his shirt starting to catch as he grabbed at the door of the Prius, setting a foot against it. The heat in the metal of the frame seared his hand, the pain coming with a hot sizzle. He yelled, pulling at the door. The metal groaned before tearing away with a shriek. He tossed the door aside, his hands hurting but the pain already starting to fade. Val bent over, his hands feeling inside the Prius — *come on Val, faster, he's not going to survive the smoke let alone the damn heat* — for the man trapped there. His hand came up against the seatbelt, and he grabbed it with his other hand, twisting the nylon—

He will be free.

—like taffy, the plastic turning white as it stretched before tearing with a snap. Val grabbed the man, dragging him clear, then turned to run back to the safety of the crowd. He was about half way when the gas tank of the Prius exploded, picking them up like a couple of dolls. Val tucked himself around the man, felt something sharp and hard stab into his back before they crashed together on the ground.

Val looked up to see the woman he'd given James to. She still held the kid, half clumsy, half protective. He looked around at the crowd. Caught a phone there, trained on him. Another phone, pointed at the inferno. *Amateur reporters — no keeping this one a secret.* Still. He hadn't changed. Not yet. He pushed himself to his feet.

"Are you — are you okay?" It was the woman holding the kid. Her eyes were wide, a hand reached out towards him, but not quite touching.

Val looked over his shoulder, saw the piece of metal lodged in his back. He coughed around the pain. "Yeah. I'll be fine." He reached around, grabbing at the edge, yanking it free. It looked like a California plate. *Of course. Only place a Prius would come from.* Val turned to go, felt the woman's hand on his arm.

"Your back," she said. "It's—" Her eyes widened as she saw his face. "Your ... your eyes," she stammered.

Val didn't need to see his reflection. He knew they'd be—

Change. Rise. Be free.

—a fierce, bright yellow. Without another word, he pushed into the crowd and away.

"WHAT'S YOUR NAME? Do you know your name?" The paramedic looked down at Rex, adjusting the air mask.

"How bad is it?"

"Bad if you can't remember your name," said the paramedic.

"Rex," said Rex. "My name's Rex."

"Like a dog?"

"Like a fucking Tyrannosaurus," said Rex.

"Got it," said the paramedic. "You'll be fine."

"Fine?"

"You got two sprained wrists and your ribs are going to be feeling everything for a couple weeks. Smoke inhalation too — don't take off the mask. We need to get you in for a scan to be sure, but your belt took the worst of it. That, and the airbag." The paramedic looked over at the emergency cordon, the firefighters still working on putting out the flames.

Damn airbag. Rex remembered the feeling of it punching up into his face. He remembered a man, too, who'd promised to get him out. What had he said? Damndest thing, like *can you keep a secret ...* or something. Rex could keep a secret, especially when he knew that it wasn't for the grace of God that he'd come out of this. The grace of something quite different. Quite, quite different.

"He's all yours," said the paramedic to an officer standing nearby. The cop walked over.

"Sir?"

"Yeah."

"Sir, do you remember how you got out of the car?"

Can you keep a secret?

"No." Rex coughed a little, adjusting his mask. "Mystery to me."

"You sure?"

"Pretty sure," said Rex. *30 years in the fire department, I should be dead, some kind of ... some kind of goddamn hero pulled me out of a car wreck it should have taken industrial machinery to crack open. Yeah, yeah. I see why you'd want to keep that a secret.*

"You're absolutely sure?" The cop was folding away his notebook, a frown on his face.

"Yeah," said Rex. "What, no one else see anything?"

"No," said the cop. "Some kid was yanked from the bus but he says he was out when it happened. Good for him too, ankle looks like it was dislocated, would have hurt like hell. You wouldn't want to remember that."

"Can I..." Rex coughed again. "Can I see him?"

"Who?"

"The kid."

"Why?"

"I figure..." Rex licked his lips. "Maybe it'll jog my memory."

"Maybe," said the cop, in a voice that said *bet it won't*.

"Thanks," said Rex. It wouldn't help his memory, not a damn bit. But maybe he could help the kid, say he was sorry, say ... well. Something. And ... and make sure they were both keeping the same secret.

CHAPTER
FOUR

The alley smelled of rotten cabbage, a dumpster sitting lazy against the wall with its lid open to the sky. Half-disgorged innards seemed to bubble up from the inside like a bad meal coming back. Phillip stared at the same sky, cold asphalt against his back, blood in his mouth.

"Fucking slope," said the man. He was stumbling over his words in his haste to spit out his hate. "Fucking *chink*." Phillip felt the boot hit his side, his body curling up around his pain, and he retched.

"You think ... you actually think you can come to our country, take our *jobs*?" The boot hit again. "You want to—" here, the boot hit him in the back, and Phillip arched, crying out "—rethink your attitude, son."

"Get him, Percy," said another voice. Phillip thought this one sounded younger, eager for the blood, for someone else's pain. *I'm going to die here, because I took out the garbage at the wrong time.* He stretched a hand out towards the black plastic sack, but a boot came down on his wrist. Phillip screamed as something snapped, and he curled up, sobbing.

Some distant part of his mind admonished him. *You should have checked. You should have looked. It's not safe here. Five men in an alley? That's a thing you shouldn't have walked in on.* They'd been arguing over a metal case, handle on the top, and their voices had dropped as he'd walked out the back of the restaurant.

Phillip looked back up along the strong, tall fingers of the buildings as they reached for the stars. Clouds snuck around a fat moon, her pale face looking down. He tried to speak, nothing but blood and a tooth coming out.

"What's that?" The man — *Percy* — leaned down over him, face broken in a smile that wasn't nice or kind or safe. He held a gun, an ugly thing of black metal and straight lines. He tapped the muzzle of the weapon against Phillip's face. *Tap, tap, tap.* Phillip flinched back at each tap. "You trying to say something, gook?"

"I'm ... I'm sorry," said Phillip. And he knew it, he *felt* it, that he was sorry. He just wished he knew what for.

Percy's face twisted into a snarl. He reached a hand up. "Give me a knife."

There was a giggle behind him, another man stepping into Phillip's view. Phillip saw the knife, the blade a foot long, a finger ring set at the base of the handle. Percy took the knife, his hand closing slow and steady around it. Percy leaned in close. "I thought you all knew karate or some shit. Hell, boy, you went down like a tall glass of water on a hot day."

"No ... karate," said Phillip. "I—"

"I don't give two shits," said Percy. "I'm going to cut you, bleed you out, and walk away. Go home, get laid, and not think about you any more. How's that sound, *boy*?"

"Sounds unfair," said a new voice from the head of the alley. "Sounds a bit fucking one-sided, if you ask me."

Percy's gaze jerked up, but the knife held steady at Phillip's throat. Phillip didn't want to turn his head, he could feel the edge of the knife kissing into his flesh already. *Please don't kill me. I don't want to die.*

Percy didn't seem to notice, maybe didn't care. "Walk away," he said. "Just walk the fuck away."

"Sure," said the voice. Phillip could hear footsteps as they came closer, his ears picking out the sounds of shoes against the asphalt. "You let him go, I'll walk away."

Percy laughed. "You for real?" He turned his head back to his entourage, the knife easing from Phillip's throat. Phillip swallowed, tossing a quick glance at the newcomer. *Another white man. Clothes look* — burned — *like he'd walked through a fire. Strong.* Phillip met the other man's eyes. *Please*, Phillip mouthed at the stranger. *Please.*

"I'm for real," said the man, ignoring Phillip. "Fair trade, I reckon. I walk away with this guy, and you don't get executed like you deserve."

"What?" Percy seemed astonished. "What?"

"What's in the case?" The man nodded a head towards the metal case. It was still on the ground. Forgotten, for a moment, before the man had drawn everyone's eyes back to it.

"Fairy dust and wishes," said Percy. He stood up and turned away, Phillip momentarily forgotten. The ugly pistol was in his hand again. "You picked the wrong night to be a hero."

"You shoot me with that and—" said the man, and was cut off as Percy pulled the trigger. Six shots rang out, hard and violent in the alley, the flashes from the weapon throwing strong shadows against the wall each time. Phillip cried out, curling up again, a hand against his head.

Silence. No, not silence: Phillip's hearing came back in stolen fits and starts, overlaid with ragged breathing, the sound of cars, a siren somewhere — *nowhere close* — and the shuffling of feet against the grime and muck of the alley floor. He opened his eyes.

"You finished?" The man with burned clothes was still standing, slightly to the left of where he'd been before. Phillip turned his head to look at Percy — the man was looking between his gun and the man with burned clothes as if he couldn't believe it.

"I shot you," he said. "I shot you five times."

The other man held up a hand, palm out. "Look, I don't want to be that guy," he said, "but it was six times, and you shot *at* me."

"What?"

"Six times. You missed."

"I don't ... I don't miss," said Percy. A sort of honest disbelief was in his voice, a thing that said *now there's something you don't see every day*. "I *shot* you. I shot *you*."

"At," said the man, again. "Nearly got me on the fourth one."

"What?"

"The thing is," said the man, tugging at his burnt shirt, "I was done for the day. It's been a long one, you know? I've already been shot once tonight, and I was in an explosion downtown. I thought, 'Hey Val, maybe you should go home, put your feet up, grab a Coke and a smile, just let the dawn creep up on you and the sofa,' and then I come down here and—"

"Your name's Val?" Percy took a half step forward, then thought better of it. "You're a dead man. You'll never—"

"Right," said Val, nodding. "You'll kill my wife, my kids, my cat. Whatever." He ran a hand through his hair, and Phillip thought the man looked so *tired* right then. "You didn't get my surname."

"I've got Google," said the man.

"Google's not sorcery," said Val. "You need to give it something to work with."

"Don't you ... seriously? We're having this conversation?" Phillip caught the movement as Percy flourished his gun in a sudden motion and pulled the trigger. Another shot rang out, but Phillip was looking right at Val, saw the other man already leaning out of the way.

"The thing is," said Val, "when I got shot earlier this evening, it was because I was trying to talk someone out of doing something stupid. Kind of like this."

"I—"

"The way I see it," said Val, "is that you can pick up your wounded pride and get out of here, leaving this poor guy—" and here, he jerked a thumb in Phillip's direction "— alone."

"Or?" Percy was shifting from foot to foot, the men behind him standing still as stones.

"We'll need to get creative," said Val.

"Creative," said Percy. "I like creative." He looked at his gun, then—

Heartbeat.

Val was already moving, running towards Phillip. Phillip could see it before it—

Heartbeat.

—happened, how the gun would come down towards his head, how the last—

Heartbeat.

—thing he saw would be the bright flash of eternity from the barrel of a Western gun. He just wanted to—

Heartbeat.

—tell his family that it was over now, and he closed his eyes. For him he would be free of this tired kingdom of liars and cheats—

The shot rang out, but the tired kingdom rolled on. Phillip felt a splash of wet, opened his eyes to the back of the man Val standing above him, standing *between* him and Percy. Phillip could see red was blooming on the back of Val's burned and tattered shirt.

This man took a bullet for me. He is going to die for a stranger. Phillip wanted to get up then, to rise and help this man. He started to push himself off the cold ground, Western words trying to form on his lips, and then—

Val turned to him, his eyes a yellow hue. There was something wrong with his face, his teeth, and the words he spoke sounded like they were spat out, their taste and shape unfamiliar. "Get. Away."

"I—" Phillip reached a tentative hand out. "You're hurt."

"Can't," said Val, something animal, something awful, in his voice. "Stop." Then he lifted Percy off his feet, tossing the man into the side of the dumpster.

Phillip scrambled to his feet and ran.

THE UNFAMILIAR LIMBS felt weak and slow. There were no claws at the ends of his hand, nothing to rend with, and the teeth in his head felt blunt and small. He was tied to this tiny body and its weak and frail ways. He looked out at the men around him, their puny weapons held high. He heard the stuttering, frantic beat of their hearts, and caught—

We don't have to kill them.

—the smells of an unfamiliar place around him. This wasn't a forest, a place to run free, and he felt the low, roiling burn of anger. Anger at being *caged* here. He longed to take those loping, easy strides under a night sky free from these tall structures of stone and iron that rose up all around. A small pain nudged at his stomach where the insect had done something to him with a weapon that spat fire. It was nothing, and the insect—

There's another way. Please listen.

—would die. They all stood before him, ready to toss their lives into the ever black of nothing, and for what? He caught the glint of metal, a rectangle made by weak and simple creatures. And yet ... and yet, there was this—

The other man got away. We did what we said we would do. We saved him. We don't have to kill anyone. Please.

—other voice inside him that nagged and snipped and bit at his heels like a pestering pup. He couldn't make the voice stop, but it made him question things. Where he was going. Why he was going there. It made him question his purpose.

He stepped among the four remaining creatures, grabbing at one. There were bright flashes, pain blooming in his chest, but it was small pain, insignificant, unlike the terrible burning of—

Silver. It's called silver.

—the metal the ancient enemy had cursed him with. He tossed the creature he held aside, then paused. The three left were standing around him, fear writ large on their faces, eyes wide, the beat of their hearts faster than a hunted deer. He looked closer at the one on his left, and it dropped its weapon, a tiny sliver of metal clattering to the ground.

See? They're stopping. They'll run away. We don't have to kill them. We don't have to—

That was when the one to his right stepped in, a long piece of wood in his hands. The creature smashed it against his head, the other voice falling to silence in a shattering of splintered timber.

It set him free.

PHILLIP CREPT BACK to the mouth of the alley, one tentative foot in front of the other. His hands touched the edges of old brick as he peered around the corner and into the dark. Lights were out, nothing but the night sky with its fat moon reaching silver legs down to walk faint light on ground. His eyes couldn't pierce the gloom, the blaze of street lighting at his back doing nothing to illuminate the dark unknown. Swallowing, Phillip walked into the alley. "Hello?" His voice was barely a squeak, and cleared his throat. "Is anyone there?" He let his feet take him forward.

He wanted to help the man named Val. He wanted to make sure he was okay, because one man against five was crazy, it was suicide—

Phillip slipped, stumbling forward and landing hard on his hands. He looked behind him at what he'd stepped on. His eyes started to pick out the details in the half light, small sticks connected to a thicker branch. It made no sense until he realized that he could see a leather strap, a watch band, encircling a wrist.

A severed hand.

The stump was ragged, torn. Phillip scrambled backwards like a crab trying to get away from it, but his hand connected with something warm and wet, sliding out from underneath him. He landed against a man's chest, but there was something wrong, it was—

Just a chest.

The head, arms, legs were all gone, blood gone black in the half-light. Phillip looked around, taking in the details of the alley as his eyes adjusted, the bits and pieces of what used to be men scattered around him. There, legs in the over-full dumpster. There, a head on the ground. There, another severed arm, fingers holding a gun. And there—

Something huge and full of darkness turned to look at him. Phillip couldn't comprehend what he was looking at until he caught angry, yellow eyes. That's when he was able to work out *there* was a mouth full of teeth, and *that* was a massive arm ended in claws, drenched wet and glistening in the black in the alley. Phillip saw the eyes blink at him, the yellow vanishing for — *Oh God it's seen me oh God* — a second before a growl broke the night air. The sound cut through the noise of traffic seeping in from the mouth of the alley. The noise turned his bowels to water. He took a step backward, his foot slipping on something soft. Phillip looked below him, each individual item in the pile of red wet at his feet unidentifiable. He turned and ran.

He wasn't fast enough.

CHAPTER
FIVE

She hugged her arms to her sides, shivering. She'd been outside the cabin for a long time.

"Don't you think you should just call him?" Carlisle stood off to her left, coat wrapped around her like a shroud. "Jesus, Danny. It's freezing out here. Isn't the point to make *him* suffer?"

He suffers.

Danny stood straighter. "No."

"It's not?"

"No."

Carlisle nodded, like she was agreeing, then she turned to face Danny. "Fill me in. What's the point?"

"I just..." She trailed off, then shrugged. "I don't know."

"You don't think this is the life for your kid?"

"Adalia?

"You got another kid?"

"No. I mean, yes. I mean ... no, I don't have another kid. Yes, the life is fine."

"It's fine?"

Danny shrugged. "You know it isn't."

Carlisle nodded again. "That makes no sense at all."

"You didn't have to come with me." Danny began to pick at the wall behind her, the thatch snagging against her fingertips. It was old, brittle with the cold that wrapped around her. Snow stretched out in front of the porch, painting the bare trees white. Their cottage was small, she'd grabbed it for just a few dollars online. If she thought about it, could almost feel the heat of the fire inside. Almost. "You really didn't."

"I really did." Carlisle sneezed. "You could have the decency to show you're cold. Just a little."

"I *am* cold. It's fucking freezing out here." Danny gave her head a shake, catching a flash of curls out of the corner of her eyes. She reached up, ran a hand through her hair. "God damn. I need a hair cut."

"You need to call Everard."

"I need a haircut more than that."

"You really don't," said Carlisle. "You need to get your ass back to the world."

"Why?"

"Couple of reasons I can think of," said Carlisle. "The first being that you can't be homeschooling your kid forever—"

"Why not?"

"Because she needs to get out there. In the middle of it. Meet friends."

"Meet people who want to kill her."

"Come on," said Carlisle. "Be reasonable. They don't want to kill her. Mostly, they want to kill Everard."

My Valentine. Danny felt her lips twinge upward in a smile. "You got a second reason?"

"My medical's lapsed," said Carlisle. "This weather's going to kill me."

Danny felt the smile fall away from her face. "I miss him."

"I know."

"I miss him like the desert misses the rain," she said. "But..."

Carlisle waited her out, just turning back to look into the woods, saying nothing.

"Okay," said Danny, "it's like this. I miss him, but I don't know if it's *me* that misses him."

We are the same.

Carlisle shrugged. "Does it matter?"

Danny frowned. "I—"

"I'll let you think it over," said Carlisle. "I used to get paid to catch bad people, like Batman, okay? This isn't really in my wheelhouse. I'm going back inside to watch bad TV."

"There's no TV reception out here."

"That's why it's bad," said Carlisle. "Also, they've found us."

Danny felt her breath catch. "Biomne?"

"Not unless they've opened up a resort in the Caribbean." Danny heard something wistful in her tone, but when Carlisle spoke again her voice had gone hard. "Different 'they.' Still assholes though, whoever they are."

"When?"

"Last night," said Carlisle. "They didn't follow me back here."

"You're sure?"

"No." Danny felt Carlisle shrug in the darkness. "Not really sure about much at the moment. I'm not sure if we should stay, or go. I'm not sure if I should roll into town, maybe get in a fight. I don't know if I should get drunk. I don't know about raising teenage girls—"

"You don't need to—"

"—or how to keep it all together in my head. You remember Elliot?" Carlisle's voice had gone soft in the cold.

"We never met," said Danny. She was caught off guard for a moment, felt that Carlisle was wanting something from her. "We never ... that was before all this."

"Sorta," said Carlisle. "Kinda not as well. He went missing in the middle. I saw him again last night."

"He's alive?" Danny turned to look at Carlisle. "He's okay?"

"Not really," said Carlisle. "I don't think so."

Danny felt Carlisle move, then the thud of the door as it closed behind her friend. She breathed, watching her breath misting in front of her.

The desert misses the rain. The night misses the moon. Pack mate.

"I know," she said to the empty air. "I know."

WHEN SHE CHECKED HER PHONE, there weren't any messages. Just a missed call from a number she knew by heart.

"Your phone rang again," said Adalia. Her tone was accusing.

"I know, honey," said Danny. She stamped her feet to get the blood moving. *Force of habit.* Not like she needed to. Not anymore — the blood always moved just fine. She caught a glimpse of herself in the old mirror hung over the fireplace. It was spotted with age, easy to look at. It hid so many sins she knew must be written on her face. She looked away, not wanting to meet her own eyes.

"It rang yesterday too," said Adalia.

"I know," said Danny. "I know."

"And —"

"I know!" Danny tossed the phone aside.

Adalia hunkered into the couch she was sitting on, the back of it cutting her off from Danny's view. Danny could see the tips of flames licking up into the chimney from where she stood, the couch not quite blocking her view. Adalia said something, almost too low to hear, but it'd been a long time since Danny had been able to pretend she hadn't heard something.

Still. You *needed* to pretend, sometimes. You needed to be a mother, sometimes. Or all the time. Even when you wanted to run, or hunt, or cry. "What was that?"

"He always calls," her daughter said again. "And you never answer."

Danny looked down at her hands, then at the back of the couch. Adalia hadn't surfaced again — her eyes probably on the fire. "It's complicated."

"Mom? If I had a boyfriend—"

"If?"

"*If* I had a boyfriend, and he called me and I didn't pick up for a week — or a month, or a *year* — do you know what would happen?"

Danny shrugged, even though she knew Adalia couldn't see her. "I'm a bit out of touch with the kids of today."

"I'd be *so* dumped," said Adalia. "*Dumped.* Like, he would stop calling."

The night misses the moon.

"Maybe..." Danny felt her voice catch. "Maybe I'll call him tomorrow."

"What if," said Adalia, "tomorrow is the day he stops wanting to talk?"

Danny's reply was cut off by Carlisle stamping in from the hallway. She was decked out in loose-fitting faded jeans and an old bomber jacket. "I'm out."

"You're what?" Danny blinked at her.

"Going out. Before we spend so much time together we start synchronizing periods. Shark week three at a time is hell. Just the thought of two at a time was why I'd never be a lesbian."

"I thought," said Adalia's voice from behind the couch, "you weren't lesbian because you—"

"And that's my cue," said Carlisle. "Kid? Stuff we talk about when your Mom's not here is like stuff that goes on in Vegas."

"I've never been to Vegas."

"Good," said Carlisle, as the door rattled closed behind her. The sound of their big truck starting up pattered against the outside of the cabin, fading as the distance ate the sound.

Danny looked at the door, the night falling outside. The fire popped, sending a shower of sparks up the chimney. She took a half step towards the couch where Adalia sat, then stopped, looking at her phone again.

Tomorrow. She'd call tomorrow. Because...

Because she just wasn't ready yet.

CHAPTER
SIX

Carlisle looked at the door to the bar, the snow falling around her. Her bomber jacket wasn't warm enough for this, not by a long shot, but she'd get warm inside soon enough, and she wanted to be free to move. She reached behind her to the sidearm she had tucked into the waist of her jeans, then pulled her jacket down over the top. The Eagle was big but felt comfortable against her back — an old friend, one she'd felt she'd needed since ... well, since she'd started hunting bigger game.

Your problem, she said to herself as she walked towards the entrance to the bar, *is that you can't leave shit alone. You should get Danny and her kid, get them in the truck, and drive, just fucking drive until there's no more people anywhere around you.*

Except, that's what they'd tried to do when they found this place. Drove to a point where there wasn't supposed to be a town on a map, and they'd still found her. Carlisle felt the weight of it on her shoulders. They hadn't tracked Danny, or even the kid. *Detective Carlisle*, the Caribbean man had said. He'd known who she was, *what* she was from before.

There were trucks parked out front tonight, five of them, one of them big and black. Snow was gathering against them, softening the edges of their shapes in the dark. The black truck had tinted windows that were out of place in a town where the night lasted far too long. As she got near it, she kneeled down in the snow, fishing the tracker — a small box, easy to miss unless you were looking for it — out of a pocket. Carlisle flicked a switch on the box, then stuck it up under the wheel arch. She brushed snow from her knees, then breathed the night air, the dry cold of it sharp in her nose. She didn't have Danny's gifts, but she could catch the scent of bad liquor and cheap men on the air as well as the next girl.

She looked around one more time. *Last chance. Just walk the fuck away.* She ran a hand through her hair, then walked to the door of the bar — *wrong way, wrong damn way Carlisle* — pushing it open in a smooth motion. Warmth and light and the smell of fried food hit her all at the same time, and she stood still for a moment, door open behind her, snow falling and tumbling in around her feet.

Carlisle saw them in the bar — Caribbean, perfect teeth showing as his lips started to pull up in a smile of recognition. She felt an unexpected, almost foreign twinge in her gut — *you hardly know the man, get over it Carlisle* — and pushed it aside. She looked at the two other men that stood next to him, their heads turning to look at her. She let the door close behind her as she took in the other men in the bar, all cut of the same cloth — heavy set, too much fat over muscle made strong by working outside in the cold.

"Detective Carlisle," said Caribbean. He looked genuinely pleased to see her, his eyes flicking down and back up as he—

Don't kid yourself, Carlisle. He's ten years younger than you, and was probably banging cheerleaders in college. You hate cheerleaders.

—stood up, arms wide and welcoming. "It looks like we won't need a search after all."

"I'll get to you in a second," she said, then turned to the men Caribbean and his team were talking to. "All you guys? Get out."

The one closest to her looked her up and down, nothing nice at all in it. He had a plaid shirt, some relic of twenty years ago, stains down the front. He did the glance — *eyes down, eyes up, smile in the eyes* — before speaking. "Well look what we've got here," he said. "Guys, we've—"

"No," said Carlisle. "This isn't going to be that kind of night."

Plaid started to get up, anger pulling at his face. It looked at home there. "Now listen here, missy," he said.

"No," said Carlisle again. "You'll listen to *me*." The cop came back into her tone, comfortable and natural. "These men are wanting to hire you. Easy money, they said."

Caribbean stepped forward, started to open his mouth.

"No," said Carlisle. "I haven't *finished*. Easy money, like I said, all you got to do is find some people living in a cabin. Not many tourists around here, you think you know where they are and what to look for. But what you don't know," said Carlisle, "is what happened to the last group of heroes who tried to bag 'em. You think maybe a cabin full of chicks is easy, you'll just roll up and stuff them in a bag for your new, rich friend here."

The jukebox started playing then, the same damn Johnny Cash song kicking on that was playing last night. Plaid was standing now, his jowls shaking as he spoke. "Looks like you just came to give us an advance."

"No," said Carlisle. "The problem with you people is you don't *listen*. I've come to give you an escape." She walked closer to them, trailing her fingers over a table top as she approached the group. She spoke again, looking at the group of men, but hoping Caribbean was listening. *He has to.* "She doesn't like killing them. She can't stop once she starts."

Plaid looked confused, but he was the kind of man that didn't let a little thing like that slow him down. He stepped forward, reaching a hand out towards Carlisle's arm. She watched the hand come, let the man step into kissing distance. Carlisle felt the hand close on her arm and almost let herself smile, closing her eyes and letting her breath out. She could feel it as Plaid's hand applied pressure, implied possession, as the man leaned away from her, his voice sounding like he'd turned to face the other men, heard him say, "Boys, I think we've—"

Her eyes snapped open as her hand whipped around in a *haito* strike, the blade formed by the top edge of her hand hitting the soft tissue in the man's neck. Plaid's voice was cut off and he gagged, sagging a little and turning to face her. His hand softened just enough on Carlisle's arm; she dropped her shoulder, breaking free of the grip, then rose up, using her momentum to slam a palm heel under the man's chin. He lifted up, head whipping back, then toppled out on the ground like a falling tree, glasses and bottles on the tables around her shaking and jumping.

Carlisle held her pose for a couple of heartbeats, then lowered her hand back to her side. "I said," she said, eyes on Plaid's four friends, "that this wasn't going to be that kind of night. Could be a different kind of night if you want it to be. Your call." She saw anger building in the group, a man with a Michelin jacket putting an uncertain hand on the belly that stuck out over his waistband. A friend of his with a cap that said *Welcome to Miami* pulled the hat off, slicked back his already slick hair, then put it back on. The third took a pull from his beer — *does he actually have a shirt that advertises Miller?* — while the last man reached under his vest and pulled out a small revolver. It looked like a 38 Special — she'd know the shape of the Smith & Wesson from any angle. She'd had one for years.

"If you point that gun at me," she said, "you're going home in a bag."

38 Special looked down at the gun in his hand, then back up to Carlisle. He thought about it, then raised the gun, slow and deliberate, and pointed it at Carlisle.

She frowned. "That wasn't the best call you've made tonight."

The man looked at her, then at the gun in his hand as he tipped it slightly before pointing it back at her. "What?"

"See," she said, "you think you've got a gun pointed at me, and you're in charge."

"That's right," said 38 Special, looking at her over the barrel. "I've got the gun."

"You've got the gun," Carlisle agreed, nodding. "It'd work better for you if the safety was off."

"You think I'm going to fall for that?"

"No," said Carlisle. She licked her lips, then let them part in a fierce, tight smile.

"Fuck this," said 38 Special, and pulled the trigger.

Nothing happened. Carlisle shrugged. "Safety's on." She pointed. "It's the little thing there on the side," she said. "Just above your thumb."

The man looked at the gun, then clicked the safety switch. "Now," he said, "we're—"

Carlisle stepped forward with her left leg, letting her right foot catch the base of a chair next to her. She kicked the chair across the space between them, letting her momentum take her a little to the left. The chair spun through the air, then collided with the man's arm. The revolver fired, the bullet spitting past her, shattering something made of glass behind her. 38 Special went down, the chair hitting him in the bridge of the nose. A touch of cold licked at her back — *he shot out a window* — as she pushed herself into a dash towards the three standing men.

Michelin took a swing at her as she got close, so slow it was almost comical. She stepped under his arm — *got to get him in the way, give me something to work with* — giving him a gentle push and spinning him around so his back faced her. Carlisle stamped down hard on the back of one of the man's knees, grabbing the back of his hair at the same time. He fell backward like a falling anvil, and she stepped to the side and slammed a fist into his face as he fell past her. He didn't get up.

Something behind her — some fragment of sound — drew her back around, and she saw man with the Miami cap had grabbed a pool cue. He waved it at her. "Bitch!"

Carlisle looked past him, took in Caribbean. The man was

standing in his impeccable suit, arms folded. The two men at his side watched. She shrugged, raising an eyebrow at him. He unfolded his arms, held a hand out, palm up towards Miami, a gesture that said *go ahead.*

Weird. She could solve that later. *One case at a time, Carlisle.* She took four quick steps towards Miami, then leaned back as the man swung the cue towards her head. She didn't slow herself, stepping inside his reach and grabbing the hands that held the wood. They locked together, shoulder to shoulder, and Carlisle let him see her smile. "You sure you want to do this?"

"Bitch!" said the man again, and tried to wrestle the cue from her. She let herself be tugged around, then planted her feet and swung the cue back around between them, using it like a lever. There was a crack as the man's wrist snapped, and he screamed. She took two steps away, still holding the cue, then swung it back around into the side of the man's head. He dropped like a stone, a tooth spinning across the room. It clattered against the jukebox, which skipped and started to change tracks. Probably more Johnny Cash.

She opened her hand, the cue balanced on her palm, and looked over at Caribbean. She saw a small smile playing at the man's mouth. A sound caught her attention again, and she saw 38 Special starting to rise. The gun was in his hand and pointed in her direction. Carlisle closed her fingers around the cue, planted her free hand on the side of a table, and rolled over the top. The cue came with her, she tucked it under her body as she rolled and the side of it knocked against her hip then — *goddamn* — her face as she rolled. She heard the gun fire, a bullet hitting somewhere above her as she moved. Her feet came down over the edge of the table, the cue in her hand, and she spun across the distance between the two of them. Another shot went off, tugging at the sleeve of her jacket. Carlisle reached 38 Special, his eyes were wide with fear. The gun was still in his hand — *no way he can miss at this range.* She saw it in his eyes, the moment before he made the decision to kill her, and she brought the cue down against the side of his head in a two-handed strike. It splintered against his skull and the man hit the ground, the gun firing blind. Carlisle felt her heart hammering in her chest, her ears ringing from the shot.

She let the broken cue go, then turned around, the movement slow and deliberate. *Okay Carlisle. You're still alive. This time.* She worked to bring her breathing under control. "Okay," she said after a few lungfuls of air, "now I've finished with them, I've got time to deal with you three."

Caribbean had a half-smile pulling at his mouth, but the two men with him looked at her hard. Caribbean thought for a moment, then said, "I don't know if the things we want are at odds with the things you want."

"I think," said Carlisle, "that if you want to send a group of assholes against me and mine, we're poles apart." She stepped forward, her foot crunching against some broken glass on the ground. "I think," she said again, "it's a problem we should work out, right here. Right now."

"This isn't really your style, Detective," he said to her. The two men at his side hadn't moved. "I know you—"

"You don't know shit."

"I know you graduated with good marks. Not *top* marks, but good enough to land you the job you wanted. I know your father is dead."

"So you read the papers." Carlisle took another step forward, aware of the Eagle still snug against her back. She wanted to reach for it, feel the comfortable weight in her hand, but there was something here that made her pause. It wasn't just that she didn't want to kill a man who hadn't pulled a weapon on her, no matter what it might prevent. There was something about him that was ... different. *You've seen a lot of assholes in your time, and this guy just doesn't have his asshole dial turned all the way to 11.* "Lucky you."

"I've spoken with him." Caribbean dropped the four words into the sound of Johnny Cash. "He is a man of indifferent quality."

Carlisle swallowed, something pulling at her guts. "You *what?*"

"We spoke," said Caribbean, "about you."

She didn't realize she'd pulled it out before she saw the gun in her hand, leveled at him. Carlisle could see the barrel shaking slightly, her fingers white with tension. "Say that again. I fucking *dare* you. No. I double dare you."

The men at Caribbean's side started to move, but Caribbean held a hand up. "Can we start again? I feel like we've ... I'd like to start again."

"Can I ask you a question?" Carlisle held her weapon in front of her like a shield. "I mean, aside from the question I just asked."

"Please."

"Let's say you meet a girl in a bar. Do you ask her about her dead partner, then maybe talk about her dead Dad, or do you take her out for a few drinks first?" Carlisle could feel the sweat cooling on her face, and she wiped it away with her hand. "Because if this is your usual style, I can't see you getting laid all that much."

Caribbean blinked at her, then laughed. "Raeni knew you were different."

"Who's Raeni?"

"You would call her ... my boss," said Caribbean. "Can we sit and talk about this? You can keep pointing your gun at me, if it makes you feel more comfortable."

"You don't look concerned." Carlisle shrugged. "I don't see there's much to talk about. I want you to get back in your truck and drive the hell on out of here."

"I'm not concerned," said Caribbean, "because I know where the dead go once they die."

Carlisle looked at him, her head tipped to one side as she thought about it. *Talks to dead people. Looks good in a suit. Could go either way.* "Sure, what the hell," she said. "Let's talk." She used her free arm to sweep the glasses and plates on a table aside, heard them crash as they hit the ground. She sat in a chair facing Caribbean, the gun held in her lap, then gestured with her free hand to the seat opposite her. "Have a seat."

Caribbean nodded at the other two men before stepping away from them and sitting in the chair. "My name's Ajay."

"What's the J stand for?" said Carlisle. "I mean, the A ... you look like an Adam."

"Not 'AJ,'" said Ajay. "Ajay. One word, four letters. Fourteen points in Scrabble. Ajay Lewiss." He was smiling at her, something easy in it that made her want to grind herself against him.

Carlisle looked away, licking her lips and watching as one of the two men behind Ajay took a call on a phone. She let her eyes flick back to him. "You play a lot of Scrabble?"

"No," he said. He seemed to think about something. "What is it you want from your life, Detective Carlisle?"

"Champagne and happiness," she said. "One drives the other."

"I want to live in a world where we're not hunted like dogs," said Ajay. "That's the story of my people. My family. Do you understand family?"

"You've talked to my Dad. You tell me." Carlisle watched the man on the phone behind Ajay, her eyes moving to the second man. He was working his way slow and steady around to her side. "Say. Ajay?"

"Yeah." Ajay leaned forward, his elbows on the table.

"These two guys work for you?"

"We come from the same place," he said.

"That a yes or a no?"

"The question doesn't mean anything here," he said. "You haven't asked about your father."

The man on the phone rung off, then nodded to the other off to Carlisle's side. She could feel the taste of the room change then, the other man reaching behind him, his hand coming out with something small and black, and Ajay was starting to rise, trying to say something, turning to face the man with the phone, his hands up—

Carlisle stood in a smooth motion, her chair skidding out behind her. She shot the man to her side three times — *one in the head, two in the chest* — then turned the weapon on the man with the phone. He was trying to bring something to bear on her, and she fired three more shots, his body tugging and pulling as the rounds hit. His body fell to the ground, the soft *tink* of her last spent cartridge leaving her sidearm and falling in a trail of smoke. Her eyes found the object one of the men had held, a small taser, not civilian-grade. She fed a fresh magazine into her weapon, turned the Eagle back on Ajay. That same twinge in her gut made her pause, stopped her finger from pulling the trigger. "Give me one reason why I shouldn't finish this right now."

"He said," said Ajay, "to tell you that he's sorry."

Carlisle narrowed her eyes. "Who?"

"Your father," said Ajay, "said to tell you that he's sorry. That if he hadn't placed his hands upon you, you wouldn't have run. He said to me that he did it because you—"

"Stop. Stop *talking*."

"He did it because you have your mother's eyes. He wishes you'd never seen the heart of the Night. He says it was his hands that pushed your first stumbling feet down this path."

Carlisle stood in the middle of the room, the fallen men around her and Ajay. She clenched her hand around her sidearm, hand shaking with it, until she screamed out loud, a cry of rage and pain. She pulled the gun to the side and squeezed the trigger again and again, the shots hammering out against the sound of Johnny Cash until the weapon clicked empty. She leaned over then, one hand on the table next to her, gun held to her side.

Ajay started to move towards her, his arm reaching out. "Are you—"

Carlisle yanked herself upright, hand palm-out towards Ajay. "Don't you touch me. Don't you fucking come near me."

"But ... Detective." Ajay looked lost. "He said—"

"Shut up!" She screamed the words at him. She took a half-step forward, her breathing ragged. "You want to live through the night?"

"I want to live through the night." Ajay's face softened. "Even though I know where the dead go when they die."

"Then you promise me, Ajay Lewiss. You promise me one thing."

"If it's in my power."

"You promise me," said Carlisle, her voice shaking, "that you don't talk to ... to *him* anymore. I don't know how you do it. Hell, I don't *care*. I don't know how you talk to a man dead and cold thirty years now, but if you do, I swear to God—"

"I will make a promise," said Ajay, his arms wide. "You do not need to make a vow to God."

Carlisle rubbed at her face, felt her hand come away wet with tears. She brushed her hand against her jacket, angry at herself. "I'm not."

Ajay looked puzzled. "You're not what?"

She looked at him, then turned to the door, her feet taking her across the room, around broken glass and spent cartridges. She reached the door, the cold and the wind creeping in through the broken window, then turned back to look at Ajay. "I'm not sorry. If he hadn't given me that push, I wouldn't have met the best family I've ever known. I swear to God, Ajay Lewiss, right here and right now, that if you hurt my family I will fucking *end* you. Do you hear what I'm saying?"

"I hear you." He was starting to say something else but she lost the end of it as she stepped out into the cold and the night, the door banging shut behind her.

You should have just shot him, Carlisle. You should have just put a bullet in him and been done with it. She let her feet take her a little further along, then she looked back at the door of the bar. Ajay hadn't followed her out.

She wished it had gone differently tonight. She hadn't felt that Ajay was lying to her, he thought he was doing something right. She pushed back on the feeling. *You're not a cop anymore, Carlisle. You haven't been a cop for five years.*

Still. She hated herself for it, but that twinge was still there in her gut. Carlisle wished he'd bought her a drink.

CHAPTER
SEVEN

"What is this shit?" John picked up the bun in front of him.

"It's brioche style," said Val. "I made it this morning."

"It's—"

"It's divine," said Sky. She had an arm looped through John's, the toweling of her robe crisp and white in the morning light. She leaned forward, nipping a bit of John's brioche.

"Hey," he said, realizing the loss of his prize that half second after it was gone.

"Too slow," she said around a mouthful of brioche, but her eyes were soft as she looked at John. "You didn't like it." Val didn't remember anyone ever looking at John like that. *He deserves it.*

"I didn't say that," said John, the Miles Megawatt Smile gone in favor of something softer, more honest. "I was thinking I wasn't going to eat it."

"You were going to eat it," said Val, "and then you were going to eat another one. Same as yesterday."

"I had two yesterday?"

"You had four," said Sky, leaning back but still touching John. "Two at breakfast, and—"

"Four?" said Val. "The Force is strong with your stomach." He leaned forward over the counter, the coffee jug in his hand. Sky nodded, lifting her cup. The smell of cinnamon and chocolate touched air already heavy with fresh coffee and baking.

"Is this some kind of revenge kick?" John took a bite from his brioche, then put it down. "For all those years you were fat. Carbs don't like me."

"Val was fat?" Sky looked Val up and down. "What, when you were born?"

"Think of it like carb loading," said Val. Watching Sky and John made him miss Danny, but he kept it from his face. He hoped. "I dunno. Five years?"

"It's good hangover food," said Sky. She combed her hair with her fingers, then shook it out. "Mostly because everything is good hangover food. I need to get to work."

"Stay," said John, "and get fat."

"I'd rather go," she said, "so we can make rent."

"We can make rent," said Val, pulling some grungy notes out of his pocket. "I made a little money last night." He tossed the bills onto the counter. "If you'd rather, you know. Get fat. Or ... something."

"Dirtiest thing on planet Earth," said John, picking through the pile with a finger. "Holy shit. There's a couple Ben Franklins in here."

"Big tipper," said Val. "Restored my faith in humanity."

"I still got to work," said Sky, "even if you get to sleep all day." She kissed John on the cheek then flounced off towards the bathroom. The door closed, followed by the sound of running water.

"So," said John, turning his coffee cup around. "How did the night really go? And I don't mean in some vague, 'Oh I got a couple of C-notes from a random stranger,' way, I mean—"

"I know what you mean," said Val. He turned his coffee around in his hand. "Honestly? I got no idea."

"That bad?"

"I guess," said Val. He picked up the remote, flicking the TV on, an NBC logo sitting in the corner. The news anchor was talking about a traffic jam — *how is that news?* — and he tossed the remote back on the counter. "It's never good when I wake up naked."

"Be serious," said John. "Sometimes that's good. When I wake up naked, the party's usually in full swing. Orgies don't start themselves."

Val smiled, but he couldn't put any heart in it. "I'm just trying..." He trailed off.

John leaned forward, slapping him on the shoulder, then stole another brioche. "You're trying to make a difference. I know. We've had this talk."

"Yeah."

"For the record, I'm not a fan," said John. "You'll get yourself killed."

"If only it were that easy," said Val. *I've tried. God help me, but—*

"Hey," said John. "What's that supposed to mean?"

"Nothing," said Val. "So, what did you two get up to last night?"

"Oh you know," said John, around a mouthful of pastry. "Few beers. Just my birthday."

"Christ, again?" Val grinned. "You have one of those every year?"

"Some of us still get older," said John. "And this is serious, okay, so — just listen. Last night, she—"

"Sky?"

"The very same," said John. "She says to me, 'I'm so glad you've got younger friends.' She meant you and Danny."

"Probably Carlisle too," said Val. "She's in good shape."

"Have you been told to get fucked today?" John looked down at his chest, then back up. "I mean, it's all still in perfect working order."

"I did warn you about the younger woman thing," said Val. "Not my fault if your dick got in the way of the conversation."

"You were talking to my dick?"

"I really think I was," said Val. His eyes flicked to the bathroom door, checking—

She has not hunted with Pack.

—that Sky was still out of earshot. "She's ... you know."

John put his elbows on the counter top. "She's what?"

"It's nothing," said Val.

"Tell me."

"She makes you less of a complete tool," said Val. He shrugged, grinning. "Hey! You asked me to tell you." *And she completes you. In a way no one else has, not that I've seen. It's good to see you smile ... for real.*

"Let me be the first," said John, "to say — on this fine morning, sir — to get fucked."

Val felt the grin slip from his face as something on the TV caught his attention. He grabbed at the remote and thumbed up the volume. The anchor's face was calm, her pumped hair — a thing of engineered beauty — somehow at odds with her serious tone.

"*We go live now to the scene. Younger viewers are advised to take special care. Tony? Tony, can you tell me what's going on?*"

"*Sure, Zambolina. It's like a war zone here in down town Chicago. The police have cordoned off the area and aren't letting us close. Are you getting these pictures?*"

"*Yes, Tony. What are we looking at?*"

"*I think it's bits ... well, I think it's bodies. Rumors are circulating of a gang-style massacre, five or more people left dead at the scene. We're trying—*"

The TV clicked off, and John tossed the remote back on the counter. "It's not going to make a difference if you beat yourself up."

Val swallowed. "Did they say five?"

"They weren't super specific," said John. "Look. It doesn't matter."

"It matters," said Val, picking up the remote. He clicked the TV back on.

"*...Other news, a local hero of the downtown Chicago district was*" *caught on camera as he pulled a man from the burning wreckage of this car. These images show—"*

"Hey," said John. "It's you. You're on TV. Kinda."

Val rubbed his face with his hand. "This is why superheroes wear masks."

"The good news," said John, stepping closer to the TV, "is that with all the smoke and flames, it's hard to tell it's you."

"How hard?"

"Pretty hard," said John. "You're barely recognizable. Basically just some anonymous stranger, helping his fellow man." John leaned forward a little more. "Are you ... are you wearing one of my T-shirts?"

"I can't remember," said Val. He turned the volume up.

"—Rex. I keep telling the cops I can't remember. I came through the intersection, got banged up pretty good I guess. The funny thing is—"

"Hey," said Sky, from the bathroom door. "Is that Val on TV?"

"No," said Val and John together. Val looked down at the plate of brioche stacked in front of him. "We were just saying he looks a little like me."

"Yeah, I can see why," said Sky. "He maybe looks like you, but his eyes are all weird." She turned away, toweling her hair as she walked towards the bedroom she shared with John. *That was close. She doesn't know, she shouldn't know ... too many people carry the burden of my secret already.*

"One thing that's been bugging me," said John, flicking the TV off again, "is what's in the case."

"The case?" Val blinked.

John jerked a thumb over towards the windows lining the outside wall of the apartment. "That case. Over there."

The alley was close around him, the taste of delicious copper in his mouth. He reached out with a massive hand, lifting up the tiny thing of metal.

John snapped his fingers in front of Val. "Hey. Buddy. You still with me? You kind of zoned out there for a minute."

Val blinked again. "I ... sure. I don't really remember."

"I see," said John. "Thing is, you don't usually go in for souvenirs."

"No," said Val. "I think we should get rid of it."

"Why? Let's take a peek." John was walking towards the case.

"Because," said Val, "*he* wanted to bring it back."

John froze in his steps, then tossed a look over his shoulder. "You sure?"

"No," said Val. He looked at the case, tipping his head a little as he tried to remember. The memories of last night felt so far away—

One of them grabbed the case, making a break for it on those tiny, spindly legs. So weak. He loped easy and slow next to the creature, then backhanded it across the alley. The shiny metal thing spun free, clattering against the wall. He reached to pick it up, then felt the hot spark of pain as something barked, harsh and loud. He turned towards another one of them pointing something small at him. He snarled with savage joy. The end of these creatures was always delicious.

"Okay," said Val, "yeah I'm sure. He brought it back."

"How'd he get in here?" said John.

"Maybe you need to set up a webcam," said Val.

"A webcam for what?" said Sky, coming back out of the bedroom. She had a suit jacket on over comfortable pants. She looked at John, her voice softening. "How do I look?"

"Like I'm the luckiest man alive," said John, his eyes stuck to her. "Like a million bucks."

The corners of her eyes creased into the smile, and she leaned forward to kiss him, her lips lingering. "Don't be late," she said.

"I won't," said John.

The door slammed behind her as she left. Val looked after her, then back to John. "Late for what?"

"My party," said John.

"You did that last night."

"No," said John. "We had drinks last night. Tonight we're having a party. You know how I know that?"

"Lay it on me."

"Because you're going to be there." John reached down for the case, hefting it. "It's pretty light."

"So I see," said Val. "Let's toss it in a dumpster and call it even."

"Let's open it," said John, "and be *rich*. It's got to have money in it."

"How you figure that?" Val looked at the case. "You have a very fertile imagination."

"Easy," said John. "Any movie with a metal case? It's got money in it."

"Or nuclear launch codes, or heroin, or something that wants to eat your face." Val frowned. "The eat-your-face thing I can probably deal with. I'd like another coffee first."

"I've seen all those movies," said John, "and I'm telling you, there's money in this one. I can feel it."

"Maybe," said Val. "Bit of a moot point though. It's locked, right?"

"Always with the problems," said John. "I'm going to grab a shower then I'll show you how we get it open."

"I can't wait," said Val. But he couldn't help but wonder—

They fought to save it and paid with their lives.

—whether it was something they should open at all.

CHAPTER
EIGHT

"What I'm telling you," said Carlisle's voice, small and distant, "is that they're on to us."

"They can't be on to us," said Danny. "We're in Alaska. Wait." She thought she caught a noise, something that could have been the *crump* of a footstep in snow.

"Wait for what?"

She held the phone away from her head, then put it back to her ear. "Who the hell are 'they'?"

"No clue," said Carlisle. "They're assholes, though."

Danny glanced at Adalia, asleep on the couch. The fire had burned low, and she was trying to keep her voice down. "There's a problem."

"Just the one?" Carlisle coughed a sound like a laugh. "Hit me."

"You've got our truck." Danny looked around the room, her eyes picking out the details despite the low light. "You took the damn truck, and we're in a log cabin in the woods. I can't just catch a bus."

"I get that," said Carlisle. "It's just that..."

Danny heard something catch in the other woman's voice, and she—

Fear. Shame. Pain.

—paused for a second, then said, "Carlisle?"

"Yeah?"

"What did they do?" Danny licked her lips. "What did they *say* to you?"

The line hissed and crackled for a moment, and Danny caught the sound of something that might have been Carlisle shifting gears. "They didn't say anything to me," said Carlisle. "*They* didn't do anything to me."

"Okay," said Danny. "It's just that—"

They hunt us, and we are not for hunting.

"—hell," she said. "Hell."

"I know," said Carlisle. "You know, the truck thing..."

"Yeah?"

"I figured you could give Adalia a ride. You know. Because you're like a big horse. If horses had claws, and—"

"It doesn't work like that," said Danny, but her lips pulled into a smile. Her eyes flicked to the couch where Adalia lay. "It can't ... it's not an option."

"Sure it is," said Carlisle.

"People ... it doesn't always turn out for the best," said Danny.

"Girlfriend," said Carlisle, "this situation is so far off the scale from 'best' that we're in a whole new land. Uncharted territory, even for us."

Danny reached a hand down to Adalia's head, stroking her daughter's hair. "What ... what did you *see*?"

"I saw—"

Danny heard a crack from outside and cut Carlisle off. "I'm going to have to call you back."

"Sure," said Carlisle. "Sure. And if you can't—"

"Really. I'll call you right back," said Danny, and clicked the phone off. She put it down on the small table, the phone scuffing across the old, uneven surface. She reached a hand down, her fingertips feeling the wood, the age of it, the memories in it. Her hand tapped the wood once, twice, and then she turned to the door, her face gone hard and cold like the night outside.

Her feet took her to the door without conscious thought, and she leaned against the wood, the feel of it rough against her skin. She listened, her ears straining, for the sound she thought she'd heard before. Her hand touched the knob, held it, then with a twist of her wrist she jerked it open and stepped out into the dark. The door clicked shut behind her, Adalia murmuring in her sleep. She left her daughter with the fire, the warmth, and its meager light.

The Night is for hunting.

DANNY'S STRIDES took her down the porch in two smooth steps, and she loped into the night. Her eyes picked out the trees, black and white against the stars, but it was her ears, her hearing—

Three.

—that was most improved since everything had ... *changed*. She was always aware, always hearing those sounds around her, like a ... what had her Valentine called it?

Spider Sense. We're like Jedi superhero rock stars with unlimited cocaine.

The memory of his face made her breath catch. *Focus.* She moved on whisper soft feet around the cabin, the smoke from the chimney rising into the night sky, the smell of it reaching her nose, tickling the back of her throat. On a whim, she grabbed at the ridges of wood that made up the wall of the log cabin, and pulled herself up, quick and easy, onto the roof. She padded across to the rear of the cabin, looking down on a man.

He was dressed in white, and should have been hard to pick out against the snow. He held something small and hard in both hands, a weapon of some kind. It didn't look like a gun. It wouldn't have mattered if it was. She lifted her face to the night sky, and sniffed. No—

Poisonous, burning.

—silver that she could smell. Danny grabbed at the edge of the roof, swinging herself down, and landing on the man with both feet. He let out a small noise like the sound of a pillow being plumped as he dropped into the snow. She snared the weapon he carried, holding it up. Danny wasn't an expert in weapons, not before the change, and not since, but she felt the heft of it, fingered the firing stud. She knew the taser for what it was.

It didn't make any sense. Tasers didn't work on her. Not really.

She scampered around the side of the cabin, coming up behind the second man. He was also in white. She let her feet pull her close behind him, then leaned forward so her face was almost at the back of his neck. "Hey."

The man jumped, a small yell — almost a scream — coming from him. He spun around, firing his taser, the shot going wide as she leaned out of the way. Her hands came up and batted the weapon from him, then she reached forward with one hand and grabbed the front of his jacket, lifting him off the ground.

His arms and legs flailed. Danny waited for a couple heartbeats, then gave the man a shake. "Hey. Cut it out."

She could see his eyes through the goggles he wore. Dark skin, brown eyes, wide with fear. She saw him nod, the movement on the edge of frantic.

"You're here for me, aren't you?"

A nod. *Yes.*

"And you're here for her. Me and my daughter."

A pause, then another nod.

Pup!

"That's too bad," she said, a snarl twisting her face. She slammed the man into the wall of the cabin beside her then tossed him aside, not waiting to watch as he slumped to the snow.

Danny was off at a sprint, closing the distance to the porch where she'd exited the cabin. She rounded the corner of the cabin, the porch coming into view, and saw the back of a white jacket as the door started to close behind him. The ground under her was icy, and she slid. One hand down in the—

Cold is nothing. Pup!

—snow, she bounded over the porch railing in time to snag the edge of the door just before it shut. She wrenched it open, saw the man inside had already heard her, had already *turned...*

She looked down at the taser darts stuck in the front of her shirt, the barbs in her skin. Didn't he know what would happen? He shouldn't, he *couldn't* pull the trigger, she wouldn't be able to stop it then—

Danny felt the hot white fire as the taser discharged, her teeth clamping together as her body locked. She tasted copper and heat, felt the harsh brush of the door frame on her shoulder as she fell against it. Her hands—

Tooth and claw are best.

—tore away a strip of the frame, the wood coming away in her hands, and she swatted the taser wires away. A quick step forward and she slammed the piece of wood against the man, and he stumbled back. He tried to regain his balance, his hand coming against the couch where Adalia slept, and—

HE THREATENS PACK.

She held the man above her. Danny couldn't remember — didn't *know* — how she'd crossed the room to reach him. She smashed her fist against his goggles, the plastic and metal fragmenting around her fist. She hit him again, and again, then threw him across the room to fall against the wall.

He was still moving, still trying to — *what, to get* away? — after all of this, crawling on hands and knees towards the cold hallway. She was on him quicker than a stolen kiss, lifting him up again. Danny snarled, her fist hitting him in the head, the stomach, and she could smell the blood inside him, wanted to taste the hot wet salt that would set them both free—

"Mom!" It was Adalia, her voice shrill with fear.

Danny felt the wrench inside her, her heart thudding against her ribs. The room came back into focus, the flickering light from the fire casting shadows against the black and red on her arms, her shirt. She looked down at the man she held, the piteous, mewling *thing* that pawed, weak and dying, against her grip. The white of his clothing was so red it was almost black. Danny turned slowly to look at her daughter, took in Adalia's horrified expression, her hands covering her mouth. Danny looked back down at the man she held as the life leaked away from him, his broken body growing still in her hands. She let him slump to the old wooden floors, the dry wood drinking at the red stain that started to spread.

She took an unsteady step towards the couch, her hand outstretched. Adalia shrank back from her, and Danny caught a glimpse of herself in the old mirror hung against the wall. She could see her torn shirt, the blood staining her arms up to the elbows, the red dripping down from her lips, all below lambent, yellow eyes.

It hit her then that Adalia was afraid of *her*. The shock hurt more than the taser, and she sank slowly against the floor, sitting half way between the body and the couch. She felt that midpoint, half way between damnation and salvation, as if there was a bitter seed inside her twisting everything she held dear. Danny gulped big lungfuls of air, and realized she was—

The fallen have no time to weep.

—crying, hot tears falling silent and quick down her face. She didn't know how long she sat on the floor until she felt the scratch of warm wool around her shoulders. Danny looked up, Adalia's face above her, as the blanket settled into place.

Her daughter reached out a hand to her, touching her shoulder, as delicate as a butterfly's landing. "Are you ... are you okay?"

No. Danny tried for a smile, but it caught somewhere inside her before it could reach her eyes. "I'm fine, honey."

"I ... I'm sorry," said Adalia.

"Oh, sweetie. You don't have anything to feel sorry about."

Danny pushed herself slowly to her feet, wanting to pull her daughter close, but aware — *so aware* — of the blood staining her arms, her chest. She didn't realize she was caught, frozen until she felt Adalia hug her, thin arms wrapping around Danny. It felt like—

Salvation.

—this time.

CHAPTER
NINE

"Tell me," said Val, "how you're going to get it open."

"With this," said John, hefting a brown leather bag. It was closed with a loop of worn cloth at the top, creases and scuffs all over its surface. It smelled of old oil and worn metal.

"Tell me you didn't steal that." Val crossed his arms. "Look me in the eye and—"

"Hey," said John. He jiggled the bag, the clink of metal coming from within. "It's me."

Val didn't say anything, just kept looking at his friend.

"Okay," said John, "let me correct that. I didn't steal this. I ... borrowed it."

"You stole it."

"From the guy in Maintenance. Mauricio."

"Jesus," said Val, "that's how the poor guy makes his living. You stole his bag?"

"No," said John, "I borrowed it."

"He just let you take it?"

"No," said John. He shrugged, looking at the floor. "I said you'd help him move Old Mrs. Berisha's piano later this afternoon."

63

"You said *what*?" Val took a step forward. "Why would you say that?"

"Because she's got a piano that needs moving, and you're the man for the job." John put the bag on the floor. "Hey. Don't look at me. I'm the brains of this operation."

"I hate shit like that." Val rubbed the back of his neck. "I have to pretend the piano's heavy, right, but not so heavy I can't move it."

"Poor baby." John picked up the TV remote, flicking the TV on. The news was still spinning the story of the mysterious stranger who'd dived into a burning bus to pull out a kid, and how there was this other guy who'd been pulled from a Prius moments before it exploded—

Val snatched the remote from him, clicking it off. "I hate it when you do that."

"You're hating a lot of things. Don't hate the player. Hate the game." John raised an eyebrow at him. "You know you can be heroic without leaving our apartment building. You move that piano, you'll get fresh baked cookies for a lifetime. It's like the great circle of life."

"I hate her cookies."

John looked surprised. "When did you try out Old Mrs. Berisha's famous pistachio and rum butterball cookies?"

"Last week, when I moved her piano." Val shrugged. "She said she couldn't get a hold of Mauricio so I helped her out."

"Why'd you help her out if you hate doing it?"

"I was trapped," said Val, "between her and Mr. Pospisil—"

"Who's that?"

"Czech guy on three."

"Looks about a hundred and eighty?"

"That's the guy," said Val. "Anyway—"

"How'd you get trapped?" John hefted the silver case, then laid it flat on the table.

"I think Mr. Pospisil fancies himself a bit of Old Mrs. Berisha." Val shrugged. "Seemed the fastest way to get out of the conversation.

'Hell yeah, Mrs. B, I'll shift that piano. Only can we do it now? Got to be somewhere in five.'"

"That's gross."

"Shifting the piano wasn't gross."

"No," said John, taking a hammer out of the bag. He considered it a moment before tossing it back in. "Old people. Sex."

"Jesus, man, I didn't say they were having sex. I said they were talking."

"Strongly implied," said John. He held up a chisel. "What do you think of this?"

"I think you'll hurt yourself," said Val. He bent over to look in the brown leather bag, rummaging through the contents. "She wasn't sure where to put it."

"Not surprising," said John. "When you get to her age, you forget, you know?"

"No, I mean, the piano," said Val.

"That's what I meant," said John. "What were you thinking of?"

Val stared at him, flat and steady, then looked back in the bag. He pulled out a mallet, old, chipped, heavy. He hefted it, then took the chisel from John.

John frowned. "Best let me."

"Why?"

"You ever done this before?"

Val looked down at the chisel and the mallet. "No, but I can't see this being a hard thing to do."

"That's why you'll get cut," said John. He took the mallet in his right hand, then slotted the blade of the chisel in between the lid of the silver case. "This look right?"

"You tell me," said Val, "since you've done this before."

"Always a critic," said John. He hefted the mallet, then swung it hard into the chisel. The impact spun the case away off the coffee table and into the floor. John stumbled forward, the chisel carving a groove into the surface of the table.

65

Val looked at the table, running a finger along the groove. "You sure you don't want me to try?"

"I got this," said John, standing up. He retrieved the silver case from the floor.

"It's just that this table is Sky's," said Val.

"I know," said John.

"Well," said Val, "it's possible she'll be pissed that you cut a—"

"I *know*," said John. He sighed, looking over at Val. "You want this open or not?"

"Pretty sure it was you who wanted it open." Val shrugged. "Do what you need to do."

John put the case on the ground, clasp facing up, and put the blade of the chisel in between the lid. He hefted the mallet, then slammed it down again. The chisel spun away with a metallic *ping*, and John dropped the mallet on the ground. "Son of a *bitch*," he said, putting his finger in his mouth.

Val looked on with crossed arms. "You getting anywhere?"

"I think I cut myself," said John.

Val sighed. "Okay. Hand it over."

John looked sullen, but lifted the silver case and handed it over. "Here."

Retrieving the mallet and chisel, Val put the blade of the chisel in the lid. He hefted the mallet and—

Crack the Earth.

—slammed it down onto the chisel. There was a snap and the case lid clicked open a few hairs. Val hefted the mallet again and—

Shatter the stone.

—smashed it into the chisel. The mallet head cracked, spinning off across the room, the chisel shattering. Val looked at the case. "Huh."

"You get it open?" John leaned over.

"Kinda," said Val. "Wait one sec." He lifted the case off the ground, the lid creaking, and put it on the table.

"Careful," said John.

Val paused. "What for?"

"Could be a bomb."

"Are you serious?"

"Kind of," said John. "Okay if I go wait in the hall?"

"No," said Val. He wriggled his fingers in the gap in the lid, then braced himself and *pulled*. He felt his muscles bunching, arms shaking a little with the effort. The case gave a metallic groan, the lid coming open a few more inches.

"Keep going," said John. "Almost got it."

Val put the case down. "You want to do this?"

"You're doing good," said John. "Pro job."

Val wriggled his fingers into the gap in the case again. He pulled again, the metal creaking before it pulled open in his hands with a shriek of metal. The case fell from his hands, dancing across the top of the table before it fell onto the ground.

They both looked over the edge of the table. Val reached down, snaring the case. He lifted it onto the table, then flicked it open.

"Well," said John, "I was not expecting that." The case was empty.

That's when Val started screaming.

"We can't keep it," said Carlisle. "No way."

"It's got a TV in the back seat," said Adalia. "It's got a heater that works."

"It's got a tracking device in it," said Carlisle.

"How do you know?" said Danny. She kicked snow off her boots, rubbing her bare arms more from habit than from the cold. She and Adalia had made the short drive without speaking, her daughter's teenage silence filling the cabin. "It's pretty nice to drive."

"I know," said Carlisle, "because that's what I'd do." She looked cold, tired — *old, she's getting* old — her leather jacket doing nothing to keep the freezing wind at bay. They'd met up here at a turning bay they'd agreed on, perched against the side of the mountain. The snow swirled around them. Danny could see down into the valley below, the lights of a tiny town she'd started to hope might become home twinkling in the night. *Guess we won't be sticking around. Not anymore.*

"But," said Adalia, her head sticking out through the window, woolen hat on crooked, "it's got a *TV.*"

"No one's after us," said Danny. "No one's here."

"To be fair," said Carlisle, "we've only just got here. I said a tracking device, not a device that predicts the future."

"Right," said Danny.

"Because," said Carlisle, "if we could get one of those we'd be happy. Predicting the future would be neat."

"I get it," said Danny. "They haven't caught us yet."

"Right," said Carlisle, "because no one has a device to predict the future with."

Danny pushed her foot through the snow, watching the two trucks at the side of the road. Their truck — a big old Dodge they'd picked up six or more months ago from the cash she had left — looked like the dented rust bucket it was. Next to it sat the GMC Yukon the men who'd come to their cabin had been driving. It was shiny as a new penny, the black standing strong against the white of the snow. "These guys look like they got some money."

"I'd guess," said Carlisle. "Not a lot of brains, but money, sure."

"How much you reckon one of these costs?" Danny looked up at the sky, the clouds—

Ice and wind.

—racing across the dark sky as if they were running from something. "Round figures."

"Fifty large," said Carlisle. "More or less."

"They had another one down at the bar?"

"Yeah," said Carlisle. "Where you going with this?"

"You think they might have helicopter money?"

"I don't know anyone crazy enough to fly in this weather," said Carlisle.

"Great," said Danny. "Adalia? Time to go sweetie."

"I like this one better," said Adalia. "Our truck sucks."

"Our truck doesn't have devil-worshiping Satanists tracking it," said Carlisle. "C'mon kid. Out."

Adalia hopped out of the Yukon with a glower and a slam of the door, trudging through the snow to the old Dodge. She put a gloved hand up on the handle, then turned around. "Why doesn't one of you ride in the middle?"

"Because we're not fourteen," said Danny. "I need to drive. Carlisle needs to shoot."

"No way," said Carlisle.

"What?" Danny blinked into the gentle flakes falling around them.

"You're not driving," said Carlisle.

"Why not?"

"Because you're a psycho behind the wheel," said Carlisle. She held out her sidearm. "Here."

"I can't shoot that well," said Danny. She tipped her head sideways. "Arm wrestle for it?"

"Fuck it all," said Carlisle, throwing Danny the keys. She trudged towards the Dodge, then spoke to Adalia. "Don't say I didn't try, kid."

"I heard you," said Adalia. She opened the door, getting in to the cab. "Try harder next time."

"I got to put up with this from her," said Carlisle. "Not from you. Get in." The door closed behind them. Danny could still hear Carlisle talking, starting a story about one long stakeout she'd had in a car in the snow. Danny turned her attention away, looked back out at the road, then at the GMC. She walked towards it, yanking the door open, then grabbed the keys. Danny turned and tossed the keys out over the edge of the road, watching them tumble end over end before being lost from view. Danny brushed her hands on her pants then walked over to the Dodge.

"Where to?" said Carlisle. Adalia sat between them, playing with her phone.

"I don't know," said Danny. "North, maybe."

"I think we should go south," said Carlisle.

"No," said Danny.

The desert misses the rain.

"Because," said Carlisle, "Everard and that clown Miles are south. Miles ain't good for much, but Everard—"

"No," said Danny.

The night misses the moon.

Carlisle breathed out a sigh in the cab. "It's just that—"

"I'm not ready."

"Right, because—"

"No, Melissa."

"For Christ's sake," said Carlisle. "There's not being ready, then there's being stupid."

They challenge us. "*What* did you say to me?" Danny could feel her hands clenching the steering wheel.

"You heard me," said Carlisle, "and if you think being the big bad wolf is going to help you here, I will slap you until the silly stops coming out."

Danny's teeth clenched. "Don't. Push. Me."

"Or what?" said Carlisle. "You'll throw me down the side of the mountain after those keys? I thought—"

"Mom wouldn't—" said Adalia.

"Not now, kid," said Carlisle. "You were tired of this thing making all the decisions for you. You want to run from your boyfriend who calls you every single day just hoping for the sound of your voice? Fine. Seven kinds of stupid, but fine. But I tell you, there is some shit going down here we don't have a label for, and we need to get the band back together."

They CHALLENGE us. "I. Can't." Danny was staring straight ahead, the steering wheel creaking in her grip.

"Course you can," said Carlisle, staring out the windscreen. "You just don't want to."

"I can't!" Danny yelled it at the windscreen, the steering wheel coming free in her hands with a shriek of metal. She knew her teeth were bared, tried to close her mouth. Danny felt Adalia shrink away from her on the seat.

The silence sat in the cab with them, thick and dirty. Adalia spoke first. "I want to get out."

"It's below freezing outside, kid." Carlisle frowned. "She doesn't want to hit you anyway. Not really me either."

"Who's she want to hit then?" Adalia looked between them. "I don't understand you at all."

"Makes two of us," said Carlisle, rubbing her arms in the chill of the cabin. "Nice work on the wheel, Kendrick."

Danny started to cry then, great choking sobs that shook her shoulders. She looked down at the wheel in her hands. "I never wanted this. *Never.*"

"No, I suppose not," said Carlisle. "I didn't want to be on a road trip in Alaska either. Sometimes shit happens."

"Mom?" Adalia was looking between the two of them, her face more confused than ever. She reached a hand out to Danny. "Are you okay?"

"No," said Danny.

"I guess it's good Everard's not here after all," said Carlisle.

Danny looked up, confused now. She—

We are strong. For Pack.

—wiped a hand at her face, trying to brush the tears away. "You said ... why not?"

"Because you don't cry pretty," said Carlisle, pushing her door open. "We'd best try and find those fucking keys."

THE BIG YUKON lapped up the miles, trampling the ice and asphalt as they sped along. Danny's hands were steady on the wheel as she looked over at Carlisle. "Thanks."

"Eyes on the road," said Carlisle. "Two of us can still die in an auto accident."

Danny felt herself start to smile, and she looked forward again. "Sure."

"Statistically speaking, this is a terrible idea. Driving at night in the snow with the lights off is up there for a Darwin Award."

"I'm not sure I'm the product of evolution," said Danny.

"I am," said Adalia, her voice coming from the big back seats. She was watching something on the TV in the back of Carlisle's seat. "I think I'm too young to die."

"Pretty sure I am too. Thing is, I'm just old enough to know what life's got to offer," said Carlisle. "With you, you'd never know what you're missing out on."

"You're not going to die," said Danny. "I'm a good driver."

"You're a werewolf," said Carlisle. "Being a good driver is a some-time accidental benefit. You get road rage like a rising red tide."

"If people would just pull the hell over—" Danny caught herself, then laughed.

So did Carlisle. "How'd you find the keys?"

"Knew where I threw 'em," said Danny. "More or less."

"Fair enough," said Carlisle, before turning to Adalia. "Kid. What are you playing with?"

"Facebook," said Adalia.

"Facebook?"

"Some of the time." Adalia shrugged. "Coverage is shit out here." The expletive sounded forced, like she needed practice.

"Watch your mouth," said Danny.

"Why?" said Adalia. "It's not like there's anyone to hear me except you two, and you say cu—"

"Kid," said Carlisle, "there are some words it's never safe to use."

"But—"

"Kid?"

Adalia looked sullen. "Yeah?"

"Have I ever lied to you?" Danny could *feel* Carlisle's smile in the dark of the cabin.

"No," said Adalia.

"Some words you can never use. Trust me."

"But you—"

73

"Never." Carlisle started fiddling with the radio in the dash. "You'd think for the money they spent on this there'd be satellite radio."

Adalia crossed her arms, sullen, and Danny laughed. She kept driving, the feel of the big machine around her almost alive. "Thanks," she said after a while.

"What for?" said Carlisle.

"You know," she said, still smiling.

CHAPTER
ELEVEN

"You can't say anything," the boy said. His eyelashes were long and black against his pale skin. "The Facebook line was good."

Adalia typed on her phone, knees scrunched up to her chest. The back seat of the Yukon was huge, like two couches sewn together. It must have taken a whole herd of cows to make the seats. *Why can't I just tell them?*

"They'd think you were crazy," said the boy. "You thought you were crazy, remember?"

Still do. Adalia sighed, deleted the line of text. She liked that the back seat was dark, as if she was alone in the whole world. Except for the boy. *I don't know why you're here.*

"Neither do I." The boy tossed himself back against the plush leather, the seats not indenting at all. Dark shapes of trees raced past the window, their tall black clothed in the luminous gray of snow. Warm and snug in the back seat it felt like they were sitting still, alone as the universe sprinted away behind them.

We've seen some weird shit. Adalia pointed at the phone's screen. She deleted the last word, then typed, *stuff.*

"I don't mind if you swear," he said to her. "It's not the worst thing I'll hear today."

What will be the worst?

He turned away, face to the window. No reflection was cast in the glass as he sat there looking out. "You don't want to know."

You said when we first met—

He laughed. "When we first met, you screamed." He looked abashed, ran a hand through his black hair. Adalia wanted to reach out and straighten a few of those strands, just tug one away from his face. "Remember?"

I remember. Her phone ticked as she entered the text. *I was in the shower!* She underlined the last word. *The shower is not where I thought I'd meet a boy.*

"Believe me, it's a good place to meet a…" He stopped as all his words guttered out. "If you meet the right kind of boy, is what I meant."

A shudder ran through the Yukon as a wheel scrabbled outside in the cold snow for purchase. Adalia ignored it, passing her phone from hand to hand. *Gross.*

"You won't think that in a few years." He looked down his nose at her, his face arch. His eyelashes looked very long from this angle, and Adalia smiled to herself. "You probably don't think that now."

The boys out here have webbing between their toes. She thought for a moment, then typed, *That's not it. I just don't like the boys out here. They're into shooting deer and racing snowmobiles. Boring.*

"I'd bet your Mom would be into hunting deer."

Below the belt.

He laughed. "Sorry." He shrugged, leaning back in the seat again. "I think that's why, though."

Why what? You know I hate it when you get cryptic. I get enough from the front seat not telling me anything.

"I'm not trying to be cryptic. I just don't have the words. It's like there's this place, and you can only know what it is when you've seen it."

Are you quoting The Matrix?

"The Matrix?"

An old movie, she typed. *I liked it. The sequels were shit.* She deleted the last word. *Bad.*

"I haven't seen a movie in years," he said. "I don't get called to watch them." He looked at the back of her mom's head. "I don't know why I was called to *you,* though. Can't work it out. I'd have thought it would be one of them."

They have their own problems, she typed. She deleted it, then, *I'm glad you came to me.*

He looked at the writing on her phone, then up at her. He gave a small smile, tentative as a new dawn. "Me too."

I still don't get it.

"We've been over this. It'll come out eventually."

We can work it out. Together. It's not like we've got anything else to do here.

"We could watch the snow outside. It'll be light in a few hours. Or you could get some sleep."

Not sleepy. Adalia ran a hand through hair a little too long for her liking. *Let's start with something simple. Why am I the only one who can see you?*

The boy shook his head. "Other people can see me."

They can't. She waved her phone at the front seat where Melissa and Mom were talking. *They would freak.*

The boy looked between her mom and Melissa, then nodded. "I think so, at least for a little while." A small smile tugged at his face. "You freaked."

I was in the shower! Adalia wanted to laugh, but it would have given her away. She hid a smile with her hand, then typed, *Who else can see you? Stop avoiding the question.*

"Special people," said the boy. "I don't know the rules."

I'm special?

"I guess," he said.

She looked away, crossed her arms.

"Jeeze," he said, "I didn't mean it like that. Look, pro tip, for when you meet a boy—"

She held up a hand, typed, *You're a boy.*

He looked at her phone, then up into her face. "I think I should go," he said, his voice soft.

No. I'm sorry.

He scooted away from her on the wide back seat of the Yukon. "So the pro tip is this. If a boy ever says something to you, and it can be taken two ways, see? And one of them makes you feel sad or angry, he meant it the other way."

Adalia thought about that, then gave a grudging nod. *Why can't you tell me your name?*

"I *could* tell you," he said.

Then you'd have to kill me? Overused, lame, try harder.

"Ouch," he said. "Tough crowd. It's not that."

What is it? She glared at him, then made herself relax. *I'm trying to take this the other way, but your whole fortune cookie thing isn't helping me not feel angry or sad.*

"Got it," he said. He thought for a moment, then swallowed. "I don't remember."

You don't remember any lines not full of cheese?

"I don't remember," he said, leaning forward again, "my *name.*"

Oh. Adalia looked down at the small word on her phone. *What do you remember?*

The boy seemed about to answer, taking a deep breath. His mouth opened, then snapped shut as the Yukon slewed, snow thrown up in big sheets around them. Her mom screamed in the front seat, hands wrenching at the wheel. Melissa was reaching over, yelling something at her, before the big machine shuddered as the back hit something. Adalia was tossed against the door, knocking her head, her phone falling from her hand. There was a crash and glass blew through the cabin, the cold of winter suddenly hungry on the inside, tearing at her face, her hair. Adalia screwed up her eyes, the spinning of the vehicle going on and on, like it would never stop, and she screamed—

Silence. The soft *tink* of cooling metal. Someone groaned, then her door was wrenched open and her mom was there. "Baby? Are you okay?

"I'm okay, Mom," said Adalia, blinking. The boy was still sitting next to her on the back seat. "What happened?"

"Good question, kid," said Melissa from the front. She coughed, then raised a hand to wipe some blood from her nose. The airbags in the front looked like big marshmallows. "Last time I let you drive."

Her mom looked into her face, then at Melissa still belted in the front seat. "Something terrible," she said. Adalia saw that her eyes were yellow, something feral glinting behind them.

"Mom?"

"I remember," said the boy into the silence, "that not all special people are good." Then he was gone, a wisp of memory caught by the wind and tugged away.

Her mom blinked yellow eyes at her before licking her lips. "They've stolen my Valentine."

CHAPTER

TWELVE

Something was tearing at the air, clawing and howling, pulling the walls of the room closer. John squinted as the air rushed around, picking up scattered papers, the curtains flailing long frantic fingers into the room. He saw Val next to the silver case, arms straining.

It looked like he was trying not to fall in to the case. *No — he was trying not to be* pulled *into the case.*

"Val!" John was yelling against the storm in their apartment, the sun outside the window somehow dimmer, further away. He tried to sit upright from where he'd been thrown, reaching a hand towards his friend.

Val was still screaming. It looked like the color was being drained out of him, all the light being drawn into the silver case still on the table. John could see the edges of his own hand, see the edges of his fingers blurring as if something — *essential* — was being pulled into the case.

He scrambled back. Looked at the case, looked at Val. Saw his friend screaming a long, impossible breath out.

It's times like this that John Miles knew his destiny. He knew that he wasn't fated to be the major act in the stage play of life. He wasn't going to save the world — that shit was for other people with more time and a better give-a-fuck meter. He wasn't the quarterback.

Hell, he'd *been* a quarterback, but that was a completely different thing. That was a thing with girls and beer after the game. Right here and now, Val was the quarterback, and Val was dying. Val, who carried something inside him bigger and stronger than anything John had ever seen — *that* Val — was being pulled apart, being pulled into a metal case that had arrived in their apartment sometime last night.

John Miles knew his destiny, and his destiny was to close that fucking case.

He stood up, moving towards the case. The air in the room was savage and wild, and he felt like he was being drawn towards the case, but almost accidentally. Like it wasn't him that the case wanted, but it'd take everything it could get. His feet slid on the floor, the carpet catching against the bottom of his shoes. He sank into a crouch, took another crab step closer.

Looked up at Val. Saw the gray of his face, the shape of something—

An animal, claws and teeth, with yellow eyes wide with rage and fear.

—being torn loose. It was ghostly, the edges indistinct, and it reached back towards Val with imploring claws as it scrabbled frantically for purchase. John had seen that thing a couple times before, and each time it had been solid, taking over the body of his friend.

Not this time. This time it was being pulled away like an old tooth—

Fuck that. Close the case, asshole.

John took one more step, reached out—

Don't think about it. Just grab the edge of the case, flip the lid closed, grab a beer, and go home.

—and forced the lid closed, the clasps *snicking* into the silence of the room. The edge of the metal felt hot and cold at the same time against his hand.

81

Silence?

John looked over at Val, saw his friend's eyes rolled back in their sockets, watched as he toppled over onto the ground. The room was calm, the curtains settling back into their old habit of falling straight down. Sun pushed its way back into the room, the light warm and welcome.

Raising the hand he'd used to close the case up before his eyes, John saw the burns on his fingers, the skin blistered and red. *That's gonna hurt.* He looked down at Val, then ran his other hand through his hair.

The case sat on the table, the wood underneath it blackened with heat. John coughed, then said, "Well, that could have gone better."

"Here." John held out a steaming mug. "Drink this."

"What is it?" Val was propped up on the sofa, his skin still—

Gray.

—bleached, colorless.

"It's coffee."

Val looked at the mug, then at John, and then at the otherwise empty apartment. "Who made it?"

John looked at the mug, then at Val. "Who do you think made it?"

"I think you made it."

"Why's that?"

"No one else here," said Val. He took the cup, sniffed it. "Also, it smells like pickled ass."

"Doesn't look like your brain is hurt," said John. "Your manners could use some work."

"I feel terrible."

"You look worse," said John. He rubbed the burns on his fingers, then stopped when that made it hurt more. "I mean that in a nice way."

"What happened?"

John shrugged. "Hell if I know. Above my pay grade."

Val sipped at his coffee, then winced. "This is terrible."

"You can make your own damn coffee next time you're almost killed by a suitcase," said John. "What's terrible is that a suitcase—"

"Briefcase."

"What?"

"Briefcase," said Val. "Suitcase is bigger. Has clothes 'n' shit inside it."

"Are you serious?" John looked at Val, then stood up. He gestured at the room around them. "There was a storm in here. A storm, with wind."

Val seemed to sober a little. "I remember."

"How often you see wind inside, Val?" John walked towards the window, looked outside. The world was much the same as he remembered — *humans doing things that humans do* — and the light was warm against his face. "I don't mean when you leave the window open, or—"

"I know what you mean." Val's voice was tired.

"I don't think you do." John turned around, holding up his burnt and blistered hand. "You ever see shit like this coming from a briefcase?"

What little color remained in Val's face left, and he tried to stand. The coffee spilled, black joining the blue of his jeans. "Ah, shit." He put the cup aside, then looked up. "I'm sorry, I—"

"No," said John.

"No?"

"No," said John. "You don't get to say sorry."

Val blinked up at him. "You've lost me."

"You're like some kind of really smart dumb guy," said John. He rubbed his hands together, felt the tension in his shoulders wind up a notch. "It's not often I have to explain stuff to you."

"Unless it's about women," said Val. He paused, then: "To be fair, I'm not sure I should be listening to you about women."

"I don't think this is one of those times," said John.

"One of what times?"

"Where you get to make jokes," said John. He lowered his voice a little. "This isn't going to be a situation where it's all going to be okay, and we can go out for beers and burgers after the game."

"Well, that's the thing," said Val. "I feel great."

"You look like shit," said John. "We've been over this already. And you said you felt like shit too."

"No, I'm saying it wrong," said Val. "I feel like shit, but it's great."

John blinked, then pulled over a chair, lowering himself into it. "Did you get hit on the head?"

"I don't think so."

"You need to break this one down for me," said John. "I'm not following where you're going. I want to, God as my witness, but I feel like this conversation has taken a turn towards Vegas."

"I feel like shit," said Val, a grin splitting his face, "and I haven't felt like shit for *five years*."

John sat very still. "Since—"

"Since then," said Val. "I think it's gone."

"I think you should stop smiling about it," said John.

"Why?" Val tried to stand again, then gave up. "You haven't had to live with a bloodthirsty killer in your head for five years. You don't wake up and *not know who you killed*."

"Ignoring your whole superhero savior thing for a moment," said John, "I don't think that's why you should stop smiling."

"What, you want me to keep killing?" Val's voice cracked, and he paused. "Sorry, I didn't—"

"No, you're good," said John. "Just ... can you just shut up for a second? Christ! I got to get words out of my head. It's not my wheelhouse, right? More of an action guy. And you're not helping." John rubbed his good hand through his hair, closed his eyes for a second, then looked at Val, waiting.

"I ... okay," said Val. He leaned back, then held out a hand. "Do your thing."

"This isn't happy fun times," said John. "This is serious fucking unhappy times. Something just sucked a fucking werewolf soul out through your eyes into a briefcase in our lounge, right next to the sofa we picked up from the dollar store. You look like shit, and you're too weak to stand. You're all happy and saying, 'John, it's a cure,' but you're forgetting something." John licked his lips. "I said I'm sorry because I made you open the fucking case, okay? It's my fault."

"No—"

John held up a hand. "I haven't given you back the talking stick yet." He cleared his throat. "I said I'm sorry because I think I've killed you."

Val blinked. "You've got my attention."

"Thought that might do it," said John.

"I get that you think you've killed me," said Val, rubbing at his nose, "but I don't see why."

"Because of that." John pointed at the hand Val had used to rub his nose.

Val almost laughed. "I got a running nose for the first time in five..." His words trailed off as he saw the streak of blood on the back of his hand.

"Yeah," said John. "You remember you've got a virus inside you, right? You've got a virus that turned someone to jelly in like a minute."

Val looked down at his hand again then touched a finger to his nose. "Ah."

"'Ah,'" said John. "See? I went and did something stupid, and now I've killed my best friend."

CHAPTER
THIRTEEN

Another black Yukon pushed its way through the snow towards them. The lights were on, strong and bright, but the noise of the storm hid the engine noise. It looked like a large, black whale nosing through the depths towards them.

Danny shifted at her side. "Let me—"

Carlisle held out a hand. The twinge in her gut was back, this time making her hopeful. "It's okay."

"I can—"

"Seriously," said Carlisle, "it's okay." She held up a small device, showed the screen to her friend. "See this?"

"Looks like a really cheap and shitty phone," said Danny.

"What it is, is a tracker," said Carlisle. The black Yukon had pulled to a stop on the road beside them. The lights stayed on. The tinted windows blacked out the interior, making the inhabitants invisible. "And it's tracking that." She waved at the other Yukon through the window.

"You know who's in that?"

"More or less," said Carlisle. "Give me five."

"Five what?"

Carlisle sighed and didn't answer. Instead, she brushed snow off herself — their own Yukon's windows were trashed. She spared a glance in the back seat where Danny held Adalia. "Kid."

"Yeah?" Adalia looked cold, but angry.

Good. If she was angry she'd be unlikely to be hypothermic. "Don't let your Mom get out of the car."

"Like I can—"

"Kid?"

A sullen pause. "Yeah?"

"Don't let her get out. We're in a delicate phase right now, and she could fuck it all up." Carlisle grabbed the door handle and yanked, the air biting and gnawing at her heels as she stepped out. She could hear Danny start to ask *what the hell did she mean* and *Carlisle don't you go*— before she shut the door with a satisfying thump. She let her feet shuffle her through the snow to the other Yukon, pulling her collar up against the driving snow. The leather didn't do shit, but it made her feel better.

A window cracked open in the other vehicle, the interior dark. She caught a glimpse of white teeth in a black face, and a part of her started to relax as another part tensed right back up. Ajay's familiar voice reached out to her. "Detective?"

Carlisle kicked snow off her foot — *now there's a song that will never end* — before putting it back down. "Could use a ride."

"What did you do to my car?"

"It's a truck," said Carlisle, "and *I* didn't do anything to it."

"What happened to my truck?" Ajay's voice had a smile hidden in it somewhere.

"I think the term we'd use is that, 'The vehicle failed to take the corner.' I've always hated that kind of language though, like the car decided to not turn." Carlisle hugged herself. "Could *really* use a ride."

"Okay, Detective Carlisle," he said. "Get your things. It just so happens, we're going your way."

"Which way is that?"

"Chicago," said Ajay. "Get in the car."

Carlisle sniffed at the air, then walked back to their battered machine. *It's a truck*, she thought, but a smile tugged at her face anyway, hurried there by the feeling in her gut. She knocked on the door, and Danny pushed it open.

"What's going on?"

"We're going to Chicago," said Carlisle, "and you have to promise me something."

Danny's eyes narrowed. "What's that?"

"You have to promise me you won't kill the men in that Yukon."

Danny thought about it. "You saying that means you think I'll want to kill someone in that Yukon."

"You've more or less got it," said Carlisle. "And you owe me."

"How you figure?"

"Because you crashed the only other way we've got of getting to Chicago," said Carlisle. "I've been punched in the face with an air bag, and I'm just *too tired for this shit*," she said. "So here's the way it's going down. I'm getting in that Yukon over there," and she yanked a thumb over her shoulder, "and I'm driving to Chicago. When I'm there, I'm going to look up Everard and that freak show Miles, and see what kind of trouble they've got themselves in to. Maybe save the world. Again. There's a small chance I'll also get *laid*, which is a thing that hasn't happened since coming the fuck up here in the snow surrounded by fishermen and inbreds." She paused for a breath. "The fishermen are also inbred."

Danny nodded slowly. "That's fair."

"I don't give a shit if it's fair," said Carlisle. "I need a burger and friends and I need to not be cold."

"Can I ask why I would want to kill the men in that car?"

"It's a truck," said Carlisle absently. She coughed into the cold, wiped some more snow out of her eyes. "I'm pretty sure these guys are the ones we were running from before."

"Pretty sure?"

"Tell you what," said Carlisle. "You promise me you won't kill them, and we can get in their nice warm *truck* and talk about it some more."

～

"THERE ARE DIFFERENT FACTIONS AT PLAY," Ajay said. He craned his neck from the front passenger seat to look at Danny. "Not everyone's playing by the rules."

Carlisle frowned. "There are rules?"

Ajay laughed. "No." He looked away from Danny, tried to crane around even further. Carlisle had chosen to sit behind him — if Danny had another freak out, this would provide some *necessary distance.*

Danny spoke up for the first time, the hint of anger — *or is that fear?* — in her voice. "Why won't you just leave us alone?"

Ajay sobered. "We want to save the world."

"World can save itself," said Carlisle.

"You seen the news?" Ajay turned back forward. "The world needs all the help it can get. Have you heard of a man named Talin Moray?"

"He in the news? We're a little out of touch up here," said Carlisle. "Or is he from the same place you come from?"

"More or less," said Ajay. "Except we are nothing alike."

"You're all the same," said Danny. "You try to take my *cub*..." She cut herself off. "Sorry."

Silence held for a few more beats. "So," said Carlisle, as if nothing bad was about to happen. "How'd you find us?"

"Wasn't looking for you," said Ajay. "Different orders."

"Orders, huh?" Carlisle leaned back in the darkness of the back seat. "You sure you're not a soldier?"

"Nor a sailor." There was an indeterminate shuffling from the front seat where Ajay sat. "But I did come here in a ship."

"You keep saying that," said Carlisle.

"I feel like an asshole," said Danny.

89

"Mom!" said Adalia. Then, quieter, "Language." Carlisle thought she could pick out the side of a smile on Adalia's face, but it was hard to see in the dark of the back.

"I feel like an asshole," said Danny, "because you two know each other and I don't know why."

"Talin Moray is why," said Ajay, before Carlisle could step in front of that one. "Do you believe in magic?"

"Hey," said the driver. "Boss, should you..?"

"No," said Ajay. "Thomas here believes we should be operating under the strictest secrecy. I have a different view."

"What view is that?" Carlisle saw that Danny's body had leaned forward, something challenging in the set of her shoulders. She could feel it even in the dark.

"Hey," said Carlisle. "I think we should all calm down."

"I'm calm," said Ajay.

"Me too," said Thomas, from the driver's seat.

"I'm not," said Danny. "What's going on?"

"You promised not to kill them," said Carlisle.

"I don't want to kill anyone," said Danny, something anguished in her voice. "You people keep removing the *choice* from me."

The Yukon juddered as it hit something in the road. Adalia cleared her throat, very deliberately. "I'm calm too. And I'm sure Mom is fine."

"Sweetie—"

"Because she won't want to crash another car," said Adalia. "Right, Mom?"

"Right," said Danny, after a moment. "That's why I won't kill them both and leave their bodies for the crows. Because we need a *ride*."

Ajay turned his neck again to face Danny. "We didn't come for you. Not at first."

"You're lying—"

"We came for the man named Valentine," he said, calm and still as a pane of glass. "We came hunting the world's bravest detective.

90

We needed to find Valentine Everard, find out if he was a myth. He'd fallen off the world, as if he'd shifted sideways and just ... moved on."

"Who is this brave detective?" said Carlisle.

"The detective," said Ajay, "had found the man named Valentine before. Their paths had crossed, linking them together like a chain that can't be broken. The world was saved. And we need them to do it one more time."

Silence, overlaid by the grumble of the Yukon as it nosed through the snow. Adalia leaned forward. "Ajay?"

"Yes, mistress?"

"Did your story ... did it have a heroic little girl?"

Ajay laughed then, Thomas joining him from the front. It was a clean sound. "I'm sorry, mistress," said Ajay, "but it did not. The spirits didn't say anything about a girl, or her mother. We thought that ... well, we thought that if Detective Carlisle wouldn't come willingly, we might impress upon her companions."

"At least you're honest," said Danny. "How'd that work out for you?"

"Not well at all," said Ajay. "You see—"

"You were going to kidnap us?" said Adalia.

"Not exactly," said Ajay. "We were going to ... convince you."

"With a taser," said Danny.

"With the spirits," said Ajay. "The taser was for our protection."

"You're full of shit," said Danny.

"Language," said Adalia, but there was something hesitant in her voice. "I don't—"

"He's not," said Carlisle. Her stomach was tensed around that new feeling — *or is it just so old you've forgotten it?* "He's not full of shit."

"What, because he comes in to town with a quick smile and a good story? They tried to *catch* us, Carlisle. They tried to catch my *little girl.*" There was a tearing sound in the dark, followed by a snap. Danny held out the handle for the door she'd been gripping, the edges twisted and torn. "Sorry."

"I'm—" said Ajay.

"He's not full of shit," said Carlisle, "because he *knows*."

"What does he know, Melissa? What's he got on you?"

Carlisle swallowed, then shook her head. "I don't want to talk about it." She sighed. "No one should know about it. Not anymore."

Carlisle felt Adalia's a hand on her arm — *Adalia* — and almost pulled away. Her skin wanted to run, remembering *his* touch, *his* breath, but ... *no*. Carlisle wasn't afraid. Not anymore. Least of all, not of *him*.

"I'm sorry," said Ajay. "I ... sometimes the spirits are unkind."

"They're not unkind," said Danny. "They don't fu—" a glance here in the dark that might have been at Adalia, "They don't *exist*. I don't believe in special faeries or magic friends or gypsies of the woods."

"And yet," said Ajay, "you walk with the power of the Night at your side. It shrouds you, clings to you. I can smell it on you. You are *changed*, woman, and changed for the good of us all."

Danny sat silent as a stone. Carlisle tried again. "Ajay?"

"Yes, Detective."

"I'm not a Detective anymore," she said. "I said that."

"You are always what your God has made you," he said. "The rest is between you and him."

"Right," she said. "The thing is, it's shit like that, that makes you sound crazy. You know that?"

A soft noise from the front, somewhere between a snort and a laugh, as Thomas covered his mouth. Ajay shot his driver a look, and said, "Enough from you, Thomas."

"The lady, she has a point," he said. "I've always said you scare people."

"I—"

"I'm not scared," said Carlisle. "I'm confused. There's a big difference."

"What does it look like when you are scared?" said Thomas.

"It looks," said Danny, leaning forward again, "like *death*. When she gets scared, I get angry."

"Girl?" said Carlisle. "Now's not really ... you're not helping, okay?"

"I'm not afraid of death," said Ajay.

"Because you know where the dead go when they die," said Carlisle.

"Yes," said Ajay.

"That is why they think you are crazy," said Thomas. "I've known you these ten years or more, and you still sound crazy to me."

"*She* doesn't think I'm crazy," said Ajay. "She thinks I am her strong right arm."

"Who is she?" said Danny.

"Yeah," said Carlisle. "I think this is where I'm getting interested again."

"She is my keeper, mother, my queen, my sister, and your salvation," said Ajay.

"She sounds like Jesus," said Adalia, "with a skirt."

Ajay laughed. "No, little one," he said. "Although she might talk with him, from time to time. Others, too. The *L'wha*—"

"Is this some voodoo shit?" said Danny.

"It is something," said Ajay. "*Vodou* is everything, it is—"

"Whoa," said Carlisle. "You're going all crazy again."

"You saw the spirits," said Ajay.

"What does he mean?" said Danny.

"Yeah," said Adalia. "What—"

"Kid," said Carlisle, "maybe later."

"But—"

"I don't want to talk about what I saw," said Carlisle, leaning forward and gripping Adalia's hand in hers. "Not because you can't hear it. No secrets between us, remember? I promised."

"You did," said Adalia.

"I don't want to talk about it because I need to get it straight in my head. Do you know what I mean?"

Adalia looked down. "I get it." She looked back up. "But I'm your friend too. I can help."

Oh, kid, thought Carlisle, *you don't know how much you help just by saying things like that. Your Mom, she made a good one.* But all she said was, "Sure. Maybe later, okay?"

"Okay."

"I'm still not clear," said Danny. "I'm not clear on why you're here, why you needed my Valentine, and why we're going to Chicago. Together."

"Ah," said Ajay. "That. Let me tell you a story."

CHAPTER

FOURTEEN

The thing that called itself Talin Moray sat in a big leather chair. The chair crumbled under the weight of time, strips and tatters falling away, the sides ragged with age. It had been black, once, but now sat as a mix of murky gray and sad, pale stuffing. It had power, this chair. It had seen many things, bore witness to the acts that had made Talin what he was today. He kept it always, sending it across continents ahead of him wherever he went.

The wall behind him was covered in newspaper clippings, scrawled notes, blurry photos. Pieces of old twine walked between each piece, a story stitched broad that told of wondrous things. Miracles. Men and women saved from certain death. Whole gangs killed in a single night. There, an article told of a drug lord that had eluded the FBI for years had been found — very dead — in a room full of spent shell casings. Here and there, a story of a random innocent killed. Talin let his lips curl — *there are no innocents*. The photos were grainy, always shot at night, catching a glimpse of a single man as he ran back into whichever night had birthed him. Reports of survivors talked of a man who spoke little and did much, often from behind glowing yellow eyes.

Those eyes belonged to Talin now.

The photos and clippings were overlaid atop a map of the United States, a scraggly line of clues moving from coast to coast and back again. The twine ended here, in this city called after *shikaakwa*, where the Great Lakes and the power of the Chicago River met, and merged, feeding and nurturing each other. It wasn't an old city as such things went, but rich in borrowed memory as people fought and traded and fucked at the water's edge.

Hunt.

"Soon," he said. He flipped the lid of the silver briefcase closed, the metal snapping at his fingers as it lapped shut. A wisp of smoke peeled from the side of it, caught in an eddy of air and was lost.

A man in front of him looked up. His black skin complemented the black of the weapon he held, a short machine pistol. It was perfect for loud, noisy work. *Outdated.* A relic of a time before this day.

Kill.

"I wasn't talking to you, boy," said Talin. He flexed his hands, marveling at the strength that flowed within him. All of this had been wasted, frittered away in this city at the edge of the water. "Is my driver ready?"

"Always," said the man, his teeth bright and white in a savage smile. "Shall I—"

"No," said Talin. Something else spoke with his lips. The feeling was strange, a snarl pulling at his teeth. *I like this.* The L'wha had never graced his presence, had always ridden that whore Raeni, but it had left him open for this other. This was a spirit of pure Night, a prize beyond measure. "I must ... hunt."

The smile on the man's face faltered, his weapon half-raised at his side. "But—"

"I must hunt alone," said Talin. "Leave me or die."

The other man—

96

It defies us. It challenges.

—hesitated a moment, a single moment's pause conveying a nuance of meaning across the distance that separated them. A few feet, a handful of steps was all it took for Talin to reach the man, push clawed fingers into his chest, and tear out the heart within. The other man's eyes were wide with shock, the strength leaving him as he slipped backward. Something in the other man that wouldn't let go of his useless life brought the machine pistol up as he fell back. A final spasm pulled at the trigger, a bark of sound and light and bright, hot—

It is not the metal that burns with the heat of the sun.

—fire tracking points across his chest and stomach. Talin took a step or two back, the other man's heart falling from his hand, red gore falling with a noise like wet fabric hitting the ground. He looked down at the holes on his chest, pulling aside the worn and faded shirt he wore. The holes were stitching themselves closed, knitting together. He touched the brown of his skin with a hand, delighting in the smoothness of it. He looked at his fallen lieutenant, then laughed. A big, easy—

The fallen do not matter. We must hunt.

—sound, full of promise at what a new night would bring.

He spared a glance at the silver briefcase. He had almost all of this spirit of the Night. A fragment remained, something that had fallen free of his trap, and he had not survived this long through a love of loose ends.

THE ALTAR WAS NEW, rich with red. It wasn't the brown of old blood, but freshly anointed. It had been part of an expressway support, the big concrete block needing seven men to strain and heave to get it here. Their blood had christened it, given the stone its first touch of power.

There were always more men.

Talin set a bowl of water down next to the knife. *Here* was temporary, good enough to hide him from any attention until he was ready to move to where the water met the sky, where the final reckoning would take place. Cages stood at his back, the keening of panicked animals loud around him. He loved the sound, this recognition of fate even in the lowest of creatures. The world was full of things set to be instruments for his will.

The salt fell in big, coarse chunks as he crumbled it into a pile. Smoke floated up around him, the tallow lamps burning with a smell as familiar to him as good white rum. He let his fingers find the bowl of ash, fine flakes of bone still held within. The ash was from men — if you wanted to command men, you needed the essence of men.

He turned to the cages, opening the wicker front of one and pulling out a chicken. The bird squawked and clucked, wings beating against his hand before the knife found its throat. Blood spattered against the pile of ash and salt, the smell of it mingling with the smoke of burning tallow. He breathed it in, then tossed the bird aside.

It is weak.

Another cage, this time a stoat, small and cunning. He needed its view of treachery to corrupt the hearts of men. Its blood added to the muddy mass on the altar. A third cage, an old tom cat, full of guile and pride. This one he slit down its length, ignoring its last frantic scrabbling at life as he pulled its innards clean and letting them rest atop the red, wet mass growing on the altar. The magic he made was fed by a strength he didn't know he had, his power lifting up to a new scale that—

The force of the river's fall.

—he hadn't dared dream of. When he'd sought out the Night he'd known of the physical benefits, but that it would also lift up his inner power was *delightful*. He looked between the altar and the bodies cast to the side. There was still one thing missing. Snakes, of course.

Snakes, for their devious nature. Snakes, for the lies they told to

Eve at the beginning of it all. Snakes, to make men kill their brothers, as Cain had done to Abel. Snakes, to make fathers kill their children, daughters to whore themselves to spite their mothers.

Talin took another long breath in, delighting in the smell of—

Death.

—it. *Not death,* he chided the thing inside him. *A new beginning.*

...Pack?

"Of a sort," he said to the room, the animals in their cages gone silent and still. A breeze tugged at the smoke around him, drawing it to the ground. Talin walked towards the big windows at the side of the room, the smoke dogging his heels. He threw the windows open, big frames opening against a winter sky gone gray, the hope gone with the sun.

The smoke twined around him, then reached out towards the outside air.

"Go," he said to it. "Go. Find it. Destroy it."

In a rush, the smoke poured out the window, slipping down the side of the building, and into the waiting city below.

CHAPTER
FIFTEEN

"I don't know why we're here," said John.

Val looked up. "It's a bar," he said. "They serve beer. I need a beer."

"You need a hospital."

Val sat himself down on a stool, the leather a shiny red. The air inside hissed a little as he lowered his weight into it. A familiar sound, comfortable. The stools were dotted along the front of the bar itself, brass poles at their bases anchored to the ground, islands of safety for anyone who needed a hand with the cares of the moment. "I really think I need a beer."

"You could barely walk getting down here." John sat down beside him anyway.

Val turned himself on his stool, looking around the bar. He noted the bright red, white and blue neon advertising Bud, cowgirls — *for show* — carrying trays of drinks around. The floor was covered in peanut shells, the wood of the bar under his fingers dark and worn. The place was seeded with rednecks, the kind that wore Stetsons inside.

Perfect. "I've been thinking about that." Val fished a few greasy notes from inside his jeans pocket and slapped them down on the bar, holding up a couple fingers to the bartender.

"About how you need to go to the hospital?"

"About how I can't walk." Val paused as the bartender brought their beers over. Val held one up. "What the hell is this?"

The bartender paused. "It's a beer."

"It's a wheat beer." Val put the beer back down, an almost primal level of disgust making its way to his face.

"Yeah," said the bartender. "Microbrewery. Does a great run in boutique—"

Val held up a hand. "One second." He pushed himself back from the bar, keeping his movements slow and careful. He took an exaggerated look around the bar, letting his eyes linger on the Budweiser sign. He turned back to the bartender. "The thing is, you come into a place like this to drink a regular, completely flavorless beer. Maybe it comes out warm, a little flat, doesn't matter."

The bartender looked at the bottles on the bar. "You want a flat beer?"

"I want a beer made with hops," said Val. He looked at John. "You?"

John shrugged. "I'm not really—"

"He wants a beer made of hops too," said Val.

The bartender sighed. "I figured there'd be a wider spectrum of tastes in Chicago."

"It's not that," said Val. "You've got cats and dogs living together here. Cowgirls and wheat beer."

"Got it," said the bartender. "How about a Miller?"

"You can do better," said Val.

"Bud?"

"Is it cold?"

"It's not a Miller."

"I'll take it," said Val.

Their beers arrived, the cash disappearing in their wake. Val watched John out of the corner of his eye, then sighed. "Spit it out."

"It'd be rude," said John, "because you made such a thing of getting these."

"What?"

"It's a Bud," said John. "Tastes like Drano."

"It tastes," said Val, "like nothing in particular."

"Kinda my point."

"You don't get it," said Val. "For the last five years, I've been able to taste the flavor of cereal the guy who bottled the stuff had, a thousand miles away. I've had the, what do you call them, the taste buds of some kind of super..." He gestured with his bottle.

John shifted in his seat. "Dog?"

"Sure," said Val. "Some kind of super dog."

"Or a werewolf."

"Or one of those," said Val. "Thing is, there's been no *respite*. It's always on. No stopping the sensory train. And now ... it's just *gone*."

"You can't taste the beer?"

"I can't taste it any more than you," said Val. He took a long pull. "And I'm betting something else is going to happen."

John's brow furrowed. "I can't wait to hear this one."

"I'm betting I can get *drunk*," said Val, then tipped back the bottle and drained it.

"Well, shit," said John. "It's ten in the morning, but what the hell."

Val slapped some more notes on the bar. He reached up, touching at his nose, his fingers coming away red with blood.

"You're going to want to get that looked at," said John.

"I want to get drunk first," said Val.

THE BAR TOP in front of Val held four empties. He spared a glance at John, that Miles Megawatt Smile still firmly in place. "How do you do it?"

John shrugged. "I'm not sure what you're referring to, but I'm pretty sure it's because I'm *me*."

Val smiled at that, but couldn't hold the expression on his face. "Yeah, that sounds about right."

"You okay?"

"Not really," said Val. "I'm drunk at slightly past ten in the morning, and I miss my girlfriend."

"Well, this is weird," said John.

"What?"

"I'm saying it's weird," said John. "You were never a maudlin drunk."

"Jesus," said Val, "I was just passing time. And I'm not drunk."

"Could you drive?"

"I could drive," said Val, "but not legally. Doesn't mean I'm drunk." He wiped at his nose, his hand coming away sticky with blood.

John sat in silence for a moment. "She's coming back," he said eventually.

Val dabbed at his nose with a napkin. "Sure," he said, meaning, *I think she's gone.*

John pushed a mostly empty bottle around in front of him. "I think—"

"Your friend okay?" The bartender was back, something packaged up to look like concern in his eyes. He pointed at the napkin.

John flicked him a glance. "Not a good time."

"It's just that he's *bleeding*—"

"Look," said John, "and don't take this the wrong way, but fuck off." Val saw he had the Megawatt Smile out. A smile like that could mask all manner of insults and make you feel good about getting them.

Still. The bartender wasn't sure if he should be offended or not. "Uh—"

"It's fine," said John. "He gets these nosebleeds."

"Really?"

"Had 'em all his life," said John. "Comes with migraines or some shit. Hell if I know. I look like a doctor?"

"No," said the bartender.

"What," said John, "I look too stupid to be a doctor?"

"I ... I'm going to help someone else," said the bartender, and stalked off.

"Thanks," said Val.

"Don't thank me yet," said John. "We need to talk."

"We are talking."

"We're drinking beer and your nose won't stop bleeding."

"It's stopped now," said Val.

There was a raised voice from the front of the bar, the sound of anger mingled with surprise. Val saw John look towards the front, concern briefly touching his face, before his friend leaned in a little closer. "Do you think," he said, "that your bleeding nose is the worst thing that's happened today?"

"I think it's, what do you call it, collateral damage." Val took another sip of his beer, but the taste of it had gone stale. A little too flavorless. *Hell.*

"How you figure?" There was another shout from the front, John looking away again. "Hang on a second." He moved to stand.

"No, wait," said Val, putting a hand on his arm. "You *want* me to kill people?"

"No, it's—"

"I get this, what do you call it, this *curse*—"

"Gift," said John. "It's a gift."

"Oh *fuck off*," said Val. "I kill people, John."

"Two things," said John. "First is, I'm going to cut you some slack here because you're drunk."

"I'm not—"

"Second thing is," said John, "you don't kill people. Hell, if anything, you save people."

"What?" Val blinked. "You'll have to unpack that for me."

"*It* kills people," said John. "Not you. You're like some kind of Boy Scout, heading off and doing stupid shit."

"We're the same," said Val. "It's a part of me."

"Hold the phone," said John. He got up from his stool. "There's something going on at the front. While I'm gone, I've got some homework for you. If you're the same, how is it that you go out and do your hero thing on every night that ends in Y?"

"Don't change the subject," said Val.

"No, really," said John. "Can't you hear it?"

Val paused, realized he was half way off his stool. He felt caught, snagged against the edge of an unfamiliar feeling. Or *was* it familiar? Wanting to help, but being too powerless to *get involved*. "I—"

"I'll be right back," said John, pushing himself off his stool and walking towards the front of the bar. Val watched him go, turning his stool around in place, his feet skipping along the edge of the footrest. His balance skipped a beat and he almost came off. He felt a flash of embarrassment, chased away by happiness. A few hours ago, he wouldn't have been able to trip himself up if he'd tried. Something else—

A part of the Night.

—would have stepped forward, reached out through his arms and legs and his very thoughts to stop him falling. It was the same thing that left a body count in his wake, orphaned children beyond counting. Beyond remembering, except he couldn't forget either, not anymore.

There's good news, though. He picked his beer up off the bar. *It's all gone. You're* free.

A crash from the front pulled him out of his thoughts, and he was off the stool before he'd even thought about it. Something inside him—

Danger.

—tried to pull him forward, a feeling like a small hand on his arm, no stronger than a child's tug. He took a tentative step towards the front of the bar, a press of people there jockeying for position, trying to see what was going on. He picked out the back of John's head, that confident Miles swagger taking him through the press of people with ease. Val swallowed, took another step forward—

A shot rang out, and the press of bodies changed, a surge in the other direction. There were screams, shouts of alarm, and Val could see John there, standing his ground, one of the bar girls pushed behind him. He had a hand out in a *just hold the fuck on* gesture. Val followed the direction of his arm, trying to see through the people scattering and saw a man. Homeless, by the look of it, his clothes ... no, not *homeless*. He was dressed okay, casual denim and a hoodie emblazoned with *Tits Free Zone* on the front, but what made him look homeless was his eyes. Val had seen it before, something wild and lost, people who had just kind of checked out and left another thing behind instead of themselves. Something cracked by life's relentless pressure.

This guy had that look. Cracked, broken. The broken man held a gun, and his arm was swinging it around like some kind of hose with the water turned up too high, thrashing at the end of his shoulder without control. The gun went off, and there was a spray of red followed by a thud as a man was shot in the back, tumbling down against the edge of a table. The arm swung again, another shot, this one a miss. Val took another halting step forward, watching the broken man's arm swing again. Another shot, and a woman's body tumbled as the side of her face was torn away in a shower of gore. The smell of blood hung heavy on the air, but people were getting out of the way, hiding now, ducked down below tables, under chairs, one man disappearing through the doorway to the ladies' room.

Silence settled for a moment, fragile and tentative. A cough, a whisper to *shut the fuck up Jesus shut the fuck up* following it. The broken man's eyes tracked around the room, the gun held at the end of his arm like a forgotten thing. His gaze turned, catching *here* on a piece of broken glass, *there* on a barstool tumbled over, until it found—

NO.

—John, still standing up. He wasn't alone, the bar girl still held behind him, but there was no one else to stand against what was to come. The broken man's gun arm pulled itself around to point the gun at John, the movements jerky like he had Parkinson's — *hell who knows, he might, just add it to the list* — before holding steady, still, a rock in a storm of crazy. Pointed right at John.

Val saw it then, the light come on in the broken man's eyes, the childish glee as his hand tensed around the gun. Val saw as John turned away, his arms coming up around the bar girl, tugging her close to shield her with his body, his eyes squeezing shut and waiting for the hammer to fall against a round in the chamber.

The chair spun across the room, smashing against the broken man, the gun going off but the shot going wild. Val looked down at his hand, the hand that had thrown the chair without a thought. John's eyes opened, surprise on his face, and he looked up at Val. Val ignored him, stepping forward to the front of the bar. The broken man was trying to stand, tugging his gun arm free of the chair.

Val stood over him, and the man stopped moving, his eyes wide and wild. "*Stop it.*"

The broken man giggled, a scattered sound full of rough edges. "Must find. Must kill."

"Kill who?" Val leaned down. "Find what?"

The broken man giggled again, then pulled the weapon free. Val caught the man's wrist, thumb against the other man's hand, twisting it around so the barrel pointed at the broken man.

"Set you free," said the broken man. "Set me free."

"Free from—" said Val, but the broken man pulled the trigger of the gun, shooting himself. The bullet hit him in the chest, and red started to well from the front of his hoodie. The writing on the front became indistinct as blood colored it over, the letters vanishing one by one. Val felt the life draining from the man as he held his wrist. At the end, the man's eyes cleared and he looked up at Val.

"Where am I?"

"What?"

The broken man looked down at himself. "I've been shot."

"You—" said Val, wanting to say *you shot yourself*. Instead he said, "Yeah."

"Am I going to die?"

Val nodded. "I'm pretty sure."

"Okay," said the man. "Can you get a message to Louis?"

"Who is Louis?"

"He's the man I was going to marry," said the broken man, as the light faded from his eyes.

"Well, shit," said John, standing behind Val. "That was unexpected."

"Yeah," said Val.

"Guy was crazy," said John.

"No," said Val. "I don't think so."

"He came in here and started shooting," said John. "He shot himself and didn't remember doing it."

"Right," said Val. "That's not crazy."

"You'll need to help me with that," said John. He reached an arm out, and Val took it, standing up. "I'm not sure I follow."

"I know someone else who does things without remembering them," said Val. "Terrible things. Or used to."

"That's different," said John.

"How so?"

"Uh," said John.

"Do you want to phone a friend?" Val looked around the bar, then caught the eye of the bar girl who John had stood in front of. "Hey."

She took a cautious step forward. "Yes?"

"What's your name?"

"Marlie," she said.

"Marlie, I need you to call 911. Get an ambulance."

Marlie blinked at him. "Why? He's dead." She almost spat the last word.

"It's not for him," said Val. He jerked a thumb at the man who'd fallen against the edge of a table, blood still pooling around him. "That guy."

"Oh," said Marlie. "Right." She stood there, staring at the blood.

"Marlie," said Val.

"Yeah?"

"Now," said Val. "Because if you don't, he will *die*."

Marlie gave a short, nervous nod, then scurried away. Val watched her go, then cocked his head. "You hear that?"

John nodded, both of them looking to the front of the bar. There was the sound of screaming outside, a horn followed by the screech of tires. A crash of something large and metal against stone. Gun shots, the distance making them sound like *pop, pop, pop*.

Val shrugged. "Want to go take a look?"

"No," said John.

"Me neither," said Val. He—

The day brings terrors.

—shrugged. *Hell with it*. They stepped through the front door of the bar and into the broken world beyond.

CHAPTER
SIXTEEN

here are we going?

The boy looked up from where he sat on the edge of the box between the front seats, his feet on the transmission tunnel. It hurt Adalia's head to look at him, because he shouldn't have fit there. There wasn't enough room, not for a *boy* to sit there in among all of them, but *there he was*. Impossible. Perfect.

"I don't know." He shrugged. "Chicago."

You don't know, or Chicago? Her fingers moved faster on her phone, practice with this way of talking giving her speed. *There's a big difference.*

"I don't know," he said, "because I've never been to Chicago." His long lashes curled a little at the end, and Adalia wanted to reach out and touch him. "I guess my mom's there."

Adalia tipped her head sideways, looking at him. *Your mom?*

"Yeah." He looked confused. "I ... I'm sorry. I don't know." The confusion turned to frustration, and he sighed.

Adalia thought for a moment. The trick, he'd explained, was asking the questions in a way that ... *allowed* him to answer. He'd told her before that he didn't always know until he knew, and he only knew when questions were asked that didn't break the rules.

It helped him to remember.

She spun her phone between her fingers for a moment. *What happened in Chicago?* She looked at the text for a moment, not showing it to him, then deleted all but the first word. *What is going to happen in Chicago?*

He looked down at his hands. "I don't know."

Can't you see?

"I'm here," he said. "Of course I can't see. Chicago is miles away."

Her stomach growled, and she nodded. It was approaching dawn, and they'd been driving most of the night without stopping. She needed a shower. She needed breakfast. She needed sleep.

She needed to pee.

I don't understand you at all.

He laughed. "You're not supposed to. I'm a boy."

You seem much older than any boys our age.

He turned sombre. "I'm ... older." He turned to look over his shoulder at the road the Yukon was lapping up, a big animal pacing fast and sure through the night, tearing the distance up and turning it into dawn. He turned to look back at her. "I think I'm a lot older."

How much older?

His brow furrowed. "I ... that doesn't make any sense," he said. "Time doesn't..." He trailed off, swallowing.

Time doesn't work that way where you are?

"It doesn't exist," he said. "I don't think it does. It's a little confusing."

You're confused?!?!?!

He laughed. "I'm going to miss you."

She sat back, feeling cold in her stomach. She typed fast into her phone, then deleted the whole line, replacing it with a single word. *Why?*

"Because everything ends," he said. "I come out from time to time, and then I have to go again. The people I see are always different. It's just..." He sighed.

You want to stay?

"No," he said. "I never want to come back at all." He looked down, his dark lashes lowering. He looked so vulnerable that she wanted to grab him, shake him, tell him it was going to be okay. She knew it would be a lie.

Adalia looked up at her mom, saw the tension in her shoulders, her eyes staring out the window. Saw how her fingers clenched and unclenched like restless animals on her lap. *I don't want to stay either.*

"Yeah you do," he said. "The thing is ... since I met you, I want to stay as well."

Her heart gave a tiny skip. She started to type, slower this time, afraid to scare him away. *Do we have to do something?*

He looked at the words on her phone. "No," he said, then, "Well, yes. But that's not why I want to stay. I want to stay because you make me miss this world."

She wanted to type a thousand things, but settled for one line. *What do you miss about it?*

"I don't remember," he said, "but you make me want to. The rest of them never do. They always want something from *me*."

I might want something from you.

"But that's the thing," he said. "I know you don't."

How do you know?

"Because you've never asked for anything," he said. He tapped the edge of her phone. "Not with this." He reached a finger out, tentative, almost touching her chest above her heart. "Only with this." He pulled his hand back as if it had been burned, closing his fist around it and putting it between his knees.

I'm sorry, she typed.

"You don't need to be sorry," he said. "Hey, this conversation's taken a morbid turn. Let's talk about something light-hearted, like child labor in China."

She hid a smile behind her hand. *You were talking about your mom before.*

He nodded. "I don't know why."

Something about Chicago. The Yukon started up an incline, the engine's note changing a little, the big motor eager for the challenge.

"Was it? I can't tell."

You said she was there.

"I said I thought Chicago had something to do with my mom," he said. "Most of the places I go have something to do with her."

Do you know why?

"I've given it a lot of thought," he admitted. "I think it's because she misses me."

She can't see you?

"Most people can't see me," he said. His mouth pulled down a little. "Most people don't want to see me."

What's your mom doing in Chicago?

She saw it by the look on his face, the look of recognition, chased away by fear. No, not fear — *horror.* She'd asked the wrong question, but she'd asked it in the right way. "Oh," he said. "Oh." He laughed, then it choked into a sob. "Oh, Adalia. I see it now."

Adalia fought to keep her calm. She felt the presence of her mom and Carlisle, and the two men in the front, all close around her in the cabin. *What do you see?*

"Madness," he said, his voice thick with emotion. "And its twin, death."

She had so many questions. What about Val? And John? But she had to ask the questions ... right. *Can you see your mom?*

"Yes." He shuffled on his seat. "She'll be right in the middle of it. At the beginning, at least."

Can we help?

A smile broke through on his face, soft as sun peeking through on a cloudy day. "Always trying to help," he said. "Sometimes things aren't your problem."

She shook her head, angry. *Val is in Chicago. John is in Chicago.*

113

"They're not your problem," he said. "They're adults. You're a kid."

Adalia wanted to reach out and slap him. *I'm 14!*

He looked at the text on her phone, then back up at her. "Are you … are you trying to make my point for me?"

She crossed her arms, sitting back in the seat, and glared at him. After a moment she started typing again. *We're the same age. We're the same.*

He held up his fingers, counting them off. "First, we're not the same age. Second, we're not the same."

We are the same.

"I remember when life seemed that black and white."

It's good you can remember something.

He read the text, then looked sad. "I know. It's not fair. I don't understand it either."

Adalia felt something in her chest release its grip. *I'm sorry. I just want to help.*

"I'm not your problem. I guess, in a way, you're *my* problem." He looked around the Yukon, stretching out his arms. Her brain skittered away from the motion, didn't want to see how he could move like that in the small space. "I get sent to solve problems."

Well, you can help me solve the problem sitting in the front seat.

"Ajay?" He frowned, his voice changing, the cadence becoming deliberate. "Ajay Lewiss. The blind soldier. The forgotten child. A weapon of faith and hope, tarnished and rusty. He fights for someone else, and the faithless contract makes his purpose weak."

Adalia stared at him for a moment. *Wow.*

"What? What did I say?"

A bunch of weird shit. She paused, then deleted the last word. *Stuff.*

"No, really," he said. "I don't always know what I'm going to say. The words come from … somewhere else. It's like … I don't know. It's like I'm a megaphone."

What's a megaphone?

"You don't watch cartoons?" He ran a hand through his hair, the

114

black strands falling through his fingers. She wanted to reach out, straighten a stray lock that fell back across his eye.

I'm 14. I'm not a child.

"*I* watch cartoons," he said. "Anyway, they're always drawn like a big red cone. You talk through, it makes your voice louder on the other end."

Have you ever wondered?

"Wondered what?"

Whose voice you're making louder?

He stared at the tiny light of her phone screen, then sat back. "Yes."

And??!?!?!

"I think it's the Universe," he said. "It's everything, and everyone, all the time. It wants to speak to us. It tries all the time, you know."

Like God?

"God's just a name for something a lot of people don't understand," he said. "I've never met God. I ... I wanted to, for a long time. To ask him why."

She frowned. *Why what?*

He looked angry. "I don't *remember.*"

You said it tries to speak to us. I've never heard it.

He smiled at her, something gentle in it. "Yes, you have. You hear it in me. You see it in Carlisle. You feel its strength in your mom. You sense its purpose, dragging us in this gas guzzling Yukon to Chicago."

Carlisle? My mom? They're just people.

He cocked an eyebrow at her.

Okay, I mean, not "just" — they're the best people. But ... they're people. Not like comets or stars or a planet or ... whatever you are.

"What makes you think that a tired, broken down cop's affection for a lonely 14 year old girl is less miraculous than the birth of a star? And *seriously*, your mom turns into a freakin' *werewolf*. How cool is that?"

She's not tired. She's not broken.

Something gentle and sad moved across his face. "Ah," he said. "There it is."

What?

He faded from view, leaving the scent of fresh mowed grass, at odds with the new car smell of the Yukon. As he left, she heard him say, "How miraculous is it that a 14 year old girl feels the need to protect her much older, world-weary friend? I find *you* miraculous, Adalia Kendrick."

Adalia stared through the space where he'd sat, the night ahead giving way to the gentle touch of dawn. She looked down at her phone, then typed — even though no one was there to see it — *Shit.*

SEVENTEEN

"That's the thing," said Rex. "I dunno, right? I work out. I eat right. Like the song."

His driver looked back at him through the rear view mirror. *Cute, nice nose.* "What song?"

"Huey Lewis."

"Huey Lewis and the News?" She turned back to the front, watching the traffic.

"I guess. There any other bands called something like that?" Rex ran a finger under the edge of his strapping. Damn thing was itching like a poison ivy rash. He didn't like bandages as a general rule, but after the ... *accident*, well, after that he'd needed one. Paramedic had said two sprained wrists, but he'd talked them down to just one. 30 years in the Fire Department meant he knew when someone needed a good bandage, and for damn sure he wasn't walking around with two oven mitts on. They'd said it might hurt bad, as if there was a *good* kind of hurt.

"Joan Jett and the Blackhearts," she said.

"What?"

"That's a band called something like that," she said. "What you asked."

"Fine," said Rex. "They sing a song called *Hip to Be Square*?"

"I don't think so," she said. Definitely a cute nose. If he was 20 years younger... "Not really my speed, though."

"Whaddya mean?" Rex leaned forward to look out through the front seats. "What the fuck is that?"

She tossed him a look, then followed his eyes. "I mean that I'm into more of a dance scene. Looks like a guy eating a pigeon."

Rex leaned back, rubbing a hand over his face. His watch strap jingled in the quiet of the car. "You don't seem phased."

"I guess people like the music they like," she said. "It's not an age thing, if that's what you're thinking."

He blinked at her. "What?"

"The music. I get it. Huey Lewis is cool, for an older guy." She shrugged, adjusted her seat belt. There was a half-smile on her face as she remembered something. Or someone. "I mean, my boyfriend's a little bit older."

"No," said Rex. "The guy. Eating the pigeon."

"It's Chicago," she said, as if it explained everything.

"How much you make in a day?" said Rex. "I mean, round numbers. I'm not trying to rob you or something like that."

"Wouldn't matter," she said. "It's an Uber. No cash, right?"

"Right," said Rex. "So what, about five hundred a day?"

"Hookers make five hundred a day," she said. "Me, after gas I'm packing a couple hundred a day."

"You drive assholes like me for two hundred a day?"

"More or less," she said. "It depends."

"I saw an article," said Rex. "Said Uber drivers make up to one fifty large."

"I saw an article," she said, "that said you could get rich on Amway."

"Fair point," said Rex. "Whatever. You ever get hungry enough to eat a pigeon on a couple hundred a day?"

The car moved forward a few more feet, then stopped again as the gridlocked traffic bunched again. "No," she said. "I mean, I'm sure it's nice—"

"Fucking sky rats," said Rex. "Psittacosis."

"Right," she said, like she knew what he was talking about. "You eaten one before?"

"I look like I'm that hungry?" Rex frowned. "Thing is, that guy is wearing an Armani suit."

"Right," she said, less certain now.

"You ever bought an Armani suit?"

"I've got some Armani sunglasses."

"Okay, we'll use that," said Rex. "You never got hungry enough to eat a pigeon on two hundred a day and you're buying Armani shades. That guy's got a whole *suit* made of Armani — a lot more than your shades cost, believe me — and he's eating a sky rat."

She nodded, silent for a moment. Her hands tapped against the steering wheel. "He *is* making kind of a mess of it."

Rex saw movement out the left of the car, a person running past them down between the line of cars. He tracked the motion, turning around in his seat, watching until the man disappeared from view. "Huh."

He saw her eyes flick up to the rear view mirror again. "'Huh?' What's, 'Huh?'"

"That guy," said Rex. "Ran right past."

"Yeah," she said. They both watched as a woman ran between the line of stopped cars, her face frantic. "That is unusual. Won't cost you extra though."

"What?" Rex saw the man who'd been eating the pigeon drop from view as he crouched down low. *Weird.* "I mean, they're running down the line of cars. On the road. Get you killed."

"Not in this traffic," she said. "I mean, doesn't matter how long it takes to get where we're going. Won't cost you extra."

"I know," said Rex. "Uber, right?"

"Right," she said, distracted now. "Uh. What's that over there?"

Rex watched for a moment, frowning. "That looks like a woman hitting a man with a doll."

"It's not a doll," she said, her voice gone quiet. "It's a child."

"Can't be," said Rex. But a voice in his head said, *You've seen weird shit these past couple days, Rex.*

"Can't be," she said, wanting to agree.

"Say," said Rex. You mind if I crack a window?"

"Why?"

He pressed the control anyway, the window sliding open a couple inches. As the air from Chicago — rich with the smell of smog in the morning's traffic — came in, they both heard it. The sound of screams, of fear.

Of panic.

"Hey," she said. "Could you close the window?"

"Good idea," said Rex, flicking the control the other way. The window slid closed, a soft mechanical *thump* as it sealed them back in. "Good idea—"

A man collided with the front of their car, his hands leaving a red smear against the windscreen. He looked in at them, and his eyes locked with Rex's. His voice was faint through the glass, but Rex heard him anyway. "Run! For God's sake, get—"

He was interrupted as a shape collided with him, knocking him over. The driver let out a scream, her hands stabbing at the car's dash. The doors locked with a satisfying *clunk*. A hand rose up over the edge of the door, fingers hooked like claws. Rex thought he could see the fingernails broken under hot pink nail polish. A face rose up after, a woman—

What the actual fuck.

—looking in at them. Young, no more than 25 if she was a day. She had some meat in her teeth and was chewing it as her hand clawed and scrabbled at the window, leaving bloody tracks against the glass. She swallowed whatever—

Jesus. Is she ... eating a part of that guy?

—was in her mouth, then bared her teeth at them. Her face

twisted into a snarl, and she started to slam her fist into the glass of the window.

Rex's driver scrabbled for the glove box. It fell open with a clatter, insurance papers falling out, a makeup case, a phone, finally a taser. She pulled it up from the floor, holding it to her chest with both hands.

"Hey," said Rex, in between thumps of the woman's hand against the glass. "She can't get in here."

"Right," she said. "Right." She didn't loosen her grip on the taser.

There was a crack, a spider's web fracture crawling up the glass. "Uh," said Rex.

There was a sound like wood on wood, and the woman's face disappeared. Rex looked up into the eyes of a large man, six four and angry with it. He held a baseball bat, the end covered in gore. He locked eyes with Rex, nodded to him, then tried the door handle on the passenger side. "Let me in," he said. "They're—"

Another shape careened into him, a man screaming and yelling, and then both went down. Rex turned to his driver. "Get us the fuck out of here."

Her eyes were wide. "Where? There's—"

He grabbed her shoulder. "Miss?"

"Yeah?"

"What's your name?"

"Skyler," she said. "Sky."

He frowned. "Which the fuck one is it?"

"My friends call me Sky," she said.

"Rex," said Rex, jerking a thumb at his chest. "Sky, we've got—"

"Rex, like a dog?" There was an edge of hysteria in her voice.

He sighed. *Keep her calm. Don't let her think about what's out* there. "Like a fucking Tyrannosaurus."

She nodded at him, mute, eyes wide.

"So, we've got what is called a *situation* here." said Rex. "What we're going to do is use this big ol' car of yours to make a gap."

"Make a gap?"

"Like a snow plow," he said. "You're going to put it in gear, and nudge a hole in the traffic. Slow and steady. Get us on the sidewalk—"

"Is that safe?"

"Sky," said Rex, "safe is in Kansas. We're in Chicago."

She nodded, set her shoulders, and turned back to the front. She was about to move the car forward when Rex spoke again. "Sky?"

"Yeah?"

"We still need to get to where we were headed."

"You really want to get to work?"

"I wasn't going to work," said Rex. "I was going to meet a friend."

"Right," she said. She placed the taser on the passenger seat, then gripped the steering wheel with both hands. "My insurance—"

A man jumped on the hood of the car, yelling at them. Sky screamed, jamming a foot on the gas, and the big town car roared forward, slamming a hole in the cars around them. It bounced onto the pavement, shooting out like a cork from a bottle, and they were away, the man tumbling off the hood.

Rex spared a look behind them. *Well, that's one way to do it.*

"Where we going?" Sky spared a glance at him over her shoulder as the big town car crawled along the sidewalk. "Can you give me directions?"

"Your phone flat?" Rex felt like his head was on a swivel as he cast about on all sides of the car. There were bodies everywhere, some fallen as if asleep, some torn apart, barely recognizable. They drove past an old Taurus, flames billowing out through the windows.

"It's not flat," she said. "I can't get a signal."

"Who you with?"

"AT&T."

"That'll be why," said Rex. "I'm with Verizon. They're..." His voice trailed off as he checked his own phone, *NO SERVICE* showing at the top. "Well, fuck me running," he said.

"Verizon not giving it to you?" She tried on a smirk, left it there. *Definitely a cute nose.*

"I'm on a plan," he said. "Got six months to run."

"Thieves, right?"

"Right," said Rex. "Look, I know the way. You need to go up another couple blocks, take a right."

"Then what?"

"Then nothing. We'll be there." Rex drummed his fingers on his leg. "Say."

"Yeah?"

"Why you doing this?" Rex pointed out the front of the car at a shopping cart full of cans. "Watch out for that."

"I see it," she said, easing the car around the cart. "People don't waste time, do they?"

"What?"

Sky jerked a thumb over her shoulder at the cart falling away behind them. "Looting."

"Oh," said Rex. "No. They never do."

"You been in places like this before?" He noticed her hands gripped the wheel so tight her fingers where white, bloodless.

"L.A. fires," said Rex. "Worked in the Department, thirty years."

"Right," said Sky. Then, "They looted in the L.A. fires?"

"People loot everywhere," said Rex. "Humans are basically jackals. Hold up here."

"Why—" but then she saw it. A pack of people loping, shoulders hunched over. Five of them, skittering around the edges of stopped and empty cars. He watched as Sky put the car in park, left the engine idling. "Do you—"

"Hush now," said Rex. He reached forward, put a hand on her arm. "Don't move."

They sat still and silent in the car as the five people — *if that's what they are* — moved like a pack of wild dogs through the stopped traffic. One of them passed close to the town car, sparing a glance inside. Rex tightened his fingers on Sky's arm, but made no other movement, not even his eyes. The face looking in at them moved on, and they both breathed out.

"They didn't see us," said Sky. "Why didn't they see us?"

"They expected to see something else," said Rex.

"Like what?"

"You ever see a lion hunting?"

"In Chicago?"

"No," said Rex. "On the nature channel, or whatever you kids watch today."

"Discovery?"

"Is that a nature channel?"

"Yes." She ran a nervous hand through her hair.

"Then Discovery," said Rex. "You see a lion hunting?"

"I've seen a show," she said.

This is why you don't date younger women, thought Rex. *No context.* "They track movement."

"Those people are lions?"

"Those people are *hunting*," said Rex. "You run, you're prey."

"Got it," said Sky. "Don't run. Except..."

"Yeah?"

"What if you *need* to run?" Sky tossed a look back at him, then slipped the big town car back into gear.

"Then," said Rex, "you run fast, Sky. You run really fast."

"It's because you seem nice," she said. "It's because you wanted to get your friend."

"What?" Rex looked at her, then back out the window. "I don't follow."

"You asked me why I was doing this," she said. "You've got a sprained wrist. You're ... don't take this the wrong way, but you're a little bit older."

"I'm retired," said Rex. "Or I thought I was, until this morning."

The town car made the right turn, edging along the sidewalk. Sky was looking out the front, focused. "That's what I mean," she said. "You don't look like you're looting the place."

"Stop here," he said as they edged next to the entrance to a brownstone. The front doors were hanging open. "This is the place."

"Who we picking up?"

Rex let out a breath. "Sky?"

"Yeah, Rex?"

"Sky, you should go now," he said. "Find your family."

"It's okay," said Sky. "They'll find me."

"How you figure?"

She thought for a moment. "I'm not sure. John just seems like the type." She seemed so certain. *That's a hell of a guy.*

"John your boyfriend?"

"Yes," she said.

"How's he going to find you?"

"Easy," she said. "He is *always* in some kind of trouble. If I'm in trouble too, we'll just..." She trailed off.

"You'll be in the eye of the storm," said Rex. "I get it. But it's okay, Sky. I got it from here."

"With your arm?"

"It's only sprained." Rex looked down at his bandage. "Even with that."

"I'll keep the engine running," she said.

"But—"

"What's your friend's name?" she asked, cutting over the top of him.

"Just James," said Rex.

"What's he like?"

"He's a good kid," said Rex. "I don't know him that well, to be honest. We were in the accident together." Rex looked at his arm. *The one I caused.* "My fault, right? I've been trying to look out for him."

She ignored everything but the first part. "He's a kid?"

"He's alone," said Rex. "His Dad's an asshole."

"We getting his Dad too?"

"Don't think that'll be an option," said Rex. "He'll be in the wind."

"You go get Just James," said Sky, "and I'll see you back down here. Then we'll go…"

"It's okay," said Rex. "We'll work it out in a bit. And Sky?"

"Yeah?"

"Thanks."

"Don't thank me yet," said Sky. "Here." She held out the taser.

He thought about refusing it, then looked up at the broken doors to the brownstone. *God damn old body, God damn seven flights of stairs, God damn people eating people.* He took it from her with a nod, then opened the door and stepped out into the smell of smoke, a scream sounding in the distance.

You left L.A. to get away from this kind of shit, he thought. *Welcome home. At least the bandage has stopped itching.* With that thought he stepped through the shadowed doorway of the brownstone and into the quiet lobby inside.

CHAPTER
EIGHTEEN

"Border Control," said Ajay. "Should be easy."

"How you figure?" Carlisle craned her neck forward. Yellow painted steel rose up to form arches across the road, *UNITED STATES BORDER INSPECTION STATION* writ large over an awning as utilitarian as it was non-functional. Rain tumbled and turned in eddies underneath the awning, promising a cold, wet, and taciturn border guard experience, if it came to that. "You see those cameras?"

"I see the cameras," Ajay said. He looked tired, his face gaunt. *An all-night drive will do that to you*, she thought. "I don't see the problem."

"Guards," said Carlisle.

"Are you wanted criminals?" Ajay tapped the steering wheel with his fingers.

Carlisle cut back an angry retort. "Uh."

"Do you have valid United States passports?" He threw a look at her over his shoulder, sparing a glance for Danny and the kid, both asleep. The kid had fallen asleep on her mom's shoulder.

"Uh," said Carlisle again. "Sure."

"And," said Ajay, "do you have a permit for that large gun you carry?"

"It's not that large," said Carlisle.

"You fired it next to me," he said. "It sounded very large."

"Oh," said Carlisle. "It fires large *bullets*."

"Will its presence about your person," said Ajay, "cause undue alarm to the officers here?"

"Probably," said Carlisle. "It's a Desert Eagle." She caught his intake of breath. "But no, I'm not carrying it *illegally*."

"Good," said Ajay. "We should have no problems."

Carlisle leaned back. "I guess. It's just..." She trailed off.

"You're used to being hunted," said Ajay. "I know the feeling."

"You do?" Carlisle closed her eyes for a moment. "Aren't you a hunter?"

"Exactly so," said Ajay.

"How you figure it feels to be hunted?" Carlisle opened her eyes, looking at Ajay in the rear view mirror.

His eyes found hers. "I was a child once too."

She bit down on her lip. "Are you telling me—"

"I'm telling you nothing, Detective Carlisle," he said, "that you don't already know."

"I'm not a cop anymore," she said, almost absently.

He shook his head. "Being a Shield of the people, the voice that speaks for victims when the wicked have stolen away their will before the coming of the dawn? That is not a job. That is what you *are*."

"What would you know about that?" She heard the bitterness in her voice, caught herself looking at Danny.

He thought for a moment before responding. The cars in front of them moved forward, and he let the big Yukon slide forward in the snow. "Names have power." His accent made the last word sound like *powa*. "I know that you need reminding of some things that you might ... prefer to forget."

"Like my fucking *father*?" She spat the last word as if it was bile.

"Like the people around you," said Ajay. "Power attracts power. The names we carry give us strength of purpose, let us share that purpose with others. The Night is a friend to you, Detective. You offered yourself as its Shield, and it has responded in kind." Ajay sighed. "It is hard to explain."

The old memory of her father sat heavy on her shoulders, and she tried to shrug it off. "Why is it so important to you?"

"The woman I ... work for has enemies," he said. "We share a common purpose."

"That's something we'll need to test a bit more," she said. "You could help by giving me names. You know how you say in your world names have power?" She looked out the window at one of the cameras attached to a pole. "Same in my world."

"Raeni Williams," said Ajay.

"What?"

"Raeni Williams is her name," said Ajay, "but it doesn't tell her purpose. You would call her a witch. I call her my mother."

"Your ... mother," said Carlisle, trailing off. "You mentioned her. Before." *Back at the bar.* "Most people *have* mothers. They don't *call* people mother. Well, not unless they tag the end of it with something else, like *fucker.*"

"Is that the detective asking?"

"I'm not asking," said Carlisle. "I'm saying how the world works."

"Who are you," said Ajay, "to tell me how the world works? We spin on around the sun regardless of your thoughts on it." He seemed almost dismissive.

Carlisle wanted his approval, recognized it for what it was and crushed it down like a bent cigarette under her boot. "Yeah," she said. "I'm telling you how it is."

"Tell me who you call mother," said Ajay, "when your own mother is torn away in a fire-filled night, bullets snapping around you like rabid dogs."

"I don't know much about that," said Carlisle.

"Just so," said Ajay.

She felt the stir of anger in her chest. "What I *can* tell you is what happens when your alcoholic father beats your mother to an early grave. She dies, and she leaves you alone with him, forever." She rubbed at her face. "Forever, or until there's an end to it. Father still wants a woman around, more or less."

"Is this why you don't want me to speak with him?"

"No," said Carlisle. Then, "Yes. Well, it's more like this: when I ... made sure he was gone, I did it because I didn't want to speak to him ever again."

"You didn't want him to use his voice." She watched the back of his head nod. "You didn't want him to speak to you."

"I didn't want," she said, "for him to speak to *anyone*. He stole away my voice. Least I could do was to return the favor." She looked at her hand clenched on the leather seat in front of her, made herself relax it.

Ajay let the car roll forward once more as the line moved. "I understand," he said.

"You can't," she said.

"I understand," he said. "I'm not trying to fight with you. Fighting's what you know. It's what you are."

"I thought you said I was a detective."

"You who claim to know how the world works don't yet know that we can be more than just one thing?"

Carlisle thought about that. "I didn't choose to be a fighter," she said. Her voice grew quiet. "I just wanted to be able to use my own voice again."

"And you may get your chance," said Ajay, his voice brightening in counterpart to hers, "because this fine border control officer wants to speak with us."

"What?" But it was true, a man in uniform was making his way towards their car. "Okay," she said. "One question."

"Just one?" She heard the smile in his voice, for all the gravitas in the cabin.

"How is it you know so much about the world?"

"I find things," said Ajay. "It's what I am."

"Just one thing?" said Carlisle. "You're not more than one thing?"

"I am many things," said Ajay. "Perhaps I can even be a friend."

"Don't push your luck," said Carlisle, but she wanted it too. That feeling in her gut made her feel like she was sixteen again. "And slide down your window."

Ajay turned his head to the window and the border control officer standing outside it. The man was leaned forward a little, head ducked against the half rain, half ice falling from the sky. Carlisle watched as Ajay cracked the window. "Hello, my friend," he said. "It is unpleasant, yes?"

Carlisle let Ajay talk with the officer, turning to find Danny's eyes on her. They were warm and dark, not the yellow that made Carlisle … concerned.

"I…" said Danny.

"You heard," said Carlisle, her voice low.

"Don't get the chance to miss much," said Danny, turning away. "I'm sorry. I—"

"Hey," said Carlisle. *Last thing I need is a pity parade.* "Save it."

"Okay," said Danny, stroking Adalia's hair. Carlisle felt like the motion was from a time when Adalia was younger, the world simpler. "It's just—"

"I know," said Carlisle.

"Okay," said Danny, turning to look out the window. Carlisle watched the muscles in her jaw bunch as she clenched her teeth. "You don't know what it's like," she said after a while. Her eyes moved to the officer, still talking with Ajay.

"What's what like?"

"When someone hurts someone in your Pack—"

"Family," said Carlisle, looking at Adalia. "Humans call them family."

"When someone hurts someone in your family, it wants … *you* want to hurt them back," said Danny, her voice low.

Carlisle made her voice light, felt how brittle it was around the words. "He didn't hurt me," she said. "He *made* me."

The car rolled through the border gates, the window sliding back up. Ajay turned to say something, looked at the two of them, and closed his mouth.

The man has wisdom. Carlisle turned back to Danny. "It's old history."

Danny nodded like she was agreeing. Carlisle couldn't stand to look at the sympathy in her friend's eyes, found herself looking at the floor of the Yukon, food wrappers — *here's a trick question: is a Moon Pie food?* — and Coke cans on the ground. *How do teenagers eat that kind of shit?*

"Well," said Danny, "there's probably something else we should talk about."

Thank God. Carlisle turned back to the front. "What is it?"

Danny jerked a thumb outside the truck at the trees on the edge of the road. "We're in Minnesota," she said.

"The capital of inbreeding," said Carlisle. "What of it?"

"Minnesota," said Danny, slower this time.

"I don't follow," said Carlisle, "unless you don't think I'm being fair with the inbreeding comment."

Danny ran a hand through her curls — *God damn but how does she look like a supermodel after sleeping in the back of a truck for six hours* — before she spoke again. "Alaska," she said, "is over two *thousand* miles from Minnesota."

Carlisle blinked. "That can't be right," she said.

"Which part?" said Danny. "The part where the planet is always the same size, or the part where we did it in a night?"

"The part where we're in Minnesota," said Carlisle.

"We are," said Ajay, "in Minnesota."

"We didn't pass through border control at the Alaska border," said Danny. "Did we?"

"No," said Carlisle and Ajay together.

Ajay cleared his throat. Carlisle could see his face was still ashen.

More than just tired. More than just not sleeping for a night. "We didn't have the time," he said, "to do this the usual way."

"What," said Carlisle, "is the usual way?"

"Driving all night."

"What," said Carlisle, "did you *do*?"

"I made a deal," he said. "I made a trade."

Danny leaned forward, her hand resting soft and steady on the seat in front of her. Her voice was so quiet Carlisle almost couldn't hear her. "Who did you make a deal with?"

"It doesn't matter," said Ajay. "It will either all be okay, or we will all be dead. We have to get to Chicago."

"To Valentine," said Danny.

"No," said Ajay.

Carlisle sighed. "Ajay?"

"Yes."

"You know what she is, don't you?"

"Yes," he said, nodding slowly.

"Do us all a favor," said Carlisle. "Don't make her play guessing games. She's not rich on patience."

"Hey," said Danny.

"Tell me it's not true," said Carlisle.

Danny said nothing. Ajay swallowed, then said, "The monster is in Chicago."

"Val's not a monster," said Danny. "Say that again and I'll—"

"I said the *monster*," said Ajay. "Valentine is no monster."

THE YUKON TURNED into the lot of a convenience store. A paper cup, caught up in a cradle of snow, disappeared under a wheel. The machine grumbled as the engine walked them forward. Ajay slid the machine into park, dropped a hand to the brake and pulled it on. "We're here."

"Where's here?" Adalia had woken up a few miles back, but her voice was still blurry with sleep.

"Paradise," said Ajay. "I believe we can secure our entry to the promised lands."

Carlisle peered through the windscreen. They'd left Pigeon River Bridge behind them, the cold of the North giving way to the cold of the South. It hurt less, but she felt it more. It was closer to home. "This looks like a shitty convenience store."

"Exactly so," said Ajay. "I believe they sell corn dogs here." He pushed his door open, the air of Minnesota pushing into the cabin, a new breath of life Carlisle didn't know she needed.

Danny put a hand on her arm. "Careful," she said.

"Careful of what?" Carlisle's hand was on the Yukon's door, ready to follow Ajay out and into the convenience store.

"You know," she said. Her eyes found Ajay's receding form.

"Yeah, I guess I do," said Carlisle. She got out of the Yukon anyway, her feet taking her into the store. *It's destiny, Carlisle. Get a corn dog, save the world.*

She heard the clunk of the door as Danny followed her, caught two sets of footsteps as Adalia spilled out into the wide open world. Carlisle walked into the store behind Ajay, not looking behind her. Those two needed some privacy, some time to work a few things out. Come to think of it, so did she.

The inside of the store was all waxed linoleum, the faint scent of disinfectant not really overcoming the smell of old mold and bad coffee. The old cop habit wouldn't die, her eyes finding the middle aged guy with the neck beard behind the counter, an old black and white set turned on behind him, a TV show playing with the sound down low. Her eyes found the counter top crowded with opportunistic sales promises, jerky nestled alongside a couple boxes of *Snickers*. The counter would hide a weapon, some kind of shotgun unless she missed her guess. Her eyes continued their walk of the inside, finding a dark doorway out the back, plastic strips hanging down as a guard against entry. No one else inside.

Other than him. Without really wanting to, she found herself beside Ajay in an aisle that sold boxes of breakfast cereal. She cleared her throat. "I thought you wanted corn dogs."

"I do not believe corn dogs are a part of a nutritious breakfast," he said. "The little one. She needs—"

"I know," said Carlisle. Then, "Thanks."

"Don't thank me yet," he said. "Is *Cap'n Crunch* a good choice?"

"No," said Carlisle. "She'll eat it though." She knew what Adalia liked, what she would gravitate to with the endless enthusiasm of youth. "Here," she said. "This is better." She pointed at a box of *Frosted Flakes.*

"'High in Vitamin A,'" said Ajay, reading the front of the box. "Is this really *better?*"

"It's all a point of view, isn't it?" Carlisle shrugged. "She likes the tiger."

"I like him too," said Ajay. "He is very fierce."

"He's a clown," said Carlisle, but the smile pulled at her mouth despite herself. She was standing close to Ajay without wanting to. She licked her lips and made herself take a step back. Something snagged at the back of her mind, like she'd just forgotten why she'd walked into a room. "Is there ... is there something missing?"

"Missing?" said Ajay, looking at her. He put the *Frosted Flakes* in the crook of his elbow, then started to walk away. "We all want what we can't have, Detective."

That brought her up sharp and hard, like a leash around her neck. "What?"

"A promise got us here," said Ajay, "and that means that for us to get what we wanted, other people had to miss out. Our world stands on an edge, a balance point. Take from *here*, and you must give *there*. A fair trade." His tone was even but his face was sad.

"What," said Carlisle, "have you done?"

Danny walked into the store, the door swinging open, the bottom edge scraping against the linoleum. Carlisle looked at her friend, watching as she moved into the store. Danny looked distracted, Adalia following a few steps behind her, the teenager playing with her phone.

"'Sup," said Carlisle.

Danny ignored her, doing a slow walk around the inside of the store. Carlisle watched her for a moment, then looked back at Ajay. "Do I need to ask again?"

"It's not so much what I did," said Ajay, "as what was *done*."

"You're a really frustrating guy to have a conversation with," said Carlisle. "Anyone ever told you that?"

"Yes," said Ajay.

After a moment, Carlisle said, "See? It's that shit. This is where you step in and say something *else* that *makes sense*."

"Everything I say makes sense," said Ajay. "You just don't know the dance yet, Detective. Do you want to?"

"Dance?" said Carlisle, distracted. She found herself looking at Danny again, the other woman still walking around the store. The clerk had noticed too, was standing up a little taller, his posture speaking volumes. "Danny?"

"There's something ... *gone*," Danny said, and Carlisle felt something colder than ice in her veins.

She turned to Ajay. "What," she said, "is going on?"

Ajay looked sad again. "What must happen, has happened."

Danny's face turned towards them, and Carlisle stopped cold. Danny's eyes had turned yellow, feral and bright. Her voice was cut with something hoarse. "Where is he?"

"Who?" said Carlisle, looking at Ajay. "Danny? Calm down."

Danny took long strides across the store to stand in front of Ajay. "Where. Is. He." Carlisle could see the strength in the set of her shoulders.

"Danny," said Carlisle. "Easy. We're just talking. You have to use your words. Remember your words?"

She could see Danny's head cock to the side a little, caught movement as Adalia stepped backward towards the front of the store where the clerk was. *One less thing to worry about.*

"One has been *taken*," said Danny. "It won't be long before he tries to take one of us."

"You can only take," said Ajay, "what is freely given."

"Who's been taken?" said Carlisle. But she felt it, that *something* missing, gone from the edge of her mind. She could feel where it used to be, but not what it was.

"I—" said Ajay, and was cut off as Danny grabbed at him. Ajay tried to move away, his movements fast — *watch that,* something inside Carlisle said, *you might need that later* — but not fast enough. Danny lifted him off the ground by the front of his jacket, one fist bunched in the material. Her other hand was cocked back in a fist, her teeth showing.

"Where," said Danny, "is he?"

"He's gone," said Ajay. "He is ... finally *safe*. I know where the dead go when they die."

"Everyone," said the clerk, "needs to calm the fuck down." He had the weapon out — *yeah, pistol grip shotgun, right again Carlisle* — leveled across the store.

Carlisle had her sidearm out, the weapon pointed across the store in return. "Easy chief," she said. "Put the gun down."

The clerk blinked, then turned his gun across the space towards Carlisle. Such a narrow pivot range. A few degrees, a hint of movement. Enough for everything to change. Carlisle watched as the gun moved away from Danny, the end of the barrel moving a foot, no more, the mouth of it full of desperate promise. She saw the moment everything changed as the weapon shifted across a space filled with another person.

Adalia.

The girl was frozen in place, her phone still in one hand. It felt like everything was moving slower now, so slowly that it hurt to watch. Carlisle could see the change in Danny, the set of her shoulders as *fear* met *fight*. She watched her friend heft Ajay like he was a sack of meal, then tip her shoulder into the throw as she tossed him across the room towards the clerk. Seeing Ajay hit the wall felt like being punched in the gut, made Carlisle want to double over, but her training took over and she was already moving, she'd felt herself begin to run before she'd seen Danny even start to move. She sprinted across the tired linoleum, head low as the voice of an almost forgotten instructor — *head* down, *cadet, it'll get shot off* — spoke at the back of her mind. The shotgun fired, boxes of breakfast cereal showering the air around her with colored flakes and shredded cardboard. Something tugged at her arm, but she was there, already at the front of the store, grabbing Adalia into a protective hug, her body closing around the girl. She heard the teenager start to scream, the noise cut off as they fell hard against the counter at the front of the store. Carlisle's gun was gone, a spin of bright metal along the floor.

The shotgun went off again, followed by a scream that turned half way — *no, no, NO* — into a roar, saw Danny walking towards them both, something wrong in her walk, something animal in the movement as red dripped and spattered along the ground in her wake. Carlisle held Adalia close, her hand over the girl's eyes as she watched Danny shift into something else. She got herself up on her knees, still holding Adalia and made a break for the door. The shotgun went off again behind her, and there was no scream when the shot hit, just something that roared out its primal anger.

Carlisle bounced against the door on her way out, the glass in the frame shattering around her. Her hip collided with the Yukon out the front and she stumbled, catching herself before she went over. She stood in the lee of the vehicle, then held Adalia out in front of her. "Are you okay?"

The girl's eyes were wide, shock and something very much like fear on her face. "I..."

"Were you hit?" Carlisle was almost shouting the words, then grabbed at the girl, turning her around. *No blood, no blood, thank God, no blood—*

"I'm okay," said Adalia. "I'm okay." There were tears in her eyes.

"Okay," said Carlisle. Her eyes went to the store. The gun had stopped firing, and only a low growl came from inside. The lights had stuttered out, leaving the inside dim in the half light of winter. "Okay," she said again. "Look, kid."

"Yeah?"

"Kid, I need to go get your mom."

Adalia bit her lip. "But—"

"Kid?"

"Yeah?"

"Kid, I *need* to go get your mom." Carlisle rubbed at her arm, her fingers coming away sticky and wet. *Huh.* "Because I promised her."

"I understand," said Adalia. "But what if—"

"Kid?"

"Yeah?"

"I know," said Carlisle. "Also, I need to get that asshole Ajay."

"Isn't he—"

"Wouldn't count on it," said Carlisle. "Get in the car. Stay down. Be back soon."

She stood up, tugging at the edge of her jacket in the cold. Her fingers flexed, wanting to hold the shape of a gun. Not that it would do anything here. *Wrong damn tool, definitely wrong damn situation.* Still keeping low, she edged towards the front of the store, then grabbed a last breath of fresh air before stepping back inside.

NINETEEN

Talin stalked back and forth in the converted warehouse, the beast pulling at his skin like a fresh new shirt. He wasn't sure if it was his imagination or desire or little pieces of both mixed together, but he thought he could hear the city screaming through the big open windows. The winds were cold, a hint of ice carried on the softness of the air, and he breathed it in, closing his eyes and reveling in it.

The sound of fluid dripping drew his attention back to the room, a faint annoyance teasing at him. His new ears let him feel the texture of the sound, a heavy liquid falling in a regular cadence to land — *spat, spat, spat* — against the cold concrete floor. Talin let his eyes open and looked back over what he'd created. It was *art*, pure and simple, something this rotted and decadent city sorely needed.

Looked at from a distance, it was hard to see where one ended and another began. There were arms, legs, torsos, all naked, mixed and matched against each other. Nature had created them wrong, this one's belly too fat for his frame, that one's legs stick-thin against a long body that craved a catwalk. He'd found them all outside, just walking about, living their tiny lives one beat at a time. Together, in his masterpiece, they formed something bigger, bolder than they could ever have been.

Still. It was missing something. Another piece. Or pieces. He wasn't sure — he wouldn't know until he'd—

Hunt.

—managed to complete it, one bit at a time. Talin let his eyes wander to the sides of the room, piles of discarded clothing, hand-bags, briefcases, shoes, and jewelry cast aside like the dross they were. This new power he'd taken—

Stolen.

He shook his head. This new power — he gritted his teeth, forcing himself to think as *he* wanted — he'd *taken* let him act as he should, without consequence or fear or petty desire. All his ambitions were pure, although he wasn't sure when he'd wanted to become an artist. That was—

Memory deep as stone, quiet as earth.

—something unexpected. Still. He felt it was time to gather himself up and hunt within this new city he'd made.

THE MILES LOST themselves under his feet as he loped along the sidewalk. Such a thin strip of pavement made possible by the dreams of tiny men. He would harness those dreams, yoke them to his purpose and rule this city — and then, the world.

The stumbling, seething crowd streamed along in his wake. One or two were strong enough to keep pace at his side, but even with the will of—

They will do as they are told.

—the Night inside him, urging them on — well, they failed, one by one. There, a man — perhaps once fit and hale, a body made strong by a religion of exercise — fell away, his feet stumbling as his heart gave out inside his chest. Talin marveled as a child no more than ten years old coughed and stumbled, blood bubbling from his lips as his body gave out.

Never before have I felt this strength. *The other, he wasted his gift on trying to fix the weak — the weak can never be fixed.*

His run took him into the city proper, buildings stretching up around him. *I hate the feel of this city, but it can be fixed. Changed. Forged.* He paused at an intersection, his followers stacking up around him, waiting, breathless, eager, the glory of madness in them. Talin blinked, looking across at a police blockade.

It is always the way. There are some who can resist. And for them — there is always art.

CHAPTER
TWENTY

Sergeant Willis had always tried to do the right thing. That was really how he liked to roll. Back in college, he'd thrown some balls around, dated a cheerleader, found he liked it. Walked her down the aisle, put a ring on her finger — a rock the size of a five year old child's head attached to a band of pure platinum.

It had cost him three months' salary, cold hard cash that couldn't have been used in any other way than doing the right thing — making Libby happy. Truth be told, it'd been a little more than three months of his salary, but he hadn't told Libby that. It wasn't important, you know? Fifty years from now he'd never remember how much it cost, but he'd always remember the smile on her face.

When his Dad was bailed up with that infection, he'd dropped some vacation time on the problem, moved into the old man's house for a couple weeks, spent time hammering and sawing, putting in new drywall, fixing the place up so he wouldn't get sick again. Hell, it wasn't that far away from a real vacation anyway. Libby had come along and made them iced tea to drink on the porch when it got too hot to do much else. At least people hadn't been shooting at him.

Or, really, trying to bite him. That was weird. Ten years in the force now, he'd seen some wild times, even that one where a man had used a pair of pliers to pull out his own teeth. Said they were demons in his head or something. Willis didn't know much about that, except that insurance wouldn't cover it, and that poor bastard would be left eating all his meals through a straw.

He wiped the sweat from his forehead, put his hat back on, straightened the uniform. His people standing to the left and right of him wore expressions ranging from confusion to anger, fear to something a little more blank than useful. That was okay, they'd come around, they just needed someone in charge to do the right thing. Unlike that useless prick Davis, the man had run screaming down the road thirty minutes ago and they hadn't heard from him since. Doing the right thing seemed a little harder when your superior officer was so spineless he *invited* insubordination.

Still. Libby wouldn't have liked it if he'd busted the man's jaw. Or maybe she would have, but with number two on the way they needed a steady paycheck so he rolled with it. The universe had a way of working this kind of shit out, and with Davis turning crazy with fear and running off without the squad — well, that there was a problem solving itself.

Dispatch were about as much use as teats on a bull, nothing but crazy coming out of the radio, so he'd turned it off.

"Officer Tomlin." Willis squinted a little at the new crowd gathering a couple blocks down, perched at an intersection. "Tomlin, let me see those glasses."

Tomlin handed him the binoculars, and Willis leaned against their makeshift barricade of cars, adjusting the focus so he could see what was what. Sure as sin, right there was another pack of them, looking for trouble and a place to let it free. "Tomlin?"

"Sir." Tomlin was a good one, didn't get nervous under fire. She seemed a natural, maybe the kind that would wear the sergeant's stripes herself before too long.

Willis lowered the glasses, looking at his team. "Tomlin, there's another group coming up. You know what that means."

"Yes, sir," she said. She turned away from him, starting to organize their group. Not that there was much organizing to do, Willis had seen to that, but the thing about doing the right thing was also making sure that your team felt important. Useful. *Every piece more important than the whole*, his Dad had told him once. *Make them feel useful, they'll be useful*. Words to live by.

Still. There was something strange about this new group. Willis felt his mouth form into a half smile, and he hid it by wiping some of the grime from his face. *Strange, huh?* This whole day was strange. *Let's just say it's* more *strange*. As near as Willis could tell, the whole city had gone barking mad, citizens clawing at each other. Sure, they'd had briefings on terror attacks, he knew the drill for when someone dropped a pack of white powder in the mail and called in an Anthrax scare. What he didn't have a procedure for was when citizens started hunting in packs, roaming the city, biting and clawing at each other. Willis rubbed his arm through his uniform, his sleeve hiding the mark on his forearm where one of them had sunk in teeth.

It had been Tomlin who'd pulled that one off.

Focus, Willis. He held the glasses back up, looking for what had set off his weird-shit-o-meter. He scanned the pack, doubled back. *There.* One of the freaks wasn't like the others. Seemed more focused somehow. *In charge.* Willis couldn't shake the feeling that the man was a focal point for this pack. It made a certain kind of crazy sense. If the disease — or whatever it was — that had got into the fine people of Chicago made people hunt in packs, well, maybe they needed a pack leader.

Hell if I know. That one's above my pay grade. You need to stay with the program, Willis. Your job's same as it always has been. Keep the bad people of Chicago from hurting the good. Do the right thing.

Willis rubbed at his jaw. Something about the other man kept nagging at him like an itch he couldn't scratch. Maybe a fresh set of eyes. "Tomlin?"

"Sir." She was at his elbow again, and he held out the binoculars to her.

"Check out that group over there. See the guy, kind of in the middle."

"Dirty shirt?"

Willis frowned. "I thought it was gray."

"Definitely dirty, sir." She leaned on the car in front of them. "My husband rocks a set of dreads like that."

"Bobby has dreads?" Willis paused for a second. *Need to get them over for another barbecue. Been too long.* The thought was crazy in the middle of all the rest of this crazy, so he went with it. "That I've got to see. You guys want to come over this weekend?"

"Beers and a game?"

"I figure."

"You're on," she said. "So, that guy. Seems outside of it. Blending in, maybe."

Blending in. That could be it. If he had a cure, some kind of immunity maybe, they needed to get him to safety. Do the right thing. "Maybe," he said. "I tell you what. They come this way, try not to shoot that guy first. Spread the word."

"On it," she said. "Don't shoot him first. Maybe second, third."

"Maybe," said Willis, hearing the desperate humor in her voice. "Maybe, Tomlin." Willis checked his weapon, making sure his revolver was loaded. He'd used it more today than he had in the last ten years, inside or out of a practice range.

Turned out, they didn't have long to wait. The new pack worked its way towards them, shuffling to a halt again about fifty feet away. Willis shrugged, cupped his hands around his mouth. "Hello."

The other guy — *please, God, let him be immune, let there be some kind of way to stop all this* — blinked at him across the empty distance. "Officer Willis."

Now that was strange, the man knowing his name. Willis felt that needed some kind of response. "It seems you know my name, sir. I don't think we've met."

"It's written on your shirt," the other man said. He made a vague gesture towards Willis that could have been pointing at his badge, him, the squad, or the world in general. "Clear as day."

"Clear as ... you're telling me you can read my shirt from fifty feet away?"

"The Night gives me certain privileges," the other man said. "What I want to know is how you're ... *resisting*."

"Immune?" said Willis. "We were wanting to ask you the same thing. Why those shamblers around you haven't gone wild."

"My children do as they're told," said the other man. "For some reason, you've resisted the call to become one of them." He paused, licking his lips. "One of us."

"Sir," said Willis, "if you don't mind me saying, you're not making a lot of sense."

"It might seem that way," said the man. "How are you doing it?"

"Just trying to do the right thing," said Willis. "So. Sir. If you walk slowly away from the herd..."

"Herd?" The man cocked his head, something like a smile on his face. "I think pack is a better term."

Tomlin was at his shoulder again. "Sarge? Something's not right with this one."

"You think?" Willis was only half listening. *Thing is, there's a time when you need to uphold the law, and there's a time you need to do the right thing. Right now, the right thing is getting this screwball to walk the fuck away.* "Sir, I'm going to have to ask you to move on."

"Move on?"

"Clear the area," said Willis.

"Ah," said the man. "Yes. We'll *clear the area*." He tipped his head towards Willis and his squad, and the pack surrounding him leapt forward like bulls out of the gate. Willis had time to blink once before he heard the report of Tomlin's weapon, brought his own up to bear and started squeezing the trigger.

Too damn many. Six rounds in the chamber, even assuming every shot hit there was no way they'd drop 'em all, and Brummel at least — maybe a couple others — was a lousy shot. Willis found himself looking past the rush of the pack to the other man, standing still as a stone, still fifty feet away. Fifty feet was a bad range for a pistol shot, but what the hell. Seemed like the right thing to do. Willis lifted his sidearm, breathed out, and squeezed. The shot rang out, the bullet hitting the other man right in the head.

Willis didn't have time to clap himself on the back. Sure, one in a million shot, whatever, he could write it up in the report if that ever happened. Until then, he'd need to—

The pack stopped dead, swaying on their feet. Still had crazy in their eyes, but it was like someone had put down their remote control. They looked at each other, and at Willis's squad. Some of them drooled, but none of them moved forward.

"Nice shot, Sarge," said Tomlin. "What did you do?"

"I'm not sure," said Willis. "It seemed—"

Something huge lifted itself from the pavement behind the pack. It was taller than a man, impossibly muscled, with fangs and claws and Lord knew what else. Willis stared, mouth open, then threw a glance at Tomlin. "Are you..."

"Yeah," she said. There was a kind of resigned set to her shoulders. "Yeah."

"Yeah," agreed Willis. He looked at his squad, then back at the creature. He stared into yellow eyes. *Hell with it.* He lifted his sidearm again and started firing.

Ah, he thought a few heartbeats later. *That wasn't the right thing to do.*

CHAPTER
TWENTY-ONE

Rex found the inside of the building a little dim for his tastes, the light from the open door reaching slender fingers in behind him. There was a woman lying face down on the floor, a pool of blood around her head. Probably gone, but he needed to check anyway. He crouched down, old knees protesting, and checked for a pulse at her neck. *Nope*.

He dragged himself back to his feet, heading towards the elevators. He clicked the button, but no light came on. *Great, just great*. At least he'd spent some time keeping in shape, right? The walk up seven flights of stairs wouldn't kill him. The stairs in the old building were opposite the elevators in the lobby, an open ring with a banister rising up through the core. He spared a look up, the top lost to a dim gloom.

Or maybe it was just his eyes. It's not like those were getting any younger either.

Rex started up the stairs, just the way everyone else would, except a little slower. He held the taser in one hand, thinking of Sky waiting back out in the car. She probably wouldn't wait for an old guy to get up and down seven flights of stairs, but that was okay.

She'd done her bit, and now he needed to find Just James and do his part.

Nice girl. He hoped she'd find her boyfriend. Joe? John? Something like that.

Three flights later, he came across a second body. Young man, lying face up this time, eyes open. A lot of people died with their eyes open, that was the truth, but Rex had an innate distrust of people who acted dead but had their eyes open.

"Son?" Rex shuffled a step closer. "Son, are you okay?"

The man didn't move. Rex frowned, waited a couple more beats, then said, "Son, I can see you breathing. I'm just gonna come out and say it, you're behaving in a way that makes me overly cautious. You understand what I'm saying here?"

The man's eyes flicked towards him, then he rose to his feet. Not in the old man way Rex would have, all creaking joints and a lot of cursing, but in a smooth, oiled-machine way. Like something wild. The kid's expression was empty as a gourd, and he bared teeth at Rex.

"Right," said Rex, and met the kid's charge with the taser. The weapon *tick-tick-ticked* and the kid convulsed, dropping like a pole axed steer. "That's probably enough conversation. You rest easy." He checked the kid, then turned him on his side. Recovery position, they called it. Rex had always thought that was one of those labels meant to make something bad sound not bad, and that fit the bill here. Being tased felt bad.

He kept walking, rising through the building in his own steady way. No more encounters on the way, just a forgotten mop and bucket on five. There was water in the bucket, so Rex figured it for a work in progress. That kind of job could keep for a day with more certainty in it.

The corridor leading to Just James' apartment was dark, like a night without the moon. He reached in his pocket for his phone — *no signal* — and fiddled with it until he made the flashlight app do its thing. The tiny light tried to shoulder past the dark in the corridor, doing a passable job for something that was supposed to make phone calls.

"Damn, which one is it … there it is." Rex found Just James' apartment, and reached up and rapped on the door. He took a step back and turned the light on himself so anyone inside could see through the peep hole. After a minute, he heard the chain being pulled back and the door unlocked. Just James stood there in socks and jeans and a happy smile, and not a lot else.

"Rex!" He rushed out into the corridor, grabbing Rex around the middle in a hug.

"Well, hey," said Rex. He used his free hand to return the hug, just a little more awkward than most people did it. Hugs weren't really his speed, it was a thing a younger generation did, or hippies. Rex wasn't young, and he wasn't a hippy. Not all of California was full of hippies, despite what CNN might have to say about it. "Say. Can we step inside?"

"Sure." Just James led the way back inside and Rex pushed the door closed, sliding the chain across. "You came."

"I sure did," said Rex. "We had an appointment."

"We were going for lunch," said James.

"Still can," said Rex, "as soon as you put a shirt on."

The kid's face fell a little. "About that."

"Yeah?"

"My Dad's in my room."

"You don't say," said Rex. "What's he doing there?"

"I locked him in," said Just James.

"Seems a fair thing to do," said Rex, "given a certain set of circumstances."

"Are you asking me what happened?"

Rex frowned. Just James' Dad was about two hundred pounds, not the biggest asshole Rex had ever had a conversation with, but the man was full of angry. And a coward, which didn't help, because angry cowards always wanted to prove some shit. Twenty years ago, Rex could have — but it wasn't twenty years ago. It was today, and

Rex's old bones didn't have that youthful spring anymore. "I'm not sure." He scratched a few fingers through the stubble clinging to his chin. "I was hoping we could just get a coffee." Rex frowned. "Actually, I was hoping we could get a coffee in a different city. It's not safe anymore."

"I need a shirt," said Just James. "My shirts are in my room." He looked at his feet, shuffling a little. "My Dad's in my room."

"Hell with it," said Rex. "Lead the way."

Just James padded ahead of him, socks whispering across the smooth wood of the floor. Rex hadn't really paid it much attention before, he'd only been here to pick the kid up once or twice, and each time he couldn't wait to get out. In a certain light, the old wood's richness was attractive, sombre, and out of place with the paintings lining the hallway. *Paintings, hell — these are straight out of a calendar.* Someone had taken the time to pull apart an old fitness calendar and frame the pictures along the walls.

Rex figured it wasn't Just James.

The door to Just James' room was closed, a keyhole underneath the knob. Just James held his hand out, palm up, an old black key resting there. Rex looked at it for a moment, then took it between two fingers. He held it in his hand, feeling the weight of it. The weight of what was going to happen when he opened that door.

The world is full of assholes. Rex put a hand against the wall, lowering himself with all the care and attention his knees demanded. He hunched over a little, lining up his eye with the keyhole. He tried to make sense of what he was seeing before he realized he was staring at another eyeball doing the exact same thing. Except the eyeball was full of crazy, skittering about in the tiny view window, and Rex heard a giggle on the other side of the door.

"Let me out," said a man, his voice reedy.

"I just want a shirt," said Rex. "I'd like to come in and get a shirt. Is that okay?"

The eyeball vanished from the keyhole, and Rex caught a partial glimpse of the room. Tail end of a bed, a window over it, blinds drawn. Not much to work with there. Something slammed on the other side of the door, causing Rex to jerk back, a cry of surprise coming from over his shoulder — *Just James* — before the other man screamed, *"LET ME OUT!"*

Didn't sound good, no matter which way you cut it. Rex rubbed at his chin, feeling that stubble again. Needed a shave. Could probably wait some. He turned and looked Just James square in the face. "Son?"

"Yeah?"

"I'm going to need some towels, big ones if you can get them. A bucket of water about this big," and here Rex held his hands about a foot and a half apart, "as cold as you can get it. Feel free to use ice. You got ice?" Just James nodded at him. Rex frowned. "Well okay. Off you go."

The kid padded away, socks slipping a little on the polished floor as he hurried. Rex waited a few heartbeats until he heard the kid rummaging around somewhere. If Rex had made a good guess of apartment life, towels would be an easy ask, the bucket less so. Ice water would keep the kid busy for even longer. He had maybe a couple minutes to get this resolved. *Squared away.* He put his hand back against the wall, pulling himself upright.

He still had the key in his hand. He fitted it into the lock, pausing before he turned it. "Okay," he said. "I'm going to open the door. Let you out."

"Good, good, goodgood*good*," said the other man. Rex heard a sound that could have been someone hopping from foot to foot. People didn't do stuff like that, not in the real world. Not if they weren't crazy as a sack of weasels.

Rex turned the key, the mechanism making a satisfying series of clicks as he twisted it. He had a moment to reflect on how they just didn't make stuff like that anymore before the door was yanked open in front of him, Just James' Dad — *step-Dad* — silhouetted in the frame, light from the window behind him casting his face into shadow. Rex could make out the eyes though, still full of the same damn crazy, and that carried on through the man's frame as he stood there, shoulders hunched, one side canted lower than the other.

The man leapt at Rex. A part of Rex's mind said, *Well, that's just dumb, he's two steps away, seems a lot of wasted effort*, at the same time as another part of his mind was saying, *Well, Rex, why the fuck is the taser in your jacket pocket.* The man collided with Rex and he stumbled back — *that's why he jumped, knock me off balance, makes sense* — and his back hit the wall behind him. He didn't know how he'd managed it, but he had a hand up, forearm jammed against the other man's neck. Just James' Dad was actually trying to bite him, teeth snapping, thick ropes of saliva strung between his pearly whites — *more of a beige, really, man needs a dentist* — as his mouth opened wide before each snap.

He could feel his old heart hammering inside his chest, and it'd be push and shove whether he'd make it out of this one. Rex got a moment of clarity —*you senile old man, if you don't find a solve for this, this crazy asshole is going to do something to Just James* — and he mustered himself, rolling his shoulder forward and getting some space between them. The *tick-tick-tick* of the taser sounded loud as he fired it right into the other man's neck, and Just James' Dad dropped, stretching himself long and loose against the wooden floor. Rex looked at the taser in his hand, no clear memory of how it had got there, and then let his gaze rise up to the wide-eyed stare of Just James, standing in the hallway with a bucket held low in one hand, a bundle of towels in the other.

Rex straightened up, looked around for a second, then said, "Ah, good. You got the stuff."

Just James nodded, silent and solemn.

Bending over to check the prone man, Rex said, "We won't be needing 'em after all. Just drop them where you are, son, and go get your shirt."

"Did you ... did you just tase my Dad?"

The guy had a pulse and was breathing steady, so Rex let him be. Looking up at Just James, he nodded. Hell of a thing to do to someone, especially in front of their kid. *You're an asshole, Rex. Should have handled that better. Water? Towels? Could have thought of something better than that.* Poor kid was going to be scarred for life now, all because Rex was older and slower than the kid needed him to be.

Just James stood still for a moment, then a big grin broke out across his face. "That's so *cool*," he said.

~

REX FELT the sunlight across his face, the warmth of it welcome against the cold of the air. He had Just James at his side, the kid dressed in sensible clothes against the chill. Rex had helped him pack, the job a little rushed in the face of them not being sure of when Just James' Dad was going to come to. Back in his days of working in the Department, they'd fought more fires than people, and tasers weren't really a thing.

Still, they'd got a few things together for the kid, and Rex had shown him how to fold for space — *roll 'em up, like this ... that's right, tight like a tube* — and even found space for Just James' current book to snuggle in there alongside something called a Nintendo DS. Rex had no idea what the little electronic device was for, but it seemed important to Just James so he'd thought *what the fuck* and went with it. The book was big and heavy and impractical, but it was a library copy of *The Princess Bride*. Rex didn't read much make-believe but he'd read that, and it had been so good he'd read it twice more straight after.

If that's what Just James was using space for, it was good enough for Rex.

He held the kid behind him with one arm, feeling a twinge go through his shoulder, no doubt pulled in the short fight upstairs with Just James' Dad. It'd work well enough for now, just needed to get the kid to safety, maybe find a car, and then—

Good God damn, he thought. The town car was still there, pulled in at the side of the road. He could see that young woman — *Sky* —

still inside it, windows wound up safe and snug. Rex looked to the left and right, then pulled Just James along behind him, down the steps from the brownstone, across what seemed an ocean of exposed sidewalk, and to the car. He knocked on the window, and heard the *clunk* as the central locking released the doors. Yanking the back door open, he hustled Just James inside, then sagged in behind him, pulling the door closed. Another *clunk*, and all the doors locked again.

"Hey," said Sky.

"Hey yourself," said Rex. "Didn't I tell you to get gone?"

"Strong independent woman," said Sky.

"What?"

"She means," said Just James, "that she does what she wants."

"Smart kid," said Sky. She craned her neck around. "I'm Sky."

"James," said Just James.

"Just James?"

"That's right," said Just James.

"Hell of a bill," said Rex, "for you to be sitting out here."

"It's okay," said Sky. "I've gone off the clock."

"That's not what I meant," said Rex, "but thanks."

"I know what you meant," said Sky, raising a hand to the windows of the car in a gesture that seemed to say, *City's gone to hell, but what's a girl to do?* "Got any idea of where you need to go?"

"No," said Rex, then, "Yeah."

"Which is it?"

"Well," said Rex, "I got no particular place to be, and Just James has no particular place to be either. But I figure, you got people."

Sky thought about that, nodding slowly. "I've got people."

"And," said Rex, "I figure, now we've got my people," and here he placed a hand on Just James' shoulder, "we should go get yours."

"Well okay then," said Sky.

"Okay then," said Rex. "Let's go."

"Small problem," said Sky.

"What's that?" said Rex.

"I got no clue where they are," she said. "Except maybe at the apartment."

"You've got an apartment?"

"More of a slum," said Sky, "but we do what we can."

"Okay," said Rex. "Sounds good." He leaned back in the seat, his shoulder nagging at him again, and figured the day had turned out just fine so far.

TWENTY-TWO

"We need to get back to the apartment," said John. "These crackerjack motherfuckers are getting me down."

"I don't think," said Val, "that I've ever called someone a crackerjack motherfucker."

"But you've always wanted to," said John, hefting the piece of wood like a bat. It was about three feet long, broken at one end, sawed at the other. Val had seen him grab it from a window frame that had busted out into the street, surrounded by rolls of toilet paper. God only knew why the store had had a display of toilet paper in the window, but he guessed it made a weird kind of sense. *Everyone needs it.*

"It's a good name," said Val. He gestured at the city around them. "Kind of captures the essence of it all. I guess the burning question is, 'Why?'"

"Why did I call them that? No clue, really," said John. Val watched as he stepped up on a pile of rubble that looked like it used to be a bus stop, all broken wood and metal and shattered glass.

Something — or some *things* — had hit it hard. "I think we should go this way."

"No, I meant, why are they here at all?" Val frowned. "That way looks like it's full of burning cars and dead bodies."

"Exactly," said John. "Won't be any live ones to bother us."

"Except for the ones that did the killing," said Val. He flexed the fingers of his right hand, still sore from where he'd punched the last crazy in the head. He wasn't used to the pain — never much of a fighter before, and after, well, the—

Night.

—thing inside him had done most of the swinging.

"Except for those," said John. "Also, I see cop cars."

"So?"

"Cop cars means cops," said John. "And I could use a friendly face."

"It hasn't really been my experience that cops are all that friend-ly," said Val. He fell in step with John anyway. One way was as bad as another, and what he really wanted was—

Pack mate.

—Danny. He wanted to hold her, to smell her, to know she was all right. Without her here, nothing was okay, and now he'd lost his—

Gift.

—abilities, there was a good chance he'd die. Die, and not be able to tell her how much she meant, and that he understood, and that he was sorry.

"To be fair, there was that one cop," said John. "You remember her. Used to kicking ass and taking names."

"Carlisle?"

"The devil herself," said John. He frowned. "I mean that in a good way."

"She's not a cop," said Val. "She gave all that up."

"She put it on hold," said John. "She's not the kind of—"

A man ran out of a doorway to their right, screaming — *ranting?*

— and slavering like a dog. Val caught a glimpse of wild eyes before the man was on him. Instinct took over, his hands grabbing at the lapels of an immaculate suit jacket. A button popped, spinning off to bounce against the sidewalk. The lunatic twisted away, arms free of the jacket. Val was left holding the empty suit jacket, one sleeve pulled inside out. He stared at it for a sliver—

Sickness.

—of time. He gave the jacket a few quick twists around his arm, just before the other man lunged again. Val pushed his wrapped arm against the guy's face, feeling it through the fabric as teeth tried to close on his flesh. Val clenched his fingers into a fist and punched the man in the head. It was a clumsy shot, his hand hitting more forehead than anything else, and he gave a yell of anger and pain. Val brought a knee up into the other man's groin and was rewarded by a cough as the teeth loosened, the guy stumbling back. Val eyed him up, took aim, and swung his fist in a savage cross.

John watched with a critical eye as Val's attacker fell to the ground, lights out. Rubbing at his jaw, John said, "I give you five, maybe six out of ten, but only because you look like your heart's in it."

"This isn't," said Val, panting a little, "as easy as it looks."

"Sure it is," said John. "You're just not very good at it."

Val coughed, wiping something red away from his lips. "To be fair, I've got this virus."

"I got a friend who had cancer," said John. "Came to work at the gym every day. With cancer. Emilio. You met him."

"I'm not sure I follow," said Val, bending over to search the fallen man. He pulled out a wallet. "Guy's name is actually Lionel."

"No way," said John, holding out a hand. "Lemme see that."

Val handed over the license. "So why you telling me about Emilio? You said Emilio was crazy."

"What Emilio was," said John, "was *reliable*. You got cancer?"

"No," said Val.

"Then get the fuck up," said John. "We got people we care about we got to go find."

He's right. Val straightened his shoulders. "Sorry," he said.

"No, it's cool," said John. "Your girlfriend is a werewolf. She can take care of herself. Mine drives a cab."

"It's Uber," said Val.

"It's a service that takes you places for money," said John. "But not like an escort service." He frowned. "Look, the thing is, she's—"

"Family," said Val. Like that, something—

Pack.

—clicked. "She's one of us."

"I've never told her," said John.

"Maybe we should," said Val. He looked farther down the street. "One thing, though."

"What is it?"

"I'm going to need more than my fists and harsh language. I need my own stick."

"This isn't a stick," said John. "This is Michelangelo."

"You've named your stick?"

"Mike, here," said John, "hits like the king."

"Great," said Val. "Let's go find his brother, Donatello."

"You're more a Raphael kind of guy," said John.

"Why you figure?" Val looked at his feet. "I'm the smart one, aren't I?"

"You got anger issues," said John. He nudged aside some debris with his foot. "Here."

"Is that ... is that an actual bat?" Val reached down, his fingers touching the metal. It was black, etchings through the paint marking it up and down the shaft. He let his fingers trace the autograph on the bat, then ran them over the *Big Stick* inscription at the business end. "Well I'll be."

"What?"

"This, sports fans," said Val, "is a genuine Frank Thomas bat. Autographed."

"'*Big Hurt?*'" said John. "I'd like one of those. Let me see it."

"You've got Mike there," said Val. "Me and Raph here are just fine. Shoo." He stood, hefting the bat. It felt light and right in his hand, the weight like the familiar hand of an old lover. *Weird.*

Still. Plenty of time to work out how he knew anything about the Chicago White Sox later on. *You've never been much of a sports fan, Val. Where'd this come from?*

But something in his hands knew how to hold the bat, and he felt a faint hint of memory, like the scent of smoke on the wind.

"THAT DOESN'T LOOK GOOD," said Val. He pointed with the bat at the ring of police vehicles a block further up. "Still got the lights on, but nobody's home." He walked past the door of a police cruiser — the rest of the car nowhere in sight — gouges dragged through the metal. The door had been tossed like a Frisbee, the edge of it buried in the asphalt of the road. He swallowed. *That* really *can't be good.* He only knew of one thing that could leave a memento like that.

"John."

"Yeah?"

"Check it," said Val, tapping the door with the toe of his shoe.

"Looks like one of your calling cards," said John.

"Looks like," said Val. "So here's the thing."

"Yeah?"

"The briefcase."

"Silver one?" John arched his back, working some kinks out. "Sucked the thing out through your eyeballs?"

"The very same," said Val. "What I think we have here is evidence of where it's gone."

"Like a case of herpes?"

Val sighed. "It's not ... no. Because if you give someone herpes, you don't lose it."

"You got herpes?"

"No," said Val. "I have a virus that causes human cells to turn to mush and all your blood to explode out through your chest. I think it's worse."

"So says the man," said John, "who's never had herpes."

"I got nothing," said Val. "Back on topic. I think that someone took it."

"The herpes?"

"The—"

Night.

"—Night," said Val.

"We're calling it the Night now?"

"Yeah," said Val. "Also, I vote we call anyone we meet who's crazy, well, we call them a zombie."

"It's a little clichéd," said John, "but we'll run with it for now."

What you've got here, thought Val, *is more blood on your hands. You've lost the Night, and now someone worse than you has it.* "John?"

"Yeah."

"We need to fix this," said Val. "We need to—"

"Hold up," said John, hand out. "I know."

"What?"

"We need to get the gang back together. Find Sky. Make a call. Chopper in the big guns."

"Danny?"

"And Carlisle."

"What about Adalia?" Val rubbed his face, then looked around the street. Aside from the two of them, Chicago was silent as a morgue.

John looked at his feet. "I hadn't thought that one through."

Val clapped his friend on the shoulder. "Keep working that angle. Let me know how you get on." Val hefted Raph, giving the bar a twirl. *One thing's for sure. You're not going to involve more of the people you love, Valentine. This one's on you.* "Let's go."

They walked up to the police perimeter. Val felt like his head was on a swivel, no creature inside him to warn him of danger. He felt its

163

absence like a missing tooth, an ache and a gap, something that had been wrenched out with a pair of pliers.

That's new. He'd been wanting to get rid of it for so long, to stop being *responsible* for the death around him. *Thing is, you didn't take good enough care, and now you're responsible for ... for whatever the hell this is.* He paused for a second. "John."

"Sup?"

"Do I come across as a sociopath?" Val tapped his bat against the ground, feeling the weight of it land against the ground at his feet. "It's a serious question."

"You want to do this now?" John gestured with his free hand at the cars ahead of them. "There's shit going on here."

"Sure, fine," said Val. "You don't call, you don't write..."

"Look, okay," said John. "The thing is—"

There were five of them, screaming and ranting, meaningless words tossed in front of them as they cascaded out a first story level to land on the sidewalk to their side. They surged as one, darting like a school of carnivorous fish. They boiled up and over John like he was a jungle gym — John got one good swing in with his piece of wood, a resounding *thwak* as it connected with one of the zombie's heads, the man — *man? Is that a man or a woman?* — tumbling back. The other four bore John to the ground, and he went down with a yell.

Val felt that small hand on his wrist again, a tiny helper tugging him along. He stepped forward, the Sox bat in his hand spinning like a gymnastics baton. The first hit landed with a hollow, wet noise, the skull of a — *Christ, it's a woman, don't look, just get it done* — zombie caving in. The remaining three looked up from John, all heads moving at the same time like they were operated by the same remote control. Val hefted the bat. "Get off him, you crackerjack motherfuckers! It's me you want. And you know what? You want a piece of me? Come *get some.*"

They heaved forward, a mess of scrabbling claws — *hands* — and they were on him. The bat swung like it knew the moves to this dance, a touch *there* breaking an arm, a solid hit *there* knocking the wind out of another. Val had a single, pure moment to marvel at how he knew how to move this well — *you might make it out of this alive, you might just* — before one of them sank its teeth into his arm.

He yelled, the pain cutting through everything as blood bubbled up and around the teeth in his flesh. He tried to shake it — *it's just some guy, he's got a Walmart apron on* — off, more blood welling up. Another one tackled him around his middle, and the three of them — *Christ, where's the other one, where did it go* — fell to the ground. The world shrank to immediate, bright points — the pain of his arm, a ragged end of agony attached to him, the breath knocked out of him, some piece of stone or wood or God only knew digging into his spine. Val felt the false strength of adrenaline wearing thin, his struggles becoming less effective. The virus in his veins was taking its toll, and here — *well, Val, this is how it ends. You don't get to save the world this time.*

The weight on his chest lifted, the one that had tackled him — *middle aged woman, hair in curlers, a stylist's bib still around her neck* — pulled off and up into the air. *John.* John had lifted her, raising her whole body above him. John dropped her down, spine against his knee, and the woman's movement's stilled. Val was still wrestling with Walmart, and he saw John pick up his piece of timber, step forward, and swing it. Val's free hand came up involuntarily to cover his face as John's swing connected with the back of the man's head. The grip of teeth lessened, and Val pushed the other man's body away. John held a hand out, and Val got to his feet.

They were breathing hard. Val swallowed, then said, "Thanks."

"This shit," said John between lungfuls of air, "was easier when you were super-powered."

Val pointed at the man with the Walmart apron on, blood and saliva running down the man's chin. His eyes were closed but he was still breathing. "That one's still alive."

"I don't think so," said John. "Take a closer look."

Val took a couple steps forward, bent down with his hands braced on his knees. *It's easy to forget just how much effort it is to do anything at all when you're normal.* The other man's color was chang-ing, red patches blooming over his skin. Blood began to seep out through his closed eyes, and after a moment the body began to sag, pulling itself apart from within. Val reached a hand out, but there wasn't anything to be done. He caught the shaking in his own hand. *It's only a matter of time before that happens to you. You're on the clock, Everard, and there's no snooze button at the end.* "The virus."

"I figure," said John. "The good news is that if they try to eat you, you'll take 'em with you."

"I'm not sure that's good news," said Val, "for anyone in the situ-ation you just described."

"Well, there's one piece of *genuinely* good news," said John.

"How you figure?" said Val. "The city's fucked, and I'm dying of an engineered military virus."

"Well, that's it," said John. "You're *not*. I was trying to tell you at the bar — I don't think they got it all. Like they were using a hose to siphon out all the gas, but got interrupted. There's a little left in the bottom of the tank."

"Maybe," said Val. "Makes sense. But..."

"But what?"

"It's just going to keep me alive to watch how this ends," said Val. "It's not going to *do* anything. It's not going to *help*."

"Turn that frown upside down," said John. "Let's get back to base and work this one through. We need a plan."

"We also need a base," said Val. "All we got is an apartment."

"Yeah," said John. "That's our base. Use your imagination a little. You said you were the smart one."

Val felt himself smiling, in spite of it all. The Night was gone, most of it having left him, but John was here, and together, they might just be able to save the world anyway.

CHAPTER
TWENTY-THREE

"You need to go in after her." The boy leaned against the side of the Yukon, the edges of his frame soft against the light of winter's sun. "She's not going to make it."

"She'll make it," said Adalia, meaning, *She's got to make it*. "She's Carlisle."

"That's right," said the boy. "She's *only* Carlisle."

"I've seen her save the world."

The boy thought on that for a few beats. "I don't know about that. I've only ever seen her save you guys."

It was Adalia's turn to pause, her voice hardening. "She'll be fine."

The boy spun on her, all angry eyes and black lashes. "She's just a, a person! She can *die*."

Adalia let out a noise, somewhere between a laugh and a sob. "I know," she said.

"So get in there." The boy walked a few paces away from the Yukon, then came back in front of her. "I know you want to. You're out here in the cold instead of in the car."

"I don't know what I want," said Adalia. *She would do it for you.* "I don't want my mom to hurt her."

"Your mom won't hurt you," said the boy. "You know that."

"She's not herself," said Adalia. "I'm not sure." But she found her feet taking the first nervous steps towards the front of the store, steps that turned into a halting run. She came up against the dark frame of the doorway, broken glass crunching under her feet as she looked inside.

Black, black, and more black. A hint of a fallen shelf, a bright spark from the edge of the room as something electrical hissed and spat the last of its life away. She felt him at her elbow, close enough to touch. She almost did, but reached a hand out to push the door open instead. It hissed against the shock set at the top of the frame, the bottom scraping against old linoleum and pieces of glass as she pushed it open. Water droplets tapped like a hundred tiny fingers against her hair as she stepped inside, the sprinklers raining their own misery into the room.

She felt the presence of something massive shifting in the gloom, the smell of wet fur in the air. A low growl, the bass heavy in it so as to make it almost directionless, came at her out of the gloom. Adalia swallowed. Her heart was hammering, hammering, hammering in her chest, and she felt so full of fear that she was sure it would make her burst. Adalia opened her mouth to call into the gloom, but no noise came out.

"That's probably not a good idea," he said. "I wouldn't do that."

Adalia swallowed, ignoring him. She tried to find her voice around the frail fingers of fear at her throat. "Mom?"

The darkness at the back of the store shifted as two glowing eyes turned to face her. Adalia froze, nothing conscious in it at all, she was rooted to the spot like someone had glued her feet in place. The creature moved with an urgency born of hate, stamping through the store, tossing a shelf aside, a cascade of sanitary products falling like rain. It came to stand before her. Adalia looked up at it, took in the teeth and claws, something wet and red around its muzzle. *Please, no.* "Mom?"

"Kid?" said Carlisle's voice from across the room, her voice a steady calm born of long practice. "Kid, I think you need to step back, nice and slow."

The creature turned to face Carlisle, and Adalia followed its gaze. Carlisle was standing — *she's alive, thank you thank you thank you* — behind the counter, her arm hooked under the unconscious form of Ajay. The man's head lolled, eyes closed, but he appeared otherwise unharmed. Carlisle's other arm was pointed out at the creature, her sidearm held in her hand. Adalia could see the faintest tremor in the weapon, could see Carlisle's eyes were wide with a kind of fear she'd never seen before.

"It's okay, Melissa," said Adalia. "It's—"

The creature roared, flexing its arms, the claws bared. Saliva and worse dripped from its muzzle, and it licked its lips. It took a step, then another, towards Carlisle.

"Mom!" Adalia skipped sideways, putting herself in front of the thing. She waved her arms above her head. "Mom. It's Carlisle. You remember Carlisle, don't you?"

The creature tipped its head to one side, ears forward like a curious dog. Adalia was aware that Carlisle was on the move, the sound of *shuffle drag, shuffle drag* as she pulled Ajay with her. Adalia swallowed, her eyes moving towards the boy. He shrugged, then said, "This one's a bit outside my area of expertise."

The creature's head turned whip quick to look at the boy. Its yellow eyes narrowed — *she can see him!* — and it took a step towards him.

Adalia watched him swallow, taking a nervous step back. One of his arms passed through a broken shelf, and her mind shied away from what she saw. "Mom. Don't look at him. Look at me."

"Look at who, kid?" Carlisle was close behind her. "No, doesn't matter. Go. Get gone. You've done your part."

"No," said Adalia.

"Kid—"

"*No*," she hissed. "Please, Melissa. Please go." Adalia watched as the creature — *Mom, it's Mom* — paced around the boy, low and steady like a hunting cat. It growled again.

"Your mom," said Carlisle, "will kill me if I go. She will also kill me if I stay. I'm kinda fucked here." Adalia caught the barrel of Carlisle's sidearm as it moved into her peripheral vision.

"We go together," said Adalia.

"Together," said Carlisle. Adalia could see her friend had made it close to the door. The Yukon sat, black and heavy, outside. Out of reach. "Thing is—"

The creature roared, taking a savage lunge at the boy. One of its claws passed through the space where he stood, and Adalia heard a sound like the scream of angels for the tiniest sliver of a moment before he flickered, guttering out like a candle snuffed on the wind. It turned lambent eyes at them, taking a step forward.

"No!" Carlisle's voice was heavy with — *Dread? Panic?* — and Adalia saw what was coming. Carlisle gave her one last look, and Adalia could see the decision in her eyes. *Draw it off. Be the shield.* Her friend's hand tightened on the sidearm's grip, and Adalia wanted to scream, but there wasn't time. The gun roared, the strength of the blast pushing air and heat and light past Adalia's head. Adalia could hear Carlisle shouting something — *Here! It's me you want! Not her!* — each word covered by a shot, and she felt the passing of the bullets as Carlisle fired again and again at the creature, the rounds hitting it square in the chest. It held a massive clawed hand up in front of its face, then shook its head as Carlisle's weapon clicked empty.

Adalia swallowed, turning her head between Carlisle and the creature. She could see Carlisle's face white with terrible purpose, and her friend opened her mouth to speak.

"No," said Adalia, and lunged at her friend. Carlisle was caught flat footed, the weight of Ajay held in front of her catching her off guard. Adalia put all she could into it, her small frame canted at an angle as she put both hands against Carlisle and pushed her out and through the door to stumble back into the car park.

Adalia turned back to look at the creature. Its jaws were wide, and it looked at her, at the door, at her, at the door. "Mom!" Adalia screamed the word at it. "Stop!"

The thing stopped looking at the door, focusing on her. Adalia felt the weight of its gaze, the yellow of its eyes a murky glow. It took a step towards her, one clawed hand raised, the motion slow. Gentle as a moth's wing, the clawed hand touched Adalia on the cheek. Adalia felt her terror return now her friend was out — *safe!* — and readied herself for the end.

The creature gave a *chuff, chuff,* then took a step back. Its hand pulled away like it had touched something hot, and its eyes widened before it let out a howl full of pain and loneliness. It spun, charging through the store and out the back. It shouldered aside wood and brick to burst into the air beyond, and Adalia lost sight of it as it ran into the winter air.

Adalia realized she was crying, the tears falling down her face. She felt rough hands on her shoulders, and she was spun around to face Carlisle. "Are you crazy? What were you thinking? You could have been killed!"

Adalia held her face behind her hair. "She would have killed you. He said I had to help. He said ... I didn't want to lose you too." Her voice ran out as she choked out a sob.

Carlisle's face went from hard planes of anger and fear to something softer. She pulled Adalia close in a savage embrace, and Adalia felt her shaking. Carlisle's voice was soft against her hair as she said, "Shhhh. It's okay. I'm not going anywhere. I've got you. I've got you."

"Who were you talking to?" Carlisle's hands gripped the steering wheel of the big Yukon, guiding it down the old side road, fallen debris crunching under the wheels. It was the first thing she'd said in the half hour since ... since the convenience store. Thinking of it like that made it easier, like a person hadn't died. Like it was a place, not an event.

Adalia straightened in the passenger seat next to Carlisle. "No one."

"Kid," said Carlisle, "I'm not in the mood."

Adalia knotted the edges of her sweater in her fingers, pulling at the hem, stretching it. "Promise you won't tell."

"I'm not promising shit," said Carlisle. "Today's not that kind of day."

"Then I'm not telling you shit," said Adalia, something fierce and unexpected in her tone.

Carlisle pulled the Yukon to an abrupt halt. "Here's how it is," she said. She held up a hand as Adalia was about to speak. "Just give me the floor for a second, okay?"

She's so tired. Adalia could see it in the lines on Carlisle's face, in the way her shoulders were a little less than perfectly straight. With a small nod, Adalia said, "Okay."

Carlisle ran a hand through her hair, trying to tease it out. She wasn't looking at Adalia as she started to speak. "The reason I won't promise not to tell is that's how people die." Adalia saw her friend tightening her grip on the wheel. "No. I said no lies between us, didn't I? Okay." She took in a couple deep breaths. "Okay. Okay. I don't want to tell you this, and you sure as hell don't want to hear it, but here we are in the fucking woods chasing your mother who's gone all feral. We've got an unconscious guy in the back seat, and my deodorant gave out an hour or more back." Her words ran out like a clock winding down, then she took another deep breath. "That's what he always asked," she said, at last.

"Who?"

"He always asked me not to tell. Said it was..." Carlisle broke off. Adalia could see her fingers were gripping the steering wheel so hard they were white. "He'd come into my room, sometimes with the liquor in him, sometimes not. Didn't matter if I was asleep or not. Or pretending to. And after..."

Her face was wet with tears, and Adalia reached out a hand to her. "Melissa..."

"No." Carlisle shook herself, wiping her face with an angry hand. "I said no more tears for that bastard. No more fear. No more hiding." She cleared her throat. "After he was done, he always made me promise not to tell. It was something special, he said, that other people wouldn't understand. Do you hear me? Do you hear what I'm saying?"

"Yes," said Adalia, her voice a whisper.

"So," said Carlisle, her tone turning brisk. "Who the fuck were you talking to?"

"Did you ever..." Adalia looked out at the woods around them. "Did you ever feel like people wouldn't believe you?"

"Every day," said Carlisle. "He always said that no one would believe me if I said anything. No one would believe the word of a child over the word of..." She stopped herself. "Enough of that story, but sure. I reckon people would have had trouble swallowing it down. If only because the truth of it was so monstrous."

"I ... I've met someone," said Adalia.

"Right," said Carlisle. "How'd you manage that in Hicksville, Alaska?"

"I met him in the shower," said Adalia. She saw the angry flash in Carlisle's eyes, and held up a hand. "What did you say? Give you the floor?"

Carlisle nodded, the movement slow. "There's gonna come a time when you can't use my own lines against me, kid."

"Today is not that day," said Adalia, a small smile resting on her lips. "It's not like what you think."

Slipping the Yukon back in gear, Carlisle let the big machine start to roll forward again. "Tell me what I should think, then."

Adalia let her hair fall down to cover her face, then pushed it aside. *No lies between us. No hiding.* "I don't know his name, or where he comes from. And I think Mom can see him, when she's a ... a monster."

"I've known real monsters," said Carlisle, her voice dark at the edges. "Your mom ain't no monster."

"Okay," said Adalia, "but back to the shower. So I was there, and the soap got in my eyes. I was reaching outside the curtain for a towel, and I felt something cold. Like the door had opened, right?"

"Right," said Carlisle.

"Right," said Adalia, "so I found the towel, and I wiped the soap from my eyes, and there he was."

"Who?"

"I don't know."

"You're not very good at telling stories," said Carlisle. "It's honest criticism. There's shit you need to know in a story, like how it begins, and how it ends, and the names of the fuckers in the story."

"He doesn't remember his name," said Adalia, "or it's against the rules to tell me."

"Rules?" Carlisle turned the wheel, pushing the Yukon further into the woods. Her gaze was intent, focused on tiny details that were invisible to Adalia.

"I think he's an angel," said Adalia.

"I think you're full of teenage hormones," said Carlisle. "What's he look like?"

"About my age," said Adalia. "He's got these wonderful lashes—"

"Hormones," said Carlisle, "are more dangerous than crack cocaine." She was quiet for a moment. "He was in the store."

It wasn't really a question, but Adalia rolled with it. "Yeah. And in the car."

"Which car? This one?"

"Yeah." Adalia looked down at her hands, wanting to fill them with something.

"Is he here now?"

"No," she said. "I think ... I think Mom did something to him."

"So..." Carlisle thought for a minute. "No one can see him. *I* can't see him. Your mom, under the normal order of the universe, can't see him. But you can see him."

"Yes."

"Have you..." Carlisle trailed off, before trying again. "What I mean is, what happened in the shower?"

"I screamed."

"After that?"

"We talked," said Adalia. "After I got a towel."

"Talking," said Carlisle. "That's all?"

"What would we have done?" Adalia felt her brow furrow. "Should I have done something?"

"Heavens no," said Carlisle with a nervous laugh. "No, doing something with your invisible friend would have been worse than ... well."

Adalia looked out the windscreen for a moment. "Thanks."

"For what?" Carlisle was intent on something, slowing the car down a bit.

"For not asking if I was making it up," said Adalia. "I was afraid no one would believe me."

"Kid," said Carlisle, "I've told you before. We don't lie to each other. You save that for your mom or Everard. You and I are honest, right?"

"Right." Adalia nodded around the edges of her hair.

"So when we're honest, well, you could tell me the moon was made of cream cheese and I'd just want to know whether it was a Philly spread or not."

"What about Uncle John?" said Adalia.

"What about that Mickey Mouse clown?"

"Should I lie to him?"

Carlisle breathed out a sigh. "I'm not really good at this, kid. Here's the thing. You shouldn't lie to anyone. But I get that sometimes you feel you got to. Right?"

"Right."

"But not between us."

"Right," said Adalia, feeling a little confused.

"The thing about Miles," said Carlisle, "is that he's a rock ape. He's a caricature of a man. He plays," and she swallowed, *"video games."*

"I play video games," said Adalia.

"You're a fourteen year old girl," said Carlisle. "It's expected. Miles is a forty year old man."

"Uncle John's forty?"

"None of us stay young forever," said Carlisle. "Thing is ... thing is, I'm pretty sure he'd know you were lying to him."

Adalia thought about that for a bit, then let her thoughts wander a little. The trees were thinning around them, snow appearing in more even patches on the ground. "You don't like Uncle John very much do you?"

Carlisle slammed the brakes on the Yukon, and Adalia's head jerked forward, her body held back by the seatbelt. Carlisle sat still in the car for a moment, then said, as if choosing her words with infinite care, "What makes you ask that?"

"Because," said Adalia. "Because of how you talk about him."

"Right," said Carlisle. "While we're baring souls here, I trust him. It's just ... shit's complicated."

"Why do you trust him?" Adalia thought about Uncle John, how he'd decided to stay with Valentine in Chicago. About how he'd tousled her hair before she'd hopped in the truck with her Mom. *Take it easy, kid. I know it's, well, it's a low bar, but try not to do shit I wouldn't do.* She'd laughed at the time.

"Because he's on the team," said Carlisle. "Because he'd die for me." She turned to look at Adalia. "Because he'd die for you."

Adalia turned away. "I hope it doesn't come to that. I don't want people dying for me."

"Yeah, well," said Carlisle, "I'm not a big fan of dying either. You asked."

"There," said Adalia, pointing. There was a crumpled form lying in the snow off the track, red curls against the snow. "She's there. She's okay."

"Kid," said Carlisle. "Kid, wait here."

"She's not ... she's *her*, Melissa. She's back." Adalia wanted to run from the car, just about the same time as she felt Carlisle's hand on her arm. She turned to look at the other woman.

"Kid," said Carlisle, then she paused. "Adalia? Can you leave it to me? This time. Just this once."

"Okay," said Adalia, but she felt the flush of happiness hit her. It was going to be okay. It was going to be *okay*.

CHAPTER
TWENTY-FOUR

Jessica straightened her cap on her head, checked her sidearm, then stepped out of the Humvee. She strode with a purpose, and that purpose was saving lives. *God damn civilians. It's like they don't know when to call in for support.*

Her aide, Gibson, picked up next to her. He was talented — knew when he was needed, knew when to shut up, both qualities she found worth their weight in gold. The man's pace looked hurried next to hers. It was something he'd need to work on if he wanted a command of his own one day. "Ma'am?"

"What is it, Gibson?"

"Ma'am, we've got intelligence that says—"

"Save it," she said. "I want eyes on first."

"Ma'am," said Gibson, still trying to keep up. He carried a tablet under his arm, the device held ready for when she wanted to see what he had. Thing was, she didn't really want to see what was on the tablet. In her experience, intelligence was a thing like insurance. It sucked to not have any when you needed it, but it was useless the other ninety-nine percent of the time.

She stalked to the front of the column, soldiers straightening as she passed. It was the kind of respect that she expected, her command being run with a precision that earned her the moniker *Perfect Pearce* among the men and women who served her.

Really, this was easy. She was far from perfect, and it was that memory — the knowledge of how she'd failed when it mattered most — that pushed her on. If she'd been perfect, Gabriel would still be alive.

"Gibson," she said, coming to a halt.

"Ma'am?"

"Gibson," said Jessica, "I need binoculars."

"Ma'am," said Gibson, magicking them from somewhere about his person. She wasn't sure how he managed that, but given time she'd work it out.

"Thank you," she said. She held the binoculars up to her eyes, looking out over the expressway and at the edges of the city of Chicago. She worked the glasses left to right, scanning the scene before her. "Gibson?"

"Yes, ma'am."

"I'm going to guess our intelligence says that the city has been taken over by terrorists."

"Ma'am. Yes, ma'am."

"They'd be wrong," she said. She picked out a building at the edge, the structure in flames. Another behind it had already burned low, the frame of it standing uneven against the sky like an old candle wick. "Terrorists may be involved, but one thing's for sure. No one's in charge." She scanned the skyline over the city. "No air traffic. Not even a news chopper." She brought the glasses lower, towards the streets. "Still some activity there. Is that..." She swallowed, lowering the binoculars. It hadn't even been this bad in Afghanistan. Sure, they strapped bombs to their kids and sent them into blockades, but there was a daily limit to that kind of thing. She looked at Gibson. "I'm going to need a perimeter set up. I'm going to need birds in the air. What I'm going to need," she said, "is an explanation of why they're *eating each other*."

CHAPTER
TWENTY-FIVE

Rex watched out the window of the car as Sky rolled them at a slow speed through the streets. *Where are all the people? You'd expect more people. Or more bodies. Or something.*

Right on cue, Just James cleared his throat. "Where are all the people?"

"You got me," said Sky. Her hands were steady on the wheel, the car traveling nice and easy despite the debris littering the streets.

It's not like there were *no* people. Rex saw the bodies, plenty of them. They were all the same, as if they'd been tossed to the ground right in the middle of something. That something was probably *running for your life*. Or *trying to kill someone*. There didn't seem to be much middle ground.

"How far?" asked Rex, for about the hundredth time.

"We got another few blocks yet," said Sky, like she had the other hundred times.

"We need," said Rex, "to talk about your definitions."

"I don't follow."

"'A few' seems a bit random," he said.

"It's not like I know which streets are blocked," she said.

"She's got a point," said Just James.

"Whose side are you on?" said Rex, but he let a smile hit his face anyway. The kid was doing great, all things considered. Seen his stepfather go batshit crazy and get tased. Saw a bunch of dead people. Seemed okay with all of it, more or less. Some people were just built that way.

"What's that?" said Just James, pointing out the front of the window.

"Looks like a plane," said Rex.

"Looks like," agreed Sky. "Why's it flying low over the city?" Almost before she'd finished talking, the jet blasted over the top of them, sound rattling hard against the windows of the car. A short moment later, two more jets followed after, the hard roar of turbines leaving Rex's ears ringing.

"I think," said Rex, "that we should get off the road."

"There's crazy people who eat each other outside," said Sky. "I like the car. The car is good."

"The car is good," agreed Just James.

"The car is a slow moving target," said Rex. He pointed to the detritus on the streets around them, his arm highlighting a piano on the road. *A piano. On the road.* "You need to keep driving around crap like that. I mean, how'd a piano get here? On foot we'd be smaller, faster moving targets."

"You say target like something's going to happen," said Sky.

"Those birds we just saw," said Rex, "are military. They are recon planes. They take a bunch of photos, mark targets, give intel. Back at master control, someone is reviewing footage on a TV screen right now. They're looking at that, seeing the city full of crazy people. They are going to try and do something about that, and the military have just one solve for most things."

"But the car," said Sky.

"If you were sitting safe in a bunker looking at footage of a car driving through the city safe as houses, would you think 'refugee' or

181

would you think 'terrorist?'" Rex rubbed a hand over his face. "Look, I'm not saying that the military is going to bomb the car."

"They're going to bomb the car?" Sky's voice had a hysterical edge.

"No—"

"I don't want to be in the car when they bomb it," said Just James.

"Right," said Rex. "They probably won't bomb it. But if they do, we won't want to be in it."

"The car is shit," said Sky. "I do not like the car."

"I think the car is a bad idea," said Just James, nodding. "We should lose the car."

"We're not losing the car," said Sky. "The car pays for my rent. But for now, we should leave the car in a safe location and lock it."

"Before we lose the car—" said Rex.

"Park the car," said Sky.

"Before we park the car, we need to work out where we're going and how we're going to get there. I don't like this street." Rex sniffed. "Don't like it at all."

A helicopter thudded around the corner of a tall building, blades slamming against the air. Rex felt his eyes open, the sight of a chain of humans — *God damn barrel of monkeys, is what it is* — strung out below it. The helicopter wasn't flying with the kind of precision he expected from the military, and as they watched a body fell from the side of it. It was hard to tell at this distance if it was man or woman as their arms pinwheeled during their fall. More of the people hanging from the underside were pulling themselves up into the helicopter. The note of the engine took on a desperate edge, and it started to cant to the side, tail section pulling sideways as it slewed through the air.

"Get out of the car," said Rex. "Get out of the car now."

"I thought you didn't like this street," said Just James.

"I don't like this street, but I don't like what's coming even more," said Rex. He kicked open the door of the car, grabbing Just

James by the arm and pulling the kid out. Sky was already moving, driver's door punched open as she pulled herself out. Rex started to hustle James over to the side of the road towards the door of an old dry cleaner's, the inside empty of people. He tossed a glance behind him, saw Sky vaulting the hood — *nice ass* — of the car, sliding off the edge and on to her feet. The helicopter was sliding out of the sky down the street, the machine now in a slow spin as it lost altitude. Rex pushed Just James inside the dry cleaner's ahead of him, then turned to hold the door open for Sky. He saw she was headed back to the car, scrambling back over the hood. *Definitely a nice ass.* He shook himself "Hurry! Christ, girl, now's not the time to stop for a quart of milk!"

She leaned in the car, snaring something out. She broke into a sprint as the helicopter's blades touched the asphalt of the street, the blades shearing off faster than Rex could follow. One of the blades tumbled end over end down the street, fragments of metal flying away before it bounced clear over the top of Sky's car. She made it to the doorway of the dry cleaner's, and Rex pulled the door shut behind her. "Go!"

Just James was looking at them both, wide eyed. "Where?"

"Doesn't matter," said Rex. "Towards the back." He could feel his heart hammering in his chest, old bones resisting the pressure he was putting on them. He saw Just James disappear through a line of hanging suits, Sky following him. He reached the line of clothing as the world kicked his feet out from under him, the floor tossing him up. He felt the weightless rush of air going past his face, and for a moment — *Christ, Rex, is this how it ends?* — he felt at peace. Then the floor hit him in the face as he landed on it, the breath running out of him in a rush. He felt the impossible heat of something behind him, light and fire and smoke all mingling to jar at his senses. The air seemed to be sucked out of the room, pulling right from his very lungs.

Get up, old man. Nothing worse than the gas explosion he'd taken a crew to. That job had been all barbecued bodies and fallen concrete, rebar poking out through chunks of building and people. Only real difference is he'd had a fire axe and an oxygen tank for company, and the damn tank had run dry anyway. Rex opened his eyes, coughing the smoke from his lungs, before getting a hand under himself. He levered himself — *at least your damn bones aren't popping, that or you've finally gone deaf or senile or both* — up, allowing himself a quick look over his shoulder.

The front of the dry cleaner's was gone, glass blown clear of the frames. Where Sky's car had been, there was nothing but fire and twisted metal. Rex couldn't work out which bits were car and which bits were helicopter, but it probably didn't much matter. That kind of thing was a job for insurance companies, men in cheap suits with expensive pens. Not firemen. He resisted the urge to check the wreckage. *Ain't no one there, Rex, and there's people who need you alive right now.*

He touched something wet on his back, and his hand came away sticky and red. The glass from the windows had blown inward, and he'd caught a bunch of it in his back. It had been turned into a fine powder, almost like glitter. He hated glitter, there was that one wedding invitation he'd got full of the stuff. He'd been pulling glitter out of everything for weeks afterward, even found some in his shaving cream. How's glitter get into shaving cream? That's a thing, right there.

"Rex," said a woman's voice. He let his gaze wander over towards the noise, saw a pretty young girl there. He couldn't quite put his hand on her name right now.

"Hi," he said. "What do you call yourself again?"

"Sky," she said. "It's me, Sky. Did you get hit on the head?"

"I don't think so," said Rex. "I think I fell on my face."

"Same thing," she said. "Come on. We've got to get moving."

"Where?" Rex blinked at her. "Say. Did you get what you went back to the car for?"

"The taser?" She held it up. "I got it."

"That was dumb," he said. Then, "I think I'm going to have a sit down, if that's okay."

A kid — *Just James, that's his name, it's Just James* — poked his head out around some clothes. "Rex, are you okay?"

"Pretty sure I'm not," he said. "That's okay. You kids head on out. I'll be fine." He felt the world sliding sideways, that damned ground coming up towards him again. He fought against the fall, for all the good it did. He was old and spent, but that was okay. It was nice to be needed again, and if he went out helping people, well, that's the best way in the world. The ground hit him again but this time it felt soft and warm, the blackness welcome.

CHAPTER
TWENTY-SIX

"Hey." *The woman's voice was familiar, the cold of the world giving her the breath of a dragon. It had been a long time since dragons had stood astride the surface of the Earth, the fierceness of their wars and lovemaking both making the ground tremble.*

She allowed herself to open her eyes, taking in arms cast in front of her in the snow. That can't be right. Arms, hands, not claws. The weakness of this form invaded again, taking over her being, her thoughts, starving her of will and purpose.

The color started to stain the world, the honesty of black and white fading with the clarity of her thoughts. There was another, someone else who wanted to come forward. It had a name, as if names made a difference.

Please, said the other. We have a little girl. She's all alone in this world. Let me go to her.

Pack. That was all that mattered. She looked around, past the woman — tiny, frail — in front of her. She saw the black mechanism that had carried them here, built with all their puny strength. Fragile, it stood in the snow, a face plastered against the glass of its windows.

Please, *said the other,* again. Don't you remember? She's our baby. She's our Adalia.

Adalia. She allowed her gaze to fall back on the woman in front of her, glanced down to see if there was a weapon hiding inside the woman's jacket. She remembered the sting of its pellets, the fire of them yapping at her like small dogs. She felt the flash of anger hit her, wanted to reach out and—

NO. *The other pushed at her, her mind holding the will of the hurricane.* She is not to be harmed. She is ... she is Pack.

Pack. A name formed, a concept hard to hold on to. Carlisle. Carlisle was one of pack. The Shield. The protector when ... when...

She's the one who protects our baby, *said the other,* when you make it impossible. You take my will from me, and she stands against us when you would kill our little girl.

Never. Never would we hurt Pack.

Then you won't hurt Carlisle. Give it back to me. Give me back my life.

It is not your life to have. It is ours. And we have things that need to be done. The world is broken, corrupted and black at its core, the carcass rotting in this old sun.

Give me back my life, *said the other,* and we can fix it together.

She snarled. It's not yours to have. It is mine.

If it can't be yours, and it can't be mine, then it is ours, *said Danny,* and I will not have you hurt them.

It is ours, she agreed. *The other, this* Danny, *was strong, her will burning bright. She felt herself fading again, the feeble hands at the end of her arms feeling more natural, as if they belonged.*

Do you promise? That we will fix the world.

I promise, *said Danny.* Our little girl lives in this world, and we'll make it safe for her.

Safe. Yes. Safe for Pack.

⁓

"Hey," said Carlisle. She was crouched down, the snow crunchy underfoot, the chill of the air leaving her head dry and clear. She watched as Danny's head came up, an edge to her movements that reminded Carlisle of a skittish animal. She watched the yellow eyes scan around, looking between Carlisle and the Yukon sitting behind them. Watched as Danny looked for her sidearm, and let a breath out she didn't know she'd been holding as Danny's eyes moved on, the yellow leeching away.

"I—" Danny's mouth moved around the word, as if it was unfamiliar. "Do you remember the dragons?"

"No," said Carlisle. "Also, what the fuck?"

"I ... I think I dreamed about them," said Danny. The woman rubbed her bare arms, a circle melted in the snow around her. Heat was coming off her in waves, the air shimmering with it. Her eyes found Carlisle's. "Did I hurt anyone?"

She means, did I hurt her. "You didn't hurt Adalia." Carlisle looked back at the Yukon. "She's fine."

"What about you?" Danny's eyes were hooded, something desperate in her voice. "I don't remember."

"I told you before." Carlisle rocked back on her heels. "It's going to take more than a werewolf to take me out. You're all Hulk rage, no finesse."

The ghost of a smile landed on Danny's lips. "Did she see?"

Carlisle thought about that for a little while. *How much do you tell her? What's going to help her? What's going to hurt? Your problem, Carlisle, is that you're just no damn good at this shit.* "I ... she was there. She saw. Danny? I tried to get her out. I took her out to the damn car, I actually put her inside before I came back for that waste of oxygen, Ajay. And she came back inside."

"For you."

"No," said Carlisle. "Yes. Hell, I don't know. She's a teenage girl. It's been a long time since I was a teenage girl." She shrugged her shoulders. "I understand more about nuclear physics than I do about the teenage girls of today."

"Me too," said Danny. "She's growing up too fast."

"All mothers say that."

"All mothers don't kill people in front of their children," said Danny, and something broke in her voice.

With a pop of her knees — *getting rusty on the inside* — Carlisle stood up. "Well, that's a bit shit, true. But what are you going to do?"

"It's more about what you're going to do," said Danny. She pulled herself into a sitting position, knees up to her chest, arms wrapped around. "Is it cold?"

"It's freezing," said Carlisle. She nodded at a pile of clothes in the snow. "I pulled some of your clothes out."

Danny seemed to notice her own nakedness for the first time. "I'm ... have we been having this entire conversation without clothes?"

"I've got clothes," said Carlisle. "For the record, I'm fully clothed. You're the weirdo sitting in the snow, naked as a newborn baby."

"You haven't answered my question," said Danny, starting to pull some clothes on. A pair of old denim jeans. A woolen sweater.

"I answered. I said it was cold." Carlisle rubbed her arms, trying to get some warmth back.

"I asked what you were going to do about Ajay."

"When the hell did you ask that?" Carlisle played the conversation back in her head. "You didn't ask me anything about that. Did you get hit in the head, you know, before?"

Danny gave her a flat stare, one leg poised over a pants leg. "It was implied. It's girl talk."

"I'm not real good at girl talk," said Carlisle.

"Get better," said Danny.

"I want to kill him," said Carlisle. "I ... want him."

"Those are different things," said Danny as she tugged her clothes straight. She ran a hand through her hair, perfect — *the bitch* — bouncy curls raining free. "How do I look?"

"The good news is that if you ever get tired of running from your boyfriend and changing into a hideous beast, you've got a career made in modeling. You look like you just stepped out of a fucking salon," said Carlisle. The idea of Ajay sat in her mind, a dangerous object like a grenade with a freshly pulled pin. *We wouldn't be here without him. We'd not be in this mess, but we'd also be in fucking Alaska, away from the people who need us.* "I get they're different things. He's a little young. I don't know. I guess I want to have sex with him."

"Is he in the car?"

"He's unconscious," said Carlisle. "You threw him into a wall."

Danny looked at her feet. "I don't remember that."

"It's okay," said Carlisle. "I've wanted to throw him into a wall before too. I think it's his superpower."

"Okay," said Danny. "Okay. Well. I remember … I remember something."

"What?" said Carlisle. "About throwing him into a wall?"

"I remember *why* I threw him into a wall. I remember we started this trip with five people in the Yukon, and now we've got four. When we were sleeping on the drive from Alaska to here, one person in the car went … they went somewhere else, Melissa." Something went hard in her eyes. "Let's go wake him up."

CHAPTER
TWENTY-SEVEN

Adalia sat in the Yukon, the heater whispering as the big car idled away some time in the snow. She watched her Mom and Carlisle talking outside. She spared a glance at Ajay — *yup, still unconscious, being thrown into a wall will do that* — laid out in the back seat. *He doesn't look so good.* The man's suit was rumpled, his skin a lighter shade, a hint of gray around his lips.

"He'll live," said the boy.

Adalia glanced around the cabin. There was no one else there. "Where are you?"

"I'm ... I've never had that happen before," said his voice. "I don't know where I am. It's dark. It hurts."

"My mom hit you," said Adalia. "I don't think she meant to."

"She meant to," he said. His voice seemed to come from everywhere around her. "It's crowded in here. Did you know that? I can feel them."

"How was it that she could see you?"

"I don't know," said the boy. "I think it was the Night."

"The what?"

"It doesn't matter," he said. She could imagine him lowering his

191

eyes as he said this, lashes black against his skin, and wished she could see him. "It's what it's called."

Adalia tried for a joke. "Is there a Dawn? A Day? Maybe a bunch of little Afternoons coming home from school?"

His voice left the cabin for a moment, the sound of Ajay's ragged breathing behind her overlaying the sound of the heater blowing warm air into the car. Then he said, "I don't make up the names, okay? I don't even know my own damn name."

"Sorry."

She felt his voice soften the air around her like a warm mist. "No. I'm sorry. I told you to go in to the store."

"I—"

"Wait. It was necessary. You need her to be the Shield. You'll need it before the end."

"Why?" Adalia realized that was the wrong question. "Whose shield?" She could see her mom getting dressed in the snow outside, Carlisle and her in some conversation. The set of both of their shoulders said it wasn't a conversation for *kids*.

"Adalia," he said, "your mom almost set me free. Do you understand? I was almost free of ... all of this."

"What?"

"You need to find my name," he said. "Please."

Adalia sighed in frustration. "I don't even know who you are," she said. "I don't even know what you are. I don't know if you're real."

"Yes you do," he said. "You know all of those things. You know me, as I know you. We were born in different times, but that doesn't stop us from being linked. Joined, across the Universe that spins around us."

Adalia looked down at her hands, realizing they were clenched in her lap. "I don't know how to help you," she said.

"I do," said Ajay, from behind. "I know how to help them all."

She felt the boy leave the cabin then, his presence blowing away like gossamer. She turned to face Ajay. "You made him leave."

"No," said Ajay. "He will always be with you. Until you set him free."

"Free?" said Adalia. "How?"

"It is—" Ajay was interrupted as the rear door was yanked open, her mom standing outside in the snow, her eyes wild.

"Now," said her mom, "tell me. Where the fuck is your friend?"

CHAPTER
TWENTY-EIGHT

I t's shit like this that had got Rex out of the job. It wasn't getting tossed around like a Tinkertoy, or even landing face first on the floor. Hell, that happened on any day ending in Y. It was the waking up hurting, a full body hurt from your toes to the tips of your ears. Even his damn hair hurt.

"Whuuzzz," he said. He tried to open his eyes before realizing he was lying on his face, trying to suck in blanket instead of air. He pushed a hand up, clearing the blanket away, then he opened his eyes.

"Rex?" Just James' young face was close to his, leaning down. The kid looked excited, a little glassy-eyed maybe, but otherwise okay.

Rex felt something inside him relax a little. He tried for his voice again, finding it this time. "Hey," he said. "What time is it?" His eyes focused past Just James, taking in the room they were in. Small, decent for an apartment, kind of bad for a house. Probably an apartment then, the furnishings looked new enough. Sky was standing a long way behind Just James, fussing around in a kitchen. He saw a silver briefcase standing against a wall, two men standing next to it. Possibly they'd been talking about the seven pounds of blond hash inside, possibly they were talking about the old man lying out cold on their couch. They both looked fit, somewhere between capable and dangerous. Too early to tell if they were dangerous to themselves or to others.

"Does it matter?" Just James looked around, anxious. "I mean, I can try and find a clock or something."

"You don't have a watch?"

"Watches are for old men," said Just James.

"Hey," said one of the men by the wall. "I wear a watch."

Just James turned to look at him. "John? You're an old man."

The other one standing by — *John?* — standing by John laughed, turning, and that's when Rex felt really awake, the kind of awake you only felt when someone had taken a big bucket of ice water and dumped it over you. He started up from the couch, swinging his feet under himself and swaying upright. "It's..." He took a step back, his foot catching on the couch, and he fell backwards. "It's *you*."

And it was. The man who'd pulled him and Just James from that terrible crash, the one that had been Rex's fault. Rex knew he'd never forget that face, the sense of care that came from the man. Except, this time, there was something not right. Rex felt it in his old bones, felt it in the twinge in his back.

"It's me," said the other man, stepping forward and holding out his hand. "We've never been introduced. I'm Val."

Rex looked at the extended hand, then reached up and shook it. "Rex."

"Like a dog?"

"Like a fucking Tyrannosaurus," said Rex. He didn't feel like this was real, he just sat on the couch shaking the other man's hand, a big dumb smile on his face. "I mean. Not like a *fucking* Tyrannosaurus, just an ordinary one. Dinosaur. It's a big lizard." He trailed off.

"I don't mean anything by it," said Val, easing his hand from Rex's. "You could say ... you could say that dogs and I are the best of friends."

John snorted, turning away and moving to the kitchen where Sky stood. He grabbed her in a hug, and they kissed. *That'd be her man she was keen to get to.* Rex felt something else unkink inside of him.

"Rex," said Val, "I owe you some thanks." He looked over his shoulder at John and Sky behind him, then turned back. "You brought some of my Pa... some of my family home."

"No," said Rex. "No, you don't have to thank anyone."

"I don't follow." Rex watched the concern cross Val's face. "You ... you brought her. Back to him. That's something ... I owe him a lot."

"I'm here," said Rex, it coming out in a rush, "because you pulled a dumb old man from a burning car." He reached over and ruffled Just James hair, the boy pulling away with a half grimace, half grin. "You got Just James out. You got us all out. Son? You've got a gift. I'd say it was just being paid back."

"Okay," said Val, pulling away from Rex. "Okay. It's not ... it wasn't a gift."

"What?" Rex blinked at him. "You saved me and Just James."

"He does shit like that all the time," said John, from the kitchen. "What he's trying to say—"

"John," said Val, half-turning. "John, what are you doing?"

"I got this," said John. "What he's trying to say is that five years ago—"

"John." Val's tone had turned a little hard, and Rex looked between the two of them.

"You said I could tell her," said John.

"Tell me what?" said Sky.

"I said *we* could tell *her*," said Val. "There's..." He gestured at Rex and James. "There's *other people* here."

"Oh, sorry," said John. He looked over at Rex. "What's your story?"

"This guy," said Rex, jerking a thumb at Val, "jerked me out of a burning Prius. My wife wanted it, before she died."

"A burning Prius?" John looked blank. "That's a hell of a thing to ask for on your death bed. I mean, did she stop to think about how hard it would be to get a car on fire into ... well, wherever you were.

Hospital? Nursing home?" He looked at Val. "You never said you went to a nursing home."

"Hospital," said Rex, then shook himself. Talking to this guy was like trying to follow the damn bouncing ball on karaoke after seven beers. "She wanted a Prius. She died. I set it on fire."

"That seems weird," said John. "Why'd you do that?"

"I crashed it," said Rex, then looked at Val. "Help?"

"It's his thing," said Val.

"What's my thing?" said John.

"You know," said Val.

"Okay," said John. "What I'm not clear on—"

"*You're* not clear?" said Rex. He rubbed his face, closing his eyes for a moment. "Look. It's like this. I was thinking about women—"

"With you so far," said John. He yelped as Sky punched him in the arm. "What? All I'm saying is that I empathize with the man. We've all been there." He looked at Val. "Right?"

"Right," said Val, then caught a look from Sky. "No, wait. Pretend I didn't just agree with you. Sky? Seriously. It was an honest mistake, I didn't mean to—"

Rex burst out laughing. Couldn't help himself, it came from somewhere deep in his gut, and felt good coming out. When he stopped, he could see grins and smiles around the room. He nodded at John. "I get it."

"What?" John blinked at him.

"I get what your thing is," said Rex. "I *get* it. It's ... it's good."

"It is," said Val. "Try living with it for a while before you decide, though."

"You guys have no focus," said John. He leaned his hands on the counter that stood between them. "We still haven't heard what happened to the Prius."

"So it was like this," said Rex. He looked past Just James, then back to the group. "I was driving. I was distracted, thinking about women. It's a thing that never stops, right? So I was thinking about women, or a woman in particular, and I got hit by a bus." He rubbed a hand across his head, then looked at the fragments of burnt hair in his hand. *That was a close one.* "That makes it sound like the bus was at fault, but I was pretty sure it was me. Just James was on the bus. And we were going to die. I didn't know Just James was there, I didn't know him at all. But ... but Val pulled me from the car. Just James, too." His voice softened. "News said that it exploded after, some kind of fire. Be a hell of a way to go. Hell of a way." He looked up at Val. "I promised. I didn't tell anyone."

"I know," said Val, "but it doesn't matter anymore."

"You're right," said John, "because you already know. So does Just James. In a way, the only person here who doesn't know is Sky."

"Know what?" said Sky.

"Baby?" John led Sky around the counter, sitting her on the couch next to Rex. "Baby, there's something you need to know."

"You're married," she said. Her voice was flat, her arms crossed in a way that said *and I always suspected.*

John blinked. "It's not that bad," he said after a moment. "But it's a little ... I'm going to say, it's a little odd. This might come as a surprise."

Rex looked at John, then Sky, then across at Val. Sky was angry, John worried — *which is damn strange, guys like him never get like that* — and Val was resigned. "What's going to come as a surprise?" He looked at Val. "What's going on?"

"Val has superpowers," said Just James.

Rex tried for a second laugh, but no one joined in. "Come again?"

"It's obvious, isn't it?" said the kid. "He can do things no one else can do, can't tell anyone his real identity, and has a secret lair."

"It's an apartment," said Val.

"I like the kid," said John. "Good save on that one."

"Val doesn't have superpowers," said Sky. "His girlfriend left him and he's been staying in our apartment for the last six months. That's pretty ordinary."

"Baby?" said John. "Baby, five years ago Val was bitten by a were-wolf. His girlfriend—"

"Danny," said Sky.

"Danny is a werewolf too," said John. "They turn into hideous monsters and get really angry. They don't like silver, but near as I can tell they don't get any older and they can't die."

She snorted. "There's no such things as werewolves," she said.

"That's the common theory," said John, "and usually I'd run with that. But this is real."

"You are all," said Sky, "on drugs." She held up a hand. "Wait. Prove it."

"Prove it?" said Val.

"Yeah. Turn into a werewolf."

"I can't," said Val.

She snorted again. "Of *course* you can't. Not a full moon?"

"It doesn't work like that," said Val. "It got ... it was stolen."

"Son," said Rex, "and I don't mean to intrude on what's obviously a very personal moment, but clear something up for me. Assuming — and this is a big assumption, mind — that you are, in fact, a werewolf, how does one go about having something like that stolen?"

Val jerked a thumb over at the silver case, resting against the wall. "The case," he said. "The case took it all."

CHAPTER
TWENTY-NINE

Talin wiped his hand across a mouth red with bloody drool. The Night was gaining strength each time he used it, like a muscle that wanted to be flexed. The man, Everard, that he'd tracked across half a continent and more to get to this point, had wasted this strength.

Because that's what it was. An *inner* strength, no matter how it shone to outside eyes with terror and power. Talin kicked the remains at his feet, a corpse that had been torn across the chest, teeth marks in the flesh. Some of these were large, like that of a bear or something even bigger. Others were small. Talin didn't remember when he'd changed back, or if *back* was really the right term. He was becoming something else, a blend of two things with one glorious purpose.

He grinned, red stains on his teeth marring the white. Before, he knew his teeth had started to rot, decaying. It was a thing that happened to the *houngan* — the male priests of his faith — from time to time. The power they used, that they funneled and marshaled, twisted their bodies just as it perfected the world.

A week ago, Talin had been a tiny man, scrabbling for loose coins

200

under the couch of life. His *vodou* had been weak; no *l'wha* had responded to his call. He'd had just a few simple tricks, used to turn the minds of men against themselves. Enough to bait a collection of traps, seeded along the trail of the Night. Because of that, here he was — and soon, ruler of the world.

Still. One thing at a time. He looked down over the city from his new perch high above. He'd moved to this tower, feeling drawn to the potential of this place named after the forgettable man who'd built it, a hotel for the rich. Such stories flowed through its doors, politicians and lovers and whores and thieves. The altar had stayed behind with the old leather chair, devices he had no need of anymore. Should never have needed in the first place.

The flat roof showed him all he had made in just short days. The *zombi* did as he wanted; a remarkable few of the city's rabble still scrabbling for freedom as his horde took them on the hoof. He stared down at his hands, his arms, the body he had been gifted for his audacity to steal what could not be stolen. It was changed, strength coursing along limbs made young again, the physique of an Olympian shoving aside what had been old and withered.

There were only a few things he needed to resolve before he extended his influence into the wide world, borne on the wings of Night. Three perfect quests remained. Talin held up his knife, using the blade to carve lines into his flesh. They healed almost immediately, but the marks would be graven on his soul, weighted and measured, giving him strength. Three lines, for each thing remaining. He no longer needed the snakes and rodents, the *vermin* that had powered his magics before. They were dross, the tiny implements of a tiny man. The Night was power itself, and upheld its end of every bargain without flinching.

The first line was cut the deepest for the man, Everard. He yet lived, with the merest fragment of the Night remaining inside. Something had gone wrong, the trap Talin laid falling short of the mark. He was like an almost empty bottle of rum, barely a swallow left in the bottom, but Talin wanted it all. And he would have it — and the man's lover too. She was coming and he would drain the Night from her just as easily as water from a glass. She would be left gasping and begging. Or perhaps she would join him at his side, a dark bride to walk down the centuries with. He discarded the idea almost immediately — *power is not to be shared.*

A second line joined the first, his flesh sizzling and smoking as the knife cut through it. This was for the shrew Raeni, who continued to be a thorn in his side. Always meddling, always following, dogging his heels to the end of days. She would have to be destroyed. He'd tried before, but had ... *failed.* As a *mambos* she had held the true power always denied to Talin, riding the *l'wha* like the cattle they were. She could still be a threat, and her instrument would be broken upon the rocks of the Earth before the end.

A helicopter buzzed overhead, Talin watching it thud over the city where the rivers met, this *Chicago,* another relic of squandered, forgotten power. It rode over the skies like a fat insect, lights set in nose and tail flashing as night fell across the city. They were riding higher now since his *zombi* had pulled one from the sky with a whispered urge. This one was watching from above, no doubt telling its masters what happened here. So was marked the third of his quests, his skin scorching under the blade, the third and final line for the guardians who stood against his conquest. A thin line of men and women who had given their service for a nation carelessly spending their lives. It was a coin of blood Talin understood well enough, and he would spend it himself before this night was done.

THIRTY

"His name was Thomas, and he was a soldier," said Ajay. "Not a sailor, not something ... *in between*, like me. A soldier first, last and always."

"Something ... *hurts*," said the boy, his lashes long. They'd been the first thing she'd noticed when he'd come back like a kiss of mist on the dawn. "Something is missing."

Ajay frowned as if he'd heard something faint, on the edge of the wind, then shot Adalia a look. "They do not always tell the truth."

"Who the fuck doesn't tell the truth?" said Carlisle, from the driver's seat. She was looking across at Ajay — Adalia could see the side of her face from her perch in the back passenger's side. Her mom was beside her, sitting behind Carlisle. *You sit there*, Carlisle had said, *because I don't want you punching through the seat and killing Ajay — before I do*. Her mom had given that look, the one that said things Adalia didn't understand, but had got in the back seat anyway. "You're being strange again, like you're having two conversations."

"Sorry," said Ajay. "I forget that not all of us here can see things that cannot be seen."

Carlisle said nothing for perhaps two heart beats, then, "You need to quit that shit. See, you're not making any *sense*."

"It doesn't matter," said Danny, her hand clutching at the edge of Carlisle's seat as she leaned forward. "What matters is what happened to Thomas. I can still … I can feel him, like he's standing on the edge of a cliff."

"The Cliffs of the Damned," said Ajay.

"What?" said Carlisle.

"They have a name," said Ajay. "It is where the dead go when they die."

"That doesn't … that doesn't sound nice," said Carlisle.

"It isn't always," said the boy, his feet up near his chin. He was between Adalia and her mom, somehow not touching either of them, the space in the back of the Yukon stretching in a way that made Adalia's head hurt to think about. No one seemed to notice him there except for her.

She pulled out her phone. *How do you know?*

He looked at her sideways, face pale, eyes blue against the black of his lashes. "I can't—"

Adalia waved a hand at him. *Forget it.*

"Soldiers spend their lives as a … you would call it a currency," said Ajay. "Your GIs spend their blood to buy you a freedom. Thomas spent his blood to buy something else."

"What's that?" said Danny, leaning forward, her eyes bright.

"Time," said Adalia. "He bought us time."

No one spoke inside the car for a moment, then Carlisle said, "What?"

"Yeah," said Danny. She turned to Adalia. "What do you mean, sweetie?"

Ajay sat silent, shoulders hunched as if something was bottled up inside. Adalia watched the back of his shoulders for a moment, and when he didn't say anything, she said, "Can't you see? We wouldn't have made it to Valentine in time."

"No time left," said the boy, "to save the world. The world would have turned around only a handful more times before the end, if we hadn't bought a road paved in blood." He shivered. "But I still don't ... I don't know why I'm here."

Ajay shifted in his seat. "There was no way we could have made it to the city where the rivers meet before the end unless we stole a little time back from the universe. Well, not stole. That's not right, because we needed ... *tribute*."

"Thomas," said Carlisle. "Let's say for a second that I buy your voodoo—"

"*Vodou*," said Ajay. "You say it wrong, like we are in a Hollywood movie."

Carlisle blinked. "Whatever. Let's say that I agree you're some kind of voodoo—" and here, Ajay winced "—sailor. You go and buy us some time, or whatever, because we all know we've driven further and faster than is possible even if we had the Starship fucking Enterprise. So tell me, Gandalf, and this is important. I want your full attention. Who did you buy the time from?"

"It doesn't work like that," said Ajay.

"It works exactly like that," said the boy.

Danny was looking at the space where the boy sat, blinking her eyes and turning her head. "I think I'm seeing things."

"You're not seeing things," said Ajay, "because they aren't there to be seen."

"Maybe you should have ridden in the front," said Carlisle, "because all I want to do is punch this guy."

Ajay breathed out a sigh. "I know what you want, Detective," he said. "You want what you can't have."

"Can't have?" said Carlisle. "Like, world peace?"

"No," said Ajay. He tossed his head backwards, as if in Adalia's direction. "Your job is to be her Shield. Your chance to become what you were made to be is fast approaching."

"Wait," said Danny. "Melissa's a good friend—"

"Thanks," said Carlisle.

"—But I'm Adalia's *mother*," said Danny. "And, lest we forget, a werewolf. I think I've got the job of shield."

"It doesn't work like that," said the boy.

"What do you mean?" said Adalia. "I don't understand."

"I mean that I'm going to look after you," said Danny. "It's kind of what I signed up for."

"You each play a part." Ajay's jaw clenched. "The ... *roles* we are given."

Adalia leaned forward, almost touching the boy. He looked like he wanted to pull away and stay at the same time, and she gave him a little smile before speaking. "The Shield. The Sword. The Knight." She licked her lips, wanting to stop, but the words kept tumbling from her. "Sacrifice, Guide, and the Doubtful Soldier. The Good Right Arm. The Lost Warrior."

Ajay was nodding as she spoke, until she hit the last role. *Lost Warrior.* "Who is that?" he said.

"Her," said the boy, pointing out the windscreen. They were rounding a bend formed from a bank lined with trees. On the other side of the bend was the remains of a barricade, an overturned Humvee lying on the road, wheels still turning. Carlisle slammed on the brakes, the Yukon slowing as the ABS stammered against the snowy ground. Soldiers were running around with what looked like ordinary people running among them, biting, clawing ... and *feeding*.

The hammer of automatic weapons fire sounded close to them, holes appearing in rapid succession across the hood before the windscreen of the Yukon was gone in a shower of fragments. Without it, the cold and the noise of the outskirts of Chicago poured in to the cabin, the sound of fighting and dying. The sound of war. Carlisle was wrenching the wheel, her eyes squeezed shut as the Yukon bucked and slewed across the road, tires screaming. The vehicle almost tipped before sitting back on its haunches.

Ahead of them, standing in the middle of the road, was a handful of soldiers in combat fatigues, rifles firing. In their midst was a woman, a little older than Melissa, and Adalia could see the burden that had made her lose her way pushing her to the ground and carrying her up at the same time. It gave her fear. It gave her strength. It gifted her with purpose. "There," said Adalia, a kind of nervous energy making her shift in her seat. It wasn't fear of what was happening outside the Yukon — it was something that *clicked* inside her as she saw the woman. "Right there. The Lost Warrior."

THIRTY-ONE

They were standing around, looking at the case. It sat on the table in the middle of them. The rounded metal corners of the thick case meant Val couldn't help but think of a bloated spider, heavy after feeding. The front was still chipped and scratched, the latches buckled from when Val had forced it. They'd pushed them closed, but a casual flick would set them open again.

Rex was reaching for it. Val stopped him, a hand on the old man's shoulder. "I wouldn't do that."

Rex looked at him, then at the case, then back to him. "It's just a box with a handle."

"It is," said John, "the gateway to Abaddon."

"Isn't Abaddon a dude? Like an angel?" Sky was crouched down in front of the case. Val felt a tingle of apprehension as she sat there — as they *all* sat there — around this thing that had done so much harm.

"It's a dude and a place," said John.

"Bottomless pit," said Just James, scratching behind his ear.

"My point," said John, nodding at Just James. "Thanks, kid."

"No problem," said Just James. "So, are we going to open it?"

"No," said John and Val, at the same time. Val looked at John, then said, "I think it would be a bad idea to open it again."

"Maybe," said Just James, "it was just you that had issues."

"I must say," said John, "you're taking this whole sorcery thing pretty well. Not having much trouble suspending disbelief."

"I got pulled out of a burning bus by a guy with superhuman strength," said Just James. "It got me thinking."

"The only superpower that Val has is doing our laundry," said Sky. She cocked her head to one side. "Also, the place has been spotless since he moved in."

"I lived alone for a while," said Val. "I learned some skills. Look, just don't open the case."

"Val," said Rex, looking up at him. The old man rubbed a weathered hand against stubble growing strong despite the gray in it. "We need to open it. Find out what we're dealing with."

Val turned and walked to the windows looking out over the city. Smoke was rising from down the street, cars scattered in a panicked gridlock. There had been no orderly exit, just a rush for the exits as madness descended on the city. The old man had a point — there was a responsibility to put this right. He nodded to himself, then turned around. But a bit of caution would go a long way. It seemed unlikely that just one of these cases had been in Chicago, and Val had to wonder what happened to the other ones, or the people that had found them. "Rex—" Val froze. The old man had moved away to the kitchen, the breakfast bar between them.

John was standing with an astonished look on his face. "The old timer moves pretty quick."

"I used to pull people out of buildings that were on fire," said Rex. "That kind of thing motivates you." He had the case with him, and he laid it on the breakfast bar. "I owe you one anyway," he said, his eyes on Val, before he turned his face away and flicked the lid open.

The silence held in the apartment as they all looked at Rex. The case rocked a little before it settled, lid open and hiding whatever was inside from the rest of them. Rex opened one eye, looking into the case. "Well, shit," he said, and tried to slam the lid closed.

Something was inside, clawing its way out. Legs, long like an insect — *except insects don't grow that big ... do they?* — edged out of the case. John was already moving, launching himself to land on the case, his bodyweight slamming the lid close with a snap. The legs that had come out of the case sheared off, falling to twitch against the breakfast bar. A green liquid, almost like a sap, was dripping from the ends of them.

"Don't open the case," said Rex. "Don't open—"

The case blew open, tossing John away like he weighed no more than an old sheet of newspaper. The lid wrenched free in a splinter of metal as the hinges gave, tumbling and bouncing across the floor of the apartment. Spiders the size of dogs were climbing out of the case to skitter across the bench and on to the floor, or scaling the walls. Val had Raph in his hand, no clear memory of how it had got there, and he took three quick steps across the floor before swinging the bat into the side of a spider. It burst like a piñata, green gore spraying from the end of the bat. Val caught a glimpse of Sky running into the room she shared with John, the door slamming behind her.

Another spider jumped, landing atop Just James. The kid went down with a scream, holding the spider away from his face with both arms. Val ran towards them, punting the spider away with his foot. He looked back at John, who was — *only John would do that* — using a spider as a flail against others circling him on the ground. He was alternately swinging the massive arachnid and punching it to keep it subdued.

Rex. Where's the old guy? Val hefted the bat, rounding the corner of the breakfast bar. Rex was on his knees, swinging the base of the metal case against the remains of a spider on the ground. Val looked at the bat in his hands, then turned his attention back to John, who still seemed to have the lion's share of opponents.

The door to John and Sky's room opened, Sky charging back through it holding something red in her hand. She took one look at the spiders circling John and ran straight for them. She pointed the red device at a spider and there was a crack, a hole punched through the fat body of the creature. She pointed the device at the ceiling and fired again, an arachnid falling to the ground, limbs still twitching. John was still swinging the remains of his insect as Val joined them, laying about with his bat.

With a final crack from Sky's device, followed by a thud as a spider fell from the wall, they looked around the room. Just James was poking his head up over the couch. Rex was leaning with one arm against the breakfast bar's counter top, the other braced against his back.

Sky's eyes were still wild, and she swung the red device back and forth.

"Hey," said John. "Baby. It's cool."

She looked at him. "What?"

"I said, it's cool." John let what was left of the spider he was holding fall to the ground.

She blinked at him, then laughed, the sound a hysterical bark. "Does this ... does this look *cool* to you?"

John looked around. "Truth?"

"Truth."

"More or less, this is a regular day at the office." John reached over to carefully ease her fingers away from the device. "Huh."

Val leaned forward to look at it. "Is that ... is that a Ramset gun?"

"Yeah," said John. "I bought it a couple months back."

"Why'd you buy a Ramset gun?" Val waved his arms at the room around them. "You live in an apartment. You don't need those kinds of things."

"Thank you, Val," said Sky. "That's what I said."

John looked hurt. "Two things," he said. "First, a man always needs tools. *Always.* Second, does it not look like it's come in handy?"

"Son," said Rex, his hands out in a placating gesture, "now's probably not the time to be having this conversation. This ain't how you're going to build your business case for a Skilsaw."

"You know, you're right," said John, turning to Val. "Where were you?"

"Me?" said Val. "I was helping. I helped."

"You ran around a lot." John pointed with the Ramset gun at the walls. Impaled spider corpses hung, and Sky's few misses were shown by protruding nail heads. "Sky *shot* some of these things."

"I still don't feel my best," said Val. He wiped his nose, then noticed the blood on it. "See?"

"You've got a bleeding nose?" said Sky. "That's it?"

"Hey," said Val. "We probably need to brief you on the killer virus."

"True," said John, nodding. "Before we do that, how about a Coke and a smile? Also, how the hell are we going to explain the bodies of giant killer spiders?"

Val looked around the apartment, taking in the spider corpses, the Ramset holes in the walls, the nails, the green stains on the carpet. "You know, I actually don't think anyone's going to care. I think that if giant spiders are the weirdest thing anyone sees in Chicago today, they haven't gone outside yet."

"IT STARTED WITH A WISH," said Val. "A woman named Elsie Morgan wished that her little girl wouldn't die."

"She was a complete bitch," said John. Val shot him a flat stare. John shrugged, then gestured with his Coke. "No, you're right. My bad, it's your story. You go."

"Thanks," said Val. He looked around at them — Just James, cross-legged on the floor, Sky standing back and leaning against the wall, her face turned away. Rex on the single seat across from them. John sitting next to him on the couch. They'd thrown the spider bodies out the window, then followed them with the remains of the metal case. It had been empty, the matte black interior innocuous, but Sky had said she wasn't having *that thing in her house*. It had looked okay, the general vibe of despicable evil having left it with the spiders, but out it went. "So, Birkita—"

"Wait a minute," said Rex. "Birkita? What the hell kind of name is that?"

"You want to tell the story?" said Val.

"No," said Rex. "All I'm asking is, who names their kid Birkita? She want her daughter to go into the wrestling team? Because she'd sure as shit learn to fight well, a name like that at school."

"Elsie," said Val, "was the CEO of Biomne. Sam Barnes took over ... after. Biomne is — or was, Sam and I don't really swap postcards — the largest pharmaceutical company on planet Earth. I don't think she was going to send Birkita to public school."

Rex seemed to chew that one over. "Shame. We could probably use more female pro wrestlers."

Val rubbed a hand over his face, then looked up at Rex. "Wasn't it thinking like that that got you into a car crash?"

"Fair point," said Rex.

"So," said Val, "where were we? Right, Birkita. So, near as I can tell, the kid had cancer, or some other equally shitty disease. All diseases are shitty, but any that kills a kid before they go to their prom is a special version of shit. Elsie had this wish, like I said. She wanted her girl to grow up. You got to figure a thing like that fucks with you, right? You're head of the company that makes all the drugs, yet your kid is going to die of a disease. I'm using a bit of artistic license here—"

"Artistic what?" said Sky.

"License," said Val. "It's where—"

"I know what it is," said Sky. "You're telling a story about werewolves. You're exercising your license already. Just the facts."

Val shot John a look. "She always like this?"

John looked at him, then at Sky, took in the expression on her face, then looked back at Val. "It's your story, man."

"Coward," said Val. He leaned back against his seat. "Elsie starts doing a Hitler. She looks all over the globe for things that can help, that conventional medicine doesn't know about. Somewhere in Russia, she finds a rumor. Some tiny scrap of information that leads her to some ancient cold war gulag."

"A gulag," said Rex. "An actual internment camp?"

"No clue," said Val. "I wasn't there. The person who was there was named Volk."

"Cute," said Just James.

"Say what?" Val blinked at him.

"It's Russian." Just James looked around at them all. "I mean, he's from Russia, sure, but his name means *wolf*."

"How you know that?" said Val. "That's a really weird piece of information to carry around in your head."

"My Dad — my real Dad, that is — was ... I mean, is ... heck." Just James looked at his feet for a minute, then tried again. "My Dad's Russian. I'm learning Russian, you know, so I can..." He trailed off.

Rex cleared his throat. "What the kid's trying to say," he said, "is that it's probably not his real name."

"Was," said Val.

"Was?" Rex scratched at his stubble. "You mean, he changed his name?"

"Was," said Val, "as in my girlfriend ate him."

The silence hung in the room for a little longer than was comfortable before John stepped up. "So," he said. "Who wants a beer?"

"I'll take a beer," said Val.

"Me too," said Rex.

"I'll try one," said Just James.

"No," said Rex.

"What do you mean," said Sky, "that Danny ate this Russian guy from a gulag, and what's it got to do with Elsie Morgan?" She looked at John. "Do we still have any Sol?"

John winced. "I can look." He moved around to the kitchen and began rooting through the refrigerator. "Good news, bad news."

"What's the good news?" said Val.

214

"We've got Sol."

"That's not good news," said Val.

"The *bad* news is that the power's out and all the Sol is warm," said John. He came back carrying a few bottles. He handed them around. "Back to your story."

"Thanks," said Val, taking a long pull from his beer. He made a face. "That's really terrible."

"It's the end of the world," said John. "You're going to complain about the beer?"

Val nodded. "I kept saying we should stock some Peroni. But no. You said—"

"I said that it's our apartment and you can buy Peroni when you get your own place." John shrugged. "You know how it is."

"That was cold then and it's damn cold now," said Val. "Anyway, Sky, to your point, *yes*. The delight of my life did in fact eat Volk. Or we think so. Let me explain." He looked across the room, thinking, before putting on an accent. "'*No, there is too much. Let me sum up.*'"

John tilted his head. "Inigo? Princess Bride?"

Val clinked his beer against John's. "'*Well remembered.*'"

"Tristan from Stardust?" said Sky.

"Girl's on fire," said Val. He nodded. "Elsie heard that Volk was a man who carried a virus inside him that left him immune to aging, and gave him amazing regenerative powers. She dispatched a team to extract him. Turns out, the virus was a red herring, and he was a werewolf. He and I first met at the Elephant Blues—"

"Nice bar," said Rex. "I've been there."

"Was," said Val. "It *was* a nice bar. Pretty sure it's closed down. Anyway. He turned into a hideous moon beast, killing everyone inside, except for me. Me, he bit, and here I am, werewolf."

"You've skipped a part," said Sky. "You skipped the part where Danny ate him."

"Right, sorry, I forgot." Val rubbed his face. "We tracked them—"

"Them?" said Sky.

"The bad guys," said John.

"The bad guys," said Val. "We tracked them to their facility—"

"Lair," said John. "It was totally a lair."

"We tracked them to their lair," said Val. "There was a fight. Pretty much everyone who was on Team Bad Guy died. I don't really know the details."

"You weren't there?" Rex frowned. "But—"

"I was a hideous moon beast," said Val. "And it turns out Danny was too. I remember they shot her." He remembered a shadow of what he'd felt then, the feeling of loss, and swallowed. "Sorry. As it happens, that's not an effective strategy for dealing with were-wolves. They shed their human form and kill everyone around them."

"So Danny—"

"Danny turned into a werewolf, joined the fight, and—"

"She jumped out a tall building and into a forest to track down Volk," said John. "She met back with us the next morning, and remembered eating him. More or less."

"More or less," said Val. "The details aren't important. The thing is—"

"Hold on, son," said Rex. "I figure the details are pretty important."

"Right," said Just James. "Like, why are there not more werewolves?"

Val blinked at him. "You do *not* want more of these things."

"Sure," said the kid, "but why aren't there more? I mean, how did … what's your girlfriend's name?"

"Danny," said Sky. "Her name is Danny."

"How did Danny get … turned?" Just James looked around at them. "Did you bite her?"

"If 'bite' is a euphemism," said John, "then sure. I think there was some … *action.*"

Rex worked his way to his feet. "Sorry, old bones," he said. "I need to move around a little. Kid's got a point though. Why is the world not crawling with … werewolves?" He looked like he'd swallowed a bug. "It's not that I disbelieve your story," he said, "but the mind kind of skitters away from saying that kind of thing out loud."

"I know, right?" said John. "But it's *cool* too."

"Very cool," said Just James.

"I kill people," said Val, "without control."

"Granted, there are downsides," said Rex. "Let's stick to the main trail. Why are there not more? You mentioned a virus?"

"Still got it," said Val. "We think that it was used to try and control Volk, but it seems to have no effect. If you inject the virus into a normal person..." He trailed off.

"Spencer," said John.

"That's a virus?" Rex looked at John, then at Val.

"It's a dick," said John. "Total, man-sized penis."

"There was this guy Spencer," said Val, "who got shot up with the virus. He ... melted."

"But you're fine?" Rex frowned.

"I'm not fine," said Val. "Since having the ... Night ... removed by the briefcase, I get nosebleeds all the time and I feel like I'm dying."

"You look fine," said Rex.

"Your metrics might be flawed from all the time around your octogenarian friends," said Val.

"You, son," said Rex, "have no respect."

"That is true," said Val.

"I have a theory," said John.

"God save us," said Sky.

"Maybe only certain kinds of people can get turned," said John. "It's a working theory, but Val's killed a lot of dudes, and—"

"You're not helping my peace of mind." Val turned to look out the window. "But sure. Go on."

"You've killed a lot of *bad* dudes," said John, "and no one's *turned*."

"They're not all bad," said Val. "I mean ... you know what I mean. Collateral damage." It helped if he stuck a label on it, like they weren't people but statistics. "Don't you think there'd be more of us?"

"Beats me," said John, "but every time one of you assholes pokes your head up above the parapet, a bunch of crackerjack motherfuckers comes and tries to take it. I think you're being hunted."

"That's big game," said Rex. "It'd have to be organized."

"It'd have to be organized for a long, long time," said Sky. "I'm not saying I buy your story, but if we run with it, because, you know, the *spiders*. If you just get all, 'Hulk, smash!' and destroy everything and everyone when someone shoots you, there'd have to be something ... worse, out there, wouldn't there? Something ... stronger?"

Val looked at John, then back at Sky. "I'd not really thought about it like that," he said.

"No," said Rex, "because you've been spending so much time worrying about the downsides, that you crawled right up your own ass." He fixed a steely eye on Val. "Don't sass me, son. I'm too old and too cranky. You've been running from one thing to another for so long, your head isn't on straight. You don't get that choice. This thing? You've got to get in front of it. Work it. Live it."

"I kill people!" said Val. "That is not a thing I want to live." The room was silent around him, and he realized he was breathing hard. "I kill people." He stood up and walked towards the window. Looking down at the city, he saw the smoke and the fires, the cars littered about. From somewhere, he heard a scream, and he put aside his beer. *You shouldn't be living it up large while people are out there dying because of you, Everard.*

He felt a tentative hand on his arm, and he spun — a little too fast, by the look on Just James' face. "What is it, kid?"

"You keep saying," said Just James, "how horrible you are. But I haven't seen that. I really haven't. Rex and I would be dead if it wasn't for you. You don't kill people, Val. You save people." He let his hand drop, stepping back. "I don't really have any special superpowers. No skills, really. Hell, I haven't gone to college yet. But because of you, I'll get that chance. I don't know if anyone's said this to you before, but—"

"Kid, stop," said Val. He tried to back away, but he was already hard up against the window. "Whatever you've got to say, I've said it to myself before. I'm a monster."

"You don't understand," said Just James. "All I wanted to say? Thank you." He gave a shy, crooked smile before he turned away.

THIRTY-TWO

"Stay in the car," said Carlisle. "For fuck's sake, stay in the car. Will you do that?" She looked at Danny, saw the other woman's eyes were bright with something — not fear, but *excitement*. Carlisle clicked her fingers, and Danny's eyes snapped towards her. Away from the soldiers and people outside, fighting with guns and fists and teeth. "Hey. Kendrick. This isn't a movable feast. If you go out there, people are going to get *dead*."

"It's a bit past that," said Danny, her voice taking on a dreamy edge. "It's … beautiful."

Carlisle sighed. *Use a different road. You're always too direct, Carlisle.* "They will get dead because of *you*."

That did it. Danny's eyes turned from excited to haunted in less than a heartbeat. Carlisle felt a *twinge* inside, but that was tiny compared to what Danny would feel like if she woke up after … *this*. "Danny. Stay here." She rolled her eyes towards Adalia. "With the kid."

She didn't wait for an answer, kicking her door open and spilling out into chaos. The hard, steady hammer of automatic weapons filled the air, and she looked down at her sidearm holding her hand like any good friend. Carlisle didn't remember drawing it, but that didn't matter. What mattered was being *here*, for *them*. She crouched down low next to the Yukon, looking around at the battlefield. A stray round punched a hole in the skin of the vehicle at her back, paint gone around a silver-bright pucker of wounded metal. She licked her lips, gripping her sidearm in both hands, and looked towards the—

Lost Warrior. That's what they'd called her. No problem — woman wasn't lost anymore, they'd found her. Only real problem, near as Carlisle could figure, was getting to her, and getting the hell out of Dodge. It wasn't a question of what to do, just how to get it done. Get the Lost Warrior. Get larger transport. Get out of this batshit crazy situation. Keep your friends from getting dead. Maybe grab a beer and a lie down at the end.

The scene around Carlisle was making a certain kind of crazy sense. There were civilians who were running all over the place, attacking military personnel. The military were fighting back, but they didn't have numbers on their side — down the road and stretching out towards the city was a long tongue of freeway, and it was full of people. A roaring mass of humanity, clawing up the road towards them. *Okay, that problem you can solve if you stay alive for the next two minutes.* It was clear they were in a temporary military camp because of the number of people in fatigues, but not a lot else was left of the place. No standing structures. Vehicles tipped on their sides. A lot of shit on fire.

A scream pulled her attention to the side, and she saw a teenage boy running at her, mouth an impossibly wide rictus. His eyes were bloodshot red. Her sidearm barked three times, the first round taking him in the shoulder, the second in the side, and the third in the back as he spun around to land face-first on the road. Carlisle's attention was pulled back behind her as one of the Yukon's doors slammed shut, and she poked her head up over the side, seeing Ajay standing out on the other side of the vehicle. He showed her white teeth under a face weary and stretched, then pointed with a hand at the Lost Warrior.

Carlisle nodded. Two was better than one, sure. She broke into a sprint across the tarmac, heading for the clump of soldiers. *Looks like they're trying some kind of last stand. It's that kind of thinking that kept me out of the military.*

On her right was Ajay, keeping pace but making it look effortless. Was he even running, or just moving through space? On her left, a pack of three came at her, arms pinwheeling as they clawed and pushed each other aside in their eagerness to reach her. She raised her sidearm, the Eagle heavy with comfort, and squeezed. She felt the release of the weapon, one of the zombies — *because they've got to have a name, and that seems to fit* — slamming backwards as the round took it in the chest. The momentum of its travel caused its legs to fly forward and it landed flat on its back, arms bouncing once as it came to rest. Carlisle moved her weapon sideways a hair, taking a breath, and fired again. The round went wide, clipping one of them on the shoulder — it careened to the side but still kept coming. She fired again, and its head disappeared, punched through like overripe fruit.

The third one was on her, and she ducked low under it, bringing her shoulder up into its middle and standing tall. It — a man, trim in a sports blazer — was tossed behind her. She turned, her sidearm ready, but Ajay was on it. He moved a foot through the air in an arc so graceful it could only have been capoeira. His heel connected with the zombie's jaw and it went down in a graceful pirouette.

Carlisle raised an eyebrow at him. "No soldier, huh?"

"Just a sailor," he said. "I'm a long way from shore."

"They teach you dance on ships?" Carlisle worked her shoulders under her jacket, then took aim across the road at another four running at them. The kinks were out now, and she got them one-for-one, then ejected her magazine onto the ground.

"I have learned many things," said Ajay, holding a hand out

towards the Lost Warrior's group, "except how to find our way home. After you."

"Careful," said Carlisle. She pointed at the group. "Those guys might get confused."

"Confusion is the least of their worries," said Ajay. "Hurry, Detective."

"I'm not a ... you know, fuck it," said Carlisle. She looked at the Lost Warrior's group. It didn't look like a happy team. She raised her voice. "Hey! Coming in. Hold your fire!"

One of the soldiers, a man holding onto his twenties with gritted teeth, looked at her. "Ma'am. Stand away! We will fire."

The Lost Warrior placed a hand on the soldier's shoulder. "Identify yourself."

Carlisle caught her breath, then brushed a strand of hair away from her face. "I—"

She was cut off by a ululation of sound as a wave of humanity crested around a fallen Humvee. A horde of zombies was scrabbling and clawing towards them, and she — *fuck that noise* — turned back towards the Yukon. She made two steps before what her eyes were seeing hit her brain and she stopped. The Yukon was surrounded by zombies, rocking the machine, pawing at the doors and windows.

A rear door smashed open, a human shape — *thank God, she's still human* — came out. It was Danny, and she dived into the middle of the group at the side of the Yukon. There was a surge like a wave of people that rose over her, and she seemed to be swallowed by a mass of bodies. Carlisle watched that for a heartbeat too long, then turned back to the Lost Warrior. "Do you have a vehicle?"

The other woman looked at her with surprise. "What about your friend?"

"She's fine," said Carlisle. "It's pretty important we get the fuck out of here though."

"She's ... fine?" said the Lost Warrior. "But—"

There was a triumphant yell behind them, and bodies were tossed sideways as Danny came back up for air. She was cut and bleeding from a dozen places, her hair wild, clumps having been torn loose. She raised a man's body above her, bringing him down into a backbreaker over her knee. She tossed him aside, her teeth pulled back in savage joy, then smashed a fist into a woman to her right. Carlisle watched as Danny put one foot against the leading knee of an opponent and landed an *enzuigiri*, using the man's knee as support as she brought her other foot through the air and into the back of his head. Bodies surged back over the top of her, and for a moment Danny was gone from view again, before Carlisle saw a flash of red curls as her friend broke free, holding two bodies above her in triumph. She was screaming with rage and joy at the same time.

Carlisle turned away. "Lady? She's fine!" She looked over the Lost Warrior's shoulder, seeing the horde drawing closer. "Move it. Fucking *move it!*"

They broke into a run, Ajay and Carlisle leading the charge back towards the Yukon. They heard a yell behind them, and Carlisle spared a glance to see one of the Lost Warrior's remaining group go down, men and woman on top of him, biting and chewing. She turned without breaking her momentum, firing a single shot into the fallen soldier, before turning back into a run towards the Yukon. "Danny! Clear a path! Danny!"

Whether Danny heard her or not didn't seem to make any difference. Danny was moving very fast now, kicks and punches landing with tremendous force against her opponents. One of her fists slammed into the forehead of a large man, caving his skull in. The back door of the Yukon was close, and Carlisle wrenched it open, pushing the Lost Warrior in beside Adalia. She saw the question on Adalia's face, ignored it as she slammed the door closed behind them. Ajay was already jumping over the hood, sliding across to land on the other side. He yanked the door open, slinging himself into the driver's seat, door closing behind him.

Carlisle looked around for the other soldiers of the Lost Warrior's group, but they were gone, lost to the horde. There was a brief lull, and Carlisle looked at the bodies scattered about her, then looked up at Danny. Danny's eyes were bright, yellow, feral. Carlisle took a cautious step forward. "Danny."

"*Yessss.*" Danny's voice was almost a growl, something in her jaw deformed, the word coming out wrong.

"I need to get her out of here," said Carlisle. There wasn't time, not to do this right. To get space, more distance between them. If Carlisle was going to do this, she wanted to do it from a mile or more away. She didn't have a mile. "I ... I need you to make a path."

Danny's nod was too vigorous, too eager. "*And a Path You Shall Have.*" There was weight behind the words. "*We Will Carve It Through Their Flesh.*"

Carlisle took a step back. "Uh, sure," she said. "You know what this means."

"*I MUST CHANGE.*" Danny didn't even look at the horde racing towards them, her eyes were fixed on Carlisle's weapon. Like it was the last glass of water on an Earth made of desert. "*Set me free.*"

"Yes," said Carlisle. She raised her sidearm, pointing it at Danny's heart. She tried to ignore just how eager, how *hungry*, Danny looked. *I'm so sorry. I'm so sorry.* Carlisle pulled the trigger.

With howl that cut to Carlisle's core, the beast was loose.

THIRTY-THREE

"I guess I wanted to circle back around," said Rex, "and make sure we're all on the same page."

"Old timer?" said John. "I know it's a lot to take in, especially if you're not used to change—"

"What the hell," said Rex, "is that supposed to mean?"

John blinked at him. "Well, you know," he said. "Baby Boomers, right? You guys can't set the time on a microwave oven."

"Right," said Val. "Twelve o'clock flashers."

Rex looked between the two of them. "Are you speaking English?"

"It's nothing personal," said John, showing some kind of brilliant smile that Rex just knew would make a woman swoon. He hated the man for it, just a little, if he was honest. "It's just every place I've seen that's been owned by a fossil has all the digital clocks set at double-oh, double-oh."

"A fossil?" Rex felt his face getting hot. *Relax, Rex. Relax. Boy just needs some of the silly knocked out of him.* "You think I'm a ... a fossil?"

"You prefer leatherface?" said John. "It sounds a bit Jack-the-Ripper, is all I'm saying, but we can go with it."

"John Miles," said Sky, "you *behave*." She placed a cool hand on Rex's shoulder, leaning in to kiss him gently on the cheek. "He's just feeling unmanned and has issues when he's not the center of the universe."

"I am," said John, "the center of the ... what do you mean, unmanned?"

"I mean," said Sky, "that this *fossil* managed to work with me to get Just James—" and here, she jerked a thumb over her shoulder at the kid, playing on that portable game gadget "—here, alive, in the middle of a war zone. Isn't that your job, hero?"

"Hey," said John, that brilliant smile coming back again, "I ain't no hero. I'm, what do you call it, I've got my own spin-off series."

"Like *Angel*," said Just James, not looking up.

"Like *Angel*," said John, nodding. "Exactly."

"What?" said Rex.

"From *Buffy*," said Just James, casting a wearied eye at Rex. "Don't you watch TV?"

"I watch TV," said Rex. "I don't watch kid's shows."

Sky pulled her hand from Rex's shoulder. "Are you ... what's wrong with *Buffy*?"

"What?" said Rex. *God damn, I am* definitely *too old for this shit.* "No. Hey. Wait. Let's try again," he said. He rubbed a hand over his face, as if he could reset the last minute's conversation. *Hell with it.* "What I was trying for, is to see if we're all ... if we've got a plan."

"No," said Val.

"No?" said Rex.

"No, *we* don't have a plan," said Val. "I — and by I, I mean, John and I — are going to find out what's going on."

"We are?" said John.

"And," said Val, looking Rex in the eye, "you are not going to come with us. Because you will die."

"Son," said Rex, "I'm pretty close to dead anyway, how the clock is running these days. I think you're overlooking one small issue."

"Okay," said Val, "I'll bite."

227

"That's just it," said Rex. "You won't."

"What?" Val blinked at him.

"You've lost your powers, son," said Rex. "You've got a cape made of Kryptonite. Unless I miss my count, Sky here killed more damn spiders than you did."

"It's not a competition," said John. "It's—"

"It's not a competition unless you're winning," said Rex. "Son, look, I know. I get it. You're used to the way things used to work. The thing is, this whole saving the world thing is a team sport."

"You ... you want to save the world?" said Val.

"What, you think you got exclusive rights to that?" said Rex. He scratched his head. "I've been saving people all my life. One burning building at a time. This?" He waved a hand at the window. "This is just a larger problem."

"Epic," said Just James, not looking up.

"What?" said Rex.

"We're at the boss fight," said Just James, putting his game console aside. "We've got to get all the equipment we've collected, hop on a horse, and go save the princess. But there's a boss, a big bad monster, and we've got to kill it."

Sky nudged the Ramset gun with a foot. "I don't know how much equipment we've collected."

"There is a boss," said John, nodding.

"Right," said Just James. "So, we get the party together, and we—"

"Whoa," said Rex. "What's this party?"

Just James looked surprised. "You. Val. John. Sky. Me."

"No," said Rex. "Not you."

"'What, you think you got exclusive rights to that?'" said Just James, in a fair approximation of Rex's West Coast accent. "This is my city. Of all of you, I figure I've got the most—" he shrugged, struggling for the word.

"Incentive," said Val.

"Incentive," said Just James.

"Investment," said John.

"That too," said Just James.

"Idiocy," said Sky. "I can do I-words too."

"Imbecile," said Rex. "I like this game."

Just James looked a little hurt. Then he brightened. "Seriously, though. What you've got to be wondering is what you might be able to do to stop me." He looked around the room at them. "One of you want to stay behind and babysit?" He pointed at the big screen attached to the wall, green spider ichor splashed across it. "It's not like we can grab a TV dinner and a movie."

"I hate kids," said John.

"Say," said Val. He was looking out the window.

"Yeah?" said Rex, turning to face him.

"It's got pretty quiet, hasn't it?" Rex watched as Val tilted his head, a curious movement more at home on a dog than a person. "Still a lot of smoke. Not a lot of screaming."

They all sat in silence for a moment. "Sure," said John. "It's quiet."

"Where do you suppose they've all gone?" said Val. He squinted out the window.

Rex pushed himself to his feet. *Damn these old bones.* He joined Val at the window. "You're right. Not a soul."

"Everyone's at a party," said John. No one laughed. "Tough crowd," he muttered.

Val held a hand up. "There."

Rex watched as a horde of people swarmed along the street underneath them. They were moving at a dead run, scrambling over the cars and other debris outside. He started to count, ten, twenty, thirty, then gave up when a huge clot of humanity rounded a corner and joined the stream of bodies. "Where you think they're going?"

"I think," said Val, "that my girlfriend has come back to town."

"Rock on," said John. "It's about damned time."

"How do you know this, son?" Rex searched Val's eyes.

Val looked down at his hands, then raised one — the tremble in his fingers obvious even to Rex's eyes — to touch his chest above his heart. "I feel it."

"She up for a fight like that?" Rex nodded out the window.

"More or less," said Val. "She is powered by a lithium awesome cell."

"I mean—" Rex caught himself. "Is she going to be okay?"

"It's a lot of dudes," said Just James.

"She'll be fine," said Val. "But this helps with our plan."

"What plan?" said Rex. "Hell. That's what I asked to start with."

"The plan," said Val, "is like this. One, we break into a jeweler's."

"Fucken-A," said John.

Val shot him a flat stare. "We find all the silver we can, and turn it into weapons."

"How?" said Rex. The way he saw it was, maybe Val had taken a hit in the head. He'd seen it before, men and women who'd taken the hard knock without realizing it. Gone down a line of thinking that put others in danger. Trick was, you wanted to make sure that this was … thought through. Rex shifted on his feet for a moment, then said, "I'll bite. How do you turn a silver necklace into a weapon?"

"You throw it," said Val. Give the guy credit but he didn't even pause. The way Rex saw it, that spoke of experience. Maybe crazy, but also maybe well-informed. "It hurts. Us. Things like us. A lot. Then, we go and kill the asshole in charge."

"How are we going to find him?" said Just James.

"Easy," said Val, pointing up the street from where the people were running. "We go to where all those people are coming from."

"I don't like this plan," said John.

"It's not much of a plan," said Sky. "There's not a lot to like."

"The good news is there's not a lot to *not* like," said Rex. He sighed. *One more fight before the end, Rex. Get your shit together.* "Let's do this."

CHAPTER
THIRTY-FOUR

Carlisle didn't look to see the change — *seen it before, move it,* move *it* — as she spun on her toes and dived over the hood of the Yukon. The denim of her jeans slipped over the metal surface, too fast for her to notice the cold of the metal. She landed on the other side of the machine from Danny, crouching low by the wheel arch. She held her sidearm with both hands in front of her, the weapon radiating its just-fired heat by her face. Carlisle shut her eyes, feeling the hammer of her heart — *God she'll hear it* — in her chest. She breathed in and out, trying to keep as quiet as possible.

It wouldn't help, but it helped to try. Before the end, as it were.

The creature roared, the sound loud enough to hurt, and Carlisle hunched forward. The movement was involuntary, it was baked into humans from when they'd crawled up from the primordial slime, discovering the hungry things with teeth. *Do* not *piss yourself, Carlisle. Keep it together.* The monster — not Danny anymore — would smell that, and the end would get here that much faster. Carlisle's lips were moving silently, and she didn't know if she was praying or crying or both. The crunch of massive feet against loose shale sounded to her right as the creature stalked around the front of the Yukon. Carlisle felt the machine rock as something massive and strong leaned against the hood, the machine creaking lower on its shocks. It *chuffed*, trying to find her scent, then let out a low growl.

So. Are you going down on your feet or your knees, Detective? She thought about it, turned the idea over in her mind. It wasn't whether she'd die that was the problem, so much as how she died. And not in some *budo* warrior's distorted view of honor, but for the kid. Because, like it or not, if the kid saw her Mom — hideous monster or not — kill Carlisle, well, you couldn't put that toothpaste back in the tube. No $400-an-hour therapy was going to weld that family back together.

Feet it is, then.

Carlisle wiped a shaky hand over her face, then pushed against the Yukon, rising to her feet. She turned to face the creature, her weapon held ready. God, it was a sight. Huge, muscled, with claws, and teeth. Drool hung in ropy strands from its jaws, jaws that were open to display those terrible, magnificent teeth. But it was the eyes — those sick, golden orbs — that made the breath catch in Carlisle's chest. She'd never been this close before.

Never will again, so make the most of it. Carlisle raised her weapon, prepared to fire. Her hand came up, whip quick, finger on the trigger, the squeeze already traveling from her brain to her hand.

The Eagle fired, her constant companion ever ready to stand strong against the darkness that hid in the hearts of men. Carlisle was happy that it was *this* gun she was using, not something begged or borrowed from the battlefield. She'd known this weapon since she'd paid good money for it back on the beat, something to keep under her pillow against the terrors that woke her every night. It had helped, the strong power kept within each casing a promise ready to be made. It hadn't let her down, hadn't jammed, hadn't ever stumbled in its purpose even when Carlisle might have.

Problem was, it was connected to *her*. The same weak girl who'd run away from *him*, and here she was thirty years later, and still too weak. And not just too weak.

She was too damn slow.

The creature shifted sideways as she fired, the round passing through the air where it had been. Carlisle kept firing, each round punching through empty air as the thing that had been Danny stepped past the path of each shot as if it was walking around gutter balls at a bowling alley. She kept firing right up until it slapped her hand to the side with a blow that felt like it broke the bones in her hand, the gun tumbling from numbed fingers. It reached out a clawed hand, snatching her up from the ground. Carlisle felt its fingers around her middle, the grip stronger than steel, felt the crushing force and the pain that pushed air from her lungs that wanted to come out as a scream.

It's just pain. You're used to pain.

She clenched her teeth against it, showing her own savage grin to the creature. It lifted her up in front of its face, and Carlisle pulled back a fist — *out on your feet, Carlisle* — to punch it. It shook her like a doll, and she felt something *twinge* in her spine. *That* made her scream.

The thing paused, looking down at her, then looked around it at the road. She could almost see the wheels turning in its head, counting the bodies, then looking at the city of Chicago.

"Yes," said Carlisle, the sound stretched to a whisper around her bruised body. "Valentine."

But it wasn't looking at Chicago. It was looking at the rising tide of people coming up the road towards them from the city. Its gaze passed through the shattered windscreen of the Yukon, to the wide-eyed passengers within. Looking at one in particular, a girl with pleading eyes. *Don't look Adalia, don't look honey.* Carlisle didn't want Adalia to see the end. Time seemed to stretch, like it was pliable, like it was something made of rubber rather than wheels. Then the creature gave Carlisle a yellowed look before tossing her to the ground with a *huff, huff* sound. Carlisle felt her head knock against the side of the Yukon, and she lay in a daze. Too shocked to move.

Too shocked to realize she was alive.

The creature slammed its forearms into the tarmac, cracks appearing in the road's surface, and it roared its defiance and challenge at the approaching horde. It looked back at Carlisle, then extended one clawed arm towards the city laid ahead of them, behind a clotted mass of humanity. Then it turned away from her and charged into the mob, claws and teeth unleashing red rain.

CARLISLE DIDN'T KNOW how long she'd lain there. It felt like hours, but it must have been no more than a minute. Her heart was still hammering in her chest — *I'm alive! I'm alive I'm alive I'm alive I'm alive* — as she watched the thing that used to be Danny kill, and kill, and kill.

Mowing. It's like watching a mower.

She heard the soft click of a door, the crunch of a foot on gravel. Carlisle looked up into a woman's face, lined with old worry, set fresh today. "You okay, soldier?"

Carlisle coughed, winced, tried to stand up, and fell back. She blinked against the hot spikes of pain in her chest, breathing short and shallow. "I'm fine."

The woman — *Lost Warrior* — snorted. "I guess it was a rookie question. What I'm really asking is, can you drive?" She held a hand out to Carlisle, ridges of callous on the palm. Carlisle looked at it for a second, then reached up. The woman's grip was cool and firm, confident in all the ways that a girl scared of her own father wouldn't be. Gentle, too, as she pulled Carlisle to her feet, her other hand coming around to grasp Carlisle's elbow, holding her up against the dizziness that hit her as soon as she was standing.

"Give me a moment," said Carlisle, the words coming out softer than she'd hoped. Something inside was broken, crushed, but it was only pain. She could deal with it later. She coughed, covering her mouth, and the back of her hand came away wet with blood.

The other woman's eyes softened. Or was Carlisle imagining that? It was hard to tell, with all this damn pain rattling around inside her chest. Carlisle held up a hand. "Really. I'm fine."

"Which unit were you with?" The other woman tugged the bottom of her shirt, straightening her fatigues.

"Unit?" Carlisle let a lopsided smile onto her face. "Ma'am? I've never been in a war. I'm not the enlisting type."

"Maybe not," said the other woman, after a moment's consideration of Carlisle's face. She held her hand out again. "Major Jessica Pearce. Formerly attached to the National Guard."

"Huh," said Carlisle. She shook the other woman's hand, surprised at the hope she felt. Maybe it was having another soldier on the team. Maybe it was because Jessica Pearce was another woman. Maybe it was because she was *alive*. "Melissa Carlisle. Formerly *Detective* Melissa Carlisle."

"Cop?" Pearce let her hand go.

"Cop," said Carlisle, after a long pause. *Because that's what you are, and it's taken you this long to realize it.* "Pearce? Get in the car."

"You're like no cop I've ever seen." Carlisle felt considered, measured, weighed. A small smile held a moment at Pearce's lips. "Car it is. Okay, *soldier*."

Carlisle put her hands behind her back, stretching — *oh, girl, take it slow* — then stood up strong and true, shoving the pain to a corner of her mind. She tugged at her own jacket, straightening it like a uniform. Her hand found its way to the driver's door of the Yukon, held the handle briefly, and then she let it drop.

You can't forget your old friends, Carlisle.

She walked around the side of the Yukon, seeing it — the soft glint of familiar metal, grip up, made to be held by her hand — in among the bodies strewn around. She picked up the Eagle, feeling its familiar weight — *old partner* — and hugged it to her chest, before

235

stowing it in the holster at her back. She walked to the back of the Yukon, pulling open the door to find her bag.

It was there, crumpled and old, just like her. Inside, worn clothes, a book — *The Old Man and the Sea* — on top of a bag containing her toiletries. She'd never read it, never enough time, but Danny had said she should. Carlisle tapped the cover of the book, then pushed it aside, reaching down into the bottom of the bag, her hand feeling the touch of cotton, leather, and denim as she felt through the contents. *There.* Her fingers touched metal, cool and heavy.

She pulled them out one by one, metal magazines to feed the Eagle. Painted by a nervous hand months ago, color coded, then hidden. Red magazines, full of silver promise.

Carlisle slammed the back of the Yukon closed, walking to the front of the car. A stray zombie ran at her, and she shot it, the motion habituated. The Eagle ran dry, and she flicked the empty magazine away. She slid one of the new red magazines into the grip of the weapon, re-holstered it, then yanked the driver's door open.

The machine roared to life, eager to be away. Carlisle looked to Ajay, sitting beside her, then her eyes found Adalia's in the rear view mirror. "You okay, kid?"

"No," said Adalia. The kid looked at Pearce, beside her, then back to Carlisle. Her eyes seemed hollow. "Yes."

Carlisle slipped the Yukon into gear, then dropped the hammer. Wheels scrabbled and the machine surged forward, the big engine wanting to be away.

"Where are we going?" said Pearce.

"Chicago," said Carlisle.

"After that thing?" Pearce leaned back in her seat. "You trust it?"

Carlisle laughed, then winced with the pain, gripping the wheel tighter. "Yes."

"Why?"

"Because," said Carlisle. "She's in love."

Ajay looked at her, then laid a cautious hand on her arm. She felt a feeling like butterflies, which was unexpected given the circumstances. "You're beginning to learn what it means to be the Shield," he said.

Carlisle slowed the machine as they started to hit the wake of Danny's passage, bodies falling under the Yukon's wheels. "I've only got one challenge," she said. She had to raise her voice over the rush of air through the shattered windscreen.

"What's that?" Pearce was all business, her voice steady even with the noise around them. The woman was used to commanding, yet was sitting this one out. *Why?*

"Keeping up," said Carlisle. The creature was ahead of them, driven by rage down the freeway towards Chicago. Danny was loping ahead on back legs, forelimbs swinging like rams as she battered their way clear ahead.

Towards Valentine.

THIRTY-FIVE

"This is why," Talin said, "I did not kill you before."

Assembled in front of him, some shivering in the cold of the room, were his best lieutenants. They stood beside him as he'd clawed his way up from poverty and across the world to stand here, in the city of the two rivers. They'd seen everything with him, and bore witness to his strength.

They had also seen his weakness.

Prey.

Talin clenched his teeth. *Not now.* He pushed the Night back and down, but it struggled against him, straining against the bonds that held it. So strong! Stronger than he'd ever hoped, this power. There was plenty there to do what was ... needed.

"You will have seen my armies cleansing warriors from the outskirts of our city," he said, his voice husky. "They couldn't stand against the Night. But now, another comes — another, like me." He laughed. "And yet so unlike me. She is weak with kindness, hindered by the need to protect. Her Night is confused, and that will be her undoing. She broke her own Shield."

Talin walked on legs that felt new and strong to stand before

Lyron. He looked the man in the eye, seeing the fear there. *Good. Fear is good.* He didn't want blind obedience, not from these. He needed his own warriors, warriors with thought, who would not toss themselves like waves to break upon the rocks of another's Night. He would reforge them into something stronger. Something better.

Something more like Talin himself. He let a hungry smile grow on his face. "Lyron. It is time. Do you choose to become all you were meant to be?"

Lyron looked him in the eye, the fear still there, but something else — hunger, desire for power. *Good.* "My lord. Yes."

Talin took the quick steps necessary to get to the table, equipment nestled there for just this moment. He had prepared five sets of equipment for five perfect soldiers. He let his hands rest, as if in a gentle caress, against the first vial of blood. A mixture of snake, ox, and — harder to get than he'd expected — bear. A salting of sulfur had gone in alongside ash. All ingredients to drive the change he needed. He picked up a knife made from bone, a single long sliver of white, almost transparent along its edge. It had been rendered from the leg of a horse; it felt light in his hands. Lifting his other hand from the vial, he picked up the pack of playing cards stolen from a high roller at the peak of his run. *Las Vegas*, the city conjured from the sands of the desert and the lost dreams of the hopeful, was another city imbued with power. They were ripe for the harvest, if you knew how to look.

He tossed the cards behind him, letting them fall where they would. He listened for the plastic flutter as they tumbled through the air, the sound almost like rain as they hit the cold stone of the floor. He snared the first vial of blood, then turned around to face his lieutenants, noting that all the cards had landed face down. He pointed with the tip of the knife at Lyron. The other man swallowed, then his face hardened. As if he was getting ready to die—

Why does he fear what is to come? Pack should not fear pack.

It is because, said Talin to the thing inside, he will die. Lyron was pulling his jacket off, letting it fall behind him. His sweater, then

239

shirt, joined the jacket, forming a small pile of clothing on the ground. Talin still held the knife out point first at Lyron, his arm never wavering.

We must not hurt pack.

Such strength! He almost dropped the knife, a tremor running through his arm. Talin gritted his teeth against it. He had fought with the witch Raeni and bested her. He would best this thing of Night as well. *We are making him better than he is. We are shaping him into something stronger.*

The wind does not die to become stronger. The wind grows as it fights against the land. This is how strength is made.

Talin's eyes widened a fraction. It had never spoken to him like this before. Normally it was snatches of sound, bits and pieces of nonsense spoken like a drooling shaman or an idiot child. But this, it was almost making sense. And he didn't have time for it. *You will do as I say. You are mine.*

There was no response this time, but Talin felt something watching him, something immense. Something terrible. *Good.* He needed all the terrible things of this world to do what he wanted to do, to be what he wanted to become. His arm was once again firm, the point of the bone knife leveled at Lyron. He held out the vial in his other hand.

Lyron stepped forward until the tip of the bone knife touched his sternum. He reached forward, taking the flask from Talin. "It will be done." He opened his mouth, lifting the flask, and drank. The man's throat worked, his Adam's apple bobbing as he swallowed. He lowered the flask, then tossed it aside. It landed with the crack of breaking glass. Lyron looked at him. "I have—"

Talin thrust the knife forward, the bone entering Lyron's chest. He pushed it until it was buried up to the leather-wrapped hilt, then gave it a savage twist. The blade ripped and tore inside Lyron, and the handle snapped from the blade, leaving the bone embedded inside the man. Lyron tried to scream, but only blood came from his mouth in a savage wet gush. It splattered against Talin, and he reveled in the hot wetness of it.

"Choose," said Talin, gesturing at the cards on the ground. "Choose, Lyron, and Become."

Lyron stumbled to his knees, the strength leaving him; Talin could feel *Baron Samdi* draw near. Lyron's face had turned ashen, his lips blue, as he scrabbled against the ground for a playing card. He managed to grip the edges of one briefly before it snapped away from him, sticky red fingerprints marring the back of it. Talin watched as Lyron cast about him for another card, his movements becoming weaker still. The man toppled to land face forward on the ground, his breath a gurgle.

We can save him.

We *are* saving him, thought Talin.

You can make him one with us.

Talin pushed back against the Night clamoring to be set free. *Be still.* He watched as Lyron's fingers found another card, the strength almost gone from the man. His fingernails scratched at the edge of the card, the lip of it leaving the ground before snapping back down. The man's eyes were unfocused now, *Samdi's* shadow standing tall and patient behind him. Talin crouched down, leaning his head forward until his lips were a hands' breadth from Lyron's ear. "Lyron," he said, his voice low. "Lyron, you must choose a card. There is no going back. You can either choose a card, my friend, and join my side, or you can take the long walk to the Cliffs. The Baron is *here*, Lyron. He is *here* and he is reaching for *you*."

Whether his words had an effect, or it was a last animal reflex, Lyron's fingers managed to peel the card away from the floor. It flicked up, skipping along its edge as it skittered and danced away. Lyron's last breath left his body in a rattle, as the card fell — face up — against the ground.

The Joker.

Talin reached out a hand, clapping Lyron's body on the shoulder. His other lieutenants were watching in silence and fear. Some believed, some did not. It didn't matter whether you believed in the lion; the lion was still hungry. "Rise, Lyron."

The body shook under his hand, and Talin released the man's shoulder, standing upright. "Rise, Lyron."

Lyron's frame convulsed, and the body got an arm underneath, pushing itself away from the stone. Red-rimmed eyes looked at Talin, then moved with predatory intent to the other four of Talin's lieutenants. Talin clapped his hands, and those eyes snapped back towards him. "*Rise*, Lyron."

And Lyron did, moving with slow, deliberate movements. A knee came up underneath him, and he levered himself upright. His body unfurled like a fern, coming upright to stand tall and strong before Talin. Talin gave the man a rare smile. "My friend. Today you are no longer Lyron. I take that name from you." He stepped towards the upright card of the Joker, picking it up from the ground. He turned back towards the man who had been called by his family, his friends, and even his enemies as Lyron, and held the card out. "In return, I give you another. Am I not generous?"

Was-Lyron reached out a hand, taking the card. Those red-rimmed eyes looked at the smiling face of the Joker before looking back at Talin. "What will I be called?"

"You will be called many things," said Talin. "But you will have only one name. The name I give you is Choler."

"Choler," said Choler. He turned back towards Talin's other lieu-tenants, as if the bone buried in his chest bothered him not at all. "And these?"

"Brothers and sisters yet to be born," said Talin.

"Come, then" said Choler. He gestured an impatient hand at the others, blood still trickling from the hole in his chest. "We have little time."

It didn't take long for them all to be born. Within the hour, Talin had five perfect soldiers, and he let them run free.

CHAPTER
THIRTY-SIX

The boy was watching the Lost Soldier — *Jessica*. She was sitting next to Adalia on the big back seat of the Yukon as it followed in the wake of ... of...

"It's best not to think about it," said the boy, turning dark lashes her way. "It's not your job to help her."

She's my mother. Adalia's fingers skipped over the face of her phone, the text coming up in smaller letters than it deserved. Adalia wanted a big font, lots of red. She settled for an *emoji* of an angry face.

"That's why it's not your job," said the boy, turning back to look at Jessica. "It's their job to help us."

Adalia tapped her phone against her hand. She watched the boy stare at the Lost Soldier, then keyed on her phone. *Do you know her?*

"Yes," said the boy. "And she knows me."

It was funny how they called Carlisle the Shield, and Jessica was the Lost Soldier. Carlisle, it made sense, even Adalia could see it. Being the Shield came out of every part of her, hammered bright and strong. But Jessica ... there *was* something lost about her, but Adalia couldn't see the details. Like they were blurry. *Why is she called the Lost Soldier? What war did she lose?*

The boy laughed. "As far as I know, she's never lost a war." He cocked his ear to one side, sitting in the space between the front seats — Adalia blinked and tried not to look too close — as if he was listening. "No. Never lost a war. Well, until *that* happened." He pointed out the back of the Yukon, the road stretching out behind them to a point where a bunch of soldiers and people were lying, dead under the winter sun.

The phone spun between Adalia's fingers, the screen glittering in the gloom of the cabin. *I don't think she lost. I think she's won everything.*

The boy looked at her like she was crazy. "Did you get hit in the head back there? No, that can't be it, you didn't get out of the car. She — *we* got creamed. Until, well, until your mom went all Wrecking Ball."

Adalia smiled at that. *I don't think that's how you use 'Wrecking Ball.'*

"Whatever," said the boy. "My point is, we were all going to die." He paused, then hugged his knees close. "Sorry. You. You were all going to die."

You can be hurt, typed Adalia. *I've seen it.*

"I made a good comeback," said the boy. A frown crossed his perfect, porcelain face. "But you're right. I didn't think … I didn't know the Night could do that. I don't know all the rules."

She won everything, typed Adalia, *because we're here. You're here.*

"Seems a bad trade," said the boy. "The lives of thousands of people for us."

I wish you could have met Val. Adalia held the phone close so the boy couldn't see before she'd finished typing, her fingers moving in furious rhythm across the screen. *He would have said something like how we've got to save the world. I guess if I think about how you talk about the Universe, like it's a thing that's alive, maybe this Universe needs the world saved. Maybe it thinks it's not a bad trade at all.* She shivered as she let him see the screen.

"You've got to wonder," said the boy. "I mean, it sounds right. Sounds like something it would do. But how does it decide who gets to do the saving and who gets to do the dying?"

I don't think it does. I think we do. Adalia shifted in her seat.

"Hang on," said the boy. "Not *you*. You're a ... kid."

So are you. I don't think it matters how old we are.

"I'm not ... I'm not a kid," said the boy.

I know. I think I can see it now. Adalia looked at the boy, past the long lashes, held his gaze. *Why are you watching her?*

"Oh," said the boy. "I keep hoping she'll see *me*."

I can help with that. Adalia looked at him again. *Tell me your name.*

"I can't," he said, his voice low. "You know I can't."

Then I'll find it out the hard way. Adalia flicked the screen of her phone off, turning to Jessica. "Excuse me."

"What are you doing?" said the boy.

Jessica turned her face from the window to look at Adalia. Her eyes darted towards the front of the cabin — towards Carlisle — before coming to rest on Adalia. Her face creased into that fabricated smile some adults got when they were trying to talk to a kid. Like they were trying to talk to a kid and didn't know how. "Hello, Adalia."

"Hey," said Adalia. "I know this is going to come out all weird and you're not going to understand why I'm asking this, but when did you lose him?"

Jessica's face closed down like a vault of stone, and she moved back in her seat a fraction. Adalia didn't know much about the military or the people who were in charge down there, but she figured that was a sign.

"Kid," said Carlisle. "Kid, what are you doing?"

"She is doing what must be done," said Ajay, resting his hand on Carlisle's arm. "Let it be."

"I don't think so," said Carlisle. "I—"

245

"Because my Mom's out there," said Adalia, "and so is Val, and John. And we need to go save them. But we can't do that until we're ... we can't do that alone. The Universe, and I don't really understand this, okay, but the Universe needs the world saved. So I need you to tell me when you lost him."

Nobody spoke for a long moment, then Jessica licked her lips. "I don't know what you mean."

"The other thing," said Adalia, talking faster before she could lose her nerve, "that is going to sound super weird is that I can hear it when you're not telling me the truth. It's like a kind of bell."

"Okay," said Jessica. She sat very straight in her uniform, the material looking out of place in the back of the Yukon, but perfectly suited to *her*. "Okay. I don't want to tell you about it."

Adalia thought about that. "I know I'm about his age when you lost him," she said. "I've figured that much out, but I ... we're going to need his help."

Jessica leaned forward, her voice harsh. "Who told you? How did you find out about this?"

"Major," said Ajay, his hand once again touching Carlisle's arm, "you need to know that she is under the care of a Shield. I'd be ... I'd encourage you to be cautious."

Jessica laughed, a harsh sound with no humor in it. "I don't take orders from you."

"Not orders," said Adalia. "We don't give each other orders." She looked over at the boy, then back to Jessica. "What's his name?"

"Please don't do this," said the boy. "Please don't."

"I want to get out," said Jessica. "Detective, could you stop the vehicle?"

"Can't you see it hurts her?" said the boy.

"Jessica," said Adalia, leaning close. "Jessica, I can help you carry it. You don't have to hold it by yourself."

"*Stop*," said the boy, his eyes wide. He held a hand to his chest, over his heart. "I can ... it hurts so much."

"I know it hurts," said Adalia, leaning closer. Jessica was trying to scrunch away from her in the seat, looking at Adalia like she was a cobra. Adalia reached out a hand, cautious at first.

"Don't touch me," said Jessica. "Don't—"

Adalia held Jessica's hand in the back seat of the Yukon and felt the pure touch of the Universe at last.

~

"Mommy!" A tiny body crashed into hers, arms grabbing her around her legs.

"Hello, what's this?" she said. "I was expecting my family, but instead I see a limpet. Limpet, what have you done with my son?"

The limpet gripped tighter. It spoke, voice muffled.

"I see," she said, lowering her duffel to the ground, letting her hand stray to the top of Gabriel's head, his hair silky under her fingers. Her eyes caught those of her husband, a smile passing between them. It'd been longer this time, the tour harder now they had the little one they'd worked for. There had been the rounds of careful lovemaking after glasses of wine, Bobby's gentle hands and soft words leading into nights of passion. She'd taken those words with her in her heart whenever she'd had to leave, but they hadn't helped as much as the IVF.

They'd tried for so long. So very long. And now Gabriel was here and wonderful and everything they'd wanted, and yet — she felt like the stranger. She felt like she didn't belong. She'd hurried away on another tour straight away, because ... well.

She felt like this boy wasn't her son.

Still, they'd said that this could happen. She had to be patient. She was okay with that — they had time.

The spring air was warm, and Bobby gave the screen door a shake. There was something in his eyes, a yearning, and she heard it in his voice when he spoke. "C'mon babe. It's steaks tonight. I know they don't feed you right when you're in Romania." It wasn't his cooking she craved — although that was good — but the touch of his hand. The feel of his body, next to hers. The smell of him. His heart, by her heart.

Jessica took a step forward, limpet — Gabriel — still attached. He'd stepped on one of her boots, and she swung that leg forward, causing a squeal of delight. She could feel the tension starting to release from her shoulders as she walked up the path to the familiar shingle-walled home they shared. There was a bike on the lawn, a soccer ball next to it. She felt herself grinning like a fool and didn't care.

Every time she left, she wasn't sure how she'd feel when she got home. Would they remember her? Would she remember them? As she walked past Bobby, the smell of him — the man she loved — hit her hard and she almost stopped. This is why it was worthwhile. Going away, that's what she wanted to keep her country safe. Coming home, that's what she needed to keep her soul safe.

THE DINNER HAD BEEN EXCELLENT. Bobby was a satisfactory cook, didn't pretend otherwise, but he seemed to pour his heart into it. There wasn't any specialist that had come out of the Food Service Training School who knew more about how her heart worked. The kitchen where they ate had that new linoleum on the floor — Bobby had laid that down while she was away, one of his "continuous improvement projects" that kept the house from looking old. She had thought it would be brighter, but maybe that was just the way he'd talked about it. The photos never told the story.

It was their home. They didn't live on base, because they'd both decided that wasn't where they wanted to raise their son. She fought, so he wouldn't have to. That was the plan.

Gabriel had started school while she'd been away, that gentle child she'd left still there but now bursting with curious energy. "Mom! Do you know that our sun is a star? It's really really big, bigger than all the planets even if you mushed them together."

She'd laughed. "Is that so?"

"Did you know," he said, eyes wide, "that it will blow up?"

Jessica had knelt down in mock concern. "I hadn't heard. Should I be worried?"

"No, Mom. It won't happen for years." And with that, he'd started to head back outside, to a new bike, and a new ball. She wanted to let him go play. She wanted him to stay here with her.

"Honey," she said, reaching after Gabriel. *"Time for your bath."*

He'd nodded at her. Bath time was play time, an easy trade for bike or ball. She drew the bath, warm water filling a tub that was white and clean, simple, not a line of military precision in its design. No metal shower heads, no lines of mirrors. Joy, and laughter, and — of course — bubbles. She sat at the edge of the bath while Gabriel played, building a tower of those bubbles with his hands. He had a plastic toy — it looked like the kind of thing you'd get from a Happy Meal — and he kept trying to balance it on top of the bubbles. Gravity won, and it kept falling back. Any excuse for more bubbles. More water, too — it was everywhere. She'd been deployed in places it had rained for six months at a time and she'd never got this wet. Her hair was matted to her head, the shirt she'd pulled on soaked through.

Maybe this was what it felt like to have a son. Maybe.

When Gabriel got out of the bath, she wrestled him mostly dry with a towel before he ran — shrieking with joy — back into the rest of the house.

There was a bedtime story, and the soft scent of his hair as he fell into a drowsy sleep. She left his door open a crack, the light in the hall on, and found Bobby's arms waiting for her. They talked, and kissed, and talked more, until the night turned black around them as they fell into rediscovering each other. He found the new scar on her arm where she'd been cut during a training exercise. She kissed his fingers away, finding the callouses under his fingertips from his work on the house. He felt the kinks in her back, rubbing the stress away. His touches became more insistent, urgent, their kisses fierce with remembered joy.

Later: contentment.

She drifted off to sleep knowing she had a five-year-old son, and next time she was back, she'd promised she'd get to know him better. They had time. All the time in the world.

Didn't they?

~

JESSICA FACED THE LAPTOP, the small faces of her husband and son staring back at her, half a world away. Thank God for Skype. "I wish I was with you guys." Gabriel was big now, the quiet curiosity of childhood about to be pushed aside by the brash, gangling advent of becoming a teenager. His dark eyes and dark lashes would turn heads and when he worked that out ... but not yet.

Not yet. Ten was too soon to be breaking hearts.

Ten was too late to get to know him.

"I got a new bike," Gabriel was saying. "Dad said it was from him, but I knew it was from Santa."

Bobby laughed, the sound smaller than it felt in her heart. "There's something wrong with our kid. He still believes in Santa Claus, and the Tooth Fairy."

Gabriel shrugged, the motion blurred by a hiss of data corruption, the link to Qatar functional but civilian comms shuffled around military needs. "They keep leaving me stuff. They must be real."

"That's your Dad," said Jessica, her fingers touching the screen's edge. Wanting to touch them. Wanting to know them. "He's always trying to take the credit. Why, he told me he did the floor in the bathroom himself."

"I helped!" said Gabriel.

"You drank all the Coke," said Bobby.

"That's helping," said Gabriel. The smile stayed on his face as he looked closer at the camera. "Where are you today, Mom?"

She couldn't say, of course. Couldn't even take a holiday photo for fear that something would get onto Facebook, and some Al-Quaeda asshole would use a message to her son as a weapon against the men to the left of her, and the women to the right. The people in her command. They'd said this was her last deployment. Said this was the last time she'd be up to her armpits in sand. She pushed a tired hand through close-cropped hair, then said. "Somewhere with a lot of sun."

"Oh!" said Gabriel. "Bring back a tan."

Jessica smiled at the screen. There'd be no trouble with that. Her shoul-

ders were a little burnt from the impromptu game of basketball they'd played earlier, something to work the stress out before the action started. Too much sun and laughter, but it was okay. Shaved a little off the divide she wanted to maintain between her command and her soldiers, but everyone was on edge.

No one knew why the fuck they were in Qatar.

No one would tell her why she was here, instead of back home for Christmas. Back with her family. That had been the deal — finish the last one, get a decent holiday at home. But then they'd asked her how important her career was. Said that being a woman in a man's job was hard enough, said that she'd best step up to the plate if she wanted to win.

They hadn't said that, of course. But she'd heard it in their every word.

Someone cleared their throat behind her. She turned, taking in Gibson and that damn tablet that always brought more trouble. "Just a minute."

"Ma'am." Gibson stood still as a post.

Jessica sighed. The man was efficient, but had the EQ of a stone. She turned back to the little screen. "I've got to go."

"We miss you," said Bobby.

"Will you be here next Christmas?" said Gabriel. "I'd like to give you a present instead of mailing it."

"Yes, honey," she said. It wouldn't be long before Gabriel didn't believe in Santa. It wouldn't be long before he stopped wanting to be with her. It wouldn't be long before she lost her chance to get to know her son. "I promise." Next Christmas, or she was out.

∽

THE PLANE SHOOK and trembled around her, the big transport's turbines churning their way back Stateside. Jessica looked at the empty bay around her. Nothing but a crate swaddled in cargo webbing, empty benches around the edges of the plane, the bay big and cold and harsh.

She felt inside her for something, found only an empty sort of desperation. She nudged her duffel with a boot, her eyes moving towards the front.

She wanted to stalk across the metal floor, pound on the door to the cabin, demand with all the privilege of rank that they get there faster.

Make the plane get to where her son, not quite fifteen, was dying.

The crew were doing it anyway. The plane pushed hard through the air, then engines running hard. They knew why she wanted to get home. It wasn't their fault the only bird on the ground was a hauler, built for capacity, not comfort — or speed. There would be a change of aircraft soon, something faster to get her Stateside before it was too late.

But it was already too late. She knew it in her heart. There was a price for broken promises, and her son was paying it.

IT DIDN'T MATTER. *None of it. The doctor was looking up at her face. "Do you understand what I've said, Mrs. Pearce?"*

She understood, all right. She was looking at a closed door to an OR. Civilian, not military, but it still had the same damn smell. Blood, under the disinfectant, she knew that smell as the price for sending men and women to die. There wasn't the usual sound though — the machines that monitored life were silent, the bustle and pace of surgeons at work was missing.

She wanted to go in there, scream at them to turn the machines back on. To move like they had a purpose. She turned to the doctor. "No."

"We tried as hard as we—"

"No," said Jessica. "You didn't. It was a car crash, wasn't it?"

"There was a ... there was a truck," said the doctor. He was a small man with glasses that framed eyes tired beyond measure.

"I've seen men hit by artillery fire put back together, Doctor," she said. "You're telling me a road accident can't be fixed?"

The doctor looked at her for a few moments, then pushed his glasses up the bridge of his nose. "Is there someone we can call?"

She thought of Bobby, lying cold and dead on a table. Her son, beside him. Their bodies a ruin, but their hearts broken long ago by a wife and a mother who'd never been home. So they'd left home too, Gabriel riding another new bike that Santa had brought while Bobby pedaled beside him. Building memories without her.

That bike was another one she'd bought to make the guilt go away. She'd paid with money earned by her service. By being away from them.

"Can you call God?" Jessica took a step towards the man, then clenched her teeth. It wasn't his fault. It wasn't his fault. It wasn't his fault. She relaxed the hands that had balled into fists, straightened her uniform. Her eyes were dry, her face was hard. "Can you?"

The doctor licked his lips. "No."

"Then what good are you?" She turned on her heel, boots taking her away from that terrible room of death. She saved her tears, feeling something clench inside her chest. Something that wouldn't let go, that held the pain locked away inside.

What a way to learn that — after all these years — she really did love her son.

～

"OH," said Adalia. She could feel the tears wet on her face. "Oh." She let go of Jessica's hands.

"How—" Jessica recoiled from her. "What—"

"What's going on?" said Carlisle. "This isn't a super good time, if I'm being honest."

"You have shared a part of your story," said Ajay. "You have shared the part about how you got here."

"You ... you saw that?" said Adalia.

"No," said Ajay. "I saw your face. Your eyes, mistress."

"Someone," said Carlisle, "needs to say what the fuck is going on. I'm driving a truck in the wake of a werewolf to a city full of zombies, okay, and this is about as real as shit gets."

"I wish you hadn't done that," said the boy. His eyes shone, bright with remembered tears.

Adalia looked at Jessica's eyes, saw the hardness there. It completely covered the pain, you'd never know unless ... you knew.

253

She reached out her hand again, but stopped as Jessica tried to pull further away. It would have been comical, this Warrior afraid of a girl in the back seat of a Yukon, except for what she'd seen. Where she'd been. What she was.

Letting her hand fall to her lap, Adalia looked to the front. "It's okay, Melissa. I did something I shouldn't have."

"Right," said Carlisle. After a moment, she said, "And what was that?"

"I don't know," said Adalia.

"I do," said Gabriel, his voice sad beyond measure.

CHAPTER
THIRTY-SEVEN

"We're running low on beer," said John. Val had watched him staring into the refrigerator for a good long minute. "We need to do a beer run."

"How about food?" Rex was standing by the window, staring into the street.

"We've got food," said John. "I put it on the counter."

"You put," said Rex, "peanut butter and coconut water on the counter."

"Right," said John. "Food."

"That shit," said Val, "and don't take this personally because I love you like a brother, but that shit isn't food. Not for normal people."

"Hey," said Sky. "I start the day with a tablespoon of peanut butter and a glass of coconut water."

"New diet?" said Val.

"You're a freak," said Just James. He held up his hands in defense at Sky's glacier stare. "Breakfast is *Frosted Flakes*."

"Huh," said Val. "That's weird." He was thinking about another young person he knew who liked *Frosted Flakes*. "Tiger?"

"Tiger," said Just James. "Also, there's a lot of sugar in it."

"I would eat a bowl of *Frosted Flakes*," said Rex, turning back to the window. "I think we should get some food."

"Right," said John. "I'm on it."

"No," said Sky.

"What?" said John.

"When you go shopping, you come back with beer and fitness magazines. The man said *food*."

"Two things," said John. "First, beer is a food. Second, I'm not going shopping. I'm going *looting*." He turned on the Miles Megawatt Smile. "I've never been looting before. Expanding my horizons. Seriously, it's on my bucket list."

A tired old sigh came from Rex. "I'll go. At least it'll get done."

"Hell with you, old man," said John. "You trying to steal stuff from my bucket list? How often am I going to get a legitimate, state-sponsored opportunity to loot?"

"I ... I don't think the state is sponsoring this," said Rex. "In fact..." His voice trailed off.

"What?" said Val. He could feel the ache in his bones, something inside *not right*. That damn virus was going to be the death of him.

"Cavalry," said Rex, "or damnation."

Val could hear it now, the low thud of rotors slicing the air. He moved to the window, seeing the black shapes of helicopters in the air. One scudded low enough to make out the numbers on the tail, a man perched by a chain gun at the open door. "Fuck me."

"It could be an evacuation," said Sky. "Couldn't it?"

"It could be that they want to drop boxes of money on us too," said Just James.

"Kid, you ain't gonna live to be 20," said Sky.

"At least he'll die pretty," said Val. "I don't think it changes anything."

"How you figure?" said John.

"Because he's young. Stands to reason if he dies he'll be pretty."

Val shrugged. "You're right though, I'm not a good judge. Sky? Is he going to die pretty?"

"Could be," said Sky, giving Just James a critical look, "if some girl doesn't mark up his face."

"No," said John, "I mean, how you figure it doesn't change anything?"

"Right," said Val. "Well, whether we go outside for food, or to be rescued, we need to go outside. I think if we call it a 'food' mission—"

"Looting," said John.

"If we're looting," said Val, "we'll probably get shot."

"Christ, man," said John. "We're not wearing T-shirts that say, 'Team Looter.' We're going to be subtle."

"You are probably the least subtle person I've ever met," said Rex.

"Thanks," said John.

"Wasn't a compliment," said Rex.

"So we're out on our food mission," said Val. "And if we see these guys setting down, lifting off survivors, setting up aid tents, and generally doing a Mother Teresa thing, we're copacetic."

"Copawhat?" said Just James.

"And if we see them shooting everyone," said Val, "then I have another plan."

"We're all going to die," said Just James.

"Thinking the same thing," said Rex. "Can you spell it out, son?" He looked over at Val. "It's not like I don't trust you, but last time you saved my life, by your own account, you were juiced up on magic fairy dust. Today, you're dying of a killer virus."

"I managed to get myself out of bed and to work every day before I was a werewolf," said Val. "I figure I still have some skills."

"Did any of those skills involve military training?" Rex stared hard at him.

"My boss was an asshole," said Val.

"That's a close second, I'll agree," said Rex.

"I'm going," said Val, "to *negotiate*."

VAL HEFTED RAPH — a genuine Frank Thomas bat. Kind of a big deal. Super weird thing though, right, was up until a couple of weeks ago, Val couldn't have told you who Frank Thomas was. Now? All kinds of knowledge had filtered into his head, almost as if touching the smooth knob at the end had let him know that The Big Hurt had played for the White Sox. Man had been born in Georgia. Five-time All-Star. Hell, he'd helped the White Sox to their first World Series title in eighty-eight years. Eighty-eight *years*. That was something to be proud of, make no mistake, but the odd thing was that a month back Val hadn't known whether Frank Thomas was a first baseman or a plumber.

How the hell do you start carrying around baseball cards in your head?

He gave Raph a twirl. The bat sure felt good in his hands, a satisfying weight that broke no promises. It was the kind of bat you could work your way to a .300 batting average with.

What the actual *fuck?*

Val leaned back against the alley wall, a building grimy with the air of Chicago. Graffiti walked a crazy scrawl at chest height on the wall opposite, but it seemed like nothing but right-angles compared to knowledge that was flowing into his head. About a baseball player, of all things.

A shot rang out, followed by a sound that would have been a laugh if it wasn't so nervous. *Great. Kids with guns.* Val tried to imagine how he'd feel if he was holding a gun in a city of crazy people and one more random guy walked towards him carrying a bat. Probably inclined to shoot someone, more or less. He looked down at Raph then rested the bat against the wall. He could come back for it later.

John would have kittens. He *really* wanted that bat.

Stepping out from the cover of the alley wall took a bit of doing; he was mortal now, couldn't take stray — or directed — gunfire without bleeding out like any other dude. Once it was done he felt the cold winter sun on his face, felt its touch and took it for the world's promise that everything was going to be okay.

It had to be, or there'd be no one to tell John where the bat was. Val felt a small smile tug at his face, then raised his hands into the universal sign of surrender as he walked further into the light. The helicopters had come down at the edge of Ping Tom Park. Crazy place to come down, what with the trees, Val would have put a bird down on the roof of a building and made the troops *walk* down.

Hang about. Val didn't know how to fly a helicopter. Did he?

"FREEEEEZEMOTHERFUCKER!" The shout was amplified through a loud hailer, the words strung into one long sound of anger. Val saw the bodies at a natural perimeter around the helicopters, thought for a bare second then stopped walking.

He raised his voice. "Hey."

"I said FREEZE," said the voice again. Christ, but it sounded like a kid. Could have been Just James, if Just James was high on caffeine and holding a SAW.

"I'm frozen," said Val. "Look, I got people who need—"

"I don't give a fuck what you need," said the voice. "You move, we will ventilate you."

"Got it," said Val. He stood, enjoying the sun. The little things, right? It wasn't so bad, and he figured he could stand here for a while longer without too much worry, except — well, there was the kicker.

Five guys, armed to the teeth, camo, the works. All wearing helmets. Definitely nothing like Just James, not a Nintendo DS in sight. Val looked at them as they took up positions around the helicopters. Yeah, there was one with a goddamn SAW all right, the machine gun looking ridiculous among the measured peace of Ping Tom Park.

Val wanted to scratch his head. He wasn't sure how he knew that the machine gun was called a Squad Automatic Weapon — a SAW. He figured moving his hands wouldn't be the smart play, so he stood there with the sun and a smile on his face and waited.

And waited.

After a while, he said, "Can I come closer now?"

"Shit no," said one of the soldiers. "Move the fuck along."

Val nodded like he was agreeing. "It's just, we could really use a ride."

"Who's 'we?'" said the one with the SAW.

"Shut it, Demetri," said another.

"You shut it, Pollock," said Demetri. "It's an honest question. Could be VIPs."

"Could be unicorns too," said Pollock. "Odds are about the same."

"It's not unicorns," said Val, "or VIPs. I got three people who need to be elsewhere. Rex, James, and Sky."

"Rex? Like a dog?" Demetri had lowered the barrel of the SAW a fraction.

"Like a Tyrannosaurus," said Val. "Retired firefighter."

"How about you?" said Pollock. "You on the list?"

"Not so much," said Val. "I've got things that need doing."

"So why didn't Rex, James, and Sky come and ask us for a ride?" Demetri's head was cocked to one side.

"More or less," said Val, "because we thought you'd shoot us all and leave us for dead."

"Fair enough," said Pollock, nodding his head a fraction to the side of Val. Val had a moment's confusion before he felt agony shoot through his knee. He stumbled then fell forward, catching himself on his hands. Some animal instinct—

Fight. Kill.

—made him turn, and he found himself looking down the long barrel of a — *M4A1, now that's unusual, you'd expect to see an M16A4, and how the hell do I know that* — rifle pointed at his head. He'd had the back of his knee kicked by this solder. *Keep cool, Val, keep cool.*

The soldier was wearing a sneer above camo, but the rifle was held steady — full professional. Except the kid was too close, been spending more time playing *Call of Duty* than reading his damns ops manual. *Ops manual? How the fuck..?* "Hi," said Val, after a moment's pause. He winced. "Can I get up?"

"What?" said the soldier looking down the rifle. "Hell, no."

"Okay," said Val. "What now?"

"Now," said Pollock, "you tell us where your friends are."

"Are you going to fly them out?" said Val.

"I don't think you should be concerned about that," said Pollock. "I think you should be concerned about the gun pointed at your head."

"Had guns pointed at my head before," said Val. "This isn't really that unusual for a Tuesday." He looked up at the rifle, the way the soldier was holding it. He could see a place *there* where he could grab the barrel, pushing it sideways, then use his other hand *there* on the stock. It'd switch the weapon around, and with a bit of luck he'd get a human shield for free.

"You've not had Sessle point a gun at your head," said Pollock. "Relax the man some, Sessle."

"I wouldn't do that, Sessle," said Val. He looked up the rifle barrel, looking for the man behind the gun. "Probably be the last bad decision you make. I'm sure you'd like to get back to the world, get a woman, have a bunch of kids crawling around your ankles. All we want is a ride out of here, don't want no trouble. Still, trouble comes to find me, and I will respond. You try and work me over with that rifle and I promise you I will bring all kinds of hurt you've never seen."

Fight.

Sessle blinked at him, a look of astonishment replacing the sneer. "What did you say?"

"I said," said Val, trying to remember — because Lord knows, that wasn't him talking — what he'd just said. "Look, it doesn't matter what I said. You think I'm here on my knees, you think you're in control with the rifle. Handsome weapon, that, but it won't save you. Only thing between you and God is good judgment, and you've got precious few seconds left to determine a fate that doesn't leave you all dead. Ignore Pollock. Guy's an asshole. I've had a boss like him before."

Kill.

"He's not my boss," said Sessle. The rifle still didn't move.

"Even worse, right?" Val wiped his face with a hand, but Sessle didn't move. Good. "Some asshole who's supposed to be on your goddamn *team*, and he's giving you orders? Probably disrespects you all the time, right?"

"Right," said Sessle.

"Shoot him, Sessle," said Pollock.

"Hold up," said Sessle, looking away from Val. "We're talking."

FIGHT.

That look, that spare quarter second in between words, was all that Val needed. His hand worked its own way around the barrel of Sessle's weapon, his other hand coming up to grip the stock. He gave the weapon a tug, knowing — without knowing how — that was the best way to get Sessle to tighten his grip, subconscious, immediate. Fast enough to let Val use it to pull himself to his feet, then reverse the weapon on Sessle. Val had his finger on the trigger and the weapon pointed at Sessle's stomach in less time than it took to take a breath.

He'd also — *can't remember how* — spun Sessle around, placing him between Val and the rest of Pollock's group.

"Hi," said Val. "Now, I was wondering if we could get a ride."

"*FIRE!*" screamed Pollock.

KILL.

Five shots rang out, Sessle jerking with each one, his eyes wide. Val watched as Sessle looked down at his chest, hands pawing at his body, checking for the holes he was *sure* would be there. Val lowered the rifle, smoke trickling from the barrel, the last kiss of a casing hitting the ground gone seconds past. He didn't remember consciously firing the weapon, but he'd felt it buck in his hands all the same, five perfect shots as he'd squeezed the trigger each time. Val cleared his throat. "You're fine."

"What?" said Sessle. "What?" The man looked to be in a state of permanent surprise.

"I didn't shoot you," said Val, "because you didn't ... hell, you made the right call, didn't you?"

"What?" said Sessle. "I ... sure. What?"

Val nodded over Sessle's shoulder. "Go on. Take a look."

Sessle looked at the weapon in Val's hands, then at the ground around Val's feet where five bright brass casings had fallen, then slowly turned to look behind him. The five members of Pollock's squad — including Pollock himself — were all lying on the ground, a single shot in each head.

Sessle turned back to Val. "What did you say your name was?"

"Didn't," said Val. "You know how to fly a helicopter?"

"No," said Sessle. "I mean, yes."

Val felt the hot wet on his upper lip, and wiped the blood from his nose away. *God damn, that's not going away is it?* "Which is it?"

"You're bleeding," said Sessle.

"It's a bloody nose," said Val. "It's not likely to be fatal." *Yet. Hunt them all. Kill.*

"We've no reason to kill this one," said Val.

"What?" said Sessle.

"I wasn't talking to you," said Val. "Which is it?"

"What?"

"Can you, or can you not, fly a helicopter?" Val nodded towards the two birds on the ground. "Those things are helicopters."

"Right," said Sessle. "I can fly crop dusters. Dad taught me how."

Val pivoted on his feet, his rifle barking twice more. He looked down at the weapon, astonished with himself, then over at the man who'd been creeping up on them from across Ping Tom Park. The now dead soldier was hard to see, his Gilli suit making him difficult to spot in among the grass and scattered trees.

"How'd you know he was there?" said Sessle.

"A better thing to be saying about now," said Val, turned back to Sessle, "is how many more are out there." He held up a hand. "I'm seeing two Black Hawks on the deck. You can get eleven humans in there with all their shit, and there's five dead assholes on the ground and you, standing alive and breathing, in front of me. Asshole in the grass over there—" and Val jerked his head towards the man in the Gilli suit "—makes seven. If you didn't come to evac us—"

"Who's saying we didn't come to evac you?" Sessle blinked twice. "I mean, we could. We did. We were. I mean."

Val eyed the man. "Right. If you didn't come to evac us, and you came with two full birds, there's got to be fifteen more guys."

"We didn't come with a full crew," said Sessle. He looked down at Val's rifle. "Are you going to kill me?"

"So," said Val, "I'm only going to shoot you if you can't fly a Black Hawk. Now, can you, or can you not, get in one of those aircraft and pilot it to a safe place?"

"I can," said Sessle, and made a lunge for Val's rifle. It was a good move, the man had kept his body light, center of gravity low, pouncing like a cat. Good, but not good enough; Val saw the way the man was going to move, felt the other man's strength wrestling for the weapon he held. Val gave the rifled a small twist, pulled the trigger, and watched Sessle drop to the grass. The man's eyes were wide, staring at something in the sky, before his breath came out one last time, dragging its way out.

Val looked at Sessle's body, then back at the two Black Hawks. "Fuck," he said.

JOHN LOOKED at the two helicopters, then down at the duffel bag he carried. "Okay, you win."

"Come again?" Val wasn't really paying attention, he was scanning the park around the birds, checking for soldiers or zombies or both. He was pretty sure they were safe for the moment, the rattle of automatic gunfire blocks away suggesting — but not guaranteeing, not even around Ping Tom Park — a military force.

"I got some clothes, a new iPod, and some protein bars. The Nike place down on Michigan had the shoes in that I wanted." John held out a foot. "See?"

"Very nice," said Val. "Say. Are those the new Frees?"

"I know, right?" said John. "But you still win. You looted two *helicopters.*"

"John, I need you to focus for a second." Val rubbed at his chin. "You know how we were going to get Sky, Rex, and Just James out of here?"

"I heard the plan, yeah," said John. He looked at the Black Hawks, then at the bodies around them. "Oh, neat. A SAW." He walked over to the fallen men, hefting up the heavy gun.

"There's a problem," said Val.

"Just one?" John frowned. "Truth to tell, there might be two. I couldn't find any silver. Looked everywhere. Lots of gold, if that's your thing. Some real A-grade bling, diamonds, the works, but not an ounce of silver."

"Silver?"

"For weapons," said John. "Your plan. Remember?"

"Right," said Val. *No silver is a wrinkle we don't need, but we probably need to know who the hell else is taking it all. Maybe we can solve that one after the immediate crisis is over? Focus, Val.* "Back to my problem. It's a significant one. We can't take Sky, Rex, and Just James out, *and* go kill the bad guys."

"We've got two helicopters," said John. "We can go two different ways."

"Do you know how to fly a Black Hawk?" Val stretched, arching his back, trying to get the kinks out.

"No," said John, "but how hard can it be?"

Val blinked at him. "It's a little tricky."

"It's not like you can fly one," said John. "You work in computers."

"Well, that's the thing," said Val. He felt the remembered texture of a flight stick in his hands, the helmet on his face as he looked over a battlefield. The helicopter fought him as it went down, but it was going to be okay, he wasn't going to die. After all, he *couldn't* die. The poor bastards in the back—

Fallen pack.

He jerked away from the ... whatever it was, it felt like a *memory*. He looked at John. "Uh."

"You okay, buddy?" John took a step towards him. "I kind of lost you for a second."

"Right," said Val. "You know how you said I can't fly one of those?" He jerked a thumb at the Black Hawks.

"Right," said John.

"Well," said Val, "That's the thing. I'm pretty sure I can."

CHAPTER
THIRTY-EIGHT

"Thank you for the ride, Detective," said Pearce, holding out a hand. "I'll be seeing you." Her eyes had taken on a haunted look, and they kept almost looking at Adalia, skittering around where the girl sat.

Carlisle reached forward and clasped the other woman's hand. "It's been ... actually, it's been shit, but that's not on you."

"Likewise," said Pearce. "Are you going to be okay?" What she meant, Carlisle suspected, was more like *what the fuck is going on*.

"I think I'll be fine," said Carlisle, then coughed. She reached into her pocket, pulling out the Aleve. She dry-swallowed four caps. "Don't forget to call in the cavalry. People around here are going to need help, after ... after the end."

"You call, I'll come," said Pearce. "Assuming I get out. Last I heard, there were some birds down around the city. Got to be a working radio in there somewhere."

"You could come with us," said Carlisle. "We've got a werewolf on our team."

Pearce pointed with her chin at Carlisle's chest. "How's that working out for you?"

"Better than you," said Carlisle. "We're all still alive." And then kicked herself as the guilt flashed bright and clear across Pearce's face for a second, before being pushed back behind the mask. "Hey," she said. "Hey, I didn't mean it—"

"Save it, Detective," said Pearce. The Major finally turned to Adalia. The girl was standing back from them, behind the tail of the Yukon. Almost, figured Carlisle, as if she was using the Yukon as a barrier. *A barrier against whom, though?* Pearce licked her lips, cleared her throat. "I wanted to..."

"He misses you," said Adalia. "He misses you every day."

"I miss him," said Pearce. "I—"

"He says," said Adalia, "that it was his fault."

"He was just a child," said Pearce.

Adalia shrugged. "He says he was racing Bobby. He wasn't listening. Rushing ahead."

"He liked the wind," said Pearce.

Adalia took a cautious step out from behind the Yukon. "He lives in it now. The wind, I mean."

Carlisle could see Pearce's throat work, but no sound came out. The Major took four swift steps towards Adalia, crushing her in a hug. Carlisle could see Adalia stiffen, then relax as Pearce said something to her. Pearce held Adalia out at arm's length, studying her for a moment, before turning to Carlisle. There were tears in her eyes. "You look after her. You look after her, you hear me?"

"Always will, and that's a fact," said Carlisle. "You be there when I call, is all."

"I'll be there," said Pearce, and turned away. She was clothed in military fatigues, urban camouflage for a capable warrior, armor of a sort, but near as Carlisle could tell she was probably naked for the first time in years.

"I'm sorry, Melissa," said Adalia. "I didn't want to scare her away."

"Kid," said Carlisle, "it's fine. She's got shit she needs to do."

"Language," said Adalia, with the ghost of a smile.

"Fuck that shit," said Carlisle. "What did she say to you anyway? If you don't mind me asking."

"She asked me to tell him that it was *her* fault," said Adalia. "She said thank you." The girl shuffled her feet. "What's happening to me, Melissa?"

"Something beautiful," said Carlisle.

"How do you know?" said Adalia, the edge of something anguished in her voice.

"Because," said Carlisle, "it's you." She checked her weapon, still snug against her spine, then patted the side of the Yukon. It had done them good, giving out here at the edge of the city only when the last of its fuel had run dry. Maybe she should get one when they put the world back together. Driving these last few miles without a windscreen had chapped her lips, made her eyes dry. *Thank God.* "C'mon."

"Where are we going?" Adalia looked around the city, the buildings standing tall and empty. "Where is everyone?"

"Can't help with the second one," said Carlisle. She stretched nice and slow, feeling something scrape on the inside. *God damn, but Danny owes me a bottle of something expensive.* "Let's go get your mom."

"Do you think it was a good idea sending Ajay up ahead?" Adalia pushed her hair back away from her face. "It's just that—"

"Last thing I did to your mom was shoot her," said Carlisle. "I sure as hell wasn't going."

"She threw him into a wall," said Adalia.

"He deserved it," said Carlisle. "Still does, I think." A flare sprouted up from around the corner of a building a few blocks up, it's bright red tip dancing ahead of a soft trail of smoke. "Well, there we go. He didn't try to shoot *her* with the flare, so I reckon we're good."

"Okay." Adalia reached out a small hand, snaking it inside Carlisle's larger one. "Okay."

They started walking, the pain in Carlisle's ribs dragging her steps. "Kid," she said.

"Yes?"

"Don't walk so fast," said Carlisle.

Adalia looked at her, then at the space off to Carlisle's other side, as if she was listening. "He says that talking about things can take your mind off the pain."

"He's there?" Carlisle jerked her thumb at the empty air.

"Sort of," said Adalia. "It's difficult to explain."

"Tell him," said Carlisle, "that it's going to take a lot of talking to make me forget about an entire chest full of broken bone."

"He says," said Adalia, "that when he died, his body was ground underneath the wheels of a semitrailer." She hid her face behind her hair, but Carlisle caught the edge of a smile peeking through.

"You tell him," said Carlisle, "that only proves he's a quitter."

"I'll tell him," said Adalia. "Why don't we let Mom go kill the bad guy? Or guys?"

"We will," said Carlisle, "but I want to speak to her first."

"What for?" Adalia helped Carlisle around some trash strewn in the street.

"Because," said Carlisle, "she owes me a bottle of Glenfiddich."

"THIS IS A NICE PLACE," said Ajay. After they'd caught up to him — and a human-again Danny — they'd agreed to go back to John and Sky's apartment. They'd talked about seeing their friends again, as if it was just another Sunday in the park. Not as if the apartment would be empty, their small family dead and gone. "Or, I can see that it would be, if the lights were on." He held a glow stick above his head, everything in the stairwell being washed in a luminous green color.

Carlisle coughed, then winced. *Stop doing that, Carlisle, you know it hurts.* "I just hope they're here."

"They'll be where we need them to be," said Ajay.

"Whatever, Yoda," said Carlisle. She turned around to Danny. "You okay?"

Yellow eyes looked back up at her from the dark below. "*I'm fine.*"

"Okay, Captain Creepy," said Carlisle.

"*You brought silver,*" said Danny.

"Yep," said Carlisle. "Now hurry up."

"*Why?*"

"I'm pretty sure I'm going to need to shoot someone with it," said Carlisle. She looked at Adalia, then at Ajay. "Probably not one of these two though."

Danny stalked out of the shadows into the pool of dim green light. Her eyes were bright, and she walked with the strength of an Amazonian goddess, her steps deliberate as she mounted the stairs. The blanket around her shoulders didn't make her look battered or lost — if anything, it highlighted the feral thing that sat behind her eyes. "*Us?*"

Carlisle sighed. "Do you want me to?"

Danny's yellow eyes didn't blink. "*It burns.*"

"That's not really answering the question, is it?" Carlisle sighed again. "Use your words, Kendrick. Fucking vowels and—"

"Language," said Adalia, but there was a tight tremor of fear in her voice.

"Vowels and consonants," said Carlisle. "As a werewolf you've got your uses, I'll give you that, but as a mother you're doing a shit job."

Something like a growl came from Danny, and she started to step forward.

"And as a friend," said Carlisle, "it's like you didn't read the same book the rest of us did." She wanted to scream — *you almost killed me!* — but Kendrick wasn't in a listening mood.

Probably wouldn't be for a few hours. Ajay had found her, buck naked in downtown Chicago, nothing on but a smile. And it wasn't a nice smile. They'd found a blanket — Carlisle figured they'd borrow some of Sky's clothes when they got to the apartment.

She narrowed her eyes. Come to think of it, were Sky and Danny the same damn size? *Hell if I know. Just keep breathing.* She rattled the

Aleve in her pocket. The stuff just wasn't cutting it. *Maybe Miles will have something stronger — the man cries more after a workout than anyone I've ever met.*

The noise of the Aleve drew Danny's gaze. "*Medicine.*"

"That's right." Carlisle shuffled back on the step. Damn, but those eyes were uncanny.

"*Pain?*"

"Two for two," said Carlisle. "You'll be on *Jeopardy* before you know it."

Danny's hand reached out, almost touching Carlisle's ribs. "*Because of me?*"

Carlisle sighed. "No, Kendrick." She rubbed her face. "Because of me. Because of me."

Danny's fingers were gentle as they touched Carlisle's side. "*Why?*" The yellow of her eyes was very bright, the green of the glow stick doing nothing to wash the color away. Carlisle could smell her, the primal scent of an animal underneath the smell of woman.

"Because we needed you," said Carlisle. "I couldn't do it myself." She looked at her feet, then pushed Danny's hand aside with a slow motion. "I couldn't save them, do you understand? I'm sorry. I'm too tired. Too slow. Too weak."

"Detective," said Ajay, "the entire city of Chicago was trying to kill everyone on that road. Your actions saved us."

"My actions saved *most* of us," said Carlisle. "Someone had to pay."

"Damnation," said Adalia. Her face was hidden by her hair, but Carlisle thought she was looking at her mother.

"Salvation," said Ajay. The green light washed around the stairwell as he gestured with the glow stick. "Two sides of the same coin, paid in blood. Do you not see it?"

"*No,*" said Danny. Her hand reached up to Carlisle's face. "*Why?*"

"I told you why," said Carlisle. She tried not to flinch from Danny's touch.

Danny's fingers lingered for a moment before falling away. "*Who you were is gone, dead and buried, heart of my heart, Pack of my Pack.*"

"Don't you fucking start," said Carlisle. "I've got enough mystic shit with these two." She jerked a thumb sideways at Ajay. "He's the worst."

"She is the Sword," said Ajay, eyes on Danny. "It is her place to—"

"*You carry her memory here,*" said Danny, touching Carlisle's chest above her heart. "*Listen to my words. The memory of the little girl you were nips at your heels. I tell you this: the frightened child you were has died, but you burden yourself with her carcass. I have seen dragons circle against the fingers of the sun, warring in the space between the moon and earth. Their fire burned the air, and their scales fell like rain. All were weaker than you.*" She pulled the blanket around her shoulders, then pushed up the stairwell into darkness. Her voice drifted back down to them. "*You ... let me save my only cub, heart of my heart. You will always run at my side.*"

Carlisle looked at Adalia, then at Ajay. She felt the press of the Eagle at her back, touching her spine like the fingers of a friend. "Huh," she said. She thought for a moment, before calling up into the dark above. "Don't think that pretty speech squares us. I still want my bottle of Glenfiddich."

"I GOT THIS," said Carlisle. "You look like a fucking vagrant."

"Language," said Adalia, but Danny nodded. She stepped aside, holding out her hand in a gesture of *after you*.

Carlisle stepped up to the door, taking in the plainness of the surface. It seemed like such a long trip to come to such an ordinary door. *It's what's behind the door that counts.*

"What if he's not home?" Adalia was shifting from one foot to the other. "I mean, them. What if they're not home."

"I know what you mean," said Danny.

"Everyone," said Carlisle, "needs to relax. I feel like it's my prom night, except instead of Zach Hollywood waiting for me in a tuxedo there's just John Miles." She rubbed the back of her neck. "Zach Hollywood was someone worth getting out of bed for."

"Or into bed?" Danny gave her a half-smile.

"That came later," said Carlisle, pulling her jacket straight. She rapped on the door, three quick strikes with her knuckles. They left smudges on the paint, and Carlisle held her hand up, seeing the skin missing from her knuckles. *Been a busy day.* She'd bet the smudges would be more red than black, but it was hard to see in the washed out green light from the glow stick.

"Are they home?" Adalia leaned forward. "Are they here?"

"Relax, kid," said Carlisle.

"They're home," said Danny, her smile widening in the dim light. "They're talking about whether they should open the door."

Carlisle rapped on the door again. "Miles, open the fucking door. I know you're in there."

John's muffled voice came from the other side of the door. "Oh shit, it's the pigs. Flush the stash." The door pulled open, and John was cast in silhouette from the relatively bright light streaming into the corridor. "Oh," he said. "It's just you. I thought was had a *real* problem."

Danny shouldered past Carlisle and grabbed John in a hug. He hugged her back, then seemed to pause. "Are you ... am I dreaming? Are you naked?"

Danny pulled her blanket tighter, but tossed him a tight grin. "First and last time you'll get that kind of action, John Miles." Her eyes went from him into the apartment.

"Oh," said John, after a minute. "He's back there. You know the way."

Adalia squealed, rushing at John and jumping up. He mock-staggered, then helped her down. He turned on the Miles Megawatt Smile, then knelt down a little. "Hey."

"Hey," said Adalia. Carlisle watched, feeling the tension fall away from her. Finally. Finally she had people she could trust.

If only it wasn't that clown John Miles. "Miles."

"Yo," he said, tousling Adalia's hair.

"Miles, this is—" Carlisle started, turning to Ajay.

"What have they done to you?" Danny's voice was rising to a shriek from inside the apartment. "*WHAT HAVE THEY DONE TO YOU?*"

Carlisle was past John, Adalia shoved behind her and back into the corridor, the Eagle bright and heavy in her hand before she'd even thought about it. The weight of the weapon lead her whole body, checking the doors and corners as natural as breathing. She took in the same apartment she knew, made smaller than she remembered by strangers standing among her friends. Old guy, probably harmless. A kid, all elbows in that awkward time of becoming a man — no gang patches, straight-laced type right from the pages of a home interiors magazine. Probably harmless. John's squeeze — Skyler Evans — something haunted around her eyes, holding what looked like a — *is that a fucking Ramset gun?* — power tool, trying to work out which direction to point it. Possibly dangerous through hysteria.

And there, at the breakfast bar, Valentine Everard, looking weaker than she'd seen a man look before. Pale, leaning against the counter top, a stricken look on his face that Carlisle could have pictured being one of joy three heartbeats earlier. Danny Kendrick, naked as the day she was born, blanket tossed aside in rage and confusion, eyes bright and yellow as she looked around the room for something to kill.

Carlisle lowered the Eagle, sneaking it away to sit in the comfortable place by her spine. "Kendrick," she said. Then, louder, "Danny."

Danny looked at her. "They've taken away my Valentine," she said. Carlisle had thought her naked a second ago, but saw her now as a woman who was fully clothed in pure anger and fear.

"Well," said Carlisle. "I am going to admit to being confused."

She didn't turn her head away from Danny before speaking again. "Sky? Sky, I'm going to ask you to put the Ramset gun down."

The old man spoke up as he rose from the couch. "That's a good idea," he said.

"She's crazy," said Sky. A quick glance showed she still held the weapon.

"I would say," said the old man, his voice even like the calm in the eye of the storm, "that she is about a hair's width from doing something bad."

Carlisle looked at the old guy. His very calmness spoke more than his words, his understanding of the word *bad* very clear. "Police?"

"Fire," he said.

"Figures," she said. "Sky, can you put the gun down? You can't hurt her with it."

The old guy was walking in careful steps towards Danny, palms out. "It's okay," he was saying. "It's okay."

"It's not okay," she said to him, hands balled into fists. "It's been *taken*."

"Yep," he said. He leaned down, picking up the blanket. "Thing is, we're going to get it back. Aren't we?"

"Who has it?"

The old guy put the blanket around her shoulders, tugging it together at the front. "I like a pretty girl as much as the next guy, but you're distracting John," he said.

"Priorities," said John.

"Hey," said Sky.

Val rubbed his face with a hand, then moved out from behind the breakfast bar. "It's me," he said to Danny. "It's still me."

"There's so little left," she said, something catching in her voice.

"I know," he said. "I made a mistake."

Danny reached a hand up — *good Christ, she's shaking like a leaf* — to touch the side of his face. "Is it you?"

"It's me," he said. He looked like he wanted to touch her. He looked like he hated himself — for what, Carlisle didn't know. He

276

tried for a smile, but it slid off his face. "Hey. At least you know." He started to turn away.

"Know what?" Danny hadn't moved, her hand still outstretched.

"You said you needed time," he said. "You wanted to know if it was—"

"The Night," she said.

"The Night," he said, nodding. "Well, now you know. It's the Night. Without it, I'm just ... empty." What he didn't say was, *and you don't love me without it.*

"No," said Danny.

"It's okay," said Val, as if he was readying himself to lift something heavy. "I understand."

"No," she said. "You silly, silly man." She stepped towards him.

"What?" he said.

"Without it in the way, I can see what makes the heart of you," she said. "That's what I love."

"What?" said Val again, with the tone of a man who'd just received a death row reprieve. He was touching Danny's face, and then they were kissing. The blanket fell away again. *Fuck's sake, that woman* cannot *keep her clothes on. Still, if I looked that good with 40 years on the clock I'd probably run up and down the street buck naked too.*

"So," said Carlisle. "Sky?"

"Yes?" Sky was still standing close to the Ramset gun, the tool within easy reach.

"Sky, do you have any spare clothes? Kendrick's giving me an inferiority complex." Carlisle felt the weight of the last few days heavy on her shoulders. *So tired.* "And beer. Do you have beer?"

Sky nodded. "I've got some clothes."

"I looted beer," said John. "We've got plenty of warm beer."

"Awesome," said Carlisle. "Let's let the lovebirds—" but Danny and Val were already walking towards one of the rooms, ignoring everyone else "—never mind. Go get me a bottle. Oh. Right. And introduce yourself to the man in the corridor."

"Okay," said John, "but one thing."

"For the love of Christ," said Carlisle, "I'm really not in the mood."

She could see something soften in John's gaze. "What happened?"

"Doesn't matter," she said, but couldn't stop herself from wincing.

"I'll get you a beer, and something with a little more pep." He nodded to himself. "What does matter," he said, "is that there's no one in the corridor."

"What?"

"Empty," said John.

"He's gone," said Adalia, something *other* in her voice. "He's gone to fight his last battle."

"Ah," said Carlisle. *Guess you won't be getting laid after all.* "Actually, you know what?"

"No," said the old man.

"I'd like to know," said John.

"I'm too damn tired for this," she said. "Get me that beer."

THIRTY-NINE

" I thought you were gone forever."

"Shh. I thought I had to leave."

"But you're back now?"

"I don't think I ever really left."

"I held you close. I thought about you every day."

"I know. I couldn't stop either."

"If it was something I did—"

"It wasn't anything you did. It wasn't anything you were."

"I've missed you so much."

"Yes. I ... I was missing a part of myself."

"But ... it *was* something I did. Maybe I didn't know it—"

"Shh. There's time enough for that later."

"Later?"

"Later."

CHAPTER
FORTY

The table was laid with a feast.

"Is this ... is this what spam looks like?" Adalia was poking something on a plate with a fork.

"I've only ever seen it in video games," said Just James. There was a kind of awe in his voice. "I didn't think it was real. You know. Like dragons."

"Dragons are real," said Danny. Val watched her pile a plate with anything she could, pieces of canned meat, vegetables from a can, stale bread.

"...Right," said Just James. He tossed a look at Adalia. "She your mother?"

"Yeah," said Adalia.

"Always been like this?" Just James scampered away from Danny as she bared her teeth at him. He was grinning.

Val sighed. *Family.*

Not family. Pack.

Oh, he thought. *There you are.*

Yes.

Great. Family is the same thing as Pack. He bit into a piece of stale bread, chewing it for a while before washing it down with a pull from his bottle. Danny came to sit next to him, the smell of her—

Pack mate.

—the best thing. Not even the cold shower could wipe the smile off his face.

He wiped his nose, fingers coming away red. *Well, that might wipe the smile off my face.*

Val felt her touch on his arm. Her eyes were warm. "Hey. We'll fix it."

"Yes," he said. Because otherwise the world was going to end. Again.

The den is always in peril.

Val tapped the side of his head. "Yours talk to you too?"

"Not so much talking," said Danny, the words coming out around a mouthful of canned asparagus. "Christ, what is this?"

"Canned asparagus." John tossed a bread roll to Rex across the table, before handing a laden plate to Sky. Val watched John's hand linger against Sky's, felt happy for his friend. "I went for canned stuff. Fresh isn't the best in a zombie apocalypse."

"It tastes like ... God, I don't know." Danny swallowed, with obvious effort. "Calories."

"No," said Sky. "It doesn't taste like calories. It tastes like—"

"Congealed snot," said Just James.

"Gross," said Adalia.

"Accurate," said Rex. The old man was putting his plate down. He leveled a fork at John. "Son? Next time you go looting, I'm coming with you."

The banter continued around the small table, people telling their stories of the past days, weeks, years. The only one who wasn't talking was Carlisle. She was leaned against a wall, her plate held on her lap with one hand. Her eyes looked out the window, but her heart looked somewhere else.

Her den is empty.

Val put his plate aside, shuffling across the room. He was feeling weaker now, the virus doing its work against what was left of the Night. He didn't know how long he had, not really, but it made him feel more alive. Like this mattered.

"Carlisle," he said. He leaned against the wall beside her.

"Hm?" She didn't stop looking out the window.

"Not hungry?" Val sighed. "I don't blame you really. I think this is the first time that I've eaten mushrooms from a can."

"What?" Carlisle sighed. "I'm sorry, Everard. I was thinking about something else." She turned to face the room, shoulder to shoulder with him.

"Someone," said Val.

"What?"

"You said some*thing*," said Val. "I'd say some*one*. The invisible man."

"Ajay," said Carlisle. "He's not invisible. He's just not here."

"Is he with us?" Val tapped his fork against his leg. "Is he one of us?"

"I don't think so," said Carlisle.

"He's against us?"

"No," she said. "I don't know."

"Do you love him?" Val spun the fork in his fingers.

"This isn't a fairy tale," said Carlisle. "Love doesn't work that way."

Val looked at John and Sky, then found Danny's eyes across the room. "Yeah," he said, "yeah it does."

"You guys are sickening," said Carlisle.

"Here's the thing," said Val. "We don't get to choose."

"Choose?" She turned her head towards him for a moment.

"Who we love." Val pointed the fork at Adalia.

"That's different," said Carlisle. "I never wanted that kind of responsibility. She just kind of ... wormed her way under my skin."

"Like I said," said Val. "We don't get to choose. Our Pack chooses us. And then we get to stand with them against all the world throws at us, until we make it okay."

"Our pack?"

"You know what I mean," said Val.

Carlisle was silent for a moment. "I know what you mean." She ran a hand through hair streaked with gray. "I don't know him at all."

"I'd like to say something without you breaking my arm," said Val.

"Is it something that I'm likely to want to break your arm over?" Carlisle's tone hid a smile.

"Maybe," said Val. "Thing is … thing is, I don't think I've seen you let someone get close. Not *us*," he said. "Someone who's not us."

"I only want the family I can choose," said Carlisle. "The real thing hurts you instead of…" She trailed off.

"Carlisle."

"What?" There was something sharp in her voice now. "I'm not looking for more touchy-feely crap. I've had days of that on a road trip with psycho Barbie and her adorable half-alien child."

"*This* is your family." Val pushed himself to his feet. "We won't hurt you. Or we'll try not to, but if we do we'll make it right." He shrugged. "We'll get him back. Then you can find out if love is a choice."

"Now I want to break your arm." She looked past him. "He came across half the world to find me." Her face twisted into something bitter. "To trap me."

"Then we'll get him back," said Val, "and you can break *his* arm."

"Now you're talking sense," said Carlisle, pushing herself to her feet with a wince. Her face was more ashen than Val had seen before.

"You okay?"

"No," said Carlisle. He watched as she slotted the bits of herself back into place in her head, pieces coming together like a suit of armor. She patted the sidearm at her back, the motion almost unconscious. "But I will be."

THE PLATES HAD BEEN CLEARED AWAY, the regular workaday tasks of eating and cleaning, done with good company, pushing aside fears for a moment's peace. *We might all be about to die*, thought Val, *but at least we've had a good meal of stale bread and spam.* There were probably worse ways to go — at least this way, they had—

Pack.

—family. They'd traded stories as they ate, about the things big and small that had happened to them. Somewhere along the way it had got too much, too wild. Rex had come up with a solution.

"So what we've got," said Rex, pointing at the scrawls on the wall behind him, "is a lot of unexplained shit."

"I think we've explained it pretty well." Sky was sitting with her arms crossed. She'd pitched a fit when Rex had started to use a Sharpie on the wall, but the old man had pointed to the Ramset nails and she'd just crossed her arms with a sigh. Val agreed with the old man though — they could fix the wall later *if* they survived. This gave them something to do; they could work the problem.

"Yeah," said John. "I know what's going on."

"Son," said Rex, "son, you don't know your ass from your elbow."

"It hurts me when you say mean things," said John. "Tell you what. Race you to 80. No, wait. You win!"

"That's cold," said Just James. "I mean, that's really cold."

Val leaned forward. "Let's see if we've got this right." He started to count on his fingers. "First up, we've got a city of zombies."

"Pretty sure that didn't come first," said Just James. "I'm pretty sure the werewolf thing came first."

"A fair point," said Val. "So, first up, we have werewolves. As far as I know, there were two left in the world as of a couple weeks ago." He looked at Danny, then down at his feet. "Now we have one, and that takes us to the second point."

"Spiders," said Sky.

"Spiders," said Val, nodding. "In a briefcase. But the briefcase did something nasty before the spiders."

"Right," said Rex, pointing to the wall behind him. He underlined a piece that said *Weird briefcase sucks all the joy out of Val.* That'd been John, of course. "Someone stole your ... son, I'm having trouble saying it."

"Superpowers," said Just James.

"Thanks," said Rex. He sighed. "It's not getting any easier."

"This is why your generation has such a problem with Snapchat," said Just James. "It's like trying to teach an old dog new tricks."

"My generation?" said Rex. "What the hell is that supposed to mean?"

"Third," said Val, pushing on, "we have some kind of mother-fucking sorcerer." He pointed to the words *motherfucking sorcerer* on the wall. Carlisle had written next to that in tight, small letters the name *Talin Moray.*

"Language," said Adalia. She was playing with her phone. No way she had coverage, so must be Angry Birds or whatever the kids played these days.

Val looked back at the wall. "This guy, Moray, comes to our town, steals the ... the—"

"Night," said Danny, leaning in to his shoulder. She smelled good.

We are the Night.

"Night," said Val. "He takes it."

"Then," said Rex, "the zombies."

"Near as I can figure, yeah," said Val. He pointed to the rough time line they'd drawn next to words on the wall. "That looks right. Mark it in there."

Rex drew on the wall with the Sharpie, Sky looking away. While Rex was drawing, he said, "Yeah. Zombies."

"See?" Just James was beaming. "I knew you could do it."

Rex sighed again. "I think," he said, "that brings us to the fourth point."

"I see dead people," said Adalia. She looked up from under her hair at the brief silence. "What? I've seen the movie."

"When?" said Danny.

"There's not much to do in the snow in Alaska, Mom," said Adalia.

"Doesn't feel related," said Val, rubbing his chin.

"Dead people and snow?" said John. "No, I can see how snow would give you dead people."

"More the dead people to werewolf thing," said Val. "I think we've skipped a step."

"Right," said Rex. He drew a thick black line — Sky looking away again — between *zombies* and *Talin Moray*. "It's like a kind of battery."

"What?" said Just James.

"Figures, doesn't it?" Rex frowned. "What. You all can't see it?"

Val thought for a moment. "I see. Because there were no zombies before."

"Right," said Rex. "Maybe I can't use Snapchat, but I can use my brain." This last was directed at Just James, who breathed a *whatever* and went back to watching his shoes. Rex pointed at the wall. "Look. All I'm saying is that if I'm the kind of sociopath who can turn the city of Chicago into a force of brainless wonders three million strong—"

"I'm not sure that *he* made them brainless," said John. "Have you seen reality TV?"

"—I'm probably not going to wait for Tuesday before I make that happen," said Rex. "What holds me back?"

"He was hunting," said Danny. She looked at Val. "He was hunting *us*."

We have ever been hunted.

"I think," said Val, "that he's not the only one. Didn't Ajay try to get you in Alaska?"

"He said," said Carlisle, her voice quiet, her chest still giving her trouble even through the *cocktail* John had given her, "that he represented a different buyer. Raeni Williams."

"What's the connection?" Val pointed at the wall. "What's the connection between the motherfucking sorcerer and—"

"Language," said Adalia.

"—this Williams chick?" Val frowned.

"There is more than one light against the dark," said Adalia.

Danny was looking over at Adalia. "Sweetie? Is ... is *he* telling you that?"

"I wish we knew Gabriel's play," said Just James. There was a hint of teenage jealousy in the air, but Val figured it was a tough rap trying to compete with a dead guy. If *compete* was the right word.

"You shouldn't say his name," said Adalia. "You shouldn't know his name." She shivered, as if trying to turn back into a 14 year old girl. "Whatever. He didn't say that. It just makes sense." She looked out from under her hair at Rex. "I can use Snapchat *and* use my brain."

"The new master race," said John.

"It makes sense, Uncle John," said Adalia, "because we can't be alone. Can we?" Her eyes moved to each of them in turn. "We can't be the only ones who want to fight what's wrong. I don't believe it."

"'Uncle John?'" Val looked at his friend.

"It's cool," said John. "Right? It's cool. I think it's cool. Is it cool?"

"It's cool," said Sky, a smile slipping between them. Her hand was on John's arm. "It's very cool."

"It makes you sound old," said Just James.

"That," said Rex, "is how you kill a beautiful moment, son."

"What I want to know," said Val, "making the broad assumption that Raeni and Ajay are on-team, is what they can *do*."

"He's got some tricks," said Carlisle, looking out the window.

"He knows things," said Danny.

"He is the Reluctant Wanderer," said Adalia.

"Right," said Val. "What's that mean?"

"I don't think that's important," said Rex. "We just need to know what he can do."

"Cause trouble," said Carlisle. "Like he's doing now."

"Okay," said Val, "wildcard. Let's ignore that for a moment. So we've got a werewolf sorcerer, and a city full of zombies. I can fly a helicopter. And we've got a dead kid on our side."

"Rock on," said John.

"What am I missing?" Val looked around the room.

"Small detail," said Rex. "I think we're in agreement: we're going to go clean this guy's clock."

"With you," said John.

"So," said Rex. "Where is he?"

"Can't you feel it?" said Adalia. "He's where the wind touches the earth. He's where the dark is strongest. He's under the world, and over it. He lives in the space between our thoughts, touches our dreams, and gives us nightmares that make us fear the fading of the sun. He sits beside the water, drawing power from it. He is the Leader of the Damned."

The room fell silent. Val looked at Danny, her face as surprised as everyone else's.

Rex stepped into the quiet first. "Okay. Where's that?"

"Shit," said John, "that's easy. He's in Trump Tower."

CHAPTER
FORTY-ONE

Talin looked out over his city, pride in his soul, hate in his heart. Such promise, a city like this, and that pack of dogs was trying to bring it down. Bring *him* down. It didn't matter what they did, of course, the city was lost — but they weren't to know that. Only he and one other could know, and she was dead.

Dead, and buried. He'd killed her himself.

It was always easier with a woman. She'd fought back, of course, her eyes bulging out as his fists closed around her throat, but her strength was ... insufficient.

He'd had only a tiny fragment of power then, enough to know that there was more to be had, and enough to make him feel powerless among the powerful. His plans had wrought an outcome, set his feet on the path that led him to today, to here, to the very *now* of life.

He'd sent his Five off to do God's work. He had so much strength now, power to spare, he could gift it to a thousand like the Five and not want for more. He stretched, marveling — again — in the youth that his body had found once more. He held the Five in the palm of his hand. Shamshoun, the strongest of them. L'inglesou, to bring night to the brightest day with a kiss of her sweet steel. Agni, who would scar and burn all in his path. Saint John, the balanced, the easy, the benign, the very devil himself. And — his first, his favorite — Choler. Choler would give them all a cloak of sweet lies, whisper into the ears of the angels themselves and make them doubt all that was true.

"You know that stolen power is never yours to keep." The voice came from behind him, familiar and strange in equal measure, and he turned to see a well-dressed man entering his domain. "Talin Moray. You know this to be true. You must trade for it, or it will consume you."

"I bow to no such rules," said Talin. "Who are you, to come in here and tell me my business?"

"I'm the one who made you," said the man.

"Oh," said Talin, laughing as he understood. "This is too rich. No, no, no. It is *I* who made *you*."

The man shrugged. "If you say so."

"I know so," said Talin. "Whose body do you wear?"

"Your son's," said the man. "Your only child."

"I have no son," said Talin.

"If you say so," said the man again. He was familiar, something scratching like an irritating insect at the back of Talin's mind.

Could it be? "Tell me," said Talin. "Tell me your story."

"You know my story," said the man. "You want to ask a different question."

"Yes, yes," said Talin, the irritation creeping into his voice. He waved a hand. "Tell me the story of my son."

"What will you trade?" said the man. "You can't take the story from me, like the power you pull around you like old curtains. It shuts out the light, Talin, and you can't see what is true in this world anymore."

"Trade?" Talin shrugged. "A moment of your life. You live a tiny sliver of time longer, at my pleasure."

"Your son's life," said the man. "You've already taken mine."

Ah. There it is. "Yes, Raeni Williams," said Talin. "I know your voice. I remember taking your life with my own hands."

"You didn't take my life," said the man. "You gave me a path to a different way of living." He looked tired, like a worn-out old photo, the colors of life fading around the edges. "Let me tell you the story of your son. He was born the product of incest after you raped your sister. Another woman you left for dead, but she — unlike me — lived. She bore her shame for years, held it up for all to see, but no one wanted to look. She grew heavy with your child. She called him Ajay, and gave him the surname of her father's house. Ajay Lewiss is your son, Talin Moray, and he stands before you."

"Then all I need to do is pull you out," said Talin, "like an oyster from its shell."

"That's one argument that can be made," said the man — Ajay Lewiss. "Another is that you tried to kill me once, and failed."

"I succeeded," said Talin. "You are a dead woman wearing a body that is not yours."

"Who are you to lecture me on taking things from people?" said Ajay. "You have robbed an entire city of will."

"Raeni, Raeni, Raeni," said Talin, *tsk*ing at the end. "I don't want to lecture you. You've come here wearing a different skin. You think I care? You think that I won't tear the life from you like I did before? This man — he is not my son. How long have you lived inside him? How much of him is left?"

"I think if you were going to tear the life from me," said Ajay, "that you would have done it already."

"You think wrong," said Talin. He paused for a moment. "Or at least, you have the wrong reasons. My son holds no place in my heart. I don't know him. But others do. He lives inside the heart of another, does he not?"

"You are blind, as always," said Ajay, but there was something hiding under the faded face he wore. *Yes,* thought Talin. *You are nervous about something.*

"We'll see," said Talin. He turned back to the windows over-looking the city.

"You mistake my words, Talin," said Ajay, his voice carrying across the room. "You think that I don't know that the Shield cares for this body. You think that I don't know that her Pack will not cross the dangers you've set against them. You think wrong."

"Wrong?" Talin turned back to Ajay. "You think they will come for you?"

"I know they will," said Ajay. "They just needed another reason. Am I a traitor they must kill? Am I a friend they must defend? Either face serves equally well. They will come here, and they will kill you."

"Because," said Talin, "you cannot."

"Because," said Ajay, "if I kill you, you'll come back like the black sickness you are. I taught you too well. You know my tricks, although you lacked the strength before. The Night, though. The Night you carry, the strength you've stolen? The Night will have its revenge." He smiled at Talin, a bitter, crooked expression. "And then, *I* will have *my* revenge."

FORTY-TWO

"It's a crappy plan," said John. He was shouting over the noise of the rotors, the wings of their Black Hawk beating the air as the machine carried them across a damned city.

This place was always lost.

"It's a great plan," said Val, the unfamiliar — yet memory perfect — flight controls around him. The cyclic stick had felt natural as soon as his hand had touched it, yet he'd never piloted a helicopter in his life.

Had he? He remembered speaking with such authority on it.

"We need to go in through the roof," said Val. "Save us walking up a hundred flights of stairs."

"You getting old?" John had looked at him across a table overlaid with a map of Chicago.

"I'm getting dead," Val said. "Virus, remember?"

"Sure, roof, whatever." John hooked a thumb at Rex. "Bet you the old guy could do a hundred flights of stairs. He's got forty years on you."

"Is he dying of a virus?" But the plan was workable — hit the top of the tower, where Talin Moray was likely to sit. He wasn't the kind of man

who lurked in the belly of a structure like that; he would want a penthouse view of the city he owned.

"Okay," said Carlisle. "Roof, I get the theory. Do we have a way to get there?"

"Helicopter," said Val. "Two Black Hawks. I found them earlier."

"You can't fly a helicopter," said Carlisle.

"Sure I can," said Val. "I used to bull's-eye womp rats in my T-16 back home."

Carlisle blinked at him. "What?"

Val sighed, rubbing his face. "Doesn't matter. Look, I can fly it."

"There's no pad at the top of Trump Tower," said Rex.

"We'll make one," said Danny. "Get me up there, and I'll get you a place to park."

Val was taking the helicopter up the Chicago River, keeping the machine right on the deck. He didn't know what made him want to do that, Talin wasn't likely to be packing radar, but it seemed ... it seemed ... *right*. He swung the machine over the water, rotors tipping in the cool air, and kicked the sound system up louder.

There was something about *Thunderstuck* that seemed fitting.

Trump Tower approached, the structure poking above Chicago's skyline in glimmering magnificence. Val had never stayed there, never really had the chance to, but he knew it was some kind of luxury hotel. The place where your moneyed betters could enjoy a stay in the heart of the city, probably get a nice view over the proletariat. Five stars all the way.

It had seen better days.

The silvered tower was pockmarked, windows shattered and open like missing teeth in an otherwise perfect smile. In some windows, curtain fabric was fluttering out into the cold air. Val tipped the helicopter into a turn, circling around the tower. The Black Hawk was loud around them — the machine had been built for a purpose, and that purpose wasn't comfort.

"It's a crappy plan, because what kind of idiot knocks on the front door?" John pointed out the open door of the helicopter. "Who punched out all the windows?"

Danny's hair was swirling around her face in a red halo. She was grinning with delight as she leaned out the open door, one hand holding the top of the door frame almost absently as the helicopter yawed away from under her. She had such an embodiment of, of—

Joy.

—that Val wanted this moment to last. Forever, if that wasn't too much to ask.

"The plan was always going to be crappy," said Carlisle, tightening the straps that held her down as she glared at Danny. "We're outnumbered what, two million to five?"

"Your math is good," shouted Rex. He was squinting against the cold of the air flowing through the cabin. "Does she have to have the door open?"

"You ask her to shut it," said Carlisle, tugging at her straps again.

"What happens if they squirrel out the bottom?" John was standing — *of course* — but bracing himself against the roof. "Shouldn't we have a team down there?"

"What team?" said Val. "This is *it*. You know we're not bringing Adalia and Just James into this."

"I just want someone there," said John, "with a catcher's mitt."

Val made the Black Hawk claw up through the air, Danny laughing as the helicopter soared. He brought the machine closer to the top of the tower. "How close you need us, baby?"

"Say," said John, looking out over Danny's shoulder. "There's a couple dudes out there."

"A who?" Val peered out the side of the cabin. "No shit."

There was a cluster of people on the roof of the building. One of them was holding a tube.

That's not a tube.

Val had a moment to wonder how you get a rocket launcher in Chicago — but hey, it's *Chicago*, right — then he was making the helicopter slew sideways through the air. He caught a spark of light as the rocket fired, the trail of smoke behind it appearing faster than thought. The shot went below them as the helicopter's engines roared.

"Wait—" said John, and Val caught a glimpse of Danny, teeth bared. She'd backed up to the other side of the cabin, dropped into a sprinter's crouch, and then ran out the open door. The last glimpse Val caught of her was the back of her shoe as she launched herself from the side of the helicopter.

"Oh," said Rex. "Oh my."

Val watched, heart in his mouth — *she'll be okay, of course she'll be okay* — as Danny's jump took her in an arc through the air to the top of the tower. She landed, rolled — and was already sprinting towards the man holding the launcher.

"That wasn't part of the plan," said John. "Was it?"

The man with the launcher had seen Danny jump, had already dropped the spent tube, but the huddle of people were raising weapons and pointing them at Danny. All but one, who was standing by a turret.

A God-damned machine gun turret. In *Chicago.* Even Trump wasn't ostentatious enough to have one of those mounted on the roof of his five-star hotel. That shit wasn't factory fitment, and it was firing right at them. Val heard the shots chew the outside of the Black Hawk and he spun the machine, turning the open door away from the line of fire. Bullets rattled against the frame of the helicopter and something groaned in the belly of the beast. The helicopter's engines started to labor, something wrong — a round luckier than most burrowing in somewhere soft and vulnerable.

Front of the building it is. He had to put the bird down before it fell out of the sky.

As the Black Hawk descended, he caught a glimpse of Danny, hair bright in the morning sun. She'd lifted the man with the launcher and tossed him over the side of the tower. He caught a glimpse of gleaming, yellow eyes before she turned back to the group around her and went to work.

CHAPTER
FORTY-THREE

"This kids' table stuff is getting old," said Just James. He was spinning his Gameboy — or whatever it was, Adalia didn't really know — between his fingers. He'd stretched out on the couch, feet hanging over the end. Adalia liked his sandy hair. She found herself watching him. She looked away, feeling guilty without knowing why.

"How can it get old?" She looked at him from under her hair. "We've only just got here."

"Right," he said, blinking. "What I mean is—"

"You want to die," said Adalia. She looked across at Gabriel, and the guilt intensified.

Just James blinked again. "Uh."

"I don't mean that in a bad way," said Adalia, but she did. She wanted it to stop this boy — this young, beautiful man — from doing something that she couldn't fix. "What I mean is—"

"He wants to show off to the girl," said Gabriel. "Guys can't help it. See a pretty girl, and you lose any hope of logical thought."

He thinks I'm pretty. "What I mean is, there's a thousand zombies out there."

"Aren't you, like, like, like," said Just James, one hand groping through the air as if he'd find the word there, "a sorcerer?"

Gabriel snorted, black lashes batting. She wanted to reach out to touch his hair, push it away from his eyes. She clenched her hands together instead, then used her fingers to straighten her shirt. "I'm nothing like that. I don't know." She looked sideways at Just James, wanting to be somewhere else. Wanting to be right here. "I don't know what I am."

"But you can see things," said Just James, pulling his long legs off the couch, planting Sketchers on the floor. He leaned forward. "You can ... can you see the future?"

"It doesn't work that way," said Gabriel, shaking his hands at Just James. Just James ignored him, because of course he couldn't see Gabriel.

"I can see the future," said Adalia.

"You can what?" said Gabriel.

"Excellent," said Just James at the same time. "What's going to happen?"

"Everyone I love is going to go through terrible pain," she said, "especially Uncle John."

Gabriel and Just James both blinked at her. Just James went first. "Why — what?"

"It's why you shouldn't go out there," she said.

"But," said Just James, "why John?"

"Uncle John," said Adalia, "is the kind of person that ... avoids the problem. Usually. He can't avoid this one. It's ... complicated."

"He wants to run away?"

"No," said Adalia. "He'll run right for it. He can't help himself."

"Uh," said Gabriel. "Oh, I get it. You're trying to scare him off."

"No," said Adalia. "I really can see the future. I mean, bits of it. Like a patchwork, without all the squares sewn in yet." *And it is terrible and beautiful and the end of all that I know.* "What am I becoming?"

"Something awesome," said Just James.

"Something beautiful," said Gabriel.

"Oh," said Adalia. She smiled behind her hair. "Someone else said that to me."

"They were right," Gabriel said, and she thought he meant something else. He looked down.

"You're ... you're having one of your moments, aren't you?" said Just James. "It's cool. I don't mind talking to myself for a bit. You know. 'Hey, James, how about them Hawks?' Or, maybe, 'James, what you need to do is grab yourself a nice cold beer.' If only there was electricity. Or something."

"He is very noisy," said Gabriel.

"He is just what I need," said Adalia.

WHEN ADALIA CAME out of the bathroom, feeling just about a million times better for having washed her face — just her face, but in clean water from a bottle in Uncle John's looted stash — the apartment was empty.

Except for Gabriel. Who wasn't really there. He was sitting on the top of the refrigerator, feet swinging against the front, heels *tap-tap-tapping* against the front. *How can he make noise if he's not really there?* "I couldn't stop him," he said.

"Of course not," she snapped. "You'd have to actually *do* something." She was already scrabbling for her jacket, her small bag of things, her useless phone.

"I can't do anything," said Gabriel. His eyes were bright, angry. "It's not my *choice*. I'm *dead*, remember?"

"I'm not," said Adalia, "and I was just in there." She pointed at the bathroom. "A closed bathroom door didn't stop you when we first met."

"This is different," said Gabriel.

"Why?" Adalia wanted to scream at him. "You could have come and got me. We could have talked him out of it."

299

"You don't know boys," said Gabriel.

"I'm starting to," said Adalia. "I don't understand the attraction."

"What would have happened," said Gabriel, "is that you would have gone with him."

"No," said Adalia. But she knew he was right. She didn't like standing here while the Universe spun around her. *She* wasn't the Sacrifice.

"Yes," said Gabriel. "And I couldn't ... I don't want that."

Adalia pulled her jacket on around her shoulders, pushed her phone into her pocket, and stormed towards the door. "Sometimes it's not about what you want," she said. "It's about what we need." The door slammed behind her, feet stomping down the corridor and towards the stairs.

She didn't see Gabriel in the apartment, staring around at the empty walls. She didn't see that he stepped across the space for living people, reaching down to lay a gentle hand against the door-knob she'd just touched. And she didn't hear him say, "I didn't want that because, Adalia Kendrick, I love you. With all that's left of my broken soul. And that is definitely against the rules."

ADALIA'S FEET MOVED, light as a scampering mouse, across the cold pavement. Abandoned cars sat empty all around her. She didn't know Chicago and felt small against the towering buildings. She tugged her jacket close against the cold wind and wondered where to go.

Where the water meets the sky.

"Oh," she said. "That way." She started her trudge across the city, thinking about her family. The Knight, his Good Right Arm, the Sword, and the Shield. Weird names, right? The Universe *clearly* didn't keep with the times. Those kinds of names were ... well, no one would actually choose to name a baby the Sword, would they?

How was she going to get across the city in time? She pushed angry fists into the pockets of her jacket, hunching her shoulders as she strode forward. The air was so cold — it felt like a dead thing trying to hold her down.

The Reluctant Wanderer had taken them thousands of miles in a single night. She could almost see how it was done, a weight on the scales that allowed them to tip a certain way. If someone wanted to be that weight, that payment to the balance, she could make it across the city in a single step. It would feel like turning the corner and she'd be there. She'd be in time to save them all.

They thought they were saving the world, but they'd all be dead if she couldn't get there in time.

A pack of zombies rounded a corner. *Great, because I need this right now.* At the head of the group was a man dressed in overalls, worn with use, some kind of maintenance worker from the guts of the city. He saw her, howled, and ran towards her.

Use his soul. Buy your passage. Pay the tithe.

"No!" said Adalia, and raised her middle finger at the sky. "People are not *coin*. They aren't to be bought and sold."

Then die.

"I don't think so," she said. The group was approaching fast, close enough now that she could see loops of drool hanging from the mouth of the maintenance worker. He was screaming, gibbering, ranting, climbing over cars rather than going around them in his frenzied attempt to get to her, to taste her flesh, to end her life.

"Hey!" said a voice, and Adalia looked across the street. Straight into the eyes of Just James.

Oh, no.

He was jumping up and down, waving at the zombies, trying to draw their attention. She could see it so clearly, like it was painted in black against the sky. He was trying to save her.

As if she needed saving, right? Melissa would have called it a *rookie mistake.* She could see the strings that held these people against their wills, taught thrumming lines stretching high into the heavens and low into the Earth. She'd been around the Night

301

long enough to see how the inner construct moved. *Like a clockwork.*

Unlike Just James, who couldn't see anything but a girl alone with zombies rushing for her. Just James, who was about to die.

She made a noise, at least half of it exasperation, the rest a plain old sigh. The horde had turned, the noise drawing them like cats at the end of a laser pointer. Just James' face flashed a moment of panic, or fear, or both, before he screamed at her to *run, Adalia, RUN!* before he turned tail himself and rabbited.

Was this what it was like when Melissa looked at Uncle John, rolled her eyes, and said *Men?*

Adalia reached into the air with a hand, grabbing at the threads against the sky. They felt like soft wool against her fingers, elastic with a hint of coarseness at the same time. This one was tethered to the mind of a man named Marcellus Samuel Kentucky, which was the coolest name she'd heard in a long time. Definitely better than the Knight, or the Sword, or the Shield, or the Good Right Arm.

Marcellus Samuel Kentucky was the one wearing the overalls, and he'd been repairing a drain when his mind was taken from him. He had a wife and two kids he never saw, working a couple shifts back to back. He liked football. No, he *loved* football, Adalia could see that in the strumming of the thread against her hand. Loved it more than his wife and two girls, because the game didn't ask when it could have new clothes or an iPhone or when he was going to take out the trash, because *God he just needed a little peace* and couldn't they see that? She saw that Marcellus Samuel Kentucky had wanted to play a little ball himself, had some luck with college football on a scholarship before a bad tackle took his left knee and most of his pride.

She pulled the threads close to her lips and breathed against them, took in their smell, felt their texture, and understood. She took a tiny step to the side, into the place that made her head hurt to think about — *don't think don't think just do* — and became. She spoke from the starless void, her voice taken from her in exchange for something older, ancient, with terrible purpose.

Marcellus Samuel Kentucky. I want to make a trade.

A trade?

Yes. Marcellus Samuel Kentucky, I will give you back to yourself. In return, you will give me your love of football.

I love football. I love that damn game.

I know. I can see it. And it's killing you. It's the cord that binds you, that he uses against you.

Who? Who uses it? What are you talking about?

Talin Moray. He is the man who takes away your will. He offers no trade. Marcellus Samuel Kentucky, he is a thief. He steals from the very Universe.

And you're different? You're just another Betty Crocker, come down here to tell me what's what. This thief? He's given me power.

He's taken away your will.

He's taken away the pain in my leg.

Marcellus Samuel Kentucky, I tell you this once. The pain in your leg is a lesson. It is a memory that makes you a better man, if you have the wit to listen. You couldn't have married her if you were on the road. You couldn't have had two beautiful girls if you were away from home. You would have died of hepatitis from a shared needle. The Universe — we kept you alive, we kept you safe, and you threw the gift back at us. And she showed him, the story of his would-have-been-life. She showed him where he fell in love with his wife, and then pointed to the moment where it would have broken her heart when he slept with someone else. She showed the places in his soul where his daughters lived, the empty void that would be left without them. *Marcellus Samuel Kentucky, this is the terrible beauty of your life. It is what you stand to lose if you take another step.*

Why should I believe you?

Why should you not? It's up to you. Here is my trade. I will give you back the pain in your leg, and take your love of football. That is all.

But ... but I get to keep them? With their needs and wants? They never leave me alone.

You get to keep them. You are a king in a kingdom you've forgotten.

A king? Oh, I see it — and here, something inside him broke with the beauty of it — *I ... I'll take your trade.*

Adalia held the thread in her hand, reaching back into the void. She found it there, the loose end of Marcellus' pain and hurt and anger and sense of failing at *everything* — and gave it back to him. In return, she took the bright, shiny thing that held his love of a game he could never play, gave it back up to the Universe. Put it into the starless void, and felt something right itself. The scales balanced a little bit, no more than a whisker, but she felt it. She had given this man something he couldn't feel through the burden of his everyday life. She'd given him back the love of his wife and his two girls.

Something unlocked inside her and she laughed.

That was, perhaps, ill-considered. The pack stuttered to a halt, turned away from where Just James had fled, turning eyes on her. Adalia looked over at them — *too many, too many, this takes too long* — and reached her hand out for another thread.

One of the zombies, clothed in worn overalls — *not a zombie, this one's a* man *again* — picked up a fallen street sign, the end of it a lump of concrete, and swung. It connected with the head of a zombie with a sound like a burst water balloon — a sound smaller than the magnitude of the action — but the man in overalls was still swinging, yelling with a voice gone hoarse. The lump of concrete at the end of the sign turned red and wet as he struck again and again. Adalia turned away, shutting her eyes tight against it, as if that would stop the noise.

Then, silence. She opened her eyes, looked over at the man in overalls, standing tall and straight against the cold air. His breath puffed out in trails of mist as he looked around at the felled bodies. He let the sign fall to the ground, held his hands up in front of his face as if seeing them for the first time. His fingers clenched, relaxed, and Adalia tried to hold her breath. *What did I do?*

The man looked over at her as if hearing her thought, moving with care around the limp that tugged at his steps. He was a big man, she could see that now that he wasn't bowed down with pain and so much horrible anger and loss. Wide shoulders. A face that should have held an easy, gentle smile, and might yet again. He held a hand out to her, and this was when she realized she'd hunkered down, crouched against the side of a car.

Adalia looked at his hand, reached up and took it. His grip was gentle and strong as he helped her up before taking a quick step back. He looked down at his hands, then put them behind his back. "Ma'am."

Well. "This isn't how it's supposed to go," she said.

"Ma'am?" His eyes met hers.

"I'm Adalia." She held out her hand again. "Not Betty Crocker."

He looked at her hand, then shook it. "Marcellus Samuel Kentucky. Or ... I was."

"You are again," she said, letting go. "Marcellus?"

"You spoke to me."

"Sort of," she said.

"I heard your voice," he said, stubborn. Of *course* he was stubborn.

"Marcellus?"

"Yeah."

"Marcellus, I need to get across the city real quick. Can you help me?"

That easy, gentle smile she'd been hoping to see broke out like the coming of dawn. "Yeah. I can help you, if you don't mind riding rough."

"Rough would be too easy," she said, "if you knew where I'd been this last week."

"You don't sound ... you don't sound like you sounded like before," he said.

"That's because," she said, then stopped. "There's this other place? Like a room, where it's dark and cold and empty. When I'm

305

there I can do things, but I can't be myself. I can't be who I should be. I don't know if I'm explaining this very well."

"I know what you mean," he said. "I know exactly what you mean." He took a step away from her, the limp snaring his walk again. "You coming?"

"We need to find Just James," she said.

"Who's that?"

"It's cool," said a voice. They both looked over to Just James, rounding the corner of a building. "It's totally cool that you're making nice with a zombie."

"Who's this asshole?" said Marcellus.

"Zombies talk?" said Just James.

"I ain't no zombie," said Marcellus, taking a heavy step forward.

Adalia put a hand on Marcellus' arm, a light touch but the man stopped. "Just James," said Adalia, "This is Marcellus Samuel Kentucky. Marcellus, this is Just James."

"Huh," said Marcellus. "He coming too?"

"Yes," said Adalia and Just James at the same time.

"That's cool," said Marcellus.

"I'm still stuck on the bit where zombies talk," said Just James.

"Oh," said Adalia. "He's not a zombie."

"But ... the thing ... what?" said Just James.

"It's like this, kid," said Marcellus. "Someone came and took something from me. She," and he jerked a thumb at Adalia, "gave it back. Now we're going to go kick seven kinds of shit out of the guy who took it. You coming?"

"You're kind of scary," said Just James. "That works."

Adalia looked around the darkening city. "How are we going to get there?"

"My truck," said Marcellus.

"A pickup's not going to help," said Just James. "Streets are clogged."

"I said a truck," said Marcellus, and set off.

"Oh," said Just James, when they reached the truck.

"Yeah," said Marcellus, pulling himself up into the cab. It was a big Kenworth dumper, metal ram bars mounted in front of the grill. "I figure, we can just push our way there."

Adalia let herself smile, gave a glance at the sky, and thought, *I don't need to trade anyone's life.* "Let's go." She piled into the cab, sitting between Just James and Marcellus Samuel Kentucky. She could feel the excitement coming off Just James in waves, something scared underneath it but hidden, buried deep — he was trying not to show her his fear. Marcellus Samuel Kentucky, on her other side, well — he had a focused feel, like a line-backer about to make his play.

Which made sense.

She felt around for Gabriel, but he wasn't anywhere near. She felt a pang of guilt, and looked at her fingers as they picked invisible lint off her jacket. She steadied her hands, smoothed the jacket flat. He wasn't here because of what she'd said, but he had been kind of a dick about the whole thing.

Hadn't he?

The guilt wouldn't go away, she needed something to take her mind off it. She looked at Just James' feet, the Sketchers laced tight. "Not Vans?"

"What?" He looked at his feet, then up at her. "No, you see, that's a misconception. Sketchers are the number two brand in the US today."

"That's why the cool kids wear Vans," she said.

"I transcend cool," said Just James. "Also, we're poor."

"Sorry," said Adalia. "Sketchers aren't exactly cheap though."

"Depends on whether you buy or loot," said Just James. "They fit. They look good. If life hands you lemons—"

"Make lemonade?" Adalia felt herself smiling. Her heart was fluttering, which was weird because they were just sitting in the cab of a truck talking about shoes. *Except you're not talking about shoes.*

"Hell no," said Marcellus Samuel Kentucky. "If life hands you lemons, buy a fucking gun."

The cab smelled of sweat and tobacco, and shook like a beast alive when Marcellus fired up the engine. He shoved the Kenworth into gear, flooring it, and the truck pulled out onto the street with a roar. They slammed aside the first car in their way, a shower of metal fragments accompanying the jarring as it bounced away. Marcellus pulled the truck onto the sidewalk, the jounce of the wheels as it mounted the curb throwing Adalia against Just James.

"Sorry," she said.

"I'm not," he said.

She smiled again, not trying to hide it behind her hair.

CHAPTER
FORTY-FOUR

The Black Hawk fought him all the way down, the machine yawing through the air. Val knew that yanking at the controls would spell certain disaster — *and how do I know that?* — but that's what most of him wanted to do.

Another part stayed calm, making small movements on the controls as if trying to steady a frightened creature. But despite the *other* helping him fly — well. He couldn't stop his fists clenching around the stick. When the machine thudded to the ground, listing to the left — John yelling half in fear and half in joy, no one else doing anything much else except praying — Val yanked off his harness. "Everyone out."

"Hey," said John. "That was some wild flying."

"*Da. Spasibo,*" said Val. "*Teper' vyyti.*"

"Uh," said John.

"Get your shit together, Everard," said Carlisle. She was pulling Sky out of her seat — Rex had already left the Black Hawk, doing a roadie run towards the entrance to Trump Tower — while John stared at him, face mostly blank.

Mostly. "*V chem tvoya problema?*" Val pointed out the open side door. "*Poshevelivaysya!*"

"Dude," said John, "I have no idea what you are saying. Did you take a knock on the head?"

"He's speaking Russian," said Carlisle, black leather jacket flashing as she ducked out the door.

"*YA ne govoryu po-russki,*" said Val. "I'm speaking *angliyskiy.*"

"You need to speak your way the fuck out of this helicopter," said Carlisle, "and get your head and ass wired correctly." With that, she was gone, pushing Sky in front of her towards the tower.

John looked at Val, then at Carlisle's receding back, then back at Val. "She's got a point." With that, he hopped out the side and jogged off, with the Miles ease that said he was totally cool with jogging from a burning Black Hawk towards a tower filled with zombies.

Val pushed open the door of the Black Hawk, the rotors still cutting the air above him as they slowed. They forced cold winter air against him, air mixed with a hint of the smoke peeling out of the top of the Black Hawk. Val gave the machine a last look — *landing on Trump Tower would have been so damn cool* — before he jogged after John.

～

"WHAT I WANT TO KNOW," Carlisle was saying as Val came through the doors, "is how we're going to get to the top." She had her sidearm out, smoke trickling from the barrel. Two bodies were splayed backward — one dressed as a security guard, another in a suit. Concierge, maybe? Didn't matter.

"What I want to know," said John, "is why Val is speaking Russian."

"What I want to know," said Rex, "is why we don't just wait here and let them come to us."

"Back to the Russian part," said John. "Val doesn't speak Russian."

"He does now," said Carlisle.

"*Nyet*," said Val. "*YA ne govoryu po-russki.*"

"Son," said Rex, "if you just said you don't speak Russian, you said that in Russian."

"Oh," said Val.

"Is 'oh' universal?" said John. "Like, do Russians say that shit?"

Sky took a couple of slow paces that brought her close to Val. She looked into his face. "You couldn't fly a helicopter either, could you?"

"*Nyet*," said Val. He heard it this time and wanted to slap himself.

"Stands to reason," she said, "that you're getting the Russian from the same place."

"Same place?" said Carlisle.

"Like a library," said Sky.

"Oh hey, neat," said John. "Like the Matrix. Do you know kung fu?"

"No," said Val. He scratched at his jaw. "I think I can wrestle."

"Makes sense," said Carlisle. "I was watching Kendrick fight, and she was doing some moves that I thought might be non-typical for a marine biologist."

"Danny's a marine biologist?" said Sky.

"She's a werewolf," said Carlisle. "I think that other stuff is secondary."

"So ... so you all shop at the same store?" said John. "Like, you know the same things?"

"I used to be an actor," said Val, "a very long time ago." His mind skated around the rim of something ancient, and he—

—*walked along the edge of a stream, the wagon on the road beside him. His wife looked up from the driver's seat, the charms braided in her hair twinkling. He smiled at her, pointing up the road at the town ahead. There would be work there where they could ply their mummer's trade, a place to get off the road for a spell. A place to get away from the thing that followed them from the cover of the trees, something he'd never seen. Not all of it. Two nights back, he thought he'd seen two yellow eyes staring at him from beyond the edge of their campfire, but she'd called him a dreamer and a fool and kissed him quiet. Still, he couldn't shake the feeling that he was hunted, that he—*

—fell to the floor, hand on his chest, gasping for breath. John was crouched down beside him. "It's cool," he said. "It's cool to not try to remember, okay?"

"I think he should try to remember," said Carlisle.

"Why?" said John. "What possible reason could you have to make him go through that again?"

"I dunno," said Carlisle, "but maybe it's because the last werewolf I heard speaking Russian was a psychopath named Volk."

No one spoke for a moment, the wind outside pushing at the glass windows around the foyer. The Black Hawk's rotors were still moving in a lazy circle outside, not another soul in sight.

"Oh," said John. "I get you."

"Right," said Carlisle.

"Hold up," said Sky. "Who is Volk?"

"I'm with Sky," said Rex. "Who in the what now?"

"Real asshole," said John.

"A killer, through and through. A murderer. Used to stack bodies," said Carlisle, holding her hand above the floor, "like so, but in pieces."

"Pieces?" said Rex. "What do you mean, pieces?"

"See," said John, "he would go to a place, say a bar—"

"The Elephant Blues," said Carlisle. She let out a tired laugh, no humor in the sound. "God. That seems like a lifetime ago."

"He'd go to a bar," said John, "and he would kill everyone. Then he'd pull them apart like, I don't know, like Lego."

"'Dismembered' would be the correct term," said Carlisle. "He pulled their arms and legs and heads right off. Then he stacked them. I don't know why."

"I wanted to stop them turning," said Val. *Wait, that's not right — it wasn't* me. He shook his head.

"Say what?" said John.

"I mean—" Val's mouth worked, but no sound would come out.

He could remember it, the smell of the blood, the copper salt taste on his tongue as he tore an arm from a torso, the image as vivid as a photograph. A child's arm, the red of the blood black against the snow under his feet. "*He* wanted to stop them turning. God, please let it not have been me. Not *me*."

"Huh," said Rex. He took three steps towards Val, reached down, and pulled him to his feet. "Son? You still with us?"

But Val was drifting on another stream of memory, the small windowless cell around him—

—*black. He could see, of course, they thought this kind of thing would break him, make him do what they wanted. But it wouldn't. He missed the taste of the night wind and the feel of the stars overhead, but not enough to break.* Nikogda — *never. The smell that pervaded the air around him was of silver, he could feel it wanting to burn his skin. Every surface around him was made of it, a cage of perfect, hated metal. He waited. He would find a way. He would reach out and—*

—felt a slap against his face, and Val jolted back to the present. Rex was staring at him, arm still up. "Did you ... did you just slap me?"

"Yeah," said Rex. "Seemed the right thing to do."

"I've never been slapped by a guy before," said Val. "That's one less thing on my bucket list."

"You want another?" said Rex, cocking his arm back.

"No," said Val, holding up his hands in surrender. He worked his jaw. The old guy still had a mean swing. "No, I'm good."

"You with us?" Rex lowered his arm. "You really with us?"

"Until the end," said Val.

"Good," said Rex. "I don't want to have to keep slapping you silly." He turned away.

Sky approached Val. "Are you?" she said.

"Am I what?"

"Really with us?" she said. "You seem to ... you seem to be this other guy, too. This Volk. I don't know him, but I know *you* don't speak Russian or fly helicopters."

"The helicopters were Volk," said Val. "When I got them, the ... well, the military guards around them? I had to talk to them. To make them believe. I was acting. Through another. An ... older one, I think."

"There's more?" Sky searched his face. "How do you know so much about this Volk? How do you know where he stops and someone else begins?"

"He had gone mad, sick inside. We had to kill him. Didn't we?" Val looked at Carlisle, then at John.

"Kendrick killed him," said Carlisle, "because he was rabid. Right?"

"I know everything about him. I know where he was born. I know the wolf that bit him. I know the wife he killed, the son who starved in the snow, the village who damned him and turned him out. I know the people who caged him." Val looked at Sky. "I know where he stops and someone else begins because he was my brother, blood of my blood, Pack of my Pack. He was my maker. He was my father."

"Huh," said Sky. "That makes no sense at all."

"It's kind of hard to explain," said Val.

"Doesn't matter," said Rex. "Which stairwell you want?"

"What?" said Val.

"Well, we got to get up to the king asshole, right?" said Rex. "Doesn't matter if you were in a gulag or an actor or, really, a fairy—"

"I wasn't a fairy," said Val. "They're too small."

"Sure," said Rex. "What I'm saying is, we need to go *up*."

"We go together," said Val.

"No," said Rex. "We pick a different stair well. Go in teams. If there's a blockage, or we get... uh..."

"Killed," said Sky.

"Okay," said Rex, "let's go there. If we get killed, then there's another team."

"We stand a better chance together," said Val.

"Son," said Rex, "son, you need to get with the program. It

doesn't matter if we're together. There are *thousands* of them. And our big gun went in the top."

"He's right," said Carlisle. "I can do—" and she counted on her fingers "—maybe five at a time. Miles might account for one or two—"

"Hey," said John.

"—and no offense, but Sky doesn't look like a fighter, and Everard, and I'm saying this as a friend, Everard, you look like shit. Like you're about to die anyway."

"More or less true," admitted Val.

"I can help," said Rex.

"If your pacemaker doesn't give out, you'll be fine," said Carlisle. "I'm just saying it how it is."

"That was kind of my point," said Rex, "except I was trying to approach it from the side. A little more, what's the word, *obliquely*."

"We don't have the time for trigonometry," said Carlisle. She checked her weapon.

"Can't Danny ... can't Danny look after herself?" said Sky.

"Yes," said Carlisle, "but if you remember, she's got herself against the devil."

"Which is, at best, an even fight," said Rex, nodding. "So she'll need our help. We need to get to the top. Some of us. Alive." He looked back at Val. "Which stairwell you want?"

It was easy after that. Carlisle and Val — *someone's got to look after the invalid*, Carlisle had said — went left, Rex and John and Sky — *no way she's not on my team*, John had said — went right. And they began to climb.

CHAPTER
FORTY-FIVE

The cold touched Danny's skin, icy fingers trailing goosebumps over her exposed arms. She didn't feel an urge to shiver — *there are some benefits to being a hound of the Night, right sister?* — but it was weird. Here she was, top floors of Trump Tower Chicago — she and Val had wanted to stay at a place like this when they had a little more money, a little more time, and fewer people wanting to kill them — and it was cold.

Sure, it was no Verkhoyansk, but it was still damn cold.

Ice collected against the walls, and her breath streamed out against the air. It wasn't a lack of power. Sure, there weren't any lights on, but there was no way AC could go this low.

She found herself wishing Val was here. She'd seen the bird go down trailing fire and smoke, but she'd been watching his eyes as they fell. He'd been looking at her like he'd let her down.

How could you have left that man? She rubbed her arms and shivered anyway, more from habit and something to do than from any real need.

Pack mate.

"Yeah," she said to the empty room, "pack mate."

"He will be your undoing." The voice was from behind her and she spun, whippet-quick, to see an empty corridor stretching away. The voice had been heavy, thick as molasses, smooth as cream. It had been beautiful.

"Who's there?" Danny pitched her voice, her shoulders squaring, ready for the attack that didn't come.

"Your future," said the voice, behind her again. She spun, caught the edge of a door slipping closed with a soft click.

She took five quick strides to the door — *locked* — and tore the handle from the frame. She pushed it open, scanning the room. *Empty.* Danny ducked inside, heeled the door closed behind her, and sniffed the air. There was a hint of cinnamon and apples, and a memory of breakfast waffles came to her unbidden.

This is a trap.

"No shit," said Danny. "Stay quiet for a second. I got this." The room was large, opulent, big windows and drapes and all sorts of things rich people could afford to love. No way she could have dropped enough dimes for a room like this on her bartender's salary. Everything was coated in a layer of ice, the carpet crunching under her feet. The drapes were frozen stiff. She paced to a door, kicked it open — *bathroom, empty, nice collection of soaps though* — before moving on. The bedroom area was clean, she even dropped low to look under the bed. "I thought you were some kind of mighty hunter. So hunt this fucking thing."

On this day, we are the hunted.

She wanted to shiver, pushed it down, looked around the room again. Put her back to the bed, faced a room covered in the excess of the wealthy, coated in ice. *Where did he go?* Because it was definitely a *he*, not an it, a honeyed voice pure with the promise of fulfillment, full of—

You are falling into the trap.

"Okay," said Danny, shaking her head like a dog. "Let's try this a different way. What do you want?"

"You." She felt the breath on her neck as the word was spoken

317

right next to her ear and she spun into the punch, her hand connecting with flesh, lifting —

Adalia. Her baby girl — *no no no, not Adalia, why is she here, not her* — had been behind her. Adalia's broken body slammed against the wall, a shimmer of ice falling loose as she crumpled to the floor, neck twisted at an unnatural angle, eyes glassy as the life dimmed from them.

Danny screamed — *"NO!"* — and dropped to the floor next to her daughter. "Baby? Baby, it's me. Talk to me. You'll be okay. You'll be fine." She was stroking Adalia's hair, her hands shaking, but Adalia didn't respond, her head lolling on a broken neck. "Baby? Please. *Please*, no."

The pain hit her in the back, claws of pure fire drawing down her spine and she screamed again, her back arching as she tried to turn around. She caught the edge of a shadow ducking away as she swung, connecting with nothing but air. It didn't matter, all that mattered was Adalia, her Adalia, her daughter whom she'd *killed*—

The floor was empty. Adalia's body was gone. The only record was an outline of broken ice where her body had been. Had it been real? She'd been able to smell the shampoo she'd used, feel the texture of her hair, a texture she'd never forget.

It is as real as you make it.

Danny rose on shaky legs, wiped the tears from her eyes. She cleared her throat, then reached a tentative hand to her back. The cuts were deep, and she winced as her fingers found the edges of the wound. *Silver.* The hated metal meant the wound wasn't healing, not like it should, not *fast* enough.

What is this? She wanted to scream at the thing that lived inside her, that forced her to be something she never wanted. *I need some help.*

It is Choler.

"Is that ... is that a thing, or a person?" Danny looked around the room, dropping into a fighter's stance, hands up. She could jump right out this hotel, fall a hundred floors to the street below and walk it off. She couldn't take hits from *silver* and live.

It is Choler.

"Why did you leave, Danny?" Val stepped in from the corridor, pushing the door closed behind him. His face was a mess of burnt tissue, caked in blood. *The crash.* "We could have really done something."

"Saved the world?" She started to walk to him, her feet wanting to stand still and run at the same time.

"Made a family," he said. "But you left. You left me, left *us*, and now look what's happened. Don't you see? We're all going to *die* because you walked away."

"I didn't mean it," she said. "I—"

"Adalia will be dead by the morning," said Val. "Talin will see to it. He'll fix *us* though, so we can be together. You want to be together, don't you?"

Danny walked closer to him, this man that she loved. "Yes," she whispered.

Val reached out a hand to her, and she took it. He pulled her close, and she breathed in the smell of him, closed her eyes for a moment, then pushed herself back to look into his face.

That broken, ravaged face. One eye was gone, and she found herself raising a hand towards it, then dropping it away. She gave a rueful smile. "You're not real," said Danny.

"What?" said Val.

"You're not real," said Danny. "You know how I know?"

"I'm real," said Val. "I'm standing here. I am as real as the dawn."

Danny looked into Val's face —ravaged by a fire he could no longer heal from. A fire that only left its mark because they had not been a pack. She'd left. Walked out, because she was confused.

Uncertain.

As uncertain as she was now. If she could just turn back time — put the toothpaste back into the tube — then this would never have happened. This wouldn't be real.

This is not pack. This does not speak to us in the way we know.

The what now?

She looked at Val's face again, at the hurt in his eyes, at the need that lay there. She looked at her hands, trembling, but not from the cold. What had the Night just said? It was important, but she couldn't hold it in her head, it was so hard—

Hear. Taste. Smell. LISTEN.

Ah. There it was. She slammed a fist into Val's face, sending him staggering back, crashing through the door and into the corridor beyond. She clenched her fists as she stood over him. "You're not real," she said, "because you don't swear enough to be my Valentine."

"We can make it real," said Val, from the floor. He worked his jaw, pulled a tooth loose. "We can be together. Forever." This last was spoken in perfect, honeyed tones, and she felt the yearning inside her, for just a taste of that perfection.

It will never be real. He is not our pack mate.

"Lover?" said Danny. "I'm going to beat the stupid right out of you." And she stepped forward —

—into an empty corridor, covered in ice.

"We will be together," said Choler, his perfect voice making her groin pulse with every beat of her heart. And she wanted this togetherness, she wanted it so bad. The certainty she had felt drained away, leaving her shaking and weak.

It is Choler.

The voice inside her head was fainter now, on the edge of hearing. She didn't know what to do. She didn't know which way to go. She hung her head, then screamed again as a silver claw raked against her back. Danny fell to one knee in an empty corridor, bleeding hot red onto the frozen carpet. "Tell me what to do," she said. "Tell me." The voice in her head was silent, or ... *pushed* away. She was alone.

"Come to me," said Choler.

Danny stood, then started her slow walk down the corridor.

CHAPTER
FORTY-SIX

"It's cool," said John. "This is nothing to be worried about."

"Son," said Rex. He waved his flashlight around. "Son, you need to work that one out for me a little. We're in a hotel filled with zombies, going to fight a werewolf — if you can believe it — with nothing but our wits." He gestured at the darkened stairwell they were in, the dim green of *EXIT* signs their only guide. "Also, it's cold, and dark."

"Point of order," said John. "Two points, really."

"Shoot," said Rex. The old timer was breathing a little hard, but who wasn't? John wasn't feeling great after climbing twenty flights, and they'd barely scraped their way up a quarter of Trump Tower.

"First," said John, "I don't think we've seen anything but two zombies. Down in the lobby."

"I'll admit," said Rex, "that is a little weird."

"Where do you suppose they all are?" said Sky. She bent over on a landing, resting her hands on her knees, taking a breather. Her flashlight was resting beside her, the white beam picking out motes of dust in the air.

"Which leads me to the second point," said John, working his arm in a slow circle, trying to get the twinge out of his shoulder. "When I say, 'This is nothing to be worried about,' I'm not talking to *you*, Rex."

Rex blinked at him, then looked at Sky. Took in her pale face, wide eyes, then looked back at John. "You know? You're right. Nothing to be worried about at all."

"You're so not good at this," said Sky. "Hey. Anyone got any water?"

"No," said John.

"Me neither," said Rex.

"Could we get some?" Sky shrugged. "We're in a five star. Bound to be some Evian in here."

"Good call," said John. "I'm the king of looting."

"Got to be good at *something*," said Rex, with a face that John figured said *all looters should die*.

"Wait one," said John. He gave the corridor a quick check — *empty* — before pulling open the door all the way open on 21. The heavy fireproof door gave way to nice carpet if that was your thing, a cleaning cart standing against one wall maybe thirty feet away. No one in sight, nothing but crappy artwork hung on the walls. "Who puts those there anyway?"

"What?" Rex was looking over his shoulder.

"Art," said John. "The shit they've got hung all over the place here. I mean, you go into any hotel, there's artwork everywhere."

"I used to rent a room from a couple who were into this," said Sky, her hand finding his. "They'd go to a trade fair and grab up a contract to paint three or four hundred different paintings for the same hotel."

"My God," said John. He gave her hand a squeeze. "That's not art."

"It's not great, but what are you going to do as an art history major?" said Sky. "The way they told it, they had to make the paintings match the decor of the hotel. So they don't get to ... exercise maximum creativity."

"But," said John, "if the hotel was in red and yellow, they could do a lot of Iron Man prints."

"Son," said Rex. "Son, there's something wrong with the way your head works."

"Right," said Sky, "because Iron Man's owned by Disney."

"Because," said Rex, "no one wants to wake up with Iron Man over the bed."

"I don't know," said Sky. "I could stand to see a little more of Robert Downey. The real problem? Red and yellow — that wouldn't work."

"Tell you what," said John. "Y'all wait here. I'll take a quick look. Rex, hold the door."

"Got it," said Rex.

John crept out into the corridor, empty except for those damn art prints. He played the beam of his light around. Wall to wall luxury, carpet and dark-colored walls and light fittings that cost more than a week's salary. Each. His breath misted out in front of him, and he shivered. *Keep it cool, John.* He laughed at himself. *Cool? It's freezing in here. After this, you're taking Sky on a holiday somewhere warmer, like McMurdo Station.* He reached out to touch a handle, the brass icy under his fingers. He gave it a push, and the door opened with a soft click. Of course it was a soft click, five stars shaved the rough edges off sounds as well, right? The lock wasn't working, probably because the power was out, and that was just fine. The door opened into a luxury room, or what he reckoned a luxury room would look like if he'd ever stayed in one — drapes, tinted windows, a bed big enough to really play around in. Damn, but you could get three or four at a time in there.

The door sighed shut behind him. He started looking for a refrigerator — moneyed people wouldn't have an appliance out in plain sight, no, that would be too *easy* — and found one behind some walnut paneling. Inside was an array of imported beers, a pack of nuts — *who the hell puts nuts in a refrigerator?* — and bottles of water.

Evian. Perfect.

John snagged a few of the bottles, then grabbed the nuts as well. Seemed a shame to leave them here. The beer could wait for after, when they had something to celebrate. He gave a last look around the room — *Sky would love a stay here* — and then pulled the door open to the corridor. "So I've got good news, and better news..." His voice trailed off.

Well, there's something you don't see every day. The corridor was gone, replaced by a large open area, pillars joining the floor to the ceiling. Instead of his feet moving soundless across thick pile carpet, the soles of his shoes squeaked against polished concrete. "Sky? Baby?"

His voice echoed back to him. John looked back at the door he'd just come through, found it gone, empty space behind him stretching back to a line of old windows letting in a dim light. He looked down at the bottles of water he carried. "Well, shit."

Let's do an inventory. He broke the seal on the nuts, tossing a few in his mouth. *You're either going crazy or crazy shit is happening. You've got a couple bottles of water and some fine hotel nuts. You have no idea where your girlfriend is. Actually, you have no idea where you are either. And let's add Rex to the list, cranky old bastard he may be, but he'd be more useful if he were here.*

"Where are we?" Sky's voice carried across the room to him, echoing across the hard surfaces. John looked around, saw her coming towards him from roughly where the stairwell would have been, Rex hard on her heels. The old man was trying to pull her back, but she shrugged him off.

"Baby?" said John. "Baby, don't come over here."

"You disappeared," she said. "I heard you, but I couldn't see you."

Rex took a couple of steps after her, and the sound of a door clicking shut followed him. Both his steps and Sky's slowed, and they looked behind them at the empty room — *no door* — before Rex cleared his throat. "This some kind of elaborate mouse trap?"

"Dunno," said John, holding out the packet of nuts to the other two. "Try some. They're good."

324

"How can you eat at a time like this?" said Sky.

"I'll take some," said Rex, walking forward and grabbing a handful.

"Water?" John offered Sky a bottle. She glared at him, but took it anyway.

"*Shamshoun!*" The word thundered across the room, more a roar than a shout. The three of them turned to see a huge, muscle-bound man. Shirtless, skin taut across a frame packed with power. Sweat glistened against that skin, steaming in the cold air.

John stopped chewing. "Huh."

"You know this guy?" said Rex.

"Nope," said John. "I know a hundred like him though." He raised his voice. "Hey, buddy. What you weigh? 300? 400 pounds?"

"*Shamshoun!*" bellowed the other man — again.

"Does he know any other words?" said Sky.

"Probably not," said John. He tapped the side of his head. "It's the 'roids."

"I thought they had ... different effects," said Rex.

"Sure, whatever," said John. "I don't touch the things as a general rule."

"No complaints here," said Sky, looking at John and raising an eyebrow.

"Not the ... not the right time *or* place," said Rex. "Ever. It's *never* the right time or place for you to put that image in my head."

"Sorry," said Sky, in a voice that said she wasn't. John gave her a tight grin before turning back to the behemoth.

"*Shamshoun!*" The other man took a lumbering step forward, the weight of his steps something John could feel through his feet.

This can't end well. "Hey, pal. Are *you* Shamshoun?"

The other man — Shamshoun — nodded, slapping a meaty hand against his chest. "Shamshoun!" he said, pride in that massive voice.

"I'm going to take another leap of faith," said John, taking a few steps away from Sky and Rex. "I'm going to bet you're here to beat us to death."

"Shamshoun," agreed Shamshoun, giving a happy nod.

"Only one problem I can see," said John. He continued to walk away from Sky and Rex, getting some distance for what was going to come. *Times like this, I could really use pre-briefcase Val. Or Danny. Either one of the heavy hitters would be fine.* "There's three of us, and one of you."

Shamshoun took a lumbering step towards one of the stone supports, wound back a fist, and slammed it into the pillar. Stone shattered, fragments spraying across the room, cracks ascending up the column and into the ceiling.

"He makes a good point," said Rex. "You got this, right?"

John took a couple deep breaths, loosened up his shoulders, then slapped his chest. "Come at me, bro."

Shamshoun started a heavy run towards John, the floor shuddering with his steps. John kept himself light on his toes, then his eyes widened as Shamshoun put on a last burst of speed. John tossed himself to the side, but still took the edge of a shoulder slam as Shamshoun thundered past. That barest hint of a hit lifted him clear off his feet, tossing him into a pillar. He fell to the ground, giving a cough. *For a big guy, he can move pretty quick.* John used the pillar for support, dragging himself to his feet. He touched his lips, fingers coming away red, and he spat on the ground.

Shamshoun was staring at him a big smile splitting his face. "Shamshoun!"

"Put some hip into it next time," said John, miming a little twist of the waist. "Seriously. Do you even lift?" He saw Rex wince, the old man covering his eyes in the heartbeat of silence that followed.

The grin dropped away from Shamshoun's face, and the man gave a roar of rage. He broke into a run towards John again. *Okay, John, okay. This is the point where you* don't *let him hit you again.* The massive man rumbled towards John like an angry boulder — and John stepped to the side at the right time. Shamshoun's momentum took him into the pillar John had used to drag himself upright, flecks of stone falling to the ground. John stepped behind the man, slamming his fists into the other man's kidneys.

It felt like hitting a rock.

John pummeled the other man's kidneys one, two, three more times before Shamshoun gave a roar, spinning around with a mean hook. John stepped under it, a smooth boxer's move taking him in close for a decent uppercut. If you'd seen that uppercut on TV, maybe Tyson putting the swing into Holyfield, the guy at the other end would be down on the ground, taking at least a three count before he stopped seeing two of everything. John felt the blow run up his arm, the skin over one of his knuckles cracked open with the strength he'd put into the swing. It was an uppercut a man could be proud of.

Shamshoun didn't even blink. He grabbed John's arm at the wrist, lifting John off the ground. The big guy leered at John — *Christ, he's got bad breath* — then started slamming a fist into John's side. The good news was that John was suspended by his arm and could swing a little. The bad news was that he could only swing a *little*, and it was about here he thought of Carlisle.

Melissa would have had a solve for this. One of his ribs gave, something soft and wet inside tearing loose. Now Melissa wouldn't have stood for that, she'd have … she'd have … well, she wouldn't have fought like a boxer in a street fight, that's for sure. Melissa Carlisle, now there was a woman who didn't fight fair. Of course, she'd have said that nobody fought fair, that was just how *life was* — another hit into John's ribs made him whimper here — and only degenerates and the mentally ill expected any of that to change.

Okay, Melissa. We'll do it your way.

John used the backswing from the blow to give him a little extra momentum, and used his free hand to jab his first and index fingers into Shamshoun's eyes. It wasn't the kind of strike that a boxer would use. It wasn't even at the sort of depth of dirty that Tyson had used in The Bite Fight. No, this was a pure dick move, balls to breaches.

Melissa would have been so pleased.

327

There was a soft, wet sound as Shamshoun's eyeballs ruptured, and the big man screamed, hurling John away like he was a broken toy. John felt his shoulder pop out of its socket with the throw, and he also screamed briefly — right before he hit, spine first, into the edge of a pillar. It knocked the air out of him, silencing his scream, and — if you were being honest, looking back — that was what stopped him from being beaten to death.

As he lay on the ground, looking at the jellied red coating his fingers, trying to suck even a tiny spoonful of air into his lungs, Shamshoun was roaring, turning around in his blindness, his pain, and his rage, and swinging wild hate around him. His fists landed into pillars, into the ground, even whistled through empty air in an effort to find something, *anything*, to make pay for what had been done to his eyes.

John looked past the big man, took in Sky and Rex in cover behind a pillar. He motioned with his palm out — *stay the fuck there* — and tried to draw in a shaky breath. He got a tiny drip of air, then his diaphragm unlocked and he sucked into a huge lungful, immediately coughing back out the tiny slivers of dust and stone on the ground.

Shamshoun heard the noise and turned to run for him. *Right,* thought John, *this is how it ends. At least they won't find me dead on a toilet like Elvis. Praise be.* Shamshoun's steps made the ground jump, John scrambling to his feet — but *sweet baby Jesus* his back hurt — and away from the freight train of a man who was about to run right over him.

The bottle of Evian hit Shamshoun in the side of the head. Nothing dramatic, no save-the-day move here with a Molotov explosion — just a plastic Evian bottle.

It was enough.

Shamshoun's attention was pulled a little left of center, and his stampede took him past John. John looked over, saw Sky's arm pulling back from the throw — *thanks, babe* — and he pulled himself back to his feet. *Get back in the fight, John. The Master Chief wouldn't sit on his ass while his girl drew live fire from a psycho.* John took a couple quick steps over to the Evian bottle, snaring it from the ground, before jogging further away from Sky and Rex.

"Hey," said John. His voice came out a little on the thin and reedy side, and he cleared his throat before starting again. "Hey. Dumbass."

Shamshoun stopped his swinging around him, standing still. His face was a waste, trails of red like vile tears marking their way down from his ruined eyes. He cocked his head, listening.

"That's right, you better listen," said John. "I've coached ninety-pound weaklings who've got more staying power than you. It looks," said John, wincing and holding his side, "like you need a *hug*."

Shamshoun gave a sickly grin. "Shamshoun will not hurt you, little man."

"Sure," said John, "because you're a glass-jawed rookie."

"No," said Shamshoun. His great brow furrowed with the effort of thought. He spoke each word with deliberate intent, as if he were laying bricks. "Shamshoun will hurt those who came with you. Draw you out, yes? Like a ... trap." He gave that same sickly grin again, by all looks pleased with his own cleverness. Then his hand stretched out, straight as an arrow, pointing at where Sky and Rex huddled behind a pillar.

Ah, hell. John started running at the same time as Shamshoun did. He hurled the Evian bottle, which bounced off the side of Shamshoun's head. The other man didn't falter — *guess it was too much to expect that to work twice in a row* — and made it to where Sky and Rex huddled.

John tried. He really did. It's just that he was hurt so bad, he couldn't get there that fast. He saw the wide-eyed fear in Sky's face, saw Rex step out in front. The old man cleared his throat, and said something that sounded like, "Son," right before a massive fist caught him in the side of the head, smashing him to one side. John's view of Sky was obscured by Shamshoun's massive frame and he pushed himself harder to close the gap. Shamshoun lifted Sky up, a single hand clenched around her throat — *no, no, not Sky, no* — and hefted his prize with a shout of triumph.

John was ten paces away, could have been five if he hadn't been so busted up. Close enough to see the fear in Sky's eyes, close enough to hear Shamshoun's laugh. Too far to be useful. Too damn far. John shouted something, he couldn't have said what, and then Shamshoun stiffened, a *tick-tick-tick* sound in the air, before he toppled to the ground like a falling tree. Sky tumbled free of his hand.

John slowed dropped to his knees beside Sky. Her neck was already discolored, but she was breathing — *alive!* — and held her taser in front of her with both hands, knuckles white. John started to laugh and cry at the same time, and fell to his knees beside her. *Thank you, thank you, thank you.*

The world fell back into place around them, concrete floors sinking beneath a layer of rich carpet, old stone pillars melding together into the muted colors of hotel walls. Shamshoun's unconscious body stayed where it was at their feet.

"Huh," said John.

"Huh," said Rex, coming to stand over them. He held a hand out. Sky waved him away; John took it, pulling himself upright. "Now there's something you don't see everyday."

"True story," said John. "Say—"

Shamshoun's body started to flicker red, wisps of smoke pouring out. With a *whoosh*, it burst into flame, turning to ash within seconds. All that was left was a charred outline on the carpet. *Now that is a thing insurance companies will have kittens about.*

A ghostly laugh echoed down the corridor, gentle, almost friendly. "You have felled my brother, and now his power is mine."

"Wait, what?" said John. "This is starting to feel like a really bad Dark Souls boss fight."

"A what?" said Rex.

"It's a game," said Sky. "You play this hero who enters a dungeon and fights—"

330

"Hang about," said Rex, holding up a hand. "You're talking about a ... a *video* game?"

"Yeah," said John. "It's a pretty good one, but—"

"I will swallow your soul in the eternal fire," said the voice, softer, almost on the edge of hearing. It sounded warm, the flicker of heat and flame around the edges of it.

"Ah, shit," said Rex.

"You know this guy?" said John.

"No," said Rex. "I figure he's probably a big fucker made of flames though. You know. 'Eternal fire.'"

"Like a balrog?" said Sky.

"Sure," said Rex, his blank face showing he had *no idea* what Sky was talking about.

"Come," said the voice, "and *see*."

CHAPTER
FORTY-SEVEN

"Everard," said Carlisle, "I want you to know I don't think this is your fault."

Val looked across at her. "Thanks."

"It's because," she said, "I know you're a little bit stupid and a tiny bit on the heroic side, but you're basically not an asshole."

"Is that ... what?" said Val.

Carlisle allowed herself a smile. "Tell me the plan."

"Okay," said Val. "What we're going to do—"

Silence. Carlisle turned around in the stairwell. Val was gone. Snapped up into thin air, lost faster than a cab in New York City. Carlisle reached behind her, fingers resting on the familiar grip of the Eagle. She pulled it from its holster, the soft leather giving up its gift with an easy slip of sound.

"So," said Carlisle to the empty stairwell. "How's it going to be?"

"*Come play*," said a voice — a woman's voice, clear and strong. From the door on her right. Carlisle pushed it open into a luxury corridor just like all the rest. There was no lighting, and she played the beam of her flashlight across carpet, walls, and there — a sign. *Fitness Center*.

She pushed the door open, leading with her sidearm. Racks of fitness equipment stood in the gloom, elliptical trainers standing like skeletal soldiers in the gloom. Plenty of places to hide.

"*You're here,*" said the voice. It didn't come from a particular direction, like it was in the air around her, or the ground at her feet. "*I've been so lonely.*"

"I'm going to say it," said Carlisle. "Someone's got to. You're creepy."

"*Creepy?*" The voice sounded hurt. "*Is that the way to talk to your only friend?*"

"No," said Carlisle. "But you're not my only friend. Hell, I don't even know your name." She allowed the door to close behind her, edging her feet out into the room. The Eagle glinted in the gloom, as if it were eager to lead her further into the dark.

"*Oh,*" said the voice. "*There's no one else here. And it would be so bad to die alone. That's what being friendless is, isn't it?*"

"Lady," said Carlisle, "you crazy." *Like all crazy shit, it has an ounce of truth though doesn't it, Carlisle?*

A tinkle of laughter came from down an aisle of rowing machines, lying still and quiet. Carlisle turned to follow the noise, the beam of her flashlight playing out ahead of her. Nothing.

"*I'm not crazy,*" said the voice. "*I'm L'inglesou.*"

"Well, Lou," said Carlisle, "good to know you."

"*Not 'Lou,'*" said L'inglesou. "*L'inglesou.*"

"You say po-tay-to, I say po-tah-to," said Carlisle. "Tell me, Lou. Where are you hiding?"

There was a hiss from next to the squat rack, and a shadow slipped out almost faster than the eye could track. The Eagle barked twice, rounds snapping through the air, biting nothing. Carlisle saw the glint of something metal, pain in her shoulder blooming a heartbeat later. She sucked air in through her teeth and spared a look down. A red line, leaking blood — *my blood* — was cut through the leather arm of her jacket. Looked like it had been done with something sharp, like razor sharp. *Lou's not fucking around.*

333

"*Not good enough, my pretty girl,*" said L'inglesou. "*Isn't that what he said, in the dark? Alone, like you are now. Frail. Small. Just a scared, little girl.*"

Something sick and hollow grew in Carlisle's gut. "What did you say?"

The shadow whispered between two treadmills, and Carlisle let the Eagle have its say, bright flashes in the gloom. The shots caught nothing but exercise equipment, fragments of metal and plastic falling in the dark.

"*Come closer,*" said L'inglesou. "*Come and play. It can be our little secret.*"

Carlisle felt a line of hot agony cross her spine and she cried out, turning around. The Eagle fired, a frantic cadence to the shots, and Carlisle wondered if here — *right here, right now* — was where it'd all catch up with her. She'd been faking it, all these years. Wearing the mask of a stronger girl, then a stronger woman, hiding the girl in the dark who cried herself all the way to the next dawn. Maybe the Eagle couldn't save her.

"*What does it feel like,*" said L'inglesou, "*to know that you'll feel his weight on you again? He waits for you at the Cliffs of the Damned. Waits, and hungers. He remembers the taste of your ...* everything."

Her flashlight. It had fallen to the ground, and she scrambled after it. Carlisle held it up in front of her like a beacon, playing it around the room. The beam was shaky, light darting across the equipment, pushing back the gloom *there*, and then *there*. Nothing, until ... a patch of red. The smallest drop, no more than a paper cut's worth, but blood nonetheless. Carlisle looked down at the Eagle, gripping it tighter. "What does it feel like," she said, hating the scared little girl that was causing her words to tremble in fear, "to know that you're going to get pistol-whipped by a scared little girl?" *Not your best line, Carlisle. Keep talking. Push it back. He's not here.* "You want to play? Come fucking get some."

She was starting to get a feel for what to look for, the hint of raven's wings moving in the gloom. *There*, something skittered in the

334

dark towards her, and the Eagle roared, pushing strength into her hand with each shot. She couldn't be sure of having hit anything, but felt new pain in the arm that held the flashlight, causing her to drop it to the ground. Carlisle pulled her arm close to her body, feeling the hot welling of blood pulsing against her chest with every beat of her heart. *Nicked something important there, Carlisle. You don't have much time.*

Something hissed in the gloom before L'inglesou spoke again. *"That hurt."*

"Yeah?" said Carlisle. She ejected her magazine, the empty red cartridge clattering and dancing through the beam of her light on the ground. She pushed a fresh magazine into the weapon. "Plenty more where that came from."

"It's not very sportsmanlike," said L'inglesou. *"Didn't anyone tell you to play fair? You can't be telling anyone about us. You can't tell anyone at all."*

"Sportsmanlike?" said Carlisle. "You sound like that clown Miles."

"Do you like John Miles?" L'inglesou's voice came from behind her now, and Carlisle spun about. *Nothing.*

"I think he's a degenerate," said Carlisle.

"You shouldn't talk about people behind their backs," said L'inglesou. *"Daddy will know if you tell."*

"Thing is," said Carlisle, "I told him he was a degenerate. This morning, I think. Tell you what, Lou—" and here, Carlisle leaned against an elliptical trainer as a wave of dizziness hit her "—why don't we play a game?"

"A game?"

"Yeah, a game," said Carlisle, swallowing. She thought of John, and what he'd do. Something dumb and stupid and heroic, probably. She looked at the Eagle in her hand, thumb tracing a line against the worn grip. John wouldn't use a gun — hell, the man couldn't hit the broad side of a barn with a firearm if you put it three feet in front of his face. He'd close up his fists and go in swinging.

He'd die. Probably.

"See," said Carlisle, "since we're such good friends, Lou, I think we should finish this. Just you and me. With a game. You get one shot. I'll put my gun away. You give a good run at me, take your swing. You kill me, we're done. But if you miss ... well."

"*And then?*" There was something like glee in L'inglesou's voice.

"Well, then it'll be my turn," said Carlisle. "What do you say, Lou?"

"*I like your games,*" said L'inglesou.

"I'll take that as a yes," said Carlisle. She stepped away from the elliptical trainer, a little unsteady on her feet, and put the Eagle away. The weapon caught on the holster, like it didn't want to be silenced, but Carlisle gave it another push — *not this time, you can't help me with this fight old friend* — and slipped it home. She stood on an exercise mat, empty space at least two paces in every direction, and breathed deep.

For no good reason she thought of Elliot, of his sense of duty, of his steady partnership. She allowed a small smile to land on her face as she remembered his "gut sense" — not once right in all the years they'd worked together. It felt like he was here, now, somewhere in this room. Even though she knew it was wrong, even though she knew she'd got him killed.

What was it that Elliot had told her? *Praise no day until it's ended, that's what I always say.* Okay, Elliot. *Okay.* She closed her eyes, then said, "Today isn't over."

L'inglesou came at her, a shadow bound with fury. *Good God damn but she's fast.* L'inglesou's first pass left Carlisle with a red streak below her right eye, years of training — sweat on the mat, bruises on her flesh — giving her the reflexes to pull her head back in time to not lose an eye. Carlisle swayed in place after L'inglesou's pass, the steady *drip, drip, drip* of her own blood falling on the floor around her.

"Close," said Carlisle. "It's almost like you meant it. But Lou?

You've got to want it. You've got to really *want it.*" Carlisle flexed her fingers. "Do you know what I mean? Do you want it, Lou?"

A hiss came from her right, something in the air hinting at danger, and Carlisle let it come. This shadow that called itself L'inglesou was just another of the fallen, one of the ones that this damn world had pushed on too hard until they cracked. Carlisle had been in a hundred fights — *no, more, be honest with yourself, you like it, this is where you feel really alive, you look for trouble in every corner, welcome it home like something lost* — and knew the way a body would lean forward with a rush. She knew where the knife was going to be held, how the angle of it would come in to her throat, or under her ribs, or a handful of other ways to try and drink her life away. She could sense that Lou was a pro, not some burned out coke camel with a blade and not a lot of common sense. Could feel it, if she was being honest, like she felt Elliot watching her, feel that here she'd finally met her match.

The faintest hint of Elliot's aftershave came to her — cheap, Brut or something, his ex-wife had given it to him and he'd worn it like it was Dolce & Gabbana, if you could believe that — and she smiled again. *I'll see you soon, old friend.* "Carlisle," he said, and there he was — *Elliot!* — standing in front of her plain as day. He took her elbow. "Carlisle, I'm real sorry about this." He wound back his hand and slapped her clean across the face.

The shock of it made her suck in a lungful of air, Elliot's face gone like smoke on wind, replaced with L'inglesou's charge, all soft darkness coming to swallow her up. Carlisle screamed, her arms coming up — *too late to do anything about that knife, just make her pay for it* — to accept L'inglesou's charge. Carlisle wrapped her hands around the back of L'inglesou's head, arms bringing the other woman into a clinch as the knife entered her chest. The pain was bright and clear, shaking the edges of her fugue away. Carlisle brought her knee up once, twice, three times into L'inglesou's face. *Christ, it's like trying to hold water.* The other woman raged, but Carlisle pulled her arms together harder, putting the last of her strength into it. Her elbows locked, pressure on L'inglesou's carotid arteries, and Carlisle brought her knee up again, and again, and *again*, until L'inglesou stopped moving. Carlisle dropped her opponent to the ground, then pulled the knife out of her chest. She let it tumble to the ground beside L'inglesou's body, then drew in a shuddering breath.

"Elliot?" The name came out of Carlisle half a whisper, half a plea. "Elliot? Are you there?"

Nothing. Silence and stillness all around, not even a hint of that nasty aftershave. "Elliot? I ... I don't want you to see. Do you understand? If you're there, don't look." Another wave of dizziness hit her, and she almost dropped to one knee. *No.* Not yet. "I've had to do things ... I couldn't carry the badge anymore, Elliot. I'm too dirty for it." Carlisle slipped the Eagle free.

Whips of smoke seeped out of L'inglesou's body, pooling on the ground around her. Carlisle stood over her opponent, leveled the weapon, and fired. She kept pulling the trigger until the Eagle clicked empty, spitting its magazine to the ground at her feet.

Carlisle ran a trembling hand through her hair, then looked back at the door. Walked towards it, steps uneven, found the stairs — God knows if they were the same stairs she'd come in through, she was too tired to think about it — and began to climb, the steady *drip, drip, drip* of her own blood keeping her company.

Elliot stood in the darkness over L'inglesou's body, and watched his old friend go. "Carlisle," he said, "you're the only one who's ever been good enough to carry the badge. You know what it really means." He reached down to touch one of the red magazines lying on the ground. *"Praise no day until it's ended, Carlisle. Praise no road until you've crossed it. Praise no wife until they're buried. And praise no Shield until you've stood behind it."* He flickered out, leaving silence behind him.

FORTY-EIGHT

The truck rumbled and bounced up to the front of Trump Tower, the engine shaking the cabin. Adalia turned to Just James, saw the wideness of his eyes, and then turned to Marcellus Samuel Kentucky. "Thank you for the ride."

"That's okay," said Marcellus Samuel Kentucky. He patted the big steering wheel in front of him. "I think the truck is due for a refit now. Boys in the garage, well, I can't see them thinking this is 'wear and tear.'"

"Tell them," said Adalia, "that you were saving the world."

"Tell them," said Just James, "that you had to ride out of a zombie apocalypse. It'll sit better with your target audience."

"I like the kid," said Marcellus Samuel Kentucky. "He gets it."

"He spends all his time playing video games," said Adalia, smiling. She looked outside the cabin, the smile dying on her lips. Gabriel stood in the cold Chicago air, wearing a T-shirt and jeans. "Anyway," she said, trailing off. "I think we should go."

"Let's kick some butt," said Just James. "Hey, you go first though, okay?"

"Hey," said Marcellus Samuel Kentucky. "That's not very manly."

"I'll give you my Man Card right now," said Just James. "In case you didn't notice, she's a ... she's a sorceress."

"You're just a tall glass of water, ain't you?" said Marcellus Samuel Kentucky, looking around Adalia at Just James.

"You coming in?" said Just James.

"Hell no," said Marcellus Samuel Kentucky. "The devil's in there."

"At least I'm going in," said Just James, pushing open the door of the cabin with his foot. He had to give it a kick to unstick it, the frame jammed up from the journey to get here. "Your door needs fixing."

"Your mouth needs fixing," said Marcellus Samuel Kentucky.

Adalia put a gentle hand on Marcellus Samuel Kentucky's arm. "Thank you," she said.

"Ain't no thing," he said. "Just a little ride across the city, you know?"

"Not that," said Adalia, rolling her eyes at Just James.

"Right," he said, giving her that easy, gentle smile. "I'm coming in anyway, you know."

"No," she said.

"It's not like you can stop me," he said. "You're a slip of a girl."

Adalia lowered her eyes, then looked back at Marcellus Samuel Kentucky. "Marcellus Samuel Kentucky, do you hear me?"

"I hear you," he said, something soft in his voice.

"I name your daughters for you. They are Candice, named after your aunt, who was always gentle with you when you were small. She gave you lemonade when the weather turned hot and the sun was merciless. And Betty, sweet Betty, who is shy and quiet and loves you with all of her heart. She watches you with big eyes as you move around the home you've made. She waits for her father — her real father — to come home, so she can grow up and build the good memories of you. I give you these names, so you will never forget them. Candice and Betty. Do you hear me?" Adalia ran out of breath, shaking with the effort of holding — *something* — heavy inside her.

"I hear you," he said. "But ... I can ... I can help. I owe you."

"We made a trade," she said, following Just James out into the cold air. "You don't owe me anything." She looked over at Gabriel, who had his arms crossed, expression closed. "Marcellus Samuel Kentucky? If you go home to Candice and Betty, you are helping. Do you understand?"

"No," he said.

"That's okay," said Adalia. "Tomorrow, or the next day, or the day after, you might. If you make it home. If you don't step into this building where the devil lives."

"Hey," said Marcellus Samuel Kentucky. "Donald Trump's a lot of things, but..." The joke died as he was telling it, and he gripped the steering wheel. "It doesn't feel right leaving you here."

"It's cool," said Just James. "I'm here."

"God save us all," said Marcellus Samuel Kentucky, and reached over the cab to pull the door shut. The Kenworth roared, then shuddered as it pulled away, jouncing back onto the street. There was a sound of crumpling metal as the machine slammed through another car, and then it was free, picking up speed as it roared away.

"You realize," said Just James, his shoulders sagging as if he'd just realized something, "that he was our heavy hitter."

"My Mom's a heavy hitter," said Adalia, "and she's inside."

"Good point," said Just James. His face softened a little as he watched her hug her elbows to her side. He looked around. "Where is he?"

"Over there," she said, pointing at Gabriel with her chin.

"Can he hear me?"

"How can I not," said Gabriel, "when you are so very loud?"

"Yes," said Adalia. "He can hear you."

"Okay, cool," said Just James. "Gabriel. Gabriel? I don't even know if the mic's on, right, but here's the thing. I don't know you, and you don't know me—"

"I know you well enough," said Gabriel.

"—but I think that if you're a dead kid about my age you'll understand how special Adalia is and how we need to team up so she gets out of this alive and that really I don't know what's going on but

341

I want to help." His words came faster and faster until they ran out completely. After a moment, he added, "I think ... I think I need to do something important. For her. For you."

Gabriel blinked. "I don't know you at all," he said. He smiled, eyes widening with wonder. "And I think that's a good thing."

He thinks I'm special? Adalia started to reach out a hand, to Just James or Gabriel she couldn't rightly have said, then let her hand fall. "I don't know what's going on either."

"I do," said Gabriel. "I don't know if he knows what it means to *help* here."

"Just James," said Adalia. "Do you ... do you know what's at stake here?"

"I just said I didn't know what's going on," said Just James, looking up at Trump Tower. "But I do know that that building's seen better days. Those windows are totally smashed. It looks a lot better in photos on the Internet." He scuffed one foot across the top of the other. "We need to give everything. To make it right."

"If we go in that building," said Adalia, "someone will die."

"One of us?" said Just James. She could see it in his eyes, the understanding of what was to come.

"I don't know who the Sacrifice is," Adalia lied, "except that it's not me, and it's not Gabriel."

"Why not you?"

"Because," said Adalia, knowing it was unhelpful, but made the truth easier to hold in her heart. "That's not the way it works."

"Well," said Just James, "the way I see it is this. Standing out in the street gives us about an eighty percent chance of dying of cold if we stick around. Maybe ninety percent if the zombies come and eat our brains."

"They don't eat brains," said Gabriel. "They — never mind," he said, sighing in exasperation.

"And," said Just James, "as long as you don't die, I'm okay with that."

"What if it's you?" said Adalia. Her voice grew small. "I don't want it to be you."

"Then this Universe of yours will owe you one," said Just James, standing tall — really *tall*, in a way she'd not seen before. Like he had a purpose and a will, like he knew where his road went all of a sudden. "C'mon."

"Wait," said Adalia. "What if it's not us?"

"What do you mean?" said Just James.

"She means," said Gabriel, rolling his eyes, "that just because we go in there doesn't mean it's one of us that dies. You, I mean. I'm already dead. I mean, it could be Adalia's mom, or Uncle John, or Melissa Carlisle, or Valentine Everard, or Skyler Evans, or Rex Aubrey. The Shield can't stop it. The Sword can't break it. The Good Right Arm won't be able to lift it, and the Knight can't fight it. Do you understand?"

Just James looked right at the spot where Gabriel stood, then turned to Adalia. "I understand," he said, "that everyone you love would die for you. Do you know? Do you see? You're becoming something more beautiful." He shrugged his thin shoulders inside his jacket. "Let's go."

More beautiful? "But—" Adalia swallowed. "No one should die because of me."

"I agree," said Just James, "but things are a bit shit right now. We might need to—" and he wiggled his hands "—*compromise* here."

"Heck of a compromise," said Gabriel.

"I don't know a lot—" said Just James.

"No kidding," said Gabriel.

"—but I know that the world ends today if we don't do this." Just James held out his hand to Adalia. "Meet me half way, and let's go save the princess."

"Save the princess?" But Adalia was already taking a small step forward.

"Figure of speech," said Just James.

"Video games," said Gabriel.

Adalia took Just James' hand in hers. It was smooth and warm. She looked down at her feet, then walked with him into where the wind touched the earth, where the dark was strongest, where the Leader of the Damned sat in the space between thoughts. But she didn't fear the fading of the sun. The living and the dead walked with her, and she would end the devil's reign.

CHAPTER
FORTY-NINE

T he floor was soft under her bare feet, warm and comforting like—

You have never been in any place like this.

—the Grand Hotel in Monte Carlo. She had stayed there, with him, for a spell or two. It had been when they met, and of course it wasn't called the Grand Hotel — that's what they'd called it, laughing as they enjoyed a week away from the rest of the world.

This is a place where your thoughts go to die.

Danny brushed a red lock away from her face, ducking under the gauzy fabric that guarded the entranceway. The room smelled of lavender, sun streaming in the open bay windows. The sounds of a street far below came in with the fresh air, muted and gentle. And he was there.

Choler tells false tales with your own mind.

Choler sat on the bed — as handsome as he had ever been. He'd stripped himself to the waist, the heat of the day starting to cause sweat to prick against his golden skin. Danny smiled at him. "Where have you been all my life?"

"Waiting for you," he said, putting aside his book — had he just been holding a book? But of course he had. She hadn't seen it, the drapes around the bed hiding the minor details from view. "Come to me."

"I'm already—"

You are lost.

"—here..?" Danny's footsteps slowed, and for a moment she saw cold walls and broken windows in a room for the rich, before the sunlight returned in a blaze of white, so brilliant, so *clean*. She swayed. "I'm sorry, Choler. The day — I'm feeling a little dizzy."

"Of course, my love," he said, getting up from the bed. That young, fit body he wore hadn't aged a day since—

You never met him before this day dawned.

—they had met all those years before. She hoped she didn't disappoint him — she knew carrying a child had given her marks on her skin that she was proud to wear.

"What are those, Mommy?" Little Adalia pointed at the stretch marks on her skin.

"They are my tiger stripes," she said, laughing. "I earned these."

"How did you get them?"

"The best way," said Danny.

Adalia frowned. "Will I get them?"

"If you're lucky," said Danny, hugging her. "If you are blessed."

Except the marks were gone now, weren't they? Gone, like Adalia. Why was that name so familiar? So close to her heart, yet so far away? She stopped, then pulled up her shirt to see her smooth skin, unmarked by the bearing of a child.

Remember.

She hadn't had a child, had she? "Choler?"

"Yes, my love?" He came to stand close to her, a strong arm holding her up.

"Choler, did we have a baby?" Danny felt so confused, and her head was beginning to hurt, hurt so bad it felt like something was trying to force its way out.

Remember.

"No, my love. I wanted one, you know this, but you never did. You said you ... well, it's not important. Surely you remember?" His eyes, so full of concern, of care. How could she not remember not wanting his child?

A sharp stab of pain hit behind her eyes, and she cried out, falling—

REMEMBER.

—to the ground. Her breath came faster now, she panted with exertion, but she didn't know why—

By the moon.

—because she should be in love, she should be relaxed, shouldn't she? She clenched her head in her hands, fingers raking against her scalp, drawing—

By the stars.

—blood. The bright copper smell hit her, and she remembered running through the night, moon and stars wheeling overhead an Earth not yet cool. The game was ahead of them, running for life, and this, this was it, the test of it all. To hunt, to earn your right to stand astride the ground and howl your victory to the heavens, to the Universe that watched it all.

Remember your Pack.

"Are you all right?" Choler's voice was liquid honey, but the pain pushed it aside and she didn't answer. Such pain, she had not felt even this much in the joy of the birth of her little girl, her baby, her Adalia—

Remember. Remember. REMEMBER YOUR CUB. He cannot take her from us.

—who was so very small in her arms. Danny had held her in the hospital, whispering against Adalia's head that *it'll be okay, Daddy's gone but I'm here, I promise I won't ever leave* and yet she had done worse than leave. She had *forgotten*.

Danny screamed, and screamed, and screamed, then stood up, the sunlight falling away from her, leaving the cold and dark of Trump Tower. She stood with Choler in a luxury room, the squalor of it vile — half empty bottles of liquor cast aside, uneaten food lying on plates and trays on every surface. Her head *was* going to explode, the memories bursting back out, washing over her. Some warning, some—

Rise. Danger. FIGHT.

—sense making her *see* the knife that Choler held, that tiny sliver of agony that he was bringing towards her face. She snarled, grabbing Choler's knife hand. Her other hand she brought round in—

No claws. This body is so weak. Change, my sister.

—a fist, smashing the bones in Choler's arm again and again. The man was thrashing in her grip, the pain must have been—

He will litter this world with the empty hearts of the lost.

—exquisite. It made her hit harder, and faster. Danny pulled him in close to her, breathed in the stench of him, then lifted him off the ground, arm straight out in front of her like she was holding up a shirt she was considering wearing. The knife finally tumbled to the carpet, the hateful silver twinkling, catching stray light as it fell.

"By the moon and the stars that I hunt by," said Danny, "I remember."

"We are in love," said Choler, and Danny felt the pull of it.

She shook him like a doll. "No," she said. "You are a sickness. You tried to take my little girl from me."

"She is your weakness," said Choler.

"She is my strength," said Danny. She pulled the man close enough to kiss, saw the madness in his eyes, and adjusted her grip. Her free hand grabbed Choler's other arm. Holding both of his arms just below the shoulders, she put a foot against his chest, and braced herself.

"She will—" but his words choked into a scream as she started to pull. She leaned back into it, her teeth clenching into a snarl. Choler screamed, and screamed, until one of his arms gave with a wet tear, a shower of red spraying across the expensive carpet, the drapes, her face. Pieces of Choler rained to the ground with the sound of a wet mop hitting linoleum. Danny stumbled back, letting his body fall.

Now we hunt.

"Yes," she said, and licked her lips, tasting copper. She caught a glimpse of herself in a broken mirror against the wall. Her eyes were burning yellow, so bright, above the red of Choler's blood. "*We are the Night.*" She raised a hand to her face, touching the blood, licking it off her fingers. A shiver went through her at the taste, the sticky red sweet she hadn't glutted on in such a long, long time. She turned those bright eyes to Choler's body, and felt a terrible hunger.

We are the Night.

They'd managed to climb another few floors up through the dark tower, but the smell of fire had drawn them out of the stairwell. John had said *we should just walk the fuck on by* and Rex had said *and that's how a fire will kill us all because they go up, don't you know anything* and Sky had just pushed the door open and left them to it.

She looked down another empty corridor — *everything in this place looks the same* — except this one wasn't the same. Sure, yeah, it looked the same, down to the identical beautiful carpet and tacky artwork. The difference was the smoke blooming like a corrupt flower from down the end. Dark and thick, like someone was burning tires. It didn't smell like tires, it smelled like potpourri, and that's when Sky knew it was all wrong.

Because, if she knew anything at all, it was that potpourri was a great lie, one of those told to children as they grew up like *Santa's real* or *that quarter came from the Tooth Fairy* or *free Wi-Fi if you dine here.* Sky had seen her share of potpourri, usually in a bowl, and she'd always thought, *why the hell would you put a bunch of dead plants in a bowl.*

Unless you were making soup.

If this fire smelled like potpourri, like potpourri was *supposed to*, then it was another great lie.

The door to the stairwell creaked open behind her. "Baby?" John came up beside her, took her hand. She leaned into the closeness of him. "I wasn't sure where you'd gone."

"Is that because you were spending so much time arguing with Rex that you forgot about me?" Sky looked at him, deadpan.

John's face went through twenty different emotions before settling on the not-quite-Miles-Megawatt-Smile that she loved. The honest one, the one just for her. "Nice," he said. "Truth be told—"

"Truth be told," said Rex, "that's a fire."

"Smells like flowers," said John.

"I'll admit, that's unusual," said Rex.

"How unusual," said Sky, "on a scale of one to ten?"

"Maybe a twelve," said Rex. "I was called to this fire a while back, right? It was—"

"Is this a long story?" said John. "Because, fire."

Rex sighed. "So, I was called to this fire a while back, place called Blake Garden. Heard of it?"

"Do I look like the kind of guy who gardens?" said John.

"UC Berkeley, right?" said Sky.

"Do I look," said John, "like the kind of guy who went to college?"

"So," said Rex, pushing on, "there's this little cottage garden there."

"What's it called?" said John.

"It's called the Cottage Garden," said Rex. "Did you want this to be a long or a short story?"

"I want it to be an accurate story," said John. "You started it."

"Made me want to take a few more classes," said Rex. "You get in a place like that with summer fashions, and..." He looked at Sky, then swallowed.

"I've got no clue what you're talking about," said John.

351

"I think you should stick to the main points," said Sky, glaring at John, "because, fire."

"Speaking of," said John, "shouldn't you be getting an extinguisher and rushing up there to put that fire out, old man?"

"Two things," said Rex.

"Shoot," said John.

"First up, do you see any extinguishers?" Rex pointed at the walls. "Nice wallpaper, sure, but no extinguishers. New hotels, they've got the fire systems all built in."

"I saw a fire axe in the stairwell," said John.

"Those are good for axing open the stairwell doors," said Rex. "They're not real good at putting out fires. You can't just cut a fire down."

"So," said Sky, looking at the smoke again. "Second thing?"

"I'm retired," said Rex. "As you pointed out, I'm an old man."

Sky snorted. "UC Berkeley," she prompted.

"Some kid had decided to start a fire," said Rex. "Weed, or something. I don't know."

"Seems plausible," said Sky, "but as they're students they pretty much all major in drug discovery so it could have been anything."

"He ... the student, that is ... started the fire in this cottage garden. I don't think he meant to, it's this little place full of cottage crap. You know. Herbs. Roses." Rex gestured vaguely with his hands. "Flowers *and shit*. I don't know. Anyway, didn't smell anything like that," he said, pointing at the smoke. "Just smelled like dead plants burning. Not air freshener."

"I don't get the link," said John. "Cottage garden, check. But—"

"Jesus, Mary, and Joseph," said Rex, "it's because potpourri is made of spices and rose petals and other crap like that."

"Gotcha," said John, but he was grinning. Sky held his hand a little tighter. "So what we going to do about this fire?"

"You," said Rex, "are going to get a fire axe from the stairwell."

"Cool," said John. "What for? I thought that you couldn't put out a fire with an axe."

"You can put out a fire *starter* with an axe," said Rex.

"On it," said John, giving her hand a quick squeeze before detaching himself from her. "This day just gets better."

Sky stood, Rex at her side, and watched John walk back the way they'd come. The old man spoke up. "Nothing much gets him down, does it?"

"Not much," said Sky. She knew her voice had gone soft, couldn't help herself. Didn't want to.

"That's got to be kind of annoying," said Rex, pretending not to notice.

"It's why I love him," said Sky.

"I wondered," said Rex, "because of all the other stuff that comes along for the ride."

"That," said Sky, as the heavy stairwell door *shunked* shut behind John, "is just John Miles being John Miles. I'd sooner try to talk a hurricane down than change any of that."

"You're a special woman," said Rex. "Look me up if he dies at the end of this."

Sky laughed. "God loves a trier, Rex. God loves a trier."

John came back through the stairwell door after only a moment, jogging back towards them with a bright red fire axe in his hands. "These things are heavy," he said.

"They're not for show, that's for sure," said Rex. "Now, son, let's go find us a fire."

SKY REACHED out for the door handle. They were in the thick of the smoke, but it wasn't hard to breathe and it didn't sting her eyes. Rex reached out for her arm, stopping her from touching the handle.

"Two things," he said.

"Okay," said Sky.

"First," said Rex, "handle could be hot. Don't grab that with your bare hands unless you want to smell cooking bacon."

Sky pulled her hand back. "What's the second thing?"

"If there's a fire in there—"

"Where there's smoke," said John, "there's fire."

"*If* there's a fire in there," said Rex, "and it's just smoking low, a bit ol' gust of fresh air can set it off."

"Bigger fire?" said Sky.

"Explosion," said Rex. "Called a backdraft."

"Like the movie?" said John.

"That was a terrible movie," said Rex. "But sure, like that."

"Got it," said John.

"What movie?" said Sky.

"There's these two brothers," said John, "and they—"

"Fire," said Rex.

"Right," said John. "So, how do we get the door open?"

The handle clicked, the door easing open a crack. John dropped the axe, tackling Sky and taking her to the ground as he shielded her with his body. She felt all the air go out of her lungs with an *oomph*, and then—

Nothing. Nothing at all.

"Son," said Rex, "son, help the lady up."

John looked down at her, his face inches away, and stole a kiss before scrambling to his feet. "Sorry," he said.

"No, it's good," said Rex. "Right response to a different set of inputs. If there had been a grenade or a backdraft, that would've been about perfect. Would even have been called smooth."

Sky let John pull her up, held his hand a little longer, then pulled him in for another kiss. "It *was* perfect," she said.

The almost-Miles-Megawatt-Smile flared briefly in the dim corridor, then John snared his axe from the floor. "I'm going to find out who opened that door."

"While you're there," said Rex, "see if you can see what all the smoke is about."

"Gotcha," said John. He used the axe to push the door open, then slipped inside the room.

Sky looked at Rex. "Anything cause smokeless fires?"

"Cigalikes," said Rex. "You know, those e-sigs. Chemical spills, but they don't smell like flowers either. Maybe Hollywood, if someone's filming a movie." He scratched at his stubble. "I hate to say it, but he was probably right. Where there's smoke, there's—"

John burst back into the corridor, slamming the door closed behind him. His eyes were wild. "Run," he said, before the door exploded into fragments. Sky was tossed aside, her head hitting the wall, and she slid down into the cool black.

"C'MON KID, I'm too old to be carrying children around." The voice was familiar, but muffled, like it was coming from a long way off. "You need to get up, Sky. You've got to get up."

She opened her eyes, black edges around her vision. Sky could see a face — *Rex, like a Tyrannosaurus* — above her. She tried to speak, coughed, tried again. "You look terrible."

"That's because," said Rex, "we're getting our asses kicked." His face was covered in soot, a bright angry burn on the lower part of his jaw. His left eye was weeping and red. Rex's face pulled away as he stood up, and he reached a hand down to her. "C'mon. You've got to move."

"Where's John?" Sky took his hand, felt herself lifted up — *it feels like floating, everything feels like I'm floating* — and almost went back down as the dizziness hit.

Rex almost smiled. She could see he wanted to, but it didn't come. "Like I said. He's getting his ass kicked. So you have time. To get moving."

"What happened to you?"

"I got my ass kicked," said Rex. "I've fought a lot of fires, but..." His voice trailed away, then he shook himself out of it. "We've got to get going."

"Wait," said Sky. "Where?"

"Out," said Rex. "We've got to get out."

"Hell, no," said Sky. "My lover's here, and all my friends are here."

"We're going to die," said Rex. He looked like he meant it.

Sky pulled her taser out. "If that's what it takes." Maybe it was the hit to the head, but she meant it too, because she didn't want a life without John Miles in it.

"Right," said Rex. "Here's where we're at. There's this thing—"

The wall beside him exploded in a shower of drywall and smoke, and John came through wrestling ... *something*. It looked like a man made of fire, the whites and yellows and reds of a hearth flickering up through his body. His eyes were the brightest white, like the core of a furnace, his mouth held in a snarl. He — *it? No, definitely a he* — and John were wrestling over a fire axe held between them. The air around them shimmered with heat.

Sky raised her taser without conscious thought, pulled the trigger. In the hair's breadth of time between her raising it and firing, the man of fire looked at her and seemed to smile. The taser *tick-tick-ticked* and ... nothing.

Then it exploded in her hand, the battery inside swelling with heat. Sky screamed, hands covering her face as shards of metal and plastic flew like shrapnel.

She heard a grunt, spared a glance and saw John use the distraction to wrest the axe away from the man of fire. John gave a yell, swinging the axe into the burning figure. It passed through, but sluggish, pulling John off balance. The man of fire seemed to laugh, taking a step back. "*You can't fight fire with an axe, little man. And you should not,*" and here, he looked at Sky, "*throw batteries into a fire. It's on all the warning labels.*"

John righted himself, looked at the fire axe in his hand, and swung again. It snared on something in the man of fire, pulled him a little off center again, and those terrible bright white eyes swung away from Sky. The man of fire took a step back. "*You killed my brother.*"

356

"The big guy?" Rex was taking a couple steps back. "He didn't put up such a hard fight."

"Your view of his value doesn't stop him from being my brother. His power is now mine, and you have made me Agni. You have made me fire." Agni — the man of fire — laughed. *"You held the power of the Night for so long, squandered all it had to offer, and now you will die, with just a taste of what could have been."*

"To be fair," said John, holding up a hand as he bent over, catching his breath, "none of the three of us squandered the Night, or whatever it is."

Agni blinked, the white-hot eyes shutting off for a second. *"What?"*

"It was my buddy, Val," said John, leaning on the axe. "He had the — what do you call it? The Night? Stupid name. Anyway, Val, and, uh, I guess, Danny." John straightened, working a kink from his back. "Thing is—"

Agni's white-hot eyes moved to Rex. *"You will all die here, and you are speaking of trivialities."*

"He's like that," said Rex, putting himself in front of Sky. Rex tapped the side of his head. "I think he got hit in the head when he was a child." He shrugged, a *what-are-you-gonna-do?* gesture.

Sky looked around as they talked to Agni, distracting the thing that had eaten the power of his dead brother to stand, burning like a bonfire, in front of them. *He can't be killed with the axe. How do you fight fires?* Her eyes moved to the walls of the room, the rich drapes hanging in silken promise. *You smother them.*

"Really," said John, "it wasn't like that. My mother was very loving."

"You're just lucky you didn't drown in the bath," said Rex.

"ENOUGH!" Agni blazed, heat making both Rex and John stumble back. John — her John, her beautiful man — raised the axe. She could see it in the set of his face, the way he held his shoulders, just how he lifted the axe. He was going to die, he was going to do something to buy them a precious second to get free.

357

That just wouldn't do. Not this time. She felt something lurch in her stomach, knew with a sick feeling what she had to do. After this, she wouldn't feel his touch, or see his face, or taste his kisses. She wouldn't know what it was like to be his wife, and she wouldn't see — again — how he ignored other women, his eyes for her alone.

Sky grabbed the drapes off the wall, the heavy material coming free with a tear. The sound made all three of the men turn, John's eyes starting to widen, Rex's face one of confusion. Agni's eyes, those white coals, narrowing. And before she could think about it anymore, she was running. Running at Agni, the drapes in her arms causing her to stumble, just once, before she got her stride. Sky hit Agni at a run, the drapes falling over the blazing man like a shroud, and she could feel the heat of the man burning the fabric she held.

But she'd got a good speed up, hit Agni off balance, and her rush carried her clear to one of the broken windows at the room's edge. She could hear John screaming behind her—

Baby, no!

—as she carried Agni out into the cold Chicago air, held against her like a prize. She burst into the cold day in a shower of broken glass, the building's solid tears falling like rain, sharing her descent. The drapes were on fire now, her skin was blistering, and she held Agni tighter as the living flame thrashed against her, the air pulling at her hair as she fell.

"Hi," he'd said. "I'm John."

"I don't care," she'd said. She'd taken one look at that megawatt smile, at the easy way he stood, and knew he was trouble.

The smile didn't falter. "This is usually where you tell me your name. Because we're introducing each other."

"Imagine," she said. "Imagine a world where you go into a mall where everyone's got advertising, right. And the advertising is all aimed at you. All the clerks, all the stores, hell, even the ice cream cart, they're all trying to sell you something. And that one thing is dick. You can't even buy an ice cream from the ice cream cart. They only sell dick, and that one guy at the

ice cream cart, well, he's only got one dick in stock. That's what it's like being a woman. Every man wants to sell you a dick, and I'm not buying."

"Huh," said John. "You know, that's fair enough. Can I interest you in a drink instead?"

The air was really rushing past her now, and her shirt caught on fire. The pain was so much, not the burning, but the memories as they came to her as she fell.

"I drive a cab," she said.

John was dissecting his dinner, something with chicken or fish, she didn't know. The menus were all in French. "Okay," he said.

"Okay?" Sky frowned. "Are you even listening?"

"Sure," he said. "You drive a cab."

"You're not surprised?"

He'd laughed then. "I tell you. When you get to meet my buddy Val, well, you'll understand that nothing much is really that surprising."

"What's he do?" Sky leaned forward. "Spy? Elevator technician?"

John had leaned back, savoring the wine. Or trying to. His face said yes, his lips said no. "He solves problems," he said, then put his glass down. "Say."

"Yeah?" The wine was good, and at two-fifty a bottle it had better be. It was a little earthy for her tastes, and she was already doing the mental math on how many extra fares she'd need to run to pay off this dinner. But she wanted to enjoy it, because he'd asked her here.

"Are you trying to get into my friend's pants?"

She blinked, then laughed. "I don't even know who he is."

Something sad went through his face for a second before that megawatt smile came back. "Plenty of time for that, after I sell you the full bag-o'-dicks package."

The ground was getting closer, but the tears in her eyes were making the world a soft collection of muted grays. She tried to pull in a breath, but all she got was fire and smoke.

"Baby," said John. "Baby, I've got something I need to tell you."

Sky looked up from the kitchen counter. It had been a bag-of-shit day, one of those ones where everything was a red light in your way. "John Miles, this had better be good."

He'd looked a little stunned, but swallowed. "I love you."

"You ... what?"

"I love you," he said. "See, I made a list." He led her to the bathroom, where he'd written on their mirror with a Sharpie. Number one said she had a great singing voice. Number two was that she sang in the shower every morning. Three was that she didn't hate his terrible cooking, and four was that she didn't mind him being him. It went on, memories held on that glass in black marker, until she hit the end. It said "Number 20: Because I can't stop thinking about you."

"Oh," she said. "Oh." She didn't say anything back, too afraid of what it meant.

"Oh," said Sky, the air taking her words away. "I love you, John Miles."

She hit the ground, and Skyler Evans didn't say anything after that.

CHAPTER
FIFTY-ONE

Adalia's feet crunched over broken shards of a fallen vase. It had probably been nice once, the bits and pieces just holding a hint of perfect colors and a shape that held the eye. She knew if she tried hard enough she could step sideways into that other place and see what it had been, and what it could be.

She didn't want to. Being in the other place didn't feel like being her.

"You know, there's probably going to be bad things happening up ahead." Gabriel walked in front of them, his feet making no sound.

"Do you think there are zombies here?" Just James' eyes were wide and round, his head on a swivel. "I think Ghost Boy should go first."

"He is going first," said Adalia. "His name is Gabriel."

"Loudmouth is still making too much noise." Gabriel turned away, hands in his pockets.

"Does he always call me James?" said Just James. "If he doesn't I don't have to call him Gabriel."

"Very mature," said Adalia. *Boys.* "We need to find my mom."

"Wait one," said Just James. "She's a werewolf, right? She went in ahead to bust some skulls. That was the plan?"

"Right," said Adalia. "That was the plan."

"So, and I'm kind of talking out loud here, but wouldn't she be right in the middle of the danger vortex? You know, random gunfire, sharp knives, harsh language, all kinds of scary things."

"Sounds plausible," said Gabriel. "Just said louder than it needed to be said."

"I think there's more biting and clawing from zombies, but that sounds right," said Adalia.

"Cool," said Just James. "I think we should go to where she isn't."

"We should find the Shield," said Gabriel. "She is your armor."

Adalia looked between them, then blew her breath out in a sigh. "It doesn't matter," she said. She took a peek sideways into the other place, not quite stepping there, just *looking*, then said, "They'll both be in the same place. When the time comes."

"What does that mean?" said Just James.

"I'm with Loudmouth this time," said Gabriel. "What time?"

"When the Sacrifice is made," said Adalia. "When the Guide is blind. When the Shield is sundered, the Good Right Arm is broken, and the Knight Falls."

"Sounds amazing," said Just James. "Why are we going there?"

"To save the world," said Gabriel. He still had his hands in his pockets.

"Because we must," said Adalia, "or my family will die."

"I figured it'd be something like that," said Just James. He pushed the button on the elevator in the lobby.

"That won't work," said Gabriel. "The power is out."

The elevator doors opened, a soft *ding* sounding in the lobby. Light spilled from the doors as they opened, a widening line being drawn against the dark carpet.

"Huh," said Gabriel.

A man stepped from the elevator, a white robe pulled close about him, head covered by a cowl. He looked for all the world like a monk, a book held in one hand, a rosary in the other. His face was shadowed, but Adalia could see a clean jawline, a hook nose. The man's head turned towards Gabriel. "*Begone.*"

Gabriel had a moment to look surprised before he flickered out like a candle in a gust of wind, the air snapping where he used to be.

"Hey," said Adalia. "That was my friend."

"The ghost is gone?" said Just James. "All *right.*" He looked at Adalia, caught her stare, and swallowed. "I mean, that was a total dick move."

The man stepped closer to Adalia, the light from the elevator slipping away as the doors closed behind him. His face was planes and angles inside the shadow of his cowl. "*I am—*"

"Saint John," said Adalia. "Or, that's what you call yourself now."

Saint John paused. "*Yes.*"

"You know this guy?" said Just James. "How—"

"*Be silent,*" said Saint John. Just James' mouth worked, no sound coming out. "*The Master needs you. He calls you.*"

Adalia felt cross. Who was this *thing* to tell her friends what to do? "We're coming, but not because he called."

"*You are coming because you are destined to die.*" Saint John held the book out towards Adalia. "*I am here to call you to justice.*"

"That's not how this works," said Adalia. She saw the eyes within the hood blink in surprise. She held up a hand. "Oh, I know you think you're here for justice, or whatever twisted fantasy you've got. I know you think you hold power over the living, and the dead. You think you are the Hand of God."

"*I am—*"

"What you *are,*" said Adalia, stepping sideways a fraction, just a tiny step into that other place, "is a fantasy."

"*You're not—*"

"What *I* am," said Adalia, smoothing the front of her sweater, "is a reality check. By the sun that warms us, the moon that dreams with us, and the stars across the endless Night, I call you back, Gabriel Pearce. I am not done with you."

There was a snap and Gabriel re-appeared, off balance. He held out his hands, took a faltering step. "How did—"

Adalia cut him off with a look, then turned to Just James. "James Malory, your voice is gentle and kind and spoken from your heart. I give it back to you."

Just James coughed. "Wow. That was … intense."

"*Adalia Kendrick,*" said Saint John. "*Adalia Kendrick, I take from you your power. I take it from you, and call it my own. I hold it in my hand* —" and here, he held his book in front of him like a shield "—*and in my heart.*" He held the rosary to his chest, and a low rumble of thunder crawled across the sky behind Adalia. The room darkened, leaving a small pool of light around where Gabriel stood. "*The Master calls and you will come.*"

Adalia laughed, the sound ringing from her like the peal of a bell. The light eased back into the room. "Saint John. There is not enough power in the world to bind me."

Saint John looked at the book he held, then at the rosary. "*What—*"

Adalia stepped forward, brushing her hair from her face. "Do you think I walk with the living and the dead by accident?" She felt full of energy, her skin taught with it. It felt like anger, it felt like justice. "Saint John, I call you by your line of Jones. I give you back your name, Bastian. Bastian Jones, I have given you back your name, and you will give me Saint John." Adalia held out her hand, palm up. Waiting.

The man shuddered, then sank to his knees. He retched once, twice, then threw up something black and bubbling onto the dark carpet of the lobby, where only the moneyed rich had walked. His face — a young face, now full of fear — looked at Adalia. He tried to reach a hand to hers, the fingers hooked like claws, before he fell sideways onto the ground. Blood started to seep through the robe he wore, and Bastian Jones let out one last breath before he died.

"You … you killed him," said Just James.

"You called me back," said Gabriel.

"He was already dead. Stabbed, through the heart. I gave him back himself, and took away the thing that was keeping him from dying all the way." Adalia stepped back from the other place, and almost fell. She felt strong hands and looked up to see Just James, his face full of concern. She waved him away, standing tall. "We have work to do." She pressed the button on the elevator, heard the soft chime, and walked inside.

The living and the dead followed her, the living a little more cautious than before. The doors closed with a *hush*.

None of them saw as Sky and Agni hit the pavement, a fireball rocking the street outside. The windows of the lobby shattered inward, glass and tables and chairs and pieces of the sidewalk flying through the hotel's foyer.

FIFTY-TWO

"Talin Moray. *I have come for you.*" Danny felt the words as rough stones against her lips, as something less honest than what she wanted — *needed* — to do to the man who had caused her so much pain. Who had hurt those she—

Pack.

—loved. She finished shouldering aside the broken, sundered door, splintered wood and pieces of metal falling aside, made brittle by her anger.

"Then come," said a man's voice, the lilt of the Caribbean in it. "We are well matched, you and I. What do you hope to do here? Kill me? You know you can't."

The floor, the very top floor of Trump Tower, had been cleared out. It was a penthouse suite reserved for the very best, but no gated lobby stood in her way. The walls had been cleared aside, their roots exposed through what had been rich carpet and tile. Where expensive couches and coffee tables and televisions had stood, there was rubble, detritus left here after some cataclysm. The smell of broken wood, sheared metal, powdered marble filled the air, confusing her senses. Her eyes narrowed. There was something else here, something hidden. She placed one foot in front of the other, sniffing at the air.

"Do you like it?" The man—

Deceiver. Hunt. Kill.

—stepped out from behind a pile of junk that could once have been a refrigerator, or just as easily one of a hundred other things that made up an apartment. "I've been redecorating." He laughed, strong shoulders moving easy with the sound.

"*I will kill you. I have done it before.*" Danny stalked closer, wanting to change. She wanted more than anything to be able to do that thing that her Valentine—

Pack mate.

—could do, to change when he needed it enough. But she couldn't, hadn't learned the knack. It didn't matter. She'd crush the life from this little man, send his body falling all the way to the hard Earth below.

Talin held up a hand. "You mean Volk?" He frowned, then tapped the side of his head. "I've been trying to *remember*. To see what happened. But I can't. Which means it must have been you that did the deed, not the wastrel Everard. He bit you, and so the line of memory stops there."

Danny remembered flashes, bits and pieces, the fight in a small room with her—

Cub.

—daughter, the impossible jump to a forest below, a bright flash and a race through trees, tongue lolling, teeth showing, the red rage falling around her and the sweet taste of victory as she licked her jaws. "*I remember,*" she said. "*I know how we can die.*"

"That is something we share," said Talin. He smiled. "Oh, not the way you're thinking. Not by tooth and claw. There are other ways. If you stretch your mind back, you'll see. So many ways we can die. Have you never wondered why the Earth isn't full of our kind? Why we few remain?"

"*You are not one of us.*" Danny stepped closer, cautious now. Her

367

muscles bunched and flexed. She wanted to rend this little man into pieces, couldn't understand why he wasn't fighting her, tooth against tooth, claw against claw. It was the right way. *"You have stolen from the Night."*

"True enough," said Talin. His eyes sparkled at her surprise. "You expected me to deny it? For many long years I've been watching, waiting, hunting. I knew it was out there, snatches of story, told around a hearth, pointing at impossible power. Untapped, ungoverned. All that was needed was for one of *you* to not want it. And then it could be lifted, light as a feather, soft as a dove. Transferred. I've almost got it all, and soon — when Everard comes in here in a deluded attempt to save you — I will have the last few drops."

"Save me?" Danny laughed at the absurdity of it. The sound was harsh and guttural, the change sitting just under her skin, waiting for release. *"From what? You, a fragile little man with a stolen bag of treats?"*

Talin's face darkened. "Do you know the power of this gift? How much strength you have both wasted?"

"I know it is a curse. I know it drives us from hearth and home. It makes us wander the dark places of the world, to take our Cub into places it is not safe. But for all that, it is a gift. It is the gift that will end you." Danny wiped drool from her chin, then licked her lips.

A snarl of anger twisted Talin's face. "You are so sure? I have made a city fall! I have taken the Night and crafted the tools that sundered the Shield, that broke the Good Right Arm. The Reluctant Wanderer is a petty joke, and your Guide is blind and wayward. Only the Sword and Knight remain, and we both know the Knight fell long ago. I sit here, in command of the living and the dead, and you think you can break me?"

"You waste words," said Danny. *"These names you give to our Pack hold no power under the moon and stars."* She bared her teeth, and stepped forward.

There was the clang of metal, and the trap fell shut around her. Bars of the hated metal revealed themselves from under the torn carpet, and a lid fell from the roof, plaster falling around her. The cage, the walls hidden from view by the ruin around her, snapped into place, the bright silver burning her eyes. She felt sick and weak, and held her hand up in front of her eyes.

"I waste nothing," said Talin. "And here you are, bait for the rest. The mighty Sword, held in a silvered cage. You asked what your useless Everard would save you from? Yourself, of course. Your pride. Your power. Your sense of your place in the world. And once he is drained dry, I shall take it from you as well."

Danny lunged forward, grabbing at the bars of the cage, then screamed as her hands smoked and seared against the silver. She pulled back, then tried again. Her palms started to blacken, her strength fading as the filthy, hated metal smothered her. Danny stumbled, a hand coming against silver on the ground, and she hissed and pulled back.

"The names I give to your precious Pack hold all the power in the world," said Talin, standing well clear of the cage.

"How—" Danny coughed. "How did you make this?"

"I was able to use my servants—" and Talin spoke this word as if the people in his thrall were paid a wage, willing participants all "— for most of the gathering, the smelting. But the finer work, for that I had help." He held a hand out, palm upward. Another man stepped out from behind a broken cupboard, his face familiar.

Ajay Lewiss looked down on Danny. "This is for the best. You will see — we are telling a new story, and it will change the world."

CHAPTER
FIFTY-THREE

Carlisle didn't like the sound of crying. Not a baby's, not a woman's, and not a man's either. Didn't matter if you were black or white, male or female, hell whether you were Christian, Muslim, Jew — no one cried pretty. No one. That shit on movies where someone had a few delicate tears, dabbed at them with the edge of a piece of white cotton, then gave a moving speech?

Horse shit.

Most people crying were doing that because they were in pain. Hell, Carlisle herself—

A smaller, weaker girl, afraid of the dark, and what came to her when the lights went out.

—was no stranger to tears. But this, this sound carried agony, and as she made her careful, methodical way up the stairwell, she thought she knew the man who was making that sound.

But that couldn't be. It had to be another trick, and she was so tired. She didn't know if she had enough strength to fight another one of those, those *things*, whatever they were. Not even the Eagle's wings could carry her through this. She looked down at the weapon in her hand — no idea how it had got there, she remembered holstering it, but okay — and took a break. Just a small one, leaning her head against the cold concrete walls of the stairwell.

It was funny, she expected the stairwell to be paneled in oak or some other excess like the rest of the place, but no, stairwells were the same the world over. You could still burn to death on nice carpet if you were rich, so best have the stairs bare, spartan, utilitarian.

She was thankful for it. Despite the cold she was sweating, and the chill wall felt good against her face. Maybe she could rest here for a moment, just take it easy for a little while. Maybe her work was done, the steady *drip, drip, drip* that had accompanied her on her long climb marking out the end of her contribution.

Maybe you can rest when you're dead. Get up, Carlisle. Get up. Your friend, the one with all the teeth, she needs your help, so she can be a mother again and not just something her daughter's afraid of. Your other friend, the one who's young and scared and alone in the dark, just like you were, she needs your help. Get moving.

She held the Eagle up to her eyes, picking out its familiar shape in the gloom. "I don't need you yet," she said, lips close to the metal, inhaling the scent of the weapon, all metal and oil and smoke and promise. It slipped back into the holster at her back, leaving her hands free. She pushed herself away from the wall, leaving a bloody hand print on the pale surface.

Carlisle didn't know how she got to the door, easing it open with whisper against carpet. She swayed, dizzy, her tired—

Blood loss. You're not tired, you're about to die.

—brain trying to keep up. She saw a room full of wreckage, charred holes punched clean through walls. Not much left, it was like a wrecking crew had been through here. She picked her way across carpet littered with bits of wallpaper and drywall, her boots crunching the flakes into white powder. The crying: that damn sound wouldn't stop, all sobs and pain.

She found an open door, not that it mattered here with all the holes everywhere, but it felt better, just a little easier, to walk through an open door rather than bend down around her hurt to try and fit herself through a gap. This door creaked, stuck, then gave, falling off its hinges to the carpet, the fall more thud than crash. Carlisle took in the scene, saw the broken window, no glass on the carpet — broken outward then — and the old man standing in front of it. He was holding back John Miles, who was sobbing, great wracking heaves, and John's hands were outstretched to the window. The old man was stronger than he looked, but Carlisle figured he was holding John back more by force of will and sheer orneriness than anything else.

John was trying to get to the window. *Huh.*

Carlisle looked around, swaying again, looking for the missing person. The one person who might be able to explain this.

Skyler Evans wasn't here. Carlisle's eyes went back to John, to his cries, to Rex, and to the window. *Oh.* Then, *oh no.*

Using the door frame for support for a second — just a second, God she was so tired — Carlisle pushed herself off and into the room. She felt like a ship at sea, voyaging across that space between where she was and the impossible thing that had happened. It wasn't that Sky was gone—

Died. Say it, at least to yourself. She's dead, Carlisle.

—but that she'd taken something with her. Carlisle had seen a lot of broken men before, she'd seen them in cuffs and she'd seen them in cells. She'd arrested some, punched a few, killed more than she wanted to. She knew what broken looked like, and John Miles was broken. Sky had taken a piece of him with her, down the side of Trump Tower, and Carlisle was pretty sure it was gone for good.

She was also pretty sure they didn't have time for this.

Rex looked at her, with old, sad eyes. "She ... jumped."

"She fell!" John almost screamed it, then tried to lunge around Rex. The old man was like a stone, immobile, resolute.

"She jumped," said Rex, "and saved us, son. She saved us all."

"That's not how it works," said John. "I loved her. I'm supposed to jump *for her.*"

"Miles." Carlisle's hand went out, delicate as a moth's wing. "Miles, look at me."

John spun to face her, anger and fear and pain and rage and hate and loss all rolled up into his eyes. "You — what—"

"Miles, I need you to listen to me," said Carlisle. Her right knee started to buckle, and she forced it steady. "Miles." His eyes were crazy, shifting from place to place, all over the room, looking everywhere but at her. "*John.*"

He seemed to settle then, looking at her. His shoulders bunched under his shirt, and she got a good look at him. Roughed up plenty, burnt hair and patches of red skin. Something had gone down here too, maybe something like she'd been through. Carlisle's eyes went to the window.

Maybe something worse.

"John, she's gone." Carlisle dropped each word out as soft as she knew how. She didn't know how very well, but they didn't have time for her to learn.

"No." He shook his head.

"She's gone. Sky is gone."

"*No.*" John licked his lips. "Adalia. She can see the dead. She can—"

"John," said Carlisle. "Sky's not coming back. They don't come back. You know that. Not really." Elliot hadn't come back, just a hint of what he was. "It's not fair on them, to be with us anymore."

"You're right." His voice shook, and he ran a hand through his hair, burnt bits of it flaking away. "Look, I'll just wait here. Just in case."

"John," said Carlisle. "Look at me."

He did, first at her eyes, then at the rest of her. He took in the blood, the cuts in her jacket, the pale face, the pained breathing. "What ... happened?"

"Something," said Carlisle. "I can't do this myself. Val needs you."

John barked a short, bitter laugh. "He doesn't need me. He's a fucking werewolf. He's got strength, and an invincible girlfriend, and a step-daughter who sees the dead. I'm just a washed up personal trainer trying to hustle my next gig." There was real bitterness there, a self-loathing she'd never seen before.

"Oh, John," said Carlisle, reaching out a hand to touch his face. She wondered at the motion, so unlike her, blamed it on the loss of blood. "That's why they need us so much."

"Son," said Rex. He'd been so quiet Carlisle had forgotten he was there. "Son, I don't know about werewolves, or the dead, but I know what love is. That girl of yours loved you more than life. Do you see? Actually more than life. She wanted you to ... I don't know. That's between you. But she didn't want you to jump after her."

"She didn't?" said John.

"Probably not," said Rex. "I'm not an expert on the female mind, but I'm pretty sure she would have left more clues."

Carlisle let her hand fall from John's face. "I'm a worn out ex-cop who can't walk."

"I'm a retired firefighter whose wife died of cancer," said Rex.

John looked at them both, then at the window. "Right," he said.

"Son," said Rex. "Son, we're having a moment here. Now's where you share."

Carlisle looked at John, at the pain in his eyes. She said, "You're John Miles."

"I'm John Miles," said John. He shook his head, eyes darting to the window. "It isn't enough."

Carlisle stumbled, head feeling light as a feather, empty as air. "We need to get moving."

"You need to sit down," said Rex. "You look like hell."

"Huh," said Carlisle. "Plenty of time for sitting. After."

"After what?" Rex reached out to take her arm, and she shook him off.

"After." Carlisle looked at John. "So, Miles. It's been a long day. Going to get a little longer. That girlfriend of yours—"

"Sky," said John. "Her name is — was — Sky."

"—saw something in you, Lord only knows what," said Carlisle. "I think you're a degenerate. But we need you. Do you hear me?" She jerked her head towards the open window. "She gave you a chance. For us. For all of us."

"She was everything that mattered," said John.

"Really?" Carlisle swayed, and this time she accepted Rex's hands on her arm. The man was like stone, all muscle and hard edges under that craggy exterior. "What about Val?"

"Like I said. Val can look after himself." John looked around. "Say. Wasn't he with you?"

"Now you're cooking," said Carlisle. "Good question, Miles. What about Danny?"

"Werewolf," said John. "She's got it."

"She's alone," said Carlisle. "What about Adalia?"

"Kid's clear," said John. "No problem here."

"She needs an uncle," said Carlisle. *If only you'd had one, Carlisle, if only someone else had been there...* "She needs us."

"She needs *you*," said John. His eyes were clearing though, something coming back into them. The pain was there, and so was the anger, but something else. Purpose.

"We need you," said Carlisle. Then, in a smaller voice, "I can't ... I'm too little." She licked her lips, feeling dizzy. "I can't do this alone. Please."

She watched John, his eyes, that moment where he *knew*. She could see it, see the straightening of his shoulders. His hand reached out to her face, and she shied away, breaking from Rex's grip. John looked at her for a moment before letting his hand fall. "What happened to you, Melissa?"

"Call me Carlisle."

He nodded at that, then straightened himself up, wiped his eyes. Cleared his throat, straightened his shirt, and brushed his hair straight — or straight as it could be. "Carlisle, huh?"

"Just Carlisle," she said, feeling the Eagle at her back. Always at her back.

"Well, Melissa," said John, "I guess I have a hard story. My girl-friend just jumped out a window, and I'll be honest, I'm having trouble wrapping my head around that. But having a sob story and being John Miles isn't enough."

"It's got to be," said Rex. "Son, it's got to be."

"No," said John. "You misunderstand." He cracked his knuckles, took a look at Carlisle's posture — guarded, she'd skittered like a beaten dog when he'd reached a hand towards her. "We've got a problem here." His eyes tracked hers, holding her locked in place tighter than Rex's grip. "The problem is too many people that I give a damn about are getting a bad serve. Bad, you understand, doesn't even begin to tell the story. Not the one that matters."

"So—" started Rex.

"Old man," said John, "I'm on a roll. Back up."

"Sure," said Rex, the faintest hint of something that could — just maybe — have been a smile on his lips.

"Being John Miles isn't enough," said John Miles. "I'm not just John Miles." He flexed, that impressive frame that Carlisle couldn't help admire — *despite it being attached to Miles* — looking like it wanted to get back in the fight. "I'm John *fucking* Miles," he said.

Carlisle almost laughed. *That's it,* she thought. *That's what we need. John* fucking *Miles — I've called him that myself more than once.* She turned, ready to walk to the roof, ready to get her friends, and her strength finally—

I have seen dragons circle against the fingers of the sun, warring in the space between the moon and earth. Their fire burned the air, and their scales fell like rain. All were weaker than you.

—gave out. She tripped on nothing much at all and fell, and fell, falling for a thousand years until she hit the carpet far, far below.

"Of course I don't know," said a familiar voice. "I have no idea. I lift weights for a job. I make people less fat, or stronger, or just make them feel better that they're fucking *trying*. I don't know shit about blood loss."

"Son," said a different, but still familiar, voice. "Son, just keep climbing."

"Didn't you," said the first voice — *Miles? Is that John fucking Miles? Still talking?* —with a bit of tension around the edges, "work as a fire fighter?"

"Sure did."

"They do first aid?" Definitely tension in John's voice. Like he was working hard, puffing a little, except John never puffed, so he was working hard and trying not to show it. That sounded about right. Sensations started to come back to her, the sway of motion, the feeling of something being stuck in her gut. She was — *Goddammit* — upside down or something.

"They do first aid," said the second voice. That gravelly sound was Rex, had to be, if only her head wasn't so light and hurt all at the same time.

"Then you need to get on board with the first aid facts," said John. "Don't ask me if she's lost too much blood, or if she'll survive. What I know is we couldn't leave her there, because zombies, right?"

"We're taking her upstairs to certain death," said Rex. His voice kept moving, like he was walking behind, or in front, or around her. Or, like they were climbing a stairwell and kept turning the damn corners.

Those assholes, thought Carlisle, *are taking me up to meet Doc fucking Doom in his killer castle, and I'm unconscious.*

"It's not certain," said John. "It's—"

"I'm pretty sure I'm going to die," said Rex. Carlisle wished she had the strength to open her eyes.

"You're old, of course you're going to die," said John. "It's Melissa I'm not so sure about." That was it, that was the last straw. If there was one human on the face of the Earth who knew exactly how to say what she didn't want said, it was that clown John Miles.

"Call me Carlisle," she croaked. "Please God, Miles, God, just call me Carlisle."

The sensation of something stuck in her gut gave a little jog, and she almost retched. "You're awake," said John.

"You're saying things out loud," said Carlisle, voice slurring, "at the same time as they go through your head. You don't always need to say the obvious." She was draped over someone's shoulder, she was sure of it now, and based on where the voices were coming from, she was being carried by John and Rex was bringing up the rear. If only she had the strength to open her eyes.

She felt herself being hauled upright, feet on the ground, and she almost passed out again. She cracked open an eye, took in that Miles Megawatt Smile — a little dimmer, a little darker, just a little fucking *broken* after today — and couldn't help but smile herself. "Hey."

"Hey," he said. Then, again, "Hey. Look, sorry. I had to ... I know you don't like me ... I know you didn't want to be touched, but I couldn't leave you there."

"I was going to leave you there," said Rex. She shifted her one eye to look at the old man. He was smiling too. "I figured, you'd only slow us down."

Carlisle licked her lips. "Either of you got some water?"

"Here," said John, holding up a bottle of Evian. She tried to reach for it, but her arms were just too weak. He held it for her and she drank. It tasted sweet and clean and perfect.

She managed to wipe her lips with the back of an arm, then saw a bandage — more like a ripped piece of curtain backing, if she was any judge — wrapped around her arm. She did a quick status check, a few bandages hastily applied, all of them showing more red than she liked. *It'll be fine. You'll be fine. It's not like you're alone in the dark. Not anymore.* "Status."

"It's like this," said Rex. "We're pretty much fucked."

"More detail," said Carlisle. "I need something to work with."

"Sure, okay," said Rex. "We're about two floors from the top. Got no clue where the werewolf—"

"Danny," said John.

"—is," said Rex. "Or Val. Haven't seen that guy since he crashed our helicopter."

"It was shot down," said John. "I was there."

"Was it on fire when it touched down?" Rex gave John a hard stare.

"More or less," said John.

"Crashed," said Rex. He turned to Carlisle. "Anyway. You're pretty busted up, but I've tried to tourniquet the bits of you that looked the worst. The bits I could reach. That you could tourniquet. Okay, look, you're still leaking in a lot of places. You could use a little bit of rest, maybe a couple pints of O negative, it'll see you right. Fighting the legions of the damned doesn't count as bed rest. Not sure you'll be doing much fighting for the rest of the day, or maybe the week, or ... hell, let's just say your professional fights this year are all called off. I'm old, but angry, so I can probably get in someone's way. John's the best of us, maybe superficial burns and a couple of cat scratches, but I figure he's borderline incompetent so I'm not sure what we should do."

"Cat scratches?" John blinked at him. "I was fighting a piece of living flame with an axe."

"You'll be fine," said Rex.

"You'll be fine," said Carlisle. John looked at her. "You're always going to be fine." There was no malice in her words — she just knew it was true.

"Yeah," John said, his voice turning bitter as burnt coffee. "*I'll* be fine. It's everyone else who ... dies."

"No, I ... Miles, I didn't mean it like that," said Carlisle.

"It's okay," said John. "I..."

"No," said Carlisle. "It's not okay."

"It's not?" He blinked.

"No," she said. "Help me the fuck up."

"No way," said Rex. "Not a chance."

"Was I talking to you?" Carlisle gave him a look she'd cultivated through years on the job, one she reserved for low ranking officers who said something stupid. Rex took a step back, swallowed. Carlisle turned back to John. "I was talking to Miles, because he knows we have to make it right."

"We ... *have* to," said John. He put his hands on his knees, then got up. He looked like he was considering something. "I don't know if we can."

"I do," said Carlisle. "So be a champ, and help me up."

She took his hand, warm and strong and full of life, and let herself be pulled to her feet. She tried to ignore the look of worry on Rex's face, tried to ignore the flash of dizziness that hit her. She turned to look at the wall she'd been leaning against, and then turned away. She definitely, definitely didn't want to see the red streak of her blood against the wall. *Quite a lot there, Carlisle. Not a lot more where that came from.*

"Tourniquet, huh," she said to Rex.

"Hard to tourniquet your back," he said. "You were the one who went through a blender. Don't look at me."

"Let's get this done," she said. She flexed her arms, worked a kink out through her shoulder, and then patted the Eagle at her back. "Couple more floors, right?"

"Couple more floors," said Rex. He looked at his feet. "I really think you should stay here."

"I think you should help me climb," said Carlisle. She let her voice soften. "Do you know what it's like to have a family?"

"Yeah, I think so," said Rex. He looked at John, then at her. "I really think I do."

"I didn't," said Carlisle. "Not really. Not until a few years back. I met this guy, you know, suspect on a case. I mean, sure, everyone says that cops are a family. But it's not *real*. It's ... except for Elliot. Doesn't matter. This guy, Everard, he ... had a family. One that he *made*. Can you believe it?"

Rex nodded, a wry smile tugging at his lips. "I've met him."

"The family that I got when I was born, well," said Carlisle. Her words ran dry for a moment, because she couldn't—

You can't tell. You can't ever tell. It's our secret.

—put into words, not the right way, what she wanted to say. "Doesn't matter. What matters is I've got one now. It's full of wonderful people, and," and she spared a glance at John, "the odd black sheep, but you know, every family's got one, right? And this family, it's worth everything."

"Worth dying for?" said Rex. "Because that's what's going to happen. The blood loss alone—"

"It's worth everything," said Carlisle, thinking of a young girl sitting in an apartment waiting for them to make the world safe for her again. A young girl who'd allowed a much-tarnished ex-cop to be her friend. "Do you hear?"

Rex looked at his feet, then at John. John's face was stone, but he nodded at Rex.

The old man blew out a breath. "Okay then. Guess I'll help you up the stairs."

It wasn't far, no more than two flights, like they'd said. But when they got there, Carlisle was sweating like she'd run a marathon. Not that she knew what that was like, the only *reason* people ran marathons at all was so they could brag about it, but she could imagine. The door to the penthouse lobby stood in front of them, quiet, dark, cold. She felt the air caress her, sending shivers down her spine.

"Miles," she said.

"I'm here."

"I know," she said, smiling into the gloom. *You'll always be where you're most needed.* "You're up."

"Some motherfucker," said John Miles, hefting the axe, "is going to pay." He grabbed the axe's haft, then slammed the door open with his shoulder. It rocked open, John leading the way into—

Well.

The demarcation between 'foyer' and 'penthouse suite' was gone. Walls were missing, rubble strewn everywhere. A cage of silver sat in the rough middle of the area, surrounded on all sides by an army — no other word for it — of zombies. In the cage stood Danny, looking small and frail under the terrible heat of the silver around her. At the far end of the room, near a hole that must once have been doors or windows or some other shit were two men. They were standing near the open air of Chicago, and at her quick glance looked no more concerned about the temperature than the wreckage around them.

She knew one of those men.

Danny's eyes found hers across the muddle of ruins and people, widened in shock. "Run, Melissa. *Run*."

"Yes," said the man at the far end that she didn't know. "You really should run. You're not needed, and you're not wanted."

Carlisle did a quick count. Army might have been too strong a term. Ten dudes, maybe fifteen. *No problem.* "You'd be Talin Moray." Her voice sounded weak to her own ears, and she cleared her throat.

"Ms. Kendrick said you wouldn't run. Couldn't be *reasoned with*, she put it." Talin tugged at the lapels of a suit jacket worth more than she used to make in a week. It was grubby with dirt and blood and dust. "I was hoping she was right."

"Asshole," she said, looking at Ajay. "What are you doing here?"

"I came to make it perfect," said Ajay. "I came—"

"He helped Talin finish the cage," said Danny.

"That true?" said Carlisle, the feeling in her gut turning to acid. "I thought you were on our team."

"I am," said Ajay. "It needs to be perfect before it can be broken. Before it can be fixed. All the pieces. They needed to be in the right places. Do you see?"

Carlisle sighed, tired, tired, tired. Damn, but she was *tired*. Tired of Ajay's cryptic word puzzles, tired of people not doing what they should, tired of people lying. She was tired of feeling attracted to this man who—

You'll never be good for another. You'll always be mine, Daddy's little girl.

Goddammit, but she was tired of feeling lost, even after all these years. "Ajay?"

"Yes, Detective."

You put a cage on my best friend, she wanted to say. *I want to know why you're standing shoulder to shoulder with the man who can end the world*, she wanted to say. *I want to know why you don't* want *me*, she wanted to say. *You've damned us all*, she wanted to say. She licked her lips instead. "Do you remember when I made you a promise? I promised to God."

"You said if I hurt your family, you would kill me." His face started to frown, doubt creeping in at the sides. "But—"

"That's right." Carlisle looked at Danny, weak in a cage. Thought of Adalia, hiding in an apartment. Of Everard. Their new friend Rex. Just James, another kid out of place and out of time. Even, now she could admit it in her dark and blackened heart, of John. Of all the pain they'd carried for so long. Her hands were trembling. "Time to pay up." Something had been clouding her thoughts, holding her back, checking her decisions, and she wasn't sure what she should do. What she should say. Carlisle felt her words dry up, her limbs stiffen, her need to act fall away. But the Eagle was in her hand, its strong voice shouting across the distance between her and Ajay. The Eagle held her up, as it always had. It acted when she wasn't strong enough, as it always had. It spoke three times, hurling all her anger across the space. The first round took Ajay in the head, the high caliber round turning his face into red mist. The second two took him in the chest, and Ajay's lifeless body fell to the ground. As it fell, something inside her released, let go its grip on her heart, and she staggered for a moment. *Free.* Carlisle was gasping for breath, sucking in lungfuls of air like she'd sprinted up those damn stairs.

"Bet you didn't expect that," said John to Talin, spinning his axe.

Talin's face looked astonished. "You did ... do you know ... why?"

"We weren't," said Carlisle, "on the same page." She looked at the Eagle, held out in front of her, her hand steady now despite her blood loss. She felt the strength of the weapon, her talisman against the evil in this world. "Your turn." She pulled the trigger, the Eagle roaring and screaming again, kept pulling the trigger until the magazine was empty.

Not a single round hit home. Talin moved like water, danced aside like the bullets were underarm tosses he could just move away from. She'd seen someone else — some*thing* — do that before. It struck her that this was going to be a hard fight. One she wasn't going to walk away from. And she thought about Adalia, that girl who was counting on her, and shrugged. *That's the way it's got to be? No problem.*

Talin's fingers came away from his arm, sticky red. *Oh*, thought Carlisle. *Clipped him. Not so fast after all, asshole.* Talin was looking at his fingers, face incredulous, then his features contorted into rage. "Now," he said, spittle flecking his lips, "you will *fall*."

The zombies lurched forward, some running, some walking. It looked like a mass, a wave, an avalanche, and Carlisle thought that maybe this time, *this fucking time*, she'd pushed a little too hard. Too far, because she wasn't a goddamn werewolf, she was just a *person*, and zombies didn't leave people *alive*. Her free hand fed a fresh magazine into her weapon. Carlisle swallowed, then pointed the Eagle at the horde.

Someone stepped in front of her. *John fucking Miles.* He spared her a backward glance, hefting his axe. She could have sworn he had that Miles Megawatt Smile out, pointed at *her*, just for a moment. "I *got* this," he said, then turned around and started swinging.

CHAPTER
FIFTY-FOUR

S ome of the shit that was getting old, like ancient, ice age old, was the damn blood that kept coming from his nose. And eyes. And *ears* now, if you'd believe it. Val paused for a breath on the stairs, shaking his flashlight. The beam flickered, maybe the batteries running low, maybe it was just broken. Val had some sympathy there: he felt a little broken, a little low on batteries himself. He'd been climbing these damn stairs for what seemed like forever, hadn't seen a soul, heard a thing. He hoped everyone else was having as easy a trip to the top as he scrubbed his nose against his sleeve.

A hammer of sound came from above. Carlisle's gun? Three shots right next to each other sounded a little like Carlisle, a little too much like her. Just a few more floors up, just a few more steps in front of each other. Val took a step, his foot slipping on the stairs, and he fell. The flashlight skittered away from him, bouncing in the gloom, the beam flickering as it tumbled down the stairs, so many floors down below. As he hit the ground, the sharp edge of a step hit him, something wet and soft giving way inside him. He realized it was a rib, and a second after he realized ribs shouldn't feel soft. And a second after that the pain, sweet baby Jesus the pain. It left him gasping, weak.

Carlisle's gun fired again. Not three shots, but … all of them, as near as he could work out. In around the shooting was yelling, all of it muffled by distance and doors and whatever else was in the way.

Pack is dying.

"I got that," said Val, and pushed himself to his feet. His fingers scrabbled over something wet on the stairwell, and he didn't need a light to know it was his blood. This damn Russian virus was going to do him in before he could finish climbing these damn stairs.

Pack is DYING.

That soft touch, something small and gentle, pulled at his hand. It felt like an old friend, trying to show him the way. In a way, maybe it was. "I know," he said. "We've got to get up these stairs. We've got to … do something."

Without Pack, we are alone.

Val remembered being alone. Through the memories of a hundred, a thousand, or *thousands* that came before him. He could see it, through the long lines of history, stretching back like a kaleidoscope of loneliness. Almost always just one wolf, looking for another. For a—

Pack.

—place to call home. That small touch on his hand, it was all that was left of the terrible, beautiful thing that had been inside him for five years. "*Plach' i ty plachesh' v odinochku,*" said Val. "*Da?*"

We have howled at the darkness alone.

"Yeah," said Val. He started climbing again. Reaching the top really didn't take all that long. Since Carlisle had vanished to God knows where — one minute she was there, the next minute she wasn't — he'd been climbing by himself. He was climbing mostly by feel in the stairwell, some residual influence of the creature letting him pick out small details, shapes. Nothing like the night vision he'd known days ago, but enough that he wasn't going to slip and kill himself. "We'll have a talk about loneliness later. Because a key, like a fucking *integral part* of not being alone, is not killing every-thing that comes across your path. It's like you never read *The Monstrous Glisson Glop*." Val wiped more blood from his face. "It's a story about a monster that eats everything. I'm sure you know how it ends."

No response came from inside him, and it didn't matter anyway because he was at the top. Or, as high as he was going to go. A door stood in front of him. He touched it, not knowing what—

Pack is HERE.

—would be on the other side. He opened the door, and saw—

"Huh," said Val.

The room was a mess, no two ways about it. He blinked, not sure what he was seeing at first. He was taking in wreckage, broken walls, smashed appliances and furniture, and scattered among it was bodies. Lots of bodies, more than ten. A silver—

Hated, vile metal.

—cage stood in the middle of the room, Danny inside it. He wanted to run to her, but—

It BURNS.

—he knew he wouldn't be able to help. Not in his state. Maybe together, but — no. She had slumped to the floor, pale, the curls he loved to touch lying matted against her head. It made him—

Pack mate.

—ache. His eyes kept roving the room. He saw Carlisle's body on the ground. He moved as fast as he could — more a quick shuffle than a run — to her. She was pale, cut, blood everywhere, probably half of it hers. Her gun was on the ground next to her. Val checked for a pulse, found it, breathed a sigh of relief, then reached for her gun. He ejected the magazine, something inside him knowing the motions, and it fell into his hand. It was red, the bullets inside—

Throw it.

—smelling sharp to him. His hand trembled with the urge to toss it far away, but he pushed the magazine back into the weapon and levered himself to his feet. He shuffled on across the room, finding

Rex lying unconscious under three bodies. The old man was bashed up, bleeding from his head, but — also, thank God — alive.

"Hey," said John. His voice was a whisper. "Over here." Val looked around, and saw that the blood-covered corpse he'd seen slumped against half a wall was not actually a corpse but John Miles.

Val moved to his friend. "Man, you look like shit."

"Is that true love I hear?" John coughed and wiped some blood from his face. He had a fire axe across his legs. He was covered in gashes, bruises, the circular indentations of bite marks.

"What, and I mean this in a loving way, the actual fuck happened to you?" Val looked at John, then at the room. "Did you ... did you do this?"

"Yeah," said John, "but I left the big guy for you." He started to laugh, but it turned into a sob, shoulders shaking. "Val? Val, my Sky is dead. She's dead, Val."

Val didn't know what to say. What do you say, when someone dies because you were an asshole? "I—"

"No," said John.

"What?"

"No," said John. "I don't ... listen. I don't want you to fucking say it's your fault, do you hear me? What I want you to say is that you will, and by God I hope you came here with a plan, fucking kill that fucking motherfucker. I — I can't. He's a little out of my league. But I want to. Val? When I was a kid, I never thought I'd want to kill someone. Sure, get in a fight or two, that's just guys having fun. But kill a man? I want that now, and I *can't*."

"Right," said Val. "I figured, Danny—"

"Seen the cage?"

"Saw the cage," admitted Val. "Doesn't look good."

"She passed out a little while ago," said John. "I guess it's silver."

"It's silver," said Val. "It's not the best place for one of us."

"One of you?" said John. "I thought you'd given it up."

Val looked around. Saw the empty place at John's side where Sky should have been. Saw Carlisle, lying unconscious. Saw Rex, an old man with too much heart, lying on the ground. Saw his—

Pack mate.

—Danny, caged, down under the unbearable weight of all that silver. "No," he said. "No, I don't think this is a thing I should be giving up. I think too many people get caught—"

"No," said John.

"What?"

"You're doing it again," said John, something gentle in his voice. "Look, I'm tired. I'm busted up. I am hoping, really hoping, that this is it, because then I can see Sky again. I can be with her. But, here's the thing. Someone laid a trap for you. A briefcase full of sin. And you fell into it. Maybe you didn't want to Hulk out on everyone, maybe you got fleas, I really don't know. You don't talk about it. But you help people, Val. Help yourself. Stop blaming yourself, for chrissakes, and get *angry*."

"Okay," said Val. "One question."

"Shoot," said John, then coughed.

"Who do you need killed?"

"Why," said a voice, smooth as honey, "I'm sure you know. Me, Valentine. He wants you to kill me."

Val pushed himself to his feet, unsteady. He held Carlisle's gun tight. He hadn't seen the man at first because he'd been standing so still, but there, near the far end of the room, was a man in an expensive jacket, but dirty like he slept at the dump. "You're Talin?"

"Yes," said Talin Moray. "And I've been waiting so very long for you to get here."

"Since we're sharing," said Val, "how'd you find me?"

"I followed the trail," said Talin. "The trail of stories. Videos on YouTube. Impossible tales of a single man lifting a truck, or an explosion caught on camera with a single survivor running to the trees. Pieced together, they told of a man wasting his life."

Val blinked. "Come again?"

"The Night," said Talin, "is not to be used helping the weak. It is to be used to become mighty."

"Cool story bro," said Val. "Second question. How much do you remember?"

"Remember?" said Talin.

"About us," said Val. He tapped Carlisle's gun against the side of his head. "Where we came from."

"A little," said Talin. His eyes narrowed. "More, when I get the last of it from you. I've sundered your Shield. Your Sword is sheathed. Your Good Right Arm is broken. The Guide is without purpose. The very Sky has fallen. You are the Knight, and I will make you yield."

"Yeah, about that," said Val. "I know you don't remember, so I'm going to make it easy. For you to have it all, *you've* got to kill me. Like, yourself. With your hands. You can't throw me to your wolves. If you do, I'll return. I'll be leading the fucking pack."

"Easy enough," said Talin. He took a step forward.

"Yeah, about that," said Val, again. "I think you're also missing some other important pieces."

"The Sacrifice?" said Talin. "The Prophet? I am the Prophet, and I have made my Sacrifices."

"I don't," said Val, "think you know what 'sacrifice' means. Will you wait here? I've got to talk to someone." He hefted Carlisle's gun, considering it for a moment. *Big play for a half-remembered recollection of something that came a long time ago. Still, you're out of options. You've got one play left to make.* Then he put the barrel in his mouth and pulled the trigger.

His body toppled to the floor to the chime of elevator doors opening.

FIFTY-FIVE

The elevator ride was long. Not long like it's-a-couple-of-minutes long, but long like it's-stopping-at-every-floor long. And it wasn't stopping, at all, at any floors. The elevator slid up through the long dark of Trump Tower, smooth, silent. But, like, taking its time.

"This elevator is taking a real long time," said Just James. "Is it getting paid by the hour?"

"I think," said Adalia, "that we'll get to where we need to, when we need to be there."

"I think," said Gabriel, "that we'll be too late." He was looking at his feet, then casting glances at her through those beautiful lashes.

"Why are you looking at me like that?" said Adalia.

"I'm not looking at you," said Just James.

"Who, me?" said Gabriel.

"I wasn't talking to you," said Adalia.

"Fine," said Gabriel.

"Okay," said Just James.

"God," said Adalia. She sighed. "I was talking to Gabriel."

"You just said that," said Just James. "I wish I could see him."

"I don't," said Gabriel.

"Stop changing the subject," said Adalia. "You're—"

The elevator stopped, the doors opening with a soft chime. They slipped open with a whisper onto a scene of horror. Adalia's hand went to her mouth as she tried to make sense of what she was seeing. There was Mom, in a silver cage, and down on the floor was Uncle John, and there, over there was Carlisle, so pale, so very pale. She could see Rex, and, and, and—

Oh, no.

—Val. She rushed from the elevator to crouch down at his side. There ... wasn't much left of his face, but she knew it was him. *Knew* it, because he was gone, just like Sky was gone. She rose slowly and turned to the one person left standing tall in the room. *Talin.*

"Hello, little one," he said. He was flexing one of his hands. He turned his attention to her. "You have arrived too late. As you can see."

Adalia wiped a tear from her cheek. "I arrived just when I was needed most."

"Adalia?" Her mom's voice was weak, so very weak. Adalia turned to face her. Her Mom was trying to stand. "No. *No.* Run!"

Adalia shook her head, hair whispering about her. "No, Mom. I'm done with running."

Her mom tried to get to her. She tried, Adalia could see it, but she was so weak. Danny grabbed the bars of her cage, screaming as the silver burned her, then fell back, panting.

"Kid," said Melissa. Adalia turned to face her friend.

"Hello, Melissa." Adalia gave her a small smile. "I'm sorry this happened to you."

"Melissa?" Danny's voice was a whisper, a croak. Desperate. "Melissa? You need to get her out of here. Do you hear me? Get her *out.*"

"So touching," said Talin. "So flawed. The Shield is sundered."

Carlisle was looking about for something, her eyes scanning the floor around her, then roaming the room until they came to rest on her gun, still held by Val. She swallowed. "Kid?"

"I'm sorry this happened to any of you," said Adalia. Just James was moving towards her, a look of awe, or fear, or just plain ol' stunned on his face. "I'm sorry I didn't wake up sooner."

"Adalia," said Gabriel. "Adalia, you should go. Talin is, he's *evil*."

"Yes," she said. "Yes, he is evil." She looked at Val, then at her mom, then at Carlisle. "It's what we fight, isn't it? The evil in the world."

"No, no, no," said Danny. "No, baby. You don't fight. You run. Far away. Leave the city. God. *Why did you come here?*"

"Kid," said Melissa. "Kid, help me up. We can ... we can run," she said, but her voice just kind of ran out at the end, the lie evident for all to see. Melissa wasn't running anywhere.

Just James was bending over to pick something up. Adalia ignored him, walking to Melissa. She stood just out of arm's reach. "I can't run, don't you see?"

"You've got to," said Melissa. She was so pale, so white, she looked dead already. "You can't ... I can't help you. I can't, kid. I'm done."

"I know," said Adalia. "That's why I'm here."

"Melissa," said Danny. "Please. Get up. You've got to try. She's my baby, my baby girl, and—"

"I know," said Melissa. She tried to stand, but didn't get much further than sitting upright before she fell back. "I—"

"You both need to listen," said Adalia. "I came here. I brought the living and the dead with me. You have done so much for me. Both of you. For so many, many years. I see it. I *feel* it, with my heart. I see what you've all done, but the cost, it is too much. The Shield was sundered. The Sword sheathed, the Good Right Arm broken. The Guide lies blind, the Reluctant Wanderer died long ago before his body was taken by a witch, a deceiver. All that remains is the Prophet, and her Sacrifice. Do you see? Now, well, now it's my turn.

To do the saving." But she knew it was a lie. It wasn't her that was going to do the saving. She wasn't the Sacrifice.

"How do you know?" Melissa's voice was barely a whisper. "How do you know all of this?"

"The Universe speaks to me," said Adalia. "I know everything. Like Facebook."

"You know nothing," said Talin. "And you will pay for it."

"Chill out, Ahab," said Just James. He was holding what he'd picked up from the ground — Carlisle's gun. The metal was stained and sticky with blood.

"He can't stop Talin with that," said Gabriel.

"He's not meant to," said Adalia, her voice a whisper. She wiped away another tear, then turned her back on Melissa. She went to stand next to Just James. She reached out, held his hand. "Do you know what you're doing?"

"Yeah," he said. He looked at his feet, those Sketchers he'd taken. "Can you tell me — where the dead go, when they die — is it beautiful?"

"You don't have to do this," said Adalia. She looked down at their hands, then back at Just James. "I don't want you to do this."

"Is it like you?" Just James was looking at her, but she thought he was really trying to look into her heart.

"It is like the dawn," said Adalia, "and the night, and the feeling you get just before you sleep, and just as you wake. It is warm, and soft, and harsh, and rough, and everything and nothing at the same time. It is terrible, and wonderful. You will stand at the Cliffs of the Damned, Just James, and you will want for nothing, until the stars go out and the sun gutters low, and the end of days is on us. You will forget this world and all that is in it."

"No," said Talin. "*No.*"

"I'm not really good at anything," said Just James. "I'm not really good *for* anything. My step dad says so. My mom doesn't argue. But I know one thing. I know it'll never be okay here. Not unless I do what I was made to do."

"What's going on?" said Gabriel. "What do you—"

"Please don't," said Adalia. She'd known this was coming, could see that Just James had known too. Known with the certainty of a young man who'd fallen in love with a girl he didn't know. Fallen in love because the Universe needed him to. Fallen, so he could fall again as the Sacrifice. She was crying freely now. "We can … we can make another trade. It will be okay if you don't."

Just James gave her a sad smile. "No, it won't. You know it won't." He leaned forward, kissing her on the lips. She leaned into it, stumbled when he broke away. "I love you, Adalia Kendrick, and I won't ever forget you. No matter where I am. Your Universe can't take that from me."

He lifted the Eagle to his lips, and pulled the trigger. Adalia screamed, and screamed, and screamed as the Universe opened above her, the majesty and terrible, faceless, impossible purpose of it rolling down on her. She was pulled away from Just James as his body fell, something lifting her up as it burned the tears from her face.

When she spoke, it was with the voice of a thousand, million suns. "*The Sacrifice has been made. Talin Moray, I would like to make a trade.*"

FIFTY-SIX

"This was not where I thought I'd be," said Val, getting up from the forest floor. Fallen leaves crunched under him, and he felt a warm breeze tug at his shirt. He checked his hands — *yep, still there* — and then let them rise to his face. That was still there too, which defied belief.

Super. He must be dead.

You are only as dead as you want to be.

"Ah," said Val, turning to face the creature. He'd never seen it. Sure, John had told him about it, Carlisle had even given a few clues away after she'd thrown back more drinks than was good for her. He'd seen Danny change, knew her in all her forms. But his own creature? Nope. "Together again, huh?"

You make light of things that can end our Pack.

"I make light of things that are so serious because you've got to laugh or cry," said Val. He brushed off his pants. "You're, well, you're on the outside now. How's that work?"

This is our home.

"Cryptic as always," said Val. He nodded. "I wouldn't have expected anything else."

This is my *home.*

"Better," said Val. He looked around, the tall trees stretched far above. The sunlight spotted the ground around him, and a stray beam caught his face. It was warm, and light, and felt good. "This where you go when you're not killing everyone in sight?"

The creature looked at him with those beautiful, terrible eyes. It blinked, but didn't move, the sunlight dappling against it through the trees. It was hard to make out when still. There had to be a few hundred people who died because they missed it, just because it was sitting still. It said nothing. *Did* nothing.

Val held up a hand. *No remorse, huh?* "Look. You and I both know how it works. I remember, see?" He tapped the side of his head. "This isn't the first time something like this has happened."

Nothing like this has ever happened.

"You know that's not true. You're always so ... literal."

You are always so ... tiny.

"Touché," said Val. "Doesn't matter. You can't touch me in here." He touched his chest, hand over his heart. "You can only touch me here."

You let yourself care about all the tiny things. You were made to feel pain.

Val walked around. No matter where he went, the sunlight followed him, warming him. "I thought you were nocturnal?"

All living creatures love the touch of our sun.

"When we're together," said Val, "you make me do horrible things."

I keep our Pack alive.

"Sure, by doing horrible things," said Val. "Can I tell you a story?"

I know all the world's stories.

Val blinked. "Can I tell it anyway?"

If you feel you must.

"Right," said Val. He tapped the side of his head again. "I'm starting to remember. I remember that you've been pretty much everywhere except right here. America. You've been in Russia,

England, Greece ... hell, Persia, back when that was a thing. And before then, before we had names for the families we were a part of."

The names men give to their fallen kingdoms hold no value to Pack.

"Got it," said Val. "Thing is, there's this story I want to tell. A bit of a local flavor."

The creature leaned forward on two strong arms, muscles rippling. *You would tell me a story from your new world? What could such a young world have to teach me?*

"It's not been called America for long, sure." Val shrugged. "But it's a lot older than that. Do you want to hear the story?"

The thing turned around, looking into the shade of the trees. Assent, or indifference?

Let's go with assent. "There's this old Cherokee. He's at a campfire with his grandson."

Is the fire important?

Val sighed, rubbing his face. "Don't tell me you have a sense of humor. It's been a long day. Can you ... can you let me finish?"

I only want to understand.

"The old Cherokee," said Val, "sits down next to his grandson. I don't know, maybe the kid's been in trouble, maybe he's been drinking, maybe he's got into girls in an overly enthusiastic way. Point is, he needs a life lesson."

A lesson you wish to teach me.

"The Cherokee, he sits down and he said, 'Grandson. There is a battle between two wolves in us all. One is evil. It is anger and jealousy. It knows only greed and resentment, and the inferiority that comes from a life of lies and ego. The other, well, it's good. It is joy. It's peace. It knows how to love. It gives hope to its Pack. It is humble, and kind. It tells the truth, and it does what is right even though it is hard.'"

You tell of a battle as if you know fighting.

"I've done my share," said Val. "You were there."

In your battle between two wolves, these two creatures of good and evil, which one wins?

398

"I'm glad you asked," said Val, "because that's what the grandson asked. He looks up at his grandfather, and he says, 'Grandfather? Which of these wolves wins?'" Val looked at his feet for a moment. Took a second to breathe in the gentle quiet of the forest. "The answer's simple, of course."

I see no answer.

"The grandfather, he leans down to the grandson. Takes the kid's shoulders in his old, weathered hands. I don't know, maybe he looks the kid in the eyes — it doesn't matter. But he says to the kid, 'The one you feed.'" Val stared at the creature, long and hard. "Which is it going to be? For you, good or evil?"

There is no good or evil. There is only Pack.

"No," said Val. "How we look after our family — the choices we make? That's what defines us. You were there when the dragons fell. *You saw the things that made them fall.* Has none of that time taught you anything? The world will give you back what you give it. And you've done nothing but take, and kill, and murder, for thousands upon thousands of years. What kind of debt do you think the Universe has banked up for you? For your Pack?"

There was silence in the tiny forest for a time. The creature shuffled in the shadows, then blinked those yellow eyes at Val. *What is it that you want?*

"I would like to propose a … a partnership."

You are ever bound to me.

"You know that's also not true," said Val. "We're both here, because you are bound to another."

He spoils good meat. He is not the Night.

"If you're so big and strong," said Val, "why is it that you're a slave to him?"

You let it happen.

"I didn't do any such thing," said Val. "There was a briefcase—"

Your metal toys are nothing. You have made me a slave by seeing me as you want to see me.

"As a curse."

The Night is the Night.

Val thought about that. "And I wanted to get rid of the curse."

You are ever bound to me.

"Tell you what," said Val. "You want to hear my proposal?"

I will listen.

CHAPTER
FIFTY-SEVEN

"It's not possible," said Talin. His eyes were wide, the whites showing. Adalia faced him across the ruined room, her hair being pulled about her head by wind coursing through the room.

Adalia didn't need to take that small sideways step, not anymore. The Universe filled her, surrounded her. She felt like she would burst, or fall to dust, or catch on fire, or drown, all at the same time. "*You have set each step in motion that allowed this to happen. Here is the trade I will make with you.*"

"I don't want—"

"*I will take from you your power. The Night does not belong to you. I will take it from you and keep it safe. In return, I will give you something precious, something so small, and simple, that even a child knows it. I will give you a conscience, Talin Moray. I will give you back your soul.*"

Talin had picked up a knife, a small, ugly thing, crusted in old blood. He ran for her, made quick by the Night. She watched him come, his lithe movements as he vaulted stone, broken wood, and steel. He would be on her in just a moment. Time enough.

Adalia looked down at her feet. She was floating in the air, her toes inches from the ground. Her gaze went to her Mom, her cage bleeding light and smoke in the face of the Universe. Danny's eyes were open, her yellow eyes watching, waiting. Adalia turned her gaze to Valentine.

"*Get up, Knight.*"

Val's body stirred, an arm twitching. His skin began to reform over his face, his head.

"*Get up, Valentine Everard. The Sacrifice was made. The price was paid. It is time for you to take your place in this world once more. You are not yet done.*"

Talin was close now, so close. He was going to make it, before she was finished. Adalia thought hard about how to stop him, about how to—

There was a *thwack*, and Talin staggered with a blow. An axe protruded from the side of his head, and Adalia's eyes went to Uncle John. Uncle John, standing tall in the face of the Universe, unbowed. Of course. He had always known his place in the Universe, had always known that he was one of its favored sons.

"Hi," said Uncle John, to Talin. "How's that feel? Tickles a little?"

Talin stumbled, a hand reaching for the haft of the axe. He screamed as he pulled it free, then turned on John. He raised the axe.

"Guy?" Uncle John shook his head. "*Always* look behind you."

Talin paused, just for a moment.

"I think," said Uncle John, "that you should wonder why you're still bleeding. Why you didn't *change*. Don't you think you should have changed?"

There was a low growl, guttural, and all eyes turned to Val. Where Val had been, and where the creature now stood. Its teeth were bared, its eyes bright, so bright.

"*Night is not yet ready to fall,*" said Adalia. She turned to the creature that was Val. "*I kept it for you. Until you got back. And now I need to make the trade. Are you ready?*"

The creature looked at her, took a heavy step forward, the floor shaking as it placed its feet. Talin gave a yell and made a final lunge for Adalia. She could see the knife, the edge of it as it came for her flesh, to take her life away, and she closed her eyes to welcome it. She'd done it, and she could go now. To see Just James. To stand with him on the Cliffs of the Damned.

There was a thump, and a crunch, and Adalia opened her eyes. Talin's arm, the one that had held the knife, was gone, torn free. Talin was trying to scream but he was panting, gasping, looking like he was right on the edge of noise but unable to make a sound. The creature stood next to her, holding the arm before it tossed it aside like a stick it was bored with. It growled again, then picked Talin up in one massive, clawed hand and tossed him across the room, blood trailing through the air in his wake. It looked at her, those yellow eyes ancient.

It walked to her mom's cage, grabbing the bars. It roared, smoke peeling away from its clawed hands as it bent and rent the bars. They sheared away with a squeal of metal. The thing that was Val stepped back, eyes searching the room.

John came up to it, stood before it. "I'll get her." He went into the cage, and helped Danny up. Carried her in his good, strong arms out through the broken bars, and placed her on the ground. As she got free of the bars, she looked less weak, less sallow. She stood up, eyes bright, and looked at the creature that was Val.

"*We must hunt,*" she said.

"No," said John. "You've got to kill a motherfucker."

Danny looked up at Adalia, then walked towards where Val had thrown Talin. With each step she shifted, something else coming out from within, until two massive things moved through what was left of the penthouse.

"*It is almost balanced,*" said Adalia. "*Now, Talin. Now that you have given me your power, I will give you your conscience. I will let you feel every tiny thing you have done.*" She reached for one of the thousand, thousand threads that she could see around her, finding exactly the right one, and tugged it. Not very hard, just a little pull, but it snapped and shriveled and was gone.

Talin stood, holding the stump of his missing arm. His eyes were wide. "I have..." His look was stricken, and he swallowed. He looked exactly like a man who realized he had done terrible things, but for the first time in his life. And the last.

"*You have broken the Covenant,*" said Adalia. "*Your life is forfeit.*"

The creatures that were Val and Danny fell on Talin Moray, tossing his body between them. They each took turns, shaking him until the life left him, his screams and cries nothing.

They were, after all, the Night.

FIFTY-EIGHT

The steady beat of helicopter rotors hit the air. For all that they were military craft, Adalia found the sound soothing. It was someone coming to help, or at least that's what she thought.

"Are you really okay?" Gabriel was at her side, the cold Chicago wind not affecting him at all. His T-shirt moved a little in the breeze.

Adalia scrunched into her jacket a little deeper. "Why would I not be?"

"The Universe," said Gabriel, "is pretty big."

"Yes," she said. "It's going to be okay."

The Black Hawk landed in front of their little rag tag group. There was Melissa, and Uncle John, and Rex. Her Mom and Val were—

Hunting.

—making sure of a few things. Everyone looked just about dead, except for her. She was just cold.

But she felt so alive.

The Lost Warrior got out of the helicopter. She looked at Adalia, then moved to Melissa's side. "I got your message," she said.

"I sent it," said Adalia. "You said that we should call. When it was safe."

"Is it?" said Jessica Pearce.

Gabriel's eyes were bright with what would have been tears if he were alive. "It's safe," he said.

Jessica's eyes narrowed, as if she could almost hear something. "Jessica," said Adalia. "I would like to make a trade."

"You don't have to trade," said Jessica. "I'm here to help."

"Wait until I finish," said Adalia. "This city of Chicago. It's dying. It's sick, and I need someone to make it better. All the people here, they are going to be waking up soon. And I need someone who can help them. Not just help them, but make it right for them."

"I'm a soldier," said Jessica.

"And you have access to hot meals, and tents, and … and blankets. It's cold here, Jessica," said Adalia.

"I don't know if I can do that," said Jessica. "It's a little outside my remit. I can make some calls."

"Do you want to hear the trade?" said Adalia.

"Sure, kid," said Jessica, with an indulgent smile.

"I will," said Adalia, "let you see the face of your son one more time. I will let you hear his voice, and let him speak to you."

"No," said Gabriel. "No. It is too much."

Jessica took three quick strides to stand in front of Adalia. Her hand was raised in a fist, and the look on her face said she didn't even remember how it got there. "Don't. Don't you speak of him."

Adalia brushed aside her hair. "Jessica? He's right here."

Jessica looked around, her eyes going right past where Gabriel stood. "I … I don't … I can't see him."

"Not yet," said Adalia. "Do we have a trade?"

"No," said Gabriel.

"Yes," said Jessica.

"*Jessica Pearce*," said Adalia. "*Jessica Pearce. I make this trade with you. You will give to this city aid. Food, and doctors, and whatever else it needs. It will cost you your good name and everything you've thought you wanted. In return, I give you this. I give you back your son. I give you back what you needed."*

Adalia sagged to the ground, drained. She was crying again, and she didn't know why for a moment until she realized she was feeling Gabriel's hurt, and Jessica's hurt, all rolled into one. She blinked, and looked at them. Jessica's eyes were wide, her hand stretched out to Gabriel. He — a flesh and blood *he*, made real, if only for a moment — was crying, and laughing, and crying some more.

"I'm sorry," Jessica said. "I said I'd be there."

"I'm sorry," Gabriel said. "I shouldn't have gone in front."

Then they were hugging, and talking, and laughing, and crying some more. Adalia walked away from them to stand next to Melissa, and Uncle John, and Rex.

Rex cleared his throat. "Where the fuck did that boy come from?"

"He's been here the whole time," said Adalia.

"Huh," said Rex. "That's something you don't see every day."

"I'm cool with it," said Uncle John.

"What did you do?" said Melissa.

Adalia smiled at her. "Something beautiful."

Gabriel came to stand in front of her. "I think ... I think I need to go now."

"You do," said Adalia. "You shouldn't even be here at all."

"I haven't finished though," he said. His long lashes lowered as he looked at his feet. "I was supposed to help you."

Adalia laughed. "You were never here for me, Gabriel."

"What?"

"I was here for you." She reached out to touch his hand. "I was here for you."

"Adalia Kendrick," said Gabriel. "Adalia Kendrick, I love you."

"Shhh now," she said. "That's enough."

But she was speaking to herself, as the winds plucked away

Gabriel Pearce like lost smoke, and took him to where the dead go when they die.

MELISSA WAS SITTING on the bench next to her. They looked out at a street filling with National Guard, and said nothing very much for a long time. Melissa had offered to shoot the first soldier that had tried to take her away for 'medical help', and now she was resting in their made-quiet zone.

Adalia scuffed her shoe against the ground. "You should have let them take you," she said. "You're pretty beat up."

"You're the expert now?" Melissa snorted.

"I know everything—"

"No," said Melissa.

"I—"

"It's not that I don't believe that you know things," she said, her voice so soft Adalia had to strain to hear. "It's that I don't know if you know the right things."

Adalia thought about that for a while, their pool of silence holding against the bustle of activity around them. "I know why Ajay ... did what he did."

"That's not really a thing I care about," said Melissa, in a tone that said she cared very much. Her hands were gripping her jeans, fingers white.

"No lies," said Adalia.

Melissa sighed. "No lies," she agreed. "I thought—"

"He was broken," said Adalia. She twisted her fingers together. "Like if you get two sets of Lego, and make them *into* each other. Neither can be what it was supposed to be."

"Raeni?" Melissa frowned. "That was real?"

"She burrowed in to his soul, through his heart," said Adalia. "He was Talin's son, do you know that? I thought that was weird. And she wanted to control him. And she did. And then ... she got you too. Caught you, like a fly in amber. Made you ... want him."

"Possession?" Melissa leaned forward, hugging herself. "Like a demon?"

"It's not like the movies," said Adalia.

"You shouldn't be watching those kinds of movies. You're too young."

Adalia let that sit between them for a moment. "I'm ... too young?"

"Yeah," said Melissa. "There are rules." But Adalia could see the hint of a smile on Melissa's face, and it warmed her heart to see it there.

"He wanted to love you," said Adalia.

"No lies," said Melissa.

"It's true," she said, her hair spilling around her face as she looked at the ground. "There was a piece of him left that hadn't been gnawed away. It saw the brightness of you. It's what pulled them here. It's what you saw in him. I can feel it, Melissa. I can ... *see* what might have been, if she hadn't ... broken the rules." Adalia rubbed a tear off her face. "I'm sorry. I don't know why I'm crying."

"Me neither," said Melissa, rubbing her face as well. "I'm not really the crying type, but I think today I killed a man who I wanted to ... know ... because a dead woman ate his soul."

"I let the sweetest boy I've ever met kill himself so that the Universe's trade could be made," said Adalia. "I miss him."

"Yeah," said Melissa. Then, "Yeah, that's not great."

"It wasn't that Talin was evil, that there's some cosmic balance between light and dark that needs to be maintained," said Adalia. "That's what we do. People. *We* decide. No ... it's that he broke the rules. The Universe doesn't care about us, not in the way you think. Not in a good and evil kind of way. That's what made ... that's why James Malory had to die. Something right was made wrong, so something wrong had to be done to make it right."

"Malory, huh?" Melissa looked out at the street, as if Adalia was making perfect sense. "That's a good name, for a good kid."

"He could see it," said Adalia, pleading. "Couldn't he?"

"Kid," said Melissa.

"Yes?" But she was crying now, the tears spilling out like they'd never stop.

"Kid," said Melissa. "This is one of those 'right things' you don't know. It doesn't matter if he could see it. He could see *you*."

"What have I done?" said Adalia, her breath coming faster. "What am I?"

Melissa's arms were warm around her, her friend's words soft in her ear. "Something beautiful."

CHAPTER
FIFTY-NINE

The news was full of stories of a mysterious virus, something that stole a whole city's will to live. The recovery teams were helping. They mentioned a Major Pearce who had spearheaded initial efforts before disappearing. They'd wanted to court-martial her at first, said she'd misappropriated resources, whatever that meant. When the tide of sentiment had turned, when the people had been cheering for her, for what she'd *done*, well. *Then* they'd wanted to give her a medal. Pearce, it seemed, wanted neither of those things. She'd walked off, exited stage left, leaving the city better than it was when she'd started. Walked out, didn't say *goodbye* or *thank you*. Major Jessica Pearce wasn't angry or sad. She was *done*.

Val walked into the apartment lobby, his arms heavy with bags. Danny was at—

Pack mate.

—his side, carrying more bags. They'd been out shopping. Chicago was limping back to its feet, stores opening, people getting by. It would be a while, maybe never, before the city was whole again. Until that happened, there was plenty of work to be done.

Petty crime, and other not-so-petty crime, was festering under the skin of the place, and it needed constant attention.

Val put the bags down in the foyer. There were plenty of hungry people here who could use it. Danny left hers there as well — they kept one bag back and started to climb the stairs. Electricity was still iffy, and being stuck in an elevator for an hour wasn't good, clean, family fun. They pushed open the door to their floor, the faded carpet at least clean. Danny led the way, curls bouncing, and opened the door for him.

"What'd you get?" John's eyes still held that pain, would for a long time unless Val missed his guess. "Something tasty?"

"Knock yourself out," said Val, handing over the bag. "Don't fuck it up."

"That's cold," said John. "You can cook, you know."

"I know I can cook," said Val. "You were the one who said he wanted to feel useful."

"I meant, you know, by fighting bad guys," said John.

"Lord preserve us," said Carlisle. She was still pale, but moving about. "Did you get more coffee?"

John tossed her a cardboard bag. She caught it one-handed, and inhaled the outside. "Divine."

"I need a shower," said Val.

"Yes you do," said Danny. "Don't take all the hot water."

"Maybe you should join me," he said.

"Deal," she said.

∿

"So here's the thing," said Val. They were sitting around their rickety table, empty plates in front of them. It actually hadn't been terrible, but that was only because Jessica had stepped in to help. *God dammit, Miles*, she'd said. *How do you manage to tie your shoelaces in the morning? You're borderline incompetent.*

He'd smiled, because that's what John did, and made space for her in the kitchen. Because she needed a purpose too.

Adalia pushed her phone around in front of her. "You want to go hunting."

"Young lady," said Val, "it gets annoying when you do that."

"I can't help it," she said, "if I know everything."

"You don't know when to keep your mouth shut," said Carlisle.

"The deal," said Val, "is that I'm tired of running." He let that sink in, silence falling around the table. Rex looked thoughtful. Jessica looked eager. Carlisle looked bored, like she was waiting for him to get to the point. John was John, not really paying attention. Danny squeezed his hand, so he continued. "You ever wonder why there're not more of us?"

"Werewolves?" said Rex. "I'd say there's two more than there should be. World doesn't seem quite right anymore."

"That," said John, "is racist."

"It's not racist," said Carlisle. "It's..." Her words ran out, and she narrowed her eyes. "Anyway, it's not racist."

"We remember," said Danny.

"Great," said Jessica. "What exactly do you remember? I mean, that's not really an inspirational line."

"I remember," said Danny, "when dragons filled the skies."

"I remember," said Val, "when we ran free. All of us. There were even unicorns. Can you believe it?"

"There were fairies," said Danny. She smiled at her hands, something sad in her face. She looked up at them. "They were very small."

"Point is," said Val, "they're gone. Everything wonderful. It's all gone."

"Where?" Rex leaned forward. "You remember that?"

"They were eaten," said Adalia.

The table fell silent. Val cleared his throat. "She's more or less right."

"What ... wait. Are you telling me that there was something out there that could eat *you* guys?" John stood up, walked to the window.

413

He pointed outside, at the skyscrapers, and at the snow. "Ain't nothing out there that can take you down. Not really. Not in a fair fight."

"The Night," said Danny, "is full of wonder. We're not the only members of our little club. But we're almost all that's left."

"For the longest time," said Val, "we've been on the run. My ... father, and his maker, and so on up the line. Hiding. Surviving. So, I made a deal."

"A what?" John looked around. "With whom?"

"With the Night," said Adalia. "It's why he could come back."

"You're like a small psychopath who steals all the punchlines to a guy's jokes," said Val. Danny glared at him, so he said, "I mean that in a loving way, Adalia."

"Sorry," said Adalia. "You just talk a lot slower than you should."

"Sass," said John. "I can work with that."

"No," said Danny, "you can't."

"I didn't mean it like that," said John.

"Doesn't matter," said Jessica.

"Really doesn't," said Rex.

"So, the deal," said Val, moving on. "I said, well ... I said, kinda, that the whole idea of Pack was flawed."

"You don't like family?" said Carlisle, something catching in her voice.

"Hear him out," said Danny, her hand finding Carlisle's across the table.

"I said," said Val, "that what we needed to do was ... enlarge the problem."

"Ah," said Rex. "Do an Eisenhower."

"A who?" said Adalia.

"I thought you knew everything," said John.

"Important stuff," said Adalia.

"Eisenhower was important," said Rex. "He was—"

"The deal," said Val, "is that we consider that most of the human race is broadly on our team. That we stop killing people, in order to focus on the real issue."

"Which is?" John walked back to the table, kicked his chair back, and sat down. "Space aliens?"

"No," said Danny. "The real problem is that we are hunted. And *we* are *never* hunted. We are the hunt*ers*."

Val looked around the table, meeting their eyes. He knew John would be in, whatever it took, because of Sky. Because of their history. And because he was John Miles, and the Universe was just going to have to keep owing him one for as long as it took. Carlisle wasn't watching him, she was looking between Danny and Adalia, and Val knew she'd do whatever it took to—

Shield them. Protect our Pack.

—look after her friends, her *family*. It was Rex and Jessica he watched closest of all, these new people who'd come into his life. The Guide. The Lost Warrior.

"Way I see it," said Rex, "is that there's some assholes out there been killing all that's good in the world."

"Not everything good," said Val. "We're still here."

"Right," said Rex. "But it wouldn't be such a heavy job lifting the load if there were a few more of you to go around."

"Right," said Val.

"I think that's a problem we should be solving," said Rex.

"Why?" Val leaned forward, palms on the table. "I need to hear why you'd care."

"Because it's the right thing to do," said Rex. "Because my wife would kick my ass if I didn't." He swallowed, and looked down at his plate. "Because I miss having a family."

"Jessica?" Val looked at the ex-soldier, still sitting military-straight in her chair. "You've paid your dues. You've helped Chicago, more than you should have. You lost your job. You got places you'd rather be?"

"No," she said. She looked at Adalia, then at Carlisle. "You people do incredible things," she said after a moment, looking for all the world like she was trying to choose her words with exquisite care. Like she was going for a job interview for a job she really wanted. "You change the world."

"Reckon so," said Val. "I reckon we're going to keep changing the world."

"I'm in," she said. "This will be something worthy of my service."

"You won't get to see Gabriel again," said Adalia. "That was ... I shouldn't have done that at all."

Jessica reached out a hand to grab Adalia's, holding on to her like a lifeline. "I won't forget it."

"It was a trade, that's all," said Adalia, almost mumbling. She was hiding behind her hair again, before she picked up her phone.

"Okay," said Val. "Then we're agreed?" He scanned the table, first to Danny, her purpose as clear as his own. Carlisle, her faith and strength burnished for all to see. Jessica, straight, guided, quiet, ready to serve. John, well, he was John. He was always going to make the difference, whatever was required. Rex, the old man looking astonished at his own words, like he'd expected to be in a home and here he was, playing a younger man's game, but alive with the thrill of it. And Adalia, sweet Adalia, who'd had to carry them, when they all failed her.

"You didn't fail me," she said. "It was my turn, is all."

"Okay," said Val, again. "It begins."

"Yes," said Danny. "Now, we hunt."

We are the Night.

THE LIGHTS WERE OUT, the small apartment rooms full of sleeping family. Val was standing watch, looking out at the scattered dark and light that was Chicago.

"What was the deal?" said Adalia. "Really?"

"You can see it," said Val, not turning around.

"No," she said. "I can't see into your home."

416

"Oh," said Val. He smiled. "That's too bad."

"Don't be mean," she said.

"I'm not being mean," said Val. "I just think it's funny. I think it's good for you to learn there are ... limits."

"I'm not going to become a monster," said Adalia. "I'm still Adalia."

Val turned to face her, seeing her face picked out in the lights coming in from the street. "Yes," he said. "You are, and you always will be."

"I think you should do it," she said.

"Do what?"

"Ask her what's in your heart." She tipped her head to one side.

"Will she want me to?" Val ran a hand through his hair before looking back out the window. "Do you know?"

"I ... no," she said. "Some stuff is hard, complicated. Like I shouldn't know."

"Sounds about right," said Val. "Sounds about the way the rest of us see things."

Adalia was quiet for a moment before she moved closer. Leaned her head against his shoulder, sharing a view out at the street. They stood in silence for a while before she said, "I'd like it."

"Okay," he said. "Thanks for the vote of confidence. No pressure, right?"

"No pressure," she said. Then, "What *was* the deal?"

"I'll tell you something, straight up," said Val. "You ready?"

She took a step back, then nodded. "Ready."

"Sometimes," said Val, "you don't always get to know everything. Not for certain. But if you want, we can walk the path together. Are you okay with that?"

Adalia looked at him, then she gave a small nod. "I'm okay with that."

"Good," he said. "Now go to bed. Even the Universe needs a good eight hours' sleep."

She gave an exaggerated sigh, but walked away. He watched her go for a moment, then looked out the window again. "Tomorrow," he said, "we begin the hunt."

We begin the hunt.

THE END.

THE WAR ISN'T OVER. The old powers are waking.

Val thought defeating Talin Moray would be the end of the fight. **He lacked imagination.**

The Night is hunted. **Ancient enemies are rising—creatures older than cities, older than myths, forged in blood and meant to rule.** And they're done waiting in the shadows.

The battle ahead isn't just about survival—it's about **stopping a war that was written in scripture, before it devours the world.**

The final reckoning is here. **Turn the page for a glimpse of what comes next.**

Because the monsters in the dark were only the beginning.

NIGHT'S END

A WEREWOLF SUPERNATURAL
THRILLER ADVENTURE

OVERTURE

The Russian stood in front of him like this kind of thing happened every day. Like being in front of a vampire was a thing that a man could get used to. Like he didn't really care how this turned out — maybe they could hit the bars after, shoot some pool, but they'd need to agree on what kind of drinking they'd be doing.

Dragomir liked that about him.

Of course, drinking could come later. Right now, they were in a shack, tucked between two warehouses. The lighting outside was poor, which was the idea, and the lighting inside wasn't a lot better. It didn't bother either of them. They were friends with the dark. It wasn't palatial accommodation — two chairs stood on either side of an old table. The table's sole purpose was holding some papers, which the Russian had ignored. The floor was bare concrete, the walls corrugated steel. There was no one else with them, because other people would lead to mistakes, and mistakes would lead to dying. Dying, if done at the wrong time, would undo everything. So here they were, just the two of them, in a worn-out neighborhood full of worn-out people, after dark.

"Dragomir Balan," said the Russian. "You are my good friend, *da*?"

They clasped arms, Dragomir feeling the strength there. It'd be useful not to forget that — not the sheer physical presence of that grip, but the man that stood behind it. To come this close to someone who could end your life took — well, it took some serious balls. In Dragomir's experience — his very, *very* long experience — that kind of ball quotient didn't come out of training, or the gym, or having your pet rabbit run away. It came out of everyone you'd ever known dying, horribly, and that sort of thing was a useful asset.

"I am," said Dragomir. He pulled the Russian closer into a hug. "Thank you ... thank you for coming."

"Is nothing," said the Russian. He stepped away, looking around the small room. Probably trying to work out which wall was the best one to punch through if they needed an exit. It's what Dragomir had done ten minutes ago. Dragomir noticed that the Russian hadn't sat at one of the stools set at the rickety table in the middle of the room, or even looked at the papers resting there. He was more of a man of action, this Russian, even after all this time. "Was in neighborhood."

"Since when did you live in the Bronx?"

"Since Tuesday," said the Russian. He sniffed the air. "Storm. Is coming."

"I can't ... I can't really tell when you're joking," said Dragomir. "Of *course* a fucking storm is coming. It's why you're here. To, uh, bring the rain. Look, I'll get you a room. At a nice place for a change."

"I am here," said the Russian, "to kill everyone, but most of all those that need killing. I am here to die. I do not care about nice places."

"Yeah," said Dragomir. "It's my plan, remember?"

"I remember," said the Russian. He pressed against the thin tin wall of the shack, the metal flexing slightly. "You were followed. Did you know?"

"I'm always followed," said Dragomir. "Kaylan's got plans for me. Most of them involve a box buried six feet under."

"I remember," said the Russian. "Kaylan, who wants to end everything. Before you were made, I," and he slapped his broad chest, "saw her raise her sword at Golgotha. She and her brother Maynor. Before they wore those names, they—"

"I know what happened," said Dragomir. Something nagged at his chest, an old pain, the well-worn path in his memories leading him there often. "I was there too. Just ... not quite ready, as you say."

The Russian looked at him, then sighed. "You will see her again soon, my friend. Kaylan? She cannot keep you from your Viorica. Not forever."

Dragomir clapped his hands together. "Well, this conversation's turned dark. What have you learned since Tuesday?"

"The Night is here," said the Russian. "They have tracked your kind to this marvelous city. But nothing else, *da*? They do not know where you live. Who you are. What your names are, or how to find you. Not like me." He gave Dragomir a bright smile, full of perfect white teeth. "They are hunting."

"We must help them," said Dragomir. "They cannot do it alone."

The Russian shrugged. "Maybe so. Maybe not. Do not underestimate the Night."

Dragomir thought about that for a while. "I'm not sure it's about my estimation skills, my friend. It's about a horde of unholy monsters that were designed to end the world. They ... *we* ... were *manufactured*. Two thousand years ago, to end the world when the apocalypse didn't come."

"Apocalypse wasn't meant to come," said the Russian.

"There's disagreement on that theory," said Dragomir. "If it wasn't for Liselle and Josef, we wouldn't be in this fine shack together. Anyway, it's not just the Night. They brought friends."

"Friends?" said the Russian. "The Night has ever walked alone." He pointed at himself with a thumb. "Like me, *da*?"

"Well, no," said Dragomir. He leaned his arms on the table to the sound of old metal creaking, and started flipping through the papers. Dossiers, a collection of stats and numbers and photographs that showed a little of the *what* but none of the *why* or *how*. "Actually, they're completely different, as near as I can tell. Here." He held up one dossier, a head-and-shoulders shot of a fit woman in the top right corner, a number of vital statistics detailing a military history, a *career*, that she'd left behind. "This one. Major Jessica Pearce. Discharged. Pretty clean run through the ranks, lots of medals, bet her dress uniform looks like someone threw a fruit salad at it. You know what the file doesn't say? Her reasons for leaving her promising, successful military career to join a bunch of ... of *werewolves*."

"Is not sensible, *nyet*," said the Russian.

"Not fucking sensible, no," said Dragomir. "You know what they call her? The Lost Warrior."

"I think," said the Russian, "that you have found her, *da*?"

Dragomir gave a snort. "Yeah. Okay. What she lost was her kid."

The Russian frowned for a moment. "Is difficult. The Night, it can collect the needy. Those who need protection. It is weakest when burdened by the frail."

Specialist with a fifty calibre sniper rifle, commendations out the ass. On the ground when that zombie shit hit Chicago — wouldn't call that one weak. Maybe it was a matter of perspective — when Dragomir had lived for over five thousand years maybe he'd have the Russian's point of view. "What about this one then?" he said, pushing another dossier in the Russian's direction. "Retired firefighter. Rex Aubrey."

The Russian leaned closer to read the papers. "'The Guide?'" He gave Dragomir a glance. "Is seeing eye dog?"

"I don't think it's literal. Managed to corral them all to the right place at the right time," said Dragomir. He flipped over another dossier. *The Shield*. "What about this one?"

The Russian tapped the photo. "*Da*. This one, yes. She is made of burnished metal. She will not break."

"I hope not," said Dragomir. "File says she's been in hospital a lot since meeting the rest of them."

"And yet," said the Russian, "not broken, *da*?"

"I guess," said Dragomir. "The Good Right Arm?"

The Russian squinted at the photo, then laughed. "Is like seeing old friends, these papers. Leaves nothing to imagination, *nyet*? John Miles." He frowned, like he was remembering something. "I ... I am not sure, I admit it. It is like he serves no purpose, but..."

"But," agreed Dragomir. "Let's look at these two and I'll save the best for last." He pushed two more files towards the Russian. The man looked at them, then finally sat down on the chair by the table.

"The Knight," said the Russian, "and his Sword." He traced a finger over the photo of Valentine Everard, then made his hand into a fist. "I do not like this, Dragomir Balan. This one should be dead."

"She probably should too," said Dragomir, pointing at Danielle Kendrick's photo. "But here. One more." He shuffled the dossiers, looking for the last one. A young woman, the photo grainy through distance and speed. She hadn't been on the grid, not a decent image of her on file in any system they controlled. They'd grabbed this one shot as she was getting into a car, her face turned towards the photographer. Her eyes looked right out of the page. "The Prophet."

The Russian became still, then he reached a cautious hand out towards the papers. Unclipped the photo of the young woman, held it up to the light. "Adalia," he said, sounding like he was tasting the word, savoring it. "Adalia Kendrick. So ... lost."

"That's where you come in," said Dragomir.

"I am sorry," said the Russian. "My English. Is not always the best, *da*? You think—"

"I think," said Dragomir, "that there's a bunch of bloodsucking assholes who are *right now* trying to get the information I have on this table. They are *right now* trying to capture her," and here, he snared the photograph of Adalia from the Russian, slapping it back down on the table, "so they can continue what they started. To end the world."

"They didn't start it," said the Russian. "*You* didn't start it."

"Semantics," said Dragomir. "Kaylan and Maynor started it. Made us, to finish it. If you can't get the Apocalypse to happen organically, you got to make your own luck, right? I guess in a way it's nice having a purpose. Avoids the whole mid-life crisis. Only problem here is the purpose is *ending the world*, which leads me to my therapist every week."

"Therapist," said the Russian. "Is expensive?"

"I'll give you his card later," said Dragomir. "Look, the thing we need here is some focus."

"You need guardian angel," said the Russian. He laughed, showing those perfect white teeth. "I am not angel, Dragomir Balan. I am weapon."

"Today," said Dragomir, "you're an angel. The world needs one."

"I am ... broken, Dragomir," said the Russian.

Dragomir leaned forward. "*She* needs one," he said.

The Russian was silent for a long time. The noise of the city beyond the walls came to them in muted tones, the blare of a horn turned into something softer, almost gentle. Dragomir waited, because he was used to time, and the passage of it, but also because this man was his friend, perhaps his only one, and they were planning to die, together. A little waiting wouldn't hurt. The Russian seemed to collect himself, pulling thoughts together as many people would sweep dust into a pan. "I am no angel," he said again. "But for her, I will try."

"We're going to save the world," said Dragomir.

"I do not think so," said the Russian. He tapped the photo of Adalia Kendrick. "I think she will save the world."

"Again, semantics," said Dragomir. "The plan is working. The Night is here. The vampires are all trying to find them. I've ... given a nudge. To an old friend of theirs. Sam Barnes. Head of Biomne."

"I know Biomne," said the Russian. "They tried to capture the Night." He laughed. "Was where it all started."

"Everyone knows Biomne," said Dragomir. "What everyone *doesn't* know is that we've got Sam's kid. That's providing a certain level of pressure on the man. He's already been in contact with the Night. They're going to meet him. Tomorrow."

"I will be there," said the Russian.

"No you won't," said Dragomir. "You will be finding Adalia Kendrick."

"They are not ready to fight *vampiry*," said the Russian. "They will need—"

"They'll be fine," said Dragomir. "The second thing I've done is, hell, where is..." He rifled through the papers again, pulling out Major Pearce's dossier. "Here we go. Jessie, here," and he tapped the papers, "has been sniffing around, trying to find us. So I've let it slip that there's a young vampire they can capture. What they do with him is ... up to them."

"You, the great Dragomir Balan, are leaving something to chance?" The Russian's eyes were wide with astonishment. "Tell me is not so."

"Sometimes," said Dragomir, "you gotta roll the dice. Also," and here, he fished out the Knight's dossier, holding up the photo of Valentine Everard, "this man. Given a choice, what do you think he will do?"

The Russian looked at the photo for a long time. "I think he will die," he said, but there was no satisfaction in it.

"I think you might be right," said Dragomir. "But I think he might die *for* something. And that's all we need."

CHAPTER
ONE

"What the hell is this?" Carlisle leaned on the pitted wood of the bar with an elbow, holding up the glass with her other hand. "There some kind of world shortage of gin?"

"You're working," said Danny, draining her third beer.

"I don't want to be tense when I'm working," said Carlisle, frowning into her glass. "Is there any alcohol in here at all?"

"It's what a single shot tastes like," said Danny.

"Doesn't taste like much," said Carlisle. "I don't think there's any risk of this becoming a habit."

Danny spared her a sideways glance. "You told me to make sure you didn't have too many before—"

"Hell," said Carlisle, "I remember what I said. I didn't mean I wanted to drink water." She brushed off some of the rain that lingered on the dark leather of her jacket, then flicked her hand to dry it. "There's enough of that outside."

"Relax," said Danny, starting on another beer.

Carlisle gave her a hard stare. "That's what the gin is *for*."

"I've been here for an hour," said Danny. "You don't know what waiting even means. Besides, he's not late. Yet."

You're nervous, Carlisle. You get cranky when you're nervous. "I hate waiting."

Danny shrugged, leaning back against the bar. She tugged on Carlisle's sleeve. "Here's number seven."

"Seven what?" said Carlisle, watching as a man walked towards them. Confident swagger, like his balls were so big he couldn't easily get his legs together. Carlisle wanted to punch him in the face almost immediately. She took a drink from her gin instead.

"Evening, ladies," said the man, the confidence in his walk making it to the smile on his face. "Can I—"

"Fuck off," suggested Carlisle.

The man's smile flickered slightly. Carlisle could almost see the thoughts going through his head. It'd be something like, *hey, this is unexpected*, or *maybe my fly is undone* or *these bitches are lesbians*. He rallied though, the smile coming back on in full force. "Well, it's a bit early, but—"

"Hey," said Danny. "You look like you're from out of town." She held out a folded pamphlet to the man.

"What's this?" he said.

"It's a map," said Danny, unfolding it. She pointed to a section near Times Square, circled in fat red pen. "See this point here?"

The man was still smiling, nodding along with it now. "Yeah. Yeah, I see it."

"I'd like you to go there," said Danny.

"To meet you?" said the man, his smile coming on brighter. Carlisle could almost smell the optimism pouring off him.

"No," said Danny. "I just want you to go there. Fuck off."

The man's smile snapped out like a candle flame in a hurricane, and he turned on his heel and stalked off.

Carlisle watched him go, then took another sip of her gin. "You had six more like that?"

429

"Not exactly like that," said Danny. "But similar. I'm running out of maps."

She still looks thirty, thought Carlisle. *Or twenty-five in good light.* "Let's hope Sam gets here before you bruise every ego in Manhattan."

The door at the front of the bar opened, a man ushered in by both the huge doorman — *is he technically a bouncer if he's big enough to block out the sun?* — and the rain in equal measure. Carlisle recognized the man immediately. He was a little older, a little thinner, but still the same Sam. Two men followed him in, both pretty big pieces of machinery, which made Carlisle frown a little. Even when Elsie Morgan was heading Biomne, she didn't have hired muscle following her around. Their jackets didn't fit quite right — *probably packing a little heat in a shoulder holster* — but the tailoring was otherwise immaculate. *Top shelf* pieces of machinery, then.

"I don't like those guys with him," said Danny.

"You don't have to like them," said Carlisle. "Remember, the last time he saw us his company's super-important secret base had been burned right down to the foundations. By us. It'll make him feel a little more relaxed."

"Maybe he should have a gin too," said Danny.

Sam saw them, inclining his chin and starting to make his way through the room. It was early, the night outside still fresh and new, but the bar was still filling up. When Sam made it to them, he held out a hand. "Detective."

Carlisle winced. "It's just Carlisle," she said. She shook his hand.

"I know," said Sam Barnes. "But you are what you are." She could feel something in his grip, a little like a cross between desperation and hope. Carlisle heard the catch in his voice.

She smiled, letting his hand go. "Truth," said Carlisle. *This man was in your corner when no one else was.* She — *they* — needed to find out if he was able to be saved, or if he was lost. "You remember Kendrick? Uh, I mean, Danny?"

"Ms. Kendrick," said Sam, shaking her hand in turn. He frowned. "Where is Mr. Everard?"

"You know," said Carlisle. "Important wolf stuff. You want a drink? Only, don't let her," and she jerked her head at Danny, "order for you. You'll get a glass of water with ice in it."

Sam didn't do the usual *allow me* or *I'll get one of my lackeys to get it*. He just nodded, and gave a small smile. "I'd like that."

They found a table — its availability helped along by the presence of Hulk and Gigantor — drinks arriving straight away. The table was round and small, tucked along the back wall of the bar. Hulk and Gigantor — whose names turned out to be Ben and Ernesto — turned their backs to them, watching the crowd. Giving them some space. Or, if you were the paranoid type, making sure no one heard something that would need to be ... cleaned up.

"Excuse the presence of Ben and Ernesto," said Sam. "They're not for you."

Danny's eyes flicked between the muscle and Sam, the muscle and Sam. "They're not?"

"Ms. Kendrick," said Sam, "last time we saw each other, you jumped out of a research building many floors up. A fall that would certainly kill a normal ... *person*. At the time, you were ... a little larger, if memory serves. I very much doubt that either Ben or Ernesto would be much use against you."

"Then what are they for?" Danny leaned closer. "*Who* are they for?"

Sam's eyes, nothing involuntary in the look at all, moved to Ben, then to Ernesto, and finally back to Danny. He sighed. "I'm sorry. This was a mistake. I shouldn't have agreed to come."

"Then why did you?" Danny leaned forward an inch, maybe two. "Sam, we've been hunting something—"

"How is Charlie?" said Carlisle.

Sam's eyes narrowed. "What did you say?"

"Charlie. Your kid." Carlisle played with the straw the fool bartender had put in her gin, then tossed it on the table. It was blue

431

plastic, in her experience useless for stirring and drinking both. "He's got to be ten years old."

"Eight," said Sam, who looked like he wanted to say something. The man swallowed, then said, "He's fine. Detective? Why did you come?"

"You were in town. We were in town. Seemed a good reason to catch up — on old times," said Carlisle. "Remember that time when we all went out and played pool for hours?"

About fifty emotions went across Sam's face, then he nodded. "Yes," he said. "I remember. Pool. Except I didn't know the rules — I'd never played. Still don't, really. Know the rules, that is."

Carlisle pushed her glass away. "I can teach you," she said. She looked at Danny. "We can teach you."

Danny said nothing. She knew they'd never played pool with Sam Barnes. She started making slow circles on the table with her beer bottle, the knurled bottom making a grinding sound against the wood.

"I don't think ... I don't think I can play anymore, Detective." Sam shrugged, then stood. "Well, it's been a pleasure."

"Sure it has," said Carlisle.

Sam looked to Danny, looked to her like he wanted to shake her hand or hug her or run away or all three. "Ms. Kendrick."

"Sam?" said Danny. Her voice was soft. "Sam, you take care of yourself, okay?"

He gave a harsh laugh, something nasty in it. "That's all I do these days." He shuffled towards the back, Ben and Ernesto flanking him.

"That was weird," said Danny, after a moment.

"Not really," said Carlisle. She lifted up Sam's glass, the whiskey hardly touched. She flicked aside the coaster, finding the paper she'd seen him slip under it. Creased, worn like it had been folded and refolded many times.

"What's that?" Danny picked the paper up, unfolding it with

care. She smoothed it out on the table between them. The text on it was to the point.

Know that we have your son Charles. Know that he will come to no harm if you do as we say. We are keeping him safe, and safe he will remain as long as you do as we ask. If you speak to law enforcement, he will die. If you talk to this world's media, he will die. If you seek help of any kind, he will die.

We are not without gratitude. Do as we ask, and you both shall know wealth and power everlasting. This will be handed to Charles on his twentieth birthday. Until then, he shall remain our ward, learning our ways. He will be your successor in all things. What you sow, he will reap.

Carlisle's eyes met Danny's over the table top. "You know what this means?"

Danny's lips pulled back from her teeth, baring them in what was definitely not a smile. "We've found them."

"I'm glad," said Carlisle, "because otherwise I'd have felt bad about what was about to happen to Ben and Ernesto."

"I know, right?" Danny frowned. "Still. I'm surprised at how easy this has been."

"It's not been easy," said Carlisle. "We had to get that clown Miles a job, remember? Interviews, dressing nice, trying not to talk. It was tough."

Danny smiled at her. "Right. Well." She stood up, smoothing the front of her jacket. "Time to get to work." Her eyes had found a reedy man towards the front of the bar. Danny nodded at him. "That one, I think."

"How can you tell?" Carlisle adjusted the back of her jacket, feeling the comforting weight of the Eagle at her spine. The sidearm still had her back. It always had her back.

"He's looking for someone," said Danny. "Like, really looking. And he's ... unhealthy. I don't know. It's been a long, long time. And ... Melissa? It wasn't even me. I don't know if I'm remembering this right."

Carlisle looked over at the man. Danny was right, the man *was* unhealthy. If she'd seen him elsewhere, she'd have thought he was in dire need of a burger and fries, probably supersize, washed down with a jumbo fat Coke, no ice. The guy was thin, like he didn't make eating a habit. His complexion was washed out, leaving him pale, reedy. What really got her humming was the look in his eyes, a kind of fanaticism she hadn't seen except that one time she'd had to face down a guy with a bomb strapped to his chest, another to a little kid he'd held in front of him like a shield.

That had been a bad day.

The reedy man saw them. Or really, if Carlisle was being honest, he saw Danny. Completely ignored Carlisle, eyes skipping right over the top of her like she was just a piece of furniture. Carlisle could almost see the wheels moving in the guy's head as he sized up Danny, whether to come on over and start some shit or walk the fuck away. If she was being honest with herself, Carlisle was hoping for *walk the fuck away*. Danny and Everard had talked about what these freaks were, what they could do.

If Carlisle hadn't been on the ride with them so long, she'd have called them crazy. She swallowed, looked up at Danny, and said, "I think you're remembering it right. Go kick his ass."

Danny rolled her shoulders and strode forward. The reedy man took one look at her and made a break for the door at the front of the bar. Which was more or less expected. They'd prepared a contingency for that.

The reedy man didn't run, more like he flowed around people. They'd look away, or lean forward, or spill their drink, or a dozen other things at just the right time to let him move right towards the bar's main door. Right towards Valentine Everard.

As far as contingencies go, he wasn't a bad one to have. Everard was brushing the water from his coat. The reedy man looked around him, back towards the rear exit where Carlisle and Danny were, then to the front, blocked by Everard. *Caught.*

He bared teeth at them, teeth that were just too damn long, then grabbed a passing waitress. She had a moment to say something —

it might have been *hey* or *watch it, asshole* — before the reedy man sank those teeth into the flesh at her neck. There was a bright spray of red as he sucked at the waitress, the life leaving her like water down a drain. Just like that, she was gone. Color bloomed in the reedy man's face, a flush of power as the waitress's blood gave him vigor.

The screams hit like a wave, people panicking as they surged away from the reedy man. Bouncing off walls, off each other, surging for any exit. Carlisle watched as they streamed around Everard, not moving him at all — he was like a rock.

"*Come,*" said the reedy man, hard voice carrying as he turned to Everard. "*Come and die.*"

THE END BEGINS NOW.

THE ELDER FORCES WANT THEIR WORLD BACK.

ACKNOWLEDGMENTS

I hadn't written *Night's Favor* with a sequel in mind. How the hell did we get here?

Mostly because of *you*, out *there*. More than a few of you wanted to know what happened next. I get asked a lot — and I mean, a *lot* — about whether Volk is really dead (I'm providing no more or less clarity on that here). But anyway: thank you to those who liked my first story. Thank you for wanting more. It'd be hard to write without readers.

Oh, related point. Thanks to those of you who left a review on Amazon, or a rating on Goodreads. You're doing God's work. While it's a great ego-trip for me, you're also helping guide like-minded souls through the mighty recommendations engines of the Internet. Every review (positive or negative) helps an angel get their wings.

My writer's circle — or did we settle on coven? — have been of tremendous help. Their most excellent advice has helped shaped some of the finer areas I don't have huge experience on. Having once been a teenage boy, I naturally assumed I knew everything about teenage girls through a certain set of shared experiences. As it turns out, not so much: Cassie, Kate, and Frances helped slap the silly clean out of me. Their feedback has hammered flat the the words you've just read, in a sort of water-to-wine kind of way; as my first critics, they voted a huge amount of shit right off the island. But where they really shone is in guiding me to create a character I'm particularly proud of: Adalia is a credit to them.

I'm pretty sure I've said something like this before, but writing is a team sport. It's not a solitary pursuit where you take a typewriter into a forest and emerge three months later with a finished manuscript. First of all, that's crazy because *no Internet*. But it's also crazy because *no people*. My friends and family (who've once again dived into the simmering pool of slime that is my first, second, or fortieth draft) have made *Night's Fall* relatable, bearable, and understandable. Anthony, Arran, Cheryl, Erin, Greg, Jane, Julia, Lynda, Matthew, and Raelene, you are amazing. Your comments made me think, some of them made me laugh, and all of them made this a better story. I'm humbled by your relentless drive to help me tell better stories. Thank you.

Oh. We're at the end. One more, before we go: my Rae. I don't know how you put up with me, but I'm ever thankful for it — and for you — each of these days we are given to share. I want them to last until the sun grows cold and the world stops turning. Until forever. And longer.

— R. P.
June 2016, Wellington

ABOUT THE AUTHOR

Richard Parry worked as a senior marketing manager in one of the world's top tech companies. It sounds cool, but it wasn't all cocaine parties. He lives in Wellington with the love of his life, Rae. They have two cats, Harry and Friday, who chase birds. The birds, who have the power of flight, don't seem to mind.

WAIT. DON'T GO!

Thanks for reading my book. If you enjoyed it, let's keep the party going:

📖 Join *Roll for Narrative* for reviews, storytelling breakdowns, and writing misadventures:

https://rollfornarrative.parrydox.com

✏️ Lurk, judge, or say hi:

https://www.parrydox.com

P.S. An angel still gets its wings for every five-star review, but I'm told they're on backorder.

- 🅰 amazon.com/author/richard.parry
- Ⓖ goodreads.com/richard_parry
- BB bookbub.com/authors/richard-parry-6ffc3911-9f2c-43ef-8ab4-13dc-cd7f5874
- ▶ youtube.com/@parrydigm
- 🦋 bsky.app/profile/parrydox.com
- in linkedin.com/in/therealrichardparry

ALSO BY RICHARD PARRY

DAWN'S WARDEN

The Three Faces of Fate

The Undefeated Throne

The Fury of the Betrayed

THE SPLINTERED LAND

Tomb of the Six

Blade of Glass

The Storm Within

Requiem's Justice

The Copper Bard

Heartsong

The Hymn of All

THE EZEROC WARS

The Ezeroc Wars universe is big (and growing!). Get the reading guide here:
https://www.parrydox.com/ezeroc-wars-reading-guide/

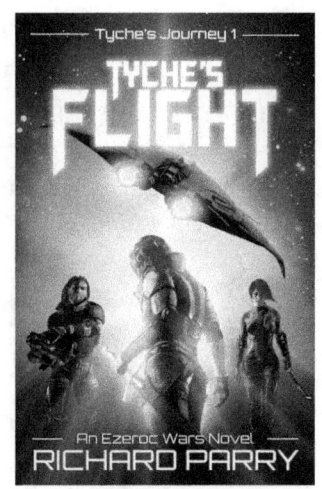

The Empire's Rogues: Volume 1

FUTURE FORFEIT

Not sure where to start? Get the reading guide here: https://www.parrydox.com/future-forfeit-reading-guide/

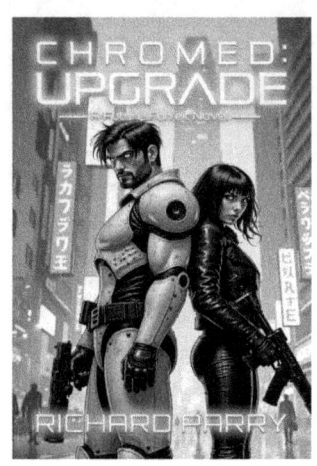

Chromed: Upgrade

Chromed: Rogue

Chromed: Restore

City Stories

Chromed: Consensus

Chromed: Delilah

Chromed: Meltdown

NIGHT'S CHAMPION

Night's Favor

Night's Fall

Night's End